I0611427

Secrets of the Sages

The World In-between Series
Book 3

IE Castellano

Laurel
Highlands
Publishing

Secrets of the Sages
Copyright © 2014 IE Castellano
All rights reserved.

Cover by JosDCreations

Laurel Highlands Publishing
Mount Pleasant, PA
USA

http://LaurelHighlandsPublishing.com

ISBN-13: 978-1-941087-05-3
ISBN-10: 1941087051

No part of this book may be reproduced or transmitted in any form or by any means, electronic or mechanical, including photocopying, recording, or by any information storage and retrieval system without the written permission of the author, except where permitted by law.

This book is a work of fiction. Names, characters, places, and incidents either are products of the author's imagination or are used fictitiously. Any resemblance to actual persons, living or dead, events, or locales is entirely coincidental.

To Brothers
Old or young, big or small
The best one of them all
Is one like no other
The man I call brother

Chapter One
In Wait

Magic infiltrated Berty's life, yet it baffled him. He had no idea how a modern invention, like the telephone, worked in the Land of Sages. Absentmindedly, he turned a page while trying not to watch his young niece talk to her parents via a telephone in the Empire Tree.

His brother and sister-in-law were in Africa, on business. Hope was left in his care for the summer. For the past half-hour, he sat at the table in her chambers, pretending to read a book. Instead, he eavesdropped on Hope's conversation.

Since bringing her to the Land of Sages, he had been keeping tabs on what she told her parents. Jon and Teresa knew nothing of the world beyond the portal or of portals at all. With Hope being a Wood Listener, keeping her away from his world was impossible. Fortunately for Berty, phone calls, thus far, had been brief.

"Uncle Berty, Mommy wants to talk to you," said Hope, holding the receiver of the old, white and brass, rotary phone towards him.

His stomach dropped, knowing that he had run out of skirting room.

Across the table, Hope's Fairy Godmother chose books for later. "Freesia, can you keep her occupied, please?" he asked her.

1

"Of course, my Lord," Freesia answered.

Peeling himself off the chair, Berty was ready to speak to her parents. He took the receiver from Hope, then held it to his head. "Teresa, Jon, how's Africa treating you?" he asked.

"Why is my daughter learning archery?" Teresa accused in response.

"Because she wanted to learn," he answered.

"She *wanted* to? I thought you were more responsible than that, Berty." He could feel her anger through the phone.

"She is very good. It's like it comes naturally to her," he said.

"She must be, since she's now practicing on moving targets."

He took a breath before saying, "She enjoys it."

"Enjoys it? It's a weapon! In the hands of a six year old!" He had to pull the phone away from his ear.

"Archery makes her happy," he countered. "You know what doesn't make her happy? The children from school."

"Berty, don't change the subject."

"Did you know that they made fun of her? They bullied her so much that she was afraid to play with the children here," he told her.

"What?" Teresa asked. Her tone softened slightly.

"I thought she made friends there," said Jon. "Her best friend is a girl named Alina."

"Only after I convinced her that the kids here were different from the ones back home," explained Berty.

"We had no idea. She never spoke about it," said Jon.

"That doesn't change the fact that she's using a bow and real arrows at a young age," Teresa reprimanded. "We can deal with the bullying when we get home."

"Archery is building her confidence and self-esteem. Is that not the best countermeasure to what she has been going through at school?" asked Berty.

2

Teresa sighed. "Yes," she admitted, "but it's so violent."

"The way Declan teaches it, it is more of an art form," Berty countered.

"Teresa, honey," Jon said sweetly, "archery isn't the only thing she's doing. She's also playing, reading and learning lots of other stuff."

"I know. I just wished Berty would have asked us first," Teresa conceded. "Those kids. Are they nice?"

"Very," assured Berty. "I'm sure she told you that Alina is sleeping over tonight."

"She did. Have you met Alina's parents?" Teresa asked like she was checking off a good parenting list.

"Cal and Natalie Rowan are good people," he answered. "Cal's mother lives with them in their ancestral home."

"Another tree house?" Jon tried to joke.

"An old cob house with a thatched roof," said Berty as he thought about the picturesque Sages' Grove surrounding the Empire Tree.

"Hope never wanted to have anyone over before," Teresa said. "I'm missing her first sleepover. Jon, I want to go home."

"I thought she had her first sleepover at what's-her-face's house," said Jon, "with all the girls from her class."

"It's not the same." Teresa sighed.

"When we get home, maybe we can have Alina stay a few days before school starts," suggested Jon.

"That would be nice," Teresa said.

Berty's stomach relaxed a little.

"Next week," Jon told Berty, "we are heading to a more remote area. Our cell phones may not work. And, we're not sure about the landline. So, we're going to call as much as possible before then. We're leaving forwarding information with Mom and Dad."

"How long are you going be out there?" Berty asked.

"At least a few weeks," Jon replied. "After that, one of our new clients is going to be taking us on a safari for a couple of weeks. Then, we'll check on the new office before heading on the first plane home."

"Sounds like quite the adventure," said Berty. "I'm sure you'll want to speak to Hope as much as possible on your next calls, so congratulations on getting the new business. Have fun, guys. I'll see you when you get home."

"Bye, Berty," said Jon.

"Can we speak to Hope one more time?" Teresa asked.

"Absolutely," he said. "Bye, guys." He placed the receiver on the small table, then looked over at his niece who was sorting games with Freesia. "Hope, your mom and dad want to talk to you again."

Jumping up off the floor, Hope ran to the phone.

He walked over to Freesia. Helping her put things away, he asked, "Are we ready?"

"Yes," she answered. "I will make sure they stay out of the Roundtable Room, the Scepter Room and off of Council Circle."

He nodded as Hope ran over to them. "Is it time yet?" she asked.

"Hmm," said Berty. "Are your bow and arrows put away?"

"Yes."

"What about your box of Fairy Dust?"

"Um." Hope looked up at him with her big, brown eyes.

"You are not allowed to show her your Fairy Dust," Berty ordered. "Alina is going to be a Witch. That is a prominent position in the Sages' Grove, which carries a lot of responsibility. Our future Witch cannot have a Fairy Dust mishap. Delyth would be forced to take away your dust privileges."

Her face fell.

"Your mom and dad want to have Alina over when they come home," said Berty. He saw her mouth widen into a smile. "She can't go through the portal if you're going to expose her to a potentially dangerous substance."

She glanced at the floor, then said, "I'll be right back."

When Hope disappeared up the steps, Freesia suggested, "I'll have them sleep down here tonight."

"Thank you," he said as he threw his claret cloak around his shoulders.

Hope galloped down the stairs at the back of the room. Seeing Freesia reach for her soft pink cloak, she scampered to the cloak tree near the door.

Enrobed in maroon, she stood next to her uncle. "Okay," she said.

With a smile, he led Hope and Freesia into a warm, early summer drizzle. The wetness darkened the rope and plank bridge that connected Hope's bundle of leafy, green branches with the massive trunk of the Empire Tree.

Hope skipped across the bridge ahead of Berty and Freesia. On the landing in front of the Scepter Room, she waited. Berty allowed Hope and Freesia to descend the staircase in front of him.

One flight down, Declan entered the trunk from the bridge that led to the chambers of the Advisory Council. Joining them on the stairs, he descended beside Berty. Quietly, he said, "This should be the last one."

"Find me when you're finished," Berty told his Advisor.

When the staircase ended, the four of them crossed the Reception Room to the stairs on the other side. A couple of large tables filled the round room while on the dais a large, ornately carved throne overlooked it all.

Hope hummed cheerfully as they descended another flight of

steps. In the Receiving Room, Declan split with them. His dark cloak billowed around him while he walked to the back of the room. Declan touched the lowest circle of one the Sages' Seals decorating the rear wall. When the large tree superimposed with seven circles split open, he stepped through the door.

"Where's he going?" Hope asked Berty.

"Empire business," he said before ushering her out into the light rain.

The warm rain darkened the thatched roofs, contrasting well with the white cob buildings. Stretched canvas protected the market stalls from getting wet. Villagers strolled from place to place with their hoods raised.

A wet dirt path led them around buildings to a white cob house in better repair than when Berty first visited the Rowan family home. Giving Hope a smile, he knocked on the old, wooden door.

A woman with a meek smile answered. "My Lord, please come in out of the rain," she said.

"Thank you," he said. The three of them crossed the threshold into the tidy home. Berty tried not to look at the worn furniture. Alina's little brother, William, sat at a wood plank table, playing with bits of dough. Next to him, his grandmother, Leena, sealed circular pieces of pastry together.

"Good afternoon, my Lord," said Leena. "William and I are making summer onion pies." She smiled brightly. "Natalie, we will make some for Cal, too."

"Good afternoon, Leena, William. That does look like fun," Berty said with a smile.

"We are hoping that William will develop a skill for making things," Natalie said as she placed a basket of cloth on a chair. "That way, he can apprentice as a smith. In a few years, he can tour the different smith guilds and see which one suits him."

6

Berty nodded politely.

"Alina will be right down. Can I offer you anything, my Lord?" Natalie asked. "Would you like to sit down?"

"Oh, no, thank you. We are fine," he said pleasantly. "Do not wish to interrupt."

"Nonsense," said Leena. "We are very grateful. Their friendship, I believe, is a blessing for both girls."

Alina thundered down the wooden steps that ran along the one side of the house. "Hope!" she squealed. Her hands clutched a large bag while a light brown cloak trailed behind her.

"What took you so long, Alina?" Natalie asked.

Her eyes found her mother sorting cloth. "Had to make sure I had everything," she said. Carefully, she placed her bag on a chair near the door. After fastening her cloak, she gave her mother a hug.

Natalie smoothed her daughter's cloak while saying, "You be good. Have fun. Love you."

"Okay, Mommy," Alina said. "Love you, too." Hurrying over to Leena, she said, "Bye, Grandma." Leena gave her granddaughter a kiss on the cheek. "See you tomorrow, Will."

Alina raised her hood, then grabbed her bag. With a wide smile and a wave to her family, she walked into the light rain next to Hope.

Glancing at Alina hugging her bag to her chest, Freesia asked her, "Would you like me to carry that for you, Alina?"

"No, thanks."

With the way Alina protected her bag, Berty wondered what she had brought. Entering the Empire Tree, Berty allowed Freesia to lead the girls through the tree to Hope's chambers.

As they crossed the Reception Room, he watched Alina's head cock in every direction. She gawked at the brass chandelier, then at the wall filling Sages' Seal behind his throne. When they

7

reached the first landing, Alina caught a glimpse of the Roundtable through the doorway.

At the top of the second flight of stairs, she peeked into the Scepter Room. "Wow," she said softly.

"Would you like to see it?" he asked. He knew that it was better if he showed them than if they ventured on their own.

Alina nodded her head.

Berty led them into the circular Scepter Room. They walked into the inner circle made by the seven carved wooden columns. Both Hope and Alina gazed at the claret crystal sitting atop of a white metal staff secured in a central carved wooden pillar.

"The Seven High Sages used their magic to craft the Scepter," he told them. "It is said that no one can touch the Scepter, except the Emperor, without certain death."

Alina took a step back.

"It is wise to keep your distance, child," said a voice behind them.

Turning his head, Berty saw a tall, elderly Elf walking towards them.

"Hello, Alfred," greeted Berty. "Please, meet Alina."

Alfred gave the girl a grandfatherly smile. "Leena's grand-daughter, of course. Nice to meet you."

She smiled at the mention of her grandmother's name. "Hel-lo," she said quietly.

"Alfred is the Empire Scholar," explained Berty. "I don't want to keep you girls from your fun day together. Hope, why don't you show Alina your chambers?"

"Okay," Hope said. "This way, Alina." They quickly walked out of the room with Freesia closely behind.

"Satiating curiosity I see," said Alfred. "Alvar has just re-ceived some information that he would like to share with you."

He walked with Alfred to the Roundtable Room. The Captain of the Empire Guard stood near the table. When the stoic Elf saw Berty, he said, "My Lord," with a bow of his head.

"What's wrong, Alvar?" Berty asked.

"May we close the door?" Alvar asked.

With a wave of Berty's hand, the door closed. He stood between the Elves, waiting.

"My men have informed me of gatherings. So far, there are at least two dozen men at each gathering point. We are aware of four such points," Alvar stated. "The gatherings look benign, but some of the people," he made a face of disgust.

"So, what you are saying is that no one has done anything wrong. It just seems suspicious," Berty said.

"Yes. What would you like us to do, my Lord?"

"Monitor the situation from afar," answered Berty. "Do not let them know they are being watched." Remembering the attack on Declan, he added, "Be aware that one or more groups could have a Watcher. They can see magic in constant use. Perching an Elf invisible in a nearby tree could be detected."

"Do you think they are planning an attack on the Empire Tree?" asked Alfred.

Berty's eyes got lost in the reflective top of the Roundtable as he mulled over Alfred's words. "I don't know," he finally admitted. "Elrick and Lida have given us a permanent Containment Unit in case of another Fairy Dust attack. However, that doesn't mean that someone isn't stupid enough to attack us again. Are there any Watchers in the Empire Guard?"

"None of which I am aware," answered Alvar.

"We could use some trusted Watchers in our perches," Berty said. "I will speak to Declan about it."

"Do you think they will use magic against us?" Alvar asked.

"Fight fire with fire," said Berty.

"Fight magic with magic," Alfred interpreted.

9

"Exactly. We cannot defend against future attacks by taking measures that only would have prevented the previous ones," stated Berty. "Has anyone spoken with Sean? He seems to be an expert on all things suspicious."

"No, my Lord," said Alvar.

Magically, Berty opened the door. "Theodore," he called.

The young Dwarf appeared in the doorway. "Yes, my Lord?" said Theodore.

"We need to speak with Sean," Berty told him.

With a bow, the Head Tender disappeared.

Berty sat in his ornately carved chair at the Roundtable. Both Alvar and Alfred took seats on either side of him.

"You wished to see me, my Lord," said the mousy voice that grated on Berty's nerves.

He studied Sean, who stood near the table in his brown Tender's uniform. Sean's dark, straight hair made his gray eyes more visible. Berty used magic to close the door before saying, "Since you were the one who informed me about those Watchers who attacked Declan, I wanted to know your thoughts about another matter that has been brought to my attention."

Standing straighter, Sean tried not to smile.

"How would you determine if a gathering of people was innocent or filled with malice?" Berty asked him.

Sean wrinkled his nose in disappointment. "If the people look to be doing nothing, then it is most likely they are planning something," he answered. His gray eyes glanced at the tabletop.

"What is it?" Berty asked.

Sean's gaze shifted to him. "There are men who will fight for money or for the thrill. They have no real honor, no cause. I never paid anyone, but I know these men exist."

"Thank you, Sean," he said. "You may return to your work."

Sean gave Berty a dignified bow before leaving.

"How long do you think we have to prepare?" asked Alvar.

"I do not know. We should fortify our defenses and increase patrols," said Berty. "Notify Irmingard and Fairyland as well."

Watching the Elves leave the table, he wondered what part Leif and Millicent played in the gatherings. How could someone who had a seat at the Roundtable betray them? "Amazing what a thirst for power can do to a person," he muttered as he rose from his chair.

Climbing the main staircase, he decided to let the girls play without his interference. When the stairs ended, he strolled down the curved hall. He found himself standing in front of an arched wooden door.

Entering the room, he merely glanced at the myriad of weapons stored around the curved room. He hung his cloak on a hook, then secured leather protective gear onto his body. With his sword securely in his grip, he looked at the practice dummy crumpled on the ground, then said, "Begin."

The dummy sprang to life. Like a marionette without strings, it attacked. With every hit, Berty released his frustrations.

"My Lord."

His eyes found Declan standing near the door.

"I have finished," said Declan.

After stabbing the dummy in the chest, Berty said, "Enough." The dummy lifelessly fell in a heap on the floor.

Declan waited as he removed his practice armor.

Throwing his cloak around his shoulders, he opened the door to the hall. "Follow me," he told Declan. Approaching a section of wall, he grabbed Declan's cloaked elbow. He stepped through the wall, pulling Declan with him.

The hallway on the other side of the wall gently curved with the large circumference of the tree. Before the hall became stairs, they turned.   Mugginess embraced them as they crossed the narrow, rope and plank bridge.

Entering his chambers, Berty hung his cloak. He motioned for Declan to do the same. "Have a seat," he said while sitting in a club chair that faced the door.

Choosing a chair across from Berty, Declan said, "The Watcher's Vault is filled with so much information that I had to take notes." He opened papers. "When I organized everything by category, I noticed that information about the Cavern was relatively small compared to everything else. But, what I've found confirms what I've read in the Guild Master's study. While the bow refers to the Bow of the Moon, the sword refers to the Gullogbrand made on the steðimyrk, or something like that. The ancient tongue is not my forte. I wrote them down."

He handed a piece of paper to Berty.

Glancing at his red stoned pinky ring, Berty wondered if the ring would allow him to translate. Reading the paper, he said, "Gullogbrand roughly means golden blaze blade and steðimyrk is anvil of darkness."

"*The* Anvil of Darkness?" asked Declan. "The one on which Edwin's new sword was forged, according to legend?"

"Golden blaze blade would translate to Blade of the Golden Flame. The very sword Edwin pulled out of that stone," he said.

"What do we tell Edwin?" Declan asked.

"As much of the truth as you can without violating the Order of the Keepers," said Berty. He gave the paper back to Declan.

Nodding, Declan said, "The Cavern does not seem to be nearly as important as magic itself. Although powerful magic originated in the Cavern, my job as Keeper and Watcher for the Empire is to protect magic's essence, so that it can be used to its full potential." He placed the paper in his pocket. "I wonder if the Watchers' Guild lost sight of that while indulging its self-interests."

"Speaking of Watchers," said Berty. "Do you trust any enough to aid the Empire Guards in looking for magic?"

The wind chimes rang.

"I will talk to the Guild Master," said Declan.

"Come in," said Berty.

Theodore entered his study, carrying dinner on a tray.

"Thank you, Theodore." After the Dwarf left, Berty said to Declan, "Join me. I will fill you in on Alvar's little discoveries."

After listening to Berty, Declan said, "It sounds as though someone or someones are amassing an army."

"I'm tempted to take Sean with us tomorrow as not to use the Empire Guards," he told Declan.

Agreeing, Declan sipped his drink. "I would like to head to Boudon," he stated. "Not only to fulfill the promise I made to my grandfather, but to see if any of them are standing on the other side."

"Sooner is better than later, but you cannot go alone," said Berty. "I will go with you."

"What if," suggested Declan, "we made it a trip to buy Hope a bow. I know that as Emperor you can use the Empire Bowsmith, but..."

"Hope won't be joining the Empire Guard. It makes sense to buy a bow for her elsewhere," Berty said.

"Exactly," said Declan. He stared at his empty plate, then at Berty. "Do you think Edwin and I should not be in the same place at the same time?"

Taking a sip of mead, Berty pondered. "When do you think we should tell the others of Leif's true plans?"

Declan sighed. "Some secrets are not meant to be kept forever."

"Have Edwin come to your study tonight. You can explain

as much as you want about the Cavern to him. I will join you as soon as I check in on the girls," said Berty. "We will have a Council meeting when we return tomorrow."

"Thank you," said Declan.

After he left, Berty placed all the dishes from dinner onto the tray that Theodore brought. He placed it near the door outside his chambers, then walked down to Hope's.

Entering, he found Hope and Alina playing with dolls on one side of the room.

"Good evening, my Lord," said Freesia. She sat at the table, drinking a cup of a steaming beverage while keeping an eye on the girls.

"How has it been going?" he asked her as he took a seat.

"Very well," she responded. "I was going to read to them before bed. Would you like any tea?"

Glancing at the teapot, he said, "Yes, thank you."

"I've been thinking," Freesia said as she poured. "Perhaps Alina should join Hope for riding lessons. It may help Hope's enthusiasm in regards to everything else she needs to know about horses."

Berty recalled Hope's impatience when it came to horseback riding. All she wanted to do was to learn how to shoot arrows from horseback instead of learning how to ride properly. Agreeing with Freesia, he answered, "As long as Alina's parents give permission."

He smiled at Hope when she looked towards the table. She gave a happy wave. Finishing his cup, he said, "I need to make sure everything is ready. I will see you in the morning. Thank you for the tea."

As he rose out of the chair, Hope asked from across the room, "Are you leaving already, Uncle Berty?"

"I am. Goodnight, girls. I'll see you after breakfast."

14

"Goodnight," they said in unison.

Berty traipsed through the tree one flight down. Standing in front of Declan's door, he pulled the cord that rang his wind chimes. As soon as Declan said, "Come in," he entered.

Edwin and Declan sat around a plain table. Upon seeing Berty, his Lieutenant stood. Standing as well, Declan said, "Please have a seat, my Lord."

He took a seat at the table in Declan's sparse study. Once the others returned to their chairs, Berty said, "Continue. I do not need a summary."

Edwin nodded, then said, "Will someone try to steal my sword like they did with your bow?"

"It is a good possibility," said Declan. "I'm not sure how much information is out there about it."

"I see." Edwin's blue eyes glanced at Berty, then at Declan. "But what about its magic?"

"Place it on the table. Let me have a look," said Declan.

Standing, Edwin unsheathed his sword. The golden hue of the blade sparkled in the lantern light. When the Elf's pale hand retracted from his sword, Berty noticed the black hilt was as dark as the blade was bright.

Declan studied it. "There is magic in this sword," he hesitated.

"But?" Berty asked.

"It's... incomplete," answered Declan. "I can't explain it. There's just something about the way the magic flows."

Berty did not fully understand how Declan saw magic or how he was different from other Watchers. Yet he relied on Declan's ability and trusted it.

"Should I write to the Dominatrix?" Edwin asked. "She should be able to explain more."

"Perhaps or perhaps not," said Declan. "As a weapons expert, even she did not know everything about the Bow of the Moon."

"But it might behoove us to know what she knows," Edwin implored.

"No," Berty said firmly. "Put nothing in writing that leaves the Empire Tree. Declan is right. The Dominatrix's knowledge may be limited. I think it is better that we go straight to the source. The Dwarves crafted this sword. While they may not have used the Blade of the Golden Flame, they reclaimed it. They also found it impossible to destroy, so they encased it in stone and hid it in one of their abandoned mines. If anyone knows anything, then it will be the Dwarves."

"Would we have to travel to Grunnan?" Edwin asked. "That is the best protected place in the Empire. I do not think any non-Dwarf has ever been there."

"Declan and I will speak to Colvin tomorrow. In the meantime, do not let your sword out of your sight. I will have Theodore add extra protection to your chambers," said Berty.

"Yes, my Lord. Thank you," Edwin said. After returning the sword to his scabbard, the Elf exited with a bow.

"He seems apprehensive," remarked Declan.

"He found a legendary weapon by chance," Berty explained. "If Telor had not been dragged off by Ogres, then we would have never been down in that mine."

Declan nodded. "And if King Elrick had not been attacked by that Fairy Eater," he added without finishing his thought. "I've been thinking about that. I would have obtained the Bow of the Moon no matter what. My grandfather had always intended to give it to me. Edwin, on the other hand... is an expert swordsman for an Elf."

Berty knew the Elves to be the best archers in the Empire. Yet, he sat in the study of the best of the best, who happened to not be an Elf. Although known for their archery skill, the Elves

16

used all sorts of weapons. They even had their own resident weapon expert—the Dominatrix.

"Do you believe in destiny?" Declan asked him.

"The idea that life is predestined means that all our choices are for naught. Freedom would be nothing than an abstract construct, which has no place in reality," answered Berty. "I like to think that our destiny is the product of what we chose to do with our innate abilities." He could see Declan digesting his words.

"I need to talk to Theodore," Berty told him. "See you in the morning."

Nodding, Declan stood when he stood. As he exited Declan's chambers, Declan grabbed his bow off a rack on the wall, then carried it to the staircase that led to his bedroom.

Berty waited until he was inside the trunk before calling for Theodore. When the young Dwarf appeared on the steps with him, he said, "Edwin's chambers need extra protection. Also, Sean will be going with us in the morning."

"Very well, my Lord," Theodore said. With a bow, he disappeared.

His eyes registered the glow from the Scepter Room spilling onto the staircase landing. As he walked to his chambers, his mind recounted the Pixie Priestess' image saying, "Seven sages. Seven seals. Seven secrets. Soon sinister steals," from the depths of the crystal Scepter. He fell asleep wondering if her last three words referred to the Bow of the Moon or the Blade of the Golden Flame.

Chapter Two
The Witch of Rowan

Freesia had the girls tidying their sleeping area when Berty entered Hope's chambers after an early breakfast. "Are we ready to go?" he asked them.

"Almost," said Hope. She scampered up the steps to her bedroom.

Alina dug into the bag she brought from home. Gently, she pulled a leather satchel from its depths. She placed the long, leather strap across her body. The satchel's flap had a tree embossed in the leather.

Hope galloped down the stairs wearing her quiver and bow. "Ooh, that's pretty," she complimented.

"Thanks," Alina said with a smile. "It was my great-great-grandmother's. This is the Rowan tree." Her fingers ran over the raised branches. "Keeps herbs and stuff."

Smiling, Hope said, "Cool."

They donned their cloaks, which covered their possessions. Berty led Freesia and the girls through the tree. In the Reception Room, they met Declan and Sean while the other inhabitants gathered for breakfast. The two men followed them into the Sages' Grove.

When they reached the gates, Berty had Hope walk next to him. "Which way?" he asked her.

She looked at the surrounding trees as if she were listening. Tugging on Berty's sleeve, she chose a direction. Leisurely, they strolled through the forest. Every now and then, Alina picked plants. She would sniff them, then place them in her satchel. When Declan found items, he would call Hope to have a look. After a quick explanation, the item went into his bag.

Finally, Hope stopped. She gazed at a large tree. The wide trunk held many branches. Cautiously, she approached the old tree. She slowly reached towards the trunk. Her little hand rested against the light grayish-brown bark. Berty could see her smile.

Stepping backwards, she looked up at its many leaves. Turning, she said, "Okay. Thank you for taking me, Uncle Berty."

"You're welcome," he replied. He remembered the wooden doll that he gave her. She named it Ashley. By her communicating with it, he knew that she was a Wood Listener. For the longest time, she wanted to visit the tree from which the doll was fashioned. "Are you ready to return?"

She nodded. With a warm smile, she skipped to Berty's side. Something only she could hear made her turn her head.

"What is it?" Berty asked.

"The Master Woodsman is coming," she said as she stared into the forest.

Declan raised his eyebrows as he looked at Berty. Before Berty could answer, a man with a long, white beard approached. His long robe matched the green of the underbrush.

"Emperor," greeted the Master Woodsman. "I have heard rumors that the Wood Listener has returned. Forgive me for wanting to meet the child."

"An honor to see you again, Master Woodsman," said Berty. He remembered meeting the man on the road to Calledin after an encounter with a rogue Wood Sprite. "Is Miradelle not with you?"

"She is forbidden to interact with the Wood Listener. A Wood Sprite in her condition is unpredictable at best," he said. "May I?"

Berty gave the Master Woodsman a nod.

Walking towards Hope, the old man said, "Hello, Hope. What an honor it is to meet you." He looked at her with a smile for a moment. "Until we meet again." With a slight nod of his head, he turned to Berty. "Thank you, Emperor. I must return to my charge before she wreaks havoc on unsuspecting travelers."

Hope watched the Master Woodsman disappear between the trees. After giving her uncle a wide smile, she led them away from the ash tree.

During their meander back to the Sages' Grove, Alina picked flowers and leaves. Hope stayed close to Declan as he explained all sorts of things to her. Berty watched Sean furrow his eyebrows every so often when glancing around the forest.

"What is it?" he asked Sean quietly.

"Directions," Sean whispered. "To the gatherings. They're subtle. A bent branch." His gray eyes scanned the trees. "The directions are for fighters for hire."

Berty's insides dropped. "Are you sure?"

"Per their instructions."

"I am sure that at least one will take the offer," he muttered. "Thank you, Sean."

Sean almost smiled as they walked out of the forest. Crossing the clearing, Alina positioned her satchel under her cloak, so that it stayed hidden from view.

As they approached the gates to the Sages' Grove, Hope walked next to Berty. "He said that I could hear the call of the Mother Wood Sprite," she said.

"Who did?" he asked.

"The Master Woodsman," she answered.

He watched her skip happily to Alina's side. Beyond the gates, the dirt path split. One direction led into the cob village while the other brought travelers to the Empire Tree and beyond to the Empire Guard barracks. In front of them, two men carried a third towards the main village.

"Cal!" shrieked Alina's mother as she ran towards the men.

"Daddy?" Alina said quietly. She began walking to her mother.

"What happened?" Natalie asked the men.

"Daddy?" Alina said louder.

"He had a bad fall," said one of the men. "We brought him home immediately."

"Daddy?" Alina screamed, running down the path.

Berty followed her. The others ran behind him. Cal's blood stained clothes could not hide his difficult breaths.

"Alina, honey, you shouldn't be here," Natalie said with a tear streaked face.

She stared at her father whose legs were not able to support him. "I'm not leaving," she said.

"Go be with your brother," Cal breathed.

She shook her head.

"Please," he labored.

Her little hands reached for her father. Both palms touched his broken body. The little girl spoke in a language that Berty did not recognize.

Watching, Declan whispered, "Wow."

When she removed her hands from her father, Cal stood on his own. Alina smiled, then collapsed.

Glancing from her husband to her daughter, Natalie cried, "Alina!" She fell to her knees. "She's so pale."

Cal crouched to pick up his daughter.

Declan placed a hand on Cal's shoulder. "She needs rest, and so do you," he said. "The Witch of Rowan has returned."

"But she is so young," Natalie said.

With a reach of his hand, Declan helped Natalie to her feet. Berty felt a tug on his cloak. Looking down, he saw Hope clutching to it. Freesia whisked the unconscious Alina off the ground.

"Sean," said Declan, beckoning him. He whispered in Sean's ear.

Giving him a slight nod, Sean hurried towards the Empire Tree.

Berty and Hope followed to the Rowan's house.

"What happened?" asked Leena as they entered the house.

"She healed without being grounded," Declan answered.

"Put her on my bed," said Leena, "under the stairs."

Freesia carefully laid her on the bed. "Thank you, Freesia," said Natalie who clutched her dress to keep her from shaking. "Is there anything we can do for her?" Dragging two chairs next to the bed, Cal had his wife sit on one while he sat on the other.

"Not really," said Declan. "She'll be weak for awhile. That was some serious magic for one so young. There is something that helps recover her strength faster, but it is hard to find."

A knock on their door made Declan stop talking. Leena opened the door, letting Sean inside the small house. He looked at Declan, then shook his head.

"As I thought," said Declan. "Thanks for looking anyway, Sean."

After Sean left, Berty asked Declan, "For what were you looking?"

"Cacao," said Declan. "It's usually found in the Witch's Trade, but I thought that it would not hurt to see if the Empire Tree had any. It will just take her longer to recover without it."

Berty repeated *cacao* over and over in his head, wondering

22

why it was familiar. Finally, he mouthed, "Cocoa." Remembering the chocolate chip cookies that Silvia had made for his first
journey through the portal, he said, "I know where you can get
some cacao products. Come with me. We'll be back soon," he
told the others.

He led Declan inside the tree. As they climbed his private
staircase, he said, "Items made from cacao are easier to get on the
other side of the portal. I hope we can find something that can
work."

They crossed the rope and plank bridge that connected to
Berty's chambers. Passing his leafy green bundle, they walked into
Silvia's. He glanced at the Sages' Seal carved into the back wall
before climbing the stairs hidden behind it. Without stopping,
they stepped through the tapestry of a stag in a woodland scene.

Emerging from the fireplace depicting the same scene, Berty
led Declan out of his Victorian era bedroom. They hurried down
a wood paneled hall. Berty paused to open a door. On a wall at
the end of the hall, a tapestry hung. It showed an owl soaring
above the trees.

"That wasn't there before," said Berty.

"It's just like the one that hangs in Hope's chambers," Declan
commented.

"Exactly?"

"The picture also moves."

Not saying another word about the tapestry, Berty galloped
down the back stairs with Declan close on his heels. "What do
you do with the cacao?" Berty asked.

"It's ground in a mortar with a pestle," said Declan. "Then it
is added to a bunch of different ingredients. I'm not sure of the
exact recipe. Geraint, the Wizard who taught me the healing arts,
told me about it. Not that I ever had a need for it." They entered the old-fashioned kitchen while Declan continued, "He

23

called it Witch's Brew."

The kitchen immediately came to life. Ingredients flew out of the wooden cabinets. A black cast iron pot heated on the old gas range.

"I guess it knows how to make it," said Berty.

"Seems that way." Declan's eyes followed the items across the room.

When an old metal goblet flew out of a cabinet, Berty said, "Can we get it to go?" A metal lid accompanied the goblet.

The pot poured its contents into the goblet. With a couple of clicks, the lid snapped over the top. Berty grabbed the goblet off the plank table, thanked the kitchen, then led Declan back the way they came.

As they hurried through the tree, Declan asked, "How did the house know how to make this? I was going to use my best guess and I've seen it being made."

"I don't know," replied Berty. "The house has yet to reveal all of its mysteries to me."

Entering the Rowan house, they found Alina barely awake. Freesia poured tea for everyone while Cal and Natalie talked to their daughter. Only Leena and Hope noticed them enter.

Magically unlocking the lid, Berty handed the goblet to Declan.

"Here, Alina, drink this," said Declan, "slowly."

"What is that?" Cal asked.

"Witch's Brew," answered Declan. "It will make her feel better."

Natalie relieved Declan of the goblet. As she held it to her daughter's lips, Alina took a sip. Alina clasped her hands over her mother's. After a couple of sips, Alina sat up in the bed.

"The color is returning to your cheeks," Natalie told Alina.

"Do I have to drink all of it?" Alina asked.

Declan smiled as if he were remembering something. "Yes," he told her. "That was some powerful magic you used on your father."

She drank more.

"Can I have some?" asked William, who sat on the bed near his sister's feet.

"You cannot," Cal said to his son.

"Only Witches can drink Witch's brew," Leena added.

"I wanna be a Witch," said William.

"Just girls can be Witches," Natalie said sweetly.

"Oh." His face fell a little. Gaping at his sister, he asked, "What does it taste like?"

"Stuff," Alina said between gulps.

"Is it good?"

"It's okay," she answered.

William briefly smirked.

Once she finished the Witch's Brew, she handed the goblet to her mother. "How are you feeling?" Natalie asked.

"Better," Alina said with a smile.

Natalie held the empty goblet towards Berty. "Thank you," she said. Taking it from her, he placed the lid on top. "How can she prevent this from happening next time?"

"From what I understand," explained Declan, "it is something that she must learn on her own. Perhaps her great-great-grandmother left instructions somewhere."

"I know where!" said Alina. She sprang from the bed. From the depths of her leather satchel, she extracted a bronze skeleton key. Crossing the room, she stopped beside the large hearth. She inserted the key into what looked like a crack between the stones. Turning the key opened the wall.

Alina gazed into the room that opened before her. "Look at all this," she said.

Through the opening, Berty was able to see shelves with books and bottles, different sized cauldrons, all sorts of tools, and glimpses of benches and a table.

Cal and Natalie stood at Alina's side. "Looks like you have a lot of books to read," Cal told her.

She walked into the room, then began to place the herbs she collected on the table. Carefully, she chose a book from a shelf. After stuffing it into her satchel, she returned to her parents. "Can I go back to Hope's?" she asked them.

Natalie smiled. "As long as you're back for dinner," she said.

Alina gave her mother a hug, then removed the key. In place of a wall was a large, wooden door.

With Alina in tow, they returned to the Empire Tree.

On the landing in front of the Roundtable Room, Berty said, "You girls go upstairs and have lunch. Declan and I have some Empire business to do."

"Okay," the girls said in unison. He watched them run up the stairs ahead of Freesia.

"You should have seen the magic she radiated," Declan said as they entered the room. "She's going to be a powerful Witch."

Declan took his seat at the table while Berty crossed to his private staircase. Stepping onto his small landing, he placed the goblet on a step so that he could retrieve it later to bring it back to the house. Before his toes touched the threshold, the goblet vanished.

He joined Declan at the Roundtable as the rest of the Advisory Council entered the room. Once they were all seated, he addressed them.

"By now, I'm sure you all are well aware of the people who are gathering in different areas of the woods. I discovered today that the organizers of these gatherings are hiring fighters," said Berty. "Alvar, have you learned anything new?"

26

The stoic Elf addressed the table. "There are rumors that these groups are looking for people who specialize in certain skills. Namely, archers and those with magic. I had a meeting with the Watchers' Guild Master today. The Watchers agreed to work with us. However, he said that because Watchers can only see magic in constant use, it limits them to only spotting magical items, not when a person uses magic."

"A magical item could be very dangerous," said Berty. "Alfred?"

"Both Irmingard and Fairyland are taking precautions," Alfred reported. "As former High Elf, I know that Irmingard is well prepared. I fear for the safety of Fairyland. No offense, Delyth, but even Fairy Dust has its limitations."

"No offense taken, Alfred," said Delyth. "I have been in contact with my mother and father. The Fairy Guard will be arriving today to escort me to Fairyland. There are a few things with which only I can help. I should return in a day or so."

Berty gave Delyth a nod. "Declan?"

"There may be an underlying reason for the gatherings," Declan began. "Watcher lore talks about a cavern which holds great magic. We believe that Leif knows about the Cavern. If he is orchestrating these gatherings, then he may be using these people to search for it."

"So we find this cavern first," said Colvin.

"It's not that easy," Declan said.

"You're a Watcher. It's your lore," Colvin reasoned.

"The Cavern is protected by secrets and puzzles and mysteries," explained Declan. "Just because I am a Watcher does not mean I know all the secrets or hold any answers at all. I am merely the holder of a locket." His light eyes pierced into Berty's as if Declan finally understood something.

Looking away from Declan, Berty said, "Hatcher?"

27

"There has been an increase in portal use," the Troll said. "I don't know if it's related or not."

"Colvin?" said Berty.

"If you need to find a cave, then I'm your Dwarf," Colvin said.

"Estelle, what do the stars say?" asked Berty.

Estelle's icy blue eyes glanced at everyone sitting around the table before she answered, "Changes are imminent. War is arriving on the doorsteps of the Sages."

"The Sages' Grove or the Land of Sages?" Alvar asked her.

"Neither," said Estelle. "The Sages themselves."

"But the Sages are long gone," said Colvin.

"Their descendants remain," Berty said. When all eyes fell on him, he continued, "The ones who wear the crystals. The Fairy Guardian Spirits called Silvia—Elder Hunter—and me wearers of the Sage Stones. In addition to the two of us, the Sages' descendants are Alfred, Prince Goscislaw, King Elrick, Queen Lida, and Sean." Out of the corner of his eye, he could see Declan's nose wrinkle slightly. "Does anyone have anything else to add?"

The Advisory Council responded with a, "No."

"Then this meeting is adjourned," he said. "Delyth, have a safe journey. Colvin, could you stay a minute, please?"

The Fairy gave Berty a smile while the Dwarf said, "Of course, my Lord."

When only Berty, Declan and Colvin remained, Berty said, "You wished to help with the Cavern situation."

"Indeed, I do," Colvin stated. "How can I be of service?"

"I want you to find out about something that Declan believes to be connected with the Cavern. And you must do so quietly," said Berty.

"Of course."

"If the legend is correct, the Dwarves hid a sword which was

28

forged on the Anvil of Darkness." He watched Colvin's dark, beady eyes grow bigger. "The sword has been released from its stone encasement. Unfortunately, not much is known about it. Perhaps you can obtain this information?"

Colvin's bright orangey-red beard hit his chest as he nodded. "I will start right away."

"Thank you, Colvin. I knew I could count on you," said Berty.

Once Colvin had exited, Berty turned to Declan. "You connected something before. What was it?"

"The way you used the Watcher's Lockets to find me after my grandfather.... I didn't think of it when you told me, but after reading the stuff in my vault, I realized that you understand the lockets better than any Watcher."

"I don't understand the lockets," Berty interrupted. "I just did what I thought I should do."

"Exactly." Declan turned in his chair to face Berty. Lowering his voice, he told him, "*You* are the Key."

Chapter Three
Golden

"The Key that is supposed to unlock the Cavern?" Berty asked. "I thought we were looking for objects."

Declan shook his head. "Magic," he said. "You possess certain magic that makes you the Key."

Looking at his friend, Berty said, "When Delyth returns, we will go to Boudon. Have you asked her to go yet?"

"I'll catch her before she leaves," said Declan.

Berty watched Declan close the door as he left. Alone, he closed his eyes. Dark red hair framed fair skin punctuated by warm, brown eyes. Silvia sat at a desk. Her fingers caressed a pen. She dipped the point into a bottle of ink. When the pen filled, she continued writing. A piece of paper was half full of her graceful handwriting. Not wanting to read her words, he opened his eyes.

He moseyed to lunch. Noticing Declan finally joining the table, his mind wandered to when Declan first told him about the Cavern. Showing him the Watcher's Symbol, Declan said, "Only when the wand, the sword and the bow unite with the past, the present and the future, will the key unlock the Cavern." He remembered Declan pointing to the eye sitting in the center of the star when he said, "Key."

"My Lord," said Colvin, interrupting Berty's thoughts. "I did as you asked," he said in hushed tones. "Prince Goscislaw requests an audience with you, Declan and the one who removed it, with the object."

"Thank you, Colvin. When would he like to meet?" asked Berty.

"I am to take you to Grunnan as soon as you are able," Colvin stated.

Berty glanced down the table. "Give me a moment," he told the Dwarf. Rising from the table, he caught Declan's eye.

Once Declan joined him away from the table, Berty said, "Are you ready to leave now?"

Declan's gaze rested on Colvin, who waited near the table. "Shall I collect Edwin?"

Berty nodded. While Declan stepped onto the bridge, Berty returned to Colvin. "We'll be ready soon."

Hearing giggling, he turned his head. Hope, Alina and Freesia descended into the Reception Room. Upon seeing her uncle, Hope ran to him.

"We're going to ride horses," said Hope. She sounded excited. "Alina's mom and dad said it was okay for her to learn, too. That's so great!"

Smiling at her enthusiasm, he said, "That's fantastic. We'll have to go riding soon. You girls be safe. I'll see you later."

He watched them disappear beneath the floor, wishing he knew how much later, later would actually be.

When Declan and Edwin reached the table, Berty told Colvin, "Lead the way."

Downstairs, Colvin led them to the back of the Receiving Room. The Dwarf touched the bottom circle of one of the Sages' Seals. When the painted seal split, the four men walked into a boxy, wooden room. After the door closed, the box plunged them deep into the earth.

"Is Delyth on her way to Fairyland?" Berty asked.

"Escorted by six Fairy Guards," said Declan. After a pause, he asked, "Is Sean really descended from a Sage?"

"You two seem to be getting along," stated Berty.

Declan shrugged. "He's becoming tolerable, but still."

Looking at his sandy haired friend, he chuckled.

"Do you like him, my Lord?" asked Colvin.

"Sean?" Berty thought about the man, who inadvertently made him Emperor, for a second. "Like is such a strong word, but he is good with a sword and has defended me. He is biding his time. When he leaves, we will not part as enemies."

The elevator like box stopped. When the doors opened, Colvin led them through a torch lighted, rough-hewn tunnel.

"There are mine carts that travel directly to Grunnan from the Empire Tree," Colvin said. "Only Dwarves can operate them."

Rounding a bend, they entered a large room full of multiple tracks. On the rough walls hung torches whose flickering light illuminated thick timber supports. They approached one of the half dozen mine carts.

As Colvin opened the cart door, Berty glimpsed at the hammer and pickaxe crossed in front of a keystone that was embossed on the metal. Inside were three benches. Two on either end, where occupants would face each other, and one in the middle on which a person could sit either way. The Dwarf had Edwin and Declan sit on the rear bench, while Berty sat on the middle bench. Closing the door, Colvin sat next to Berty.

With a push of a lever, the cart began to move. The last time Berty traveled in a mine cart, his Advisor took him to the Empire Vaults.

Before leaving the large room, the tracks converged. They entered a tunnel, which held two tracks. The wooden supports and torches started to whiz past as the cart picked up speed.

When the torches ended, cool air rustling through his hair told Berty that they moved much faster than when he visited the vault.

Every so often, he could feel the cart lean as it rounded bends. He was not sure how far they had been traveling, but his legs told him that he had been sitting in the cart for a while. Eventually, his eyes detected light somewhere up ahead. The cramps in his legs relaxed, hoping that they had reached their destination.

The cart slowed slightly. Torchlight illuminated levers between the tracks. Reaching, Colvin moved a couple. When the tunnel widened, the cart rode on the Dwarf's chosen track. Their speed decreased further, making the rough rock walls less blurry.

The tunnel opened into a gigantic cave. Rushing water echoed in the cavern. The track wove through stalagmites spiking from the ground and columns formed by the meeting of stalactites and stalagmites. Berty's eyes detected a soft light, but he could not find the source.

A forest of cave formations gave way to an imposing, expansive clearing. In the distance, Berty spied an underground El Dorado. Rays of sunlight spilled into a crack in the earth above. Mesoamerican style pyramids glittered with a golden hue. Crossing the clearing quickly, the cart zipped towards the golden city.

Some tracks led to the golden steps that cascaded down the side of the first pyramid. Their track took them inside a golden tunnel that cut through the pyramid.

"Welcome to Grunnan," said Colvin. Pulling a lever, they switched tracks. "This takes us straight to the Prince."

"Is Grunnan made entirely of gold?" asked Declan.

The Dwarf smiled under his fiery beard. "All the stone is covered with thin sheets of a gold alloy. It is a secret blend of metals that helps keep our city safe."

"Gold allows for magic to travel easily," said Declan.

"When need be," Colvin responded. "The gold also is easier

on the eyes underground."

The mine cart stopped inside a golden room. Dwarves wearing brownish-gold armor heavily guarded the room and its many exits.

Opening the door, Colvin jumped out. "Mind your head, Lieutenant. Dwarf construction does not take into account the height of Elves."

Berty carefully exited the cart. While waiting for the others, he realized that his head was very close to the gold ceiling. Declan glanced upwards at the ceiling that was also only a few inches from the top of his head. Getting out of the cart, Edwin had to hunch to stand and walk.

All three of them ducked as they followed Colvin into a claustrophobia-inducing staircase. The golden tunnel that encased the stairs looked to go on forever.

To distract himself from feeling like the gold walls were going to close in on him, Berty said to Colvin, "This area is heavily guarded, but I did not see any guards as we approached the city."

"The Royal Battalion protects only the Palace and the Royal Family," Colvin said.

"Who protects Grunnan?" asked Berty.

"The city does not have an official guard. If need be, we Dwarves will head into battle. However, Grunnan is equipped to protect itself," Colvin explained. "The Dwarves who built this place were Masters of their trades. Any Dwarf who learns their secrets and knowledge is known as a Master Tradesman in his field." He glanced at the three men following him. "Mind your heads," he told them.

Bending to avoid hitting his head, Berty stepped out of the staircase. A grandiose room with plenty of room for their heads greeted them. Gold columns supported a gold vaulted ceiling. Shining shallow bowls holding fire dotted the golden floor.

Members of the Royal Battalion stood guard throughout the room.

They approached many golden steps that led to a golden throne encrusted with large jewels.

"My Lord, welcome to the Royal Palace of Grunnan," said Goscislaw's low growl. The Dwarf Prince hurried down the many steps to greet his guests. "I am glad that you were able to come on such short notice. Please, come with me."

Goscislaw led them along the edge of the dais to a pair of tall arched doors. When they opened, they revealed a large dining hall with a very long central table. Walking to one side, the Prince stopped in front of a tall door. "Thank you, Colvin. Wait here."

Bowing, Colvin obeyed his prince. Berty, Declan and Edwin followed Goscislaw through the doorway. The Dwarf brought them through a narrow hall off of which were many doors.

Finally opening one of the doors, Goscislaw said, "After you."

Berty led his men into the room. The only light spilled in from the narrow hallway door. Two stone circles filled the center of the room. They walked around the outer stone circle that resembled an unbroken circular bench. When the door closed, darkness surrounded them.

Goscislaw growled, "*Slaga.*" A fire erupted inside the center circle of stone. Its light failed to reach much beyond the outer circle. The Dwarf stepped over the stone, then sat, facing the fire. He gestured for the others to do the same.

Once the three of them sat on the stone bench, Goscislaw said, "This is the Dark Room. There is no metal of any kind fused to the stone. What is said here will not go beyond these walls. No outside magic can reach us in here, nor can any of our magic leak out there." He studied Edwin for a moment. "So, an Elf pulled a sword from a stone. May I see it?"

Unsheathing the golden sword, Edwin handed it to the Dwarf.

"The Blade of the Golden Flame," said Goscislaw. "It was protected by an enchanted sapphire. How did you procure it?"

"We were returning from the tree line when Fairy Prince Telor was abducted by Ogres," Edwin began. "We pursued into their lair. They had him next to a pool that emitted a blue light. After smashing my bow, an Ogre threw me. I crashed into the rocks behind the waterfall. My ribs felt cracked, perhaps even broken. The pain was indescribable. Thunderous quakes of Ogre feet vibrated through my body. I needed to help them, but I was in severe pain and weaponless. My feet slid into the water, then a blue glow washed over me. My pain was gone. The only thing I had was my strength, so I climbed. Near the top of the waterfall, I saw a hilt of a sword sticking out of the rock. I decided to use it as a handle to help me climb. When I touched it, it did not feel as secure as it looked. It released easily from the rock. Sword in hand, I leapt across the pool to join the others. The Ogres retreated at the very sight of the sword."

Goscislaw turned the blade to reflect the firelight. "It was forged by Master Weaponsmith Ezard. Blind since birth, he crafted some of the best weaponry by feel and sound. This sword is an excellent example of his craftsmanship. After leaving our forges, the Blade of the Golden Flame has known a bloody history. It has aided many a bloodthirsty owner in ruthless brutality. Dwarf lives were lost confiscating this sword.

"Once it returned to our hands, we learned that its magic is great. Battling against magic is the sword's greatest asset. That is why we did not destroy it. We used it to vanquish evil magical creatures that constantly plagued our doorsteps. Only when that task was done, did we lock it away in stone. There, it waited centuries for someone worthy to claim it." He gazed at the

36

sword. Laying it on the bench, he rose, then stepped over the circle into the darkness.

When he returned, the Dwarf carried an empty scabbard as black as the sword's hilt and circular shield with a golden hue. "Without these, the sword's magic is incomplete," Goscislaw explained. "This scabbard hides the sword's magic away from the prying eyes and wands of Watchers. As long as the sword is sheathed in its scabbard, no Watcher can use a wand to find you or the sword." He handed the scabbard to the Elf. "This shield was also forged by Ezard on the Anvil of Darkness as an accompaniment to the sword. The warrior who commissioned the sword did not want the shield. It never left Grunnan. The shield deflects magic, including Dragonfire. Together, the right balance is found." The Dwarf held the shield and the sword towards Edwin. "Use them well, Lieutenant."

Edwin received them from Goscislaw. "Thank you." While Edwin removed his old scabbard and added the new one, Goscislaw ran back into the shadows.

"I almost forgot," said Goscislaw as he returned to the circle. He carried what looked like a leather harness. "This allows you to carry your shield on your back." He gave it to Edwin.

Facing Berty and Declan, Goscislaw growled, "Now, Colvin told me about a cavern. What is that about?"

"In the Watchers' Guild," said Declan, "I belong to the Order of the Keepers. We believe in a cavern from where great magic stems. There are seven elements that need to come together to open the Cavern. One of which is the Blade of the Golden Flame."

The Dwarf nodded his head. "It is known to me in the modern tongue as the Crystal Cave. My ancestor helped to craft the Scepter that sits in the Empire Tree from materials in that cave. Keepers protected the cave. I know not when or how it was sealed, just that it was and its location forgotten. What I do know is that neither the Anvil of Darkness nor the Blade of the Golden Flame were made from anything that originated from the Crystal Cave."

"Thank you, Goscislaw," said Berty.

"You are welcome, Emperor. I am glad to help," Goscislaw said. Standing, he said, "Please, stay and have dinner with us before you return."

"It would be an honor," said Berty as he stood.

Goscislaw extinguished the fire, then opened the door. Exiting the Dark Room, they followed the Dwarf Prince through the narrow, golden hallway.

When they arrived at the door through which they came, Goscislaw placed his hand on the lever. Looking at Declan and Edwin, he said, "You gentlemen take seats at the table. I wish to speak to the Emperor before we eat."

While his traveling companions entered the dining hall, Berty followed the Dwarf through another door.

They ascended a gold staircase where Berty did not have to worry about his head. Goscislaw said, "The words of the Empire Astrologer worry me. Grunnan is the eighth state of the Dwarf Kingdom. There were nine states in all."

"Were?" asked Berty.

"The Kingdom is gone. We are all that remain," Goscislaw explained. "My family has ruled Grunnan since its keystone was placed. This task will eventually pass to my daughter. The other eight states resided on the other side of the portal. The Sage from which I am descended had the foresight to make our home here. When the Kingdom fell, refugees from the other states scattered. Some took shelter here. Their descendants still live among us."

The stairs ended at a golden balcony. Berty walked with the melancholy Dwarf to its golden covered rail. A golden city of pyramids sprawled out beneath them. Tracks connecting every corner created a labyrinth like maze against the gold.

"I've never seen anything like it," Berty remarked.

Goscislaw smiled. "The last Dwarf King thought Grunnan was the most beautiful of the eight Prince or Princess run states. Because of that, we have always had the largest Royal Battalion. I suppose they are a relic of another time—sworn to protect the King wherever he may travel." The Dwarf watched his people go about their business in the city.

"Sometimes I wondered if I, too, were a relic of days past," he said to Berty. Pulling out the dark brown crystal from behind his fine shirt, he said, "This puts everything in perspective. It reminds me that the Dwarves and Grunnan are only one spoke in the wheel. Perhaps Grunnan has endured because of Sage wisdom combined with Dwarf resiliency, of course.

"I do not want war on my doorstep, my Lord. My people are good, hard working people. This city has never seen war. I want to keep it that way."

"No one wants war, Goscislaw," Berty said. "I wish I knew how to prevent it. You've heard the Pixie Priestess' warning."

With a nod, Goscislaw growled, "Aye."

"Until they make a move, uncertainty is the enemy." He gazed out at the golden city. "Without hesitation, you came to the aid of the Empire Tree when she needed it. To win this war, we, the descendants of the Seven High Sages, must band together."

"You can count on me," said Goscislaw.

"As you can me," Berty replied.

"I trust you can bring us together, even if one of us is a murdering weasel." When the Dwarf uttered those words, Berty knew he referred to Sean. "Come, Emperor, let's not make the cooks wait."

Together, they descended the steps, which returned them to the golden corridor off of the Dining Hall. When they entered, people stood. Food filled the half of the long table.

Goscislaw stood in front of his chair at the head of the table. Berty stood in front of the only empty chair, which was the first chair to the Prince's right. To Berty's right, stood Declan.

"Tonight, guests from the Empire Tree honor our dinner table," Goscislaw announced. "The Emperor, his Advisors, Declan and Colvin and his Lieutenant."

Further down the table was Edwin who towered like a Frost Giant over the Dwarves who flanked him.

"Let us feast for continued peace and prosperity in the Empire," said Goscislaw.

People took their seats. Platters of food passed from hand to hand around the table. After all the platters returned to the center of the table, Goscislaw said, "My Lord, I do not believe you have met my wife, Leosia, and my daughter, Brana."

Across from Berty sat a duo of redheads. The women's flame red hair shined brightly in the golden room.

"An honor to meet you both," said Berty with a warm smile.

"The honor is ours, my Lord," Leosia said. Brana blushed. Her cheeks almost matched her hair.

Dinner was filled with cheerful laughter and hearty food. When the plates were taken away, small cordial glasses filled with a dark liquid sat in each place.

"This is a Dwarf specialty," growled Goscislaw happily. "Dark Root Schnapps helps you sleep at night."

Berty watched the Dwarves merrily sip from their glasses. Raising the glass to his lips, the smell was familiar. His first sip reminded him of root beer soda except not as sweet and minus the carbonation.

"My Lord, do you like it?" Brana asked.

"I do," replied Berty. "It is reminiscent of something I grew up having."

Smiling, Brana blushed again. She glanced at the table before looking elsewhere.

After the glasses were empty, Berty said to his hosts, "We thank you for your hospitality. Duty now beckons us home."

"Indeed," said Goscislaw. He walked with them to the Throne Room. "Our doors are open to you anytime, my Lord."

With a nod to the Dwarf Prince, he followed his men back to the mine cart. The ride home gave Berty clarity. There was no need to keep Declan and Edwin apart from each other. The Blade of the Golden Flame's magic was complete. Their chances of keeping those who coveted them at bay were better together than apart.

As they traveled through the rough-hewn tunnel from the mine cart to the Empire Tree, Berty said, "Colvin, thank you."

"Just doing my duty for the Empire, my Lord," said Colvin. When they entered the box to the surface, he added, "If I can do anything more, let me know."

"I will," Berty replied. "Edwin, you may share today with Captain Alvar only." The Elf nodded.

When the door opened, they found the Receiving Room mostly empty. The four men climbed the steps to the Reception Room. Alfred greeted them as they crossed the room.

"My Lord," said the aged Elf, "Delyth arrived in Fairyland safely. All is well there."

"Good to hear," he said. Both he and Declan ascended higher into the tree.

"I've been thinking," said Declan as he followed Berty beyond the Roundtable Room's landing. "Edwin should accompany us to Boudon."

"I agree," he said. He stopped at the entrance to the bridge leading to Hope's chambers.

Declan stopped a step below the landing. "Good. We leave when Delyth returns?"

"Sounds good to me," said Berty. "I'll see you in the morning."

The setting summer sun cast a pinkish orange glow as he crossed the bridge to Hope's chambers. Inside, he found Hope and Freesia tidying the play area.

"Uncle Berty!" squealed Hope. "You missed Mommy and Daddy's call."

He smiled. "That's okay. They'd rather talk to you anyway. Did you and Alina have a good time?"

"The best!" When the room met Freesia's neat standards, Hope ran over to him. "She showed me the book that she took out of her Witch Room," she told him.

They sat on puffy chairs while Freesia crept upstairs. "What was that like?" he asked.

"Written in a strange language. It looked like a bunch of sticks," she said. "Alina never saw the language before, but she could read it. Why?"

"Because she's a Witch. It's part of her magic," he explained. "The book sounds as if it were written in some form of Runes."

"Can I learn to read Runes?" she asked.

"If we can find someone to teach you," he said. Her face fell a little. "If no one here knows Runes, then I'm sure we can get a book or two online when your parents come home."

"Okay."

"Did you do the Fairy Dust exercises Delyth gave you yet?"

"No."

He raised his eyebrows. "Get them done before bed. That way you'll have a clear mind for archery tomorrow."

"Okay, Uncle Berty."

"Goodnight, Hope."

Freesia quietly walked down the steps.

"Goodnight," Hope told him.

He gave Freesia a nod before returning to the Empire Tree's bridge system. Taking the direct bridge to his chambers, all he wanted to do was reflect on the day. The best way he found to reflect was to write about everything that transpired in his notebook in his fictionalized version of his life, *the Adventures of Leigh and Marcus.*

Summer mornings reminded him of his childhood. He and Jon would wake up early to ride their bikes to the neighborhood park. They played whatever game with whomever was there. No one, that Berty could recall, ever practiced archery at the park. As he watched Hope hit moving targets, he was not sure if he would have been interested in archery at her age.

At the end of her lesson, Declan said to Berty, "Hope has out mastered her training bow. I believe she is ready for a real bow."

Hope's eyes widened as she looked from Declan to Berty.

"If you say she is ready, then we are to get her a real bow," said Berty. "The Empire Bowsmith has a lot on his plate, especially helping Fairyland."

"I know of an expert Bowsmith," said Declan. "It should only take a few days ride on horseback."

Berty crouched in front of his niece. "What do you say to a little trip on a horse to get you an early birthday present?"

"Yay!" She hugged Berty so hard he almost fell on the ground. After releasing him, she asked, "When do we leave?"

"I'd like Delyth to come with us, so as soon as she returns from Fairyland," he answered. "In the meantime, get your horseback riding perfected."

"Okay, Uncle Berty," she said. "Come, Freesia," Hope tugged her Fairy Godmother's hand, "we have horses to ride!"

Chuckling, he stood. "That went well," he told Declan.

Entering the Empire Tree from the guard's practice area, Declan said, "I expect Delyth to be returning tonight. Shall I make arrangements to leave tomorrow?"

"Yes." Once inside the Reception Room, Berty climbed the few steps concealed by the long draping curtains that framed the dais. He entered the private staircase hidden behind in the wall filling Sages' Seal.

Climbing, he passed the entrance to the rooms of the other levels. When the stairs ended, he crossed the bridge to his chambers. He grabbed his notebook off his desk before returning to the sun-filled summer day.

Crossing the short bridge, he entered Silvia's chambers. Upstairs, the tapestry waited for him. Stepping through the portal, he entered his bedroom.

A warm summer breeze meandered through the old house. Draping his cloak over one of the wing back chairs, he briefly wondered who taught the house its rituals. Downstairs, he walked through the paneled hallway to the back sitting room.

He placed his spiral notebook open to the correct page onto the old, wooden desk. Next to it, he laid a stack of plain paper. Hovering his hand inches from the notebook page, his hand glided to the paper. With a swipe of his hand, the words he had written copied onto the top of the stack. Turning the page, he continued until he had run out of written words.

Berty stuffed the copies into a manila envelope. After addressing it to Martin Hunter at the newspaper, he said, "Time to mail." The envelope disappeared. Not knowing if it landed in the mailroom or on Martin's desk, he closed his notebook.

"That was easy," he muttered. Notebook in hand, he returned to the Empire Tree.

After dropping his notebook in his study, he strolled through the tree. Eventually, he came across the Elf he wished to see.

"Alfred, do you have a minute?" he asked.

"Of course, my Lord."

"My niece is interested in learning how to read Runes," Berty explained. "I thought if anyone knew how to procure that knowledge, it would be you."

The Elf rubbed his jawbone. "Runes," he repeated. "Not many have uses for Runes besides Witches and Wizards. Unfortunately, as they diminished in our world, their knowledge went with them."

"I see."

"However," said Alfred, "if Hope is interested in learning the ancient tongue, then I would be very willing to teach her."

Smiling, he said, "Thank you, Alfred. I will ask her."

Berty found his way to Hope's chambers in time for lunch. Sitting around her table with both her and Freesia, he said, "I spoke to Alfred about learning Runes."

Hope's face lit up.

"Looks like we'll have to find a book on the other side of the portal," he told her, "but Alfred offered to teach you the ancient tongue. Could be fun. Silvia knows it."

Hope thought while chewing. "Okay," she said.

"Great. You can start as soon as we return with your new bow," he said.

"Uncle Berty," Hope began, "will I be able to bring my bow through the portal to show Mommy and Daddy?"

He tried not to picture the look of abject horror on Teresa's face when she saw her daughter with a bow in her hands. "I don't see why not, but you may have to keep it at my house when you're on that side of the portal."

Smiling, she said, "Okay."

After lunch with his niece, he spent the afternoon sparring

45

with the live dummy. The clanging of metal cleared his head. He was getting to the point where he no longer had to think about the way he moved with his sword. His body began to react instinctively. When he returned to his chambers, he felt confident in his swordsmanship.

In his study, Berty readied for the trip to Boudon. Wondering how much a bow would cost, he opened a box on the shelf. His fingers loosened the leather wrapping around a hard leather pouch. Round metal glistened inside the dark leather. The cold coins rolled between his fingers. He had used quite a few since he first retrieved some from his coin vault. Afraid he would not have enough for lodging and food as well, he grabbed his leather coin purse, then stepped out of his chambers.

Remembering a ladder, he crossed the short bridge. Inside Silvia's study, he made a beeline for the Sages' Seal carved into the back wall. He touched the lowest circle on the seal. A trapdoor popped open. Climbing into the hole in Silvia's floor, he descended rung by rung.

When he reached the bottom of the ladder, a stone door opened. He stepped into his vault's antechamber. Sconces flickered to life on the rock walls, illuminating four different drawings on the rock. He gazed at the scroll, the trunk, the ladder and the coin. Pressing the picture of the coin, he waited for the rock wall to open the coin vault.

Mounds of gleaming coins greeted him inside his vault. After dumping handsful of small metal discs into the leather, he retreated to the antechamber. As the door to the coin vault closed, the scroll intrigued him.

With a glance at the ladder leading upwards, he touched the picture of the scroll. On the opposite wall, rock slid behind rock. Berty approached the scroll vault. Lanterns lighted a long, central table. Surrounding the table on three sides were rows of shelves covered with books and scrolls. Peering around the shelves, he could not see an end. The vault felt more like a library.

Immediately, he wondered if Silvia had read everything on the shelves. He plucked a book at random off a shelf. Perusing its pages, he wandered towards the table. His eyes skimmed the words, *beyond the tree line.*

He focused on the page, reading:

> *Traveling northward, the forest will eventually end. A line of trees marks the border of our land. If one goes beyond the tree line, one enters the land of the Frost Giants.*
>
> *At first glance, it looks to be a barren wasteland. However, upon closer inspection, there are signs of life. Large deer and ice bears call the frozen land home. Clusters of Frost Giants live within the sheer mountains. They tend to leave people alone unless one hunts their game. This, however, does not hold true for the Frost Giants who live in Rimpar Castle.*
>
> *The castle is constructed from large blocks of ice. The giants living within do not take kindly to strangers whether giant or non-giant. They fiercely protect their land and will not hesitate to slice anyone who approaches. If one can see the icy turrets of Rimpar Castle, then one must run to the safety of the forest.*
>
> *Caution: Never allow an Elf to cross the tree line.*
>
> *An irreversible transformation takes place.*

Berty's pocket vibrated. Extracting the large, gold locket, he pried open the gold halves. The one side said, "Delyth has returned safely."

After closing the book, he returned it to its shelf. He was sure the vault held answers about Elders and perhaps, other mysteries such as the Cavern.

Climbing the ladder, he realized that Silvia had not read everything in that vault. Silvia thought Frost Giants were myths. The book clearly stated that the creatures were as real as he remembered.

Chapter Four
Wood and Fire

Uneasiness bubbled in his stomach as he secured his sword. Checking his leather coin purse that he filled the night before, Berty fastened his cloak.

He walked down the bridge to Hope's chambers. She and Freesia stepped onto their platform. Hope's training bow contrasted against her dark maroon cloak.

Seeing Berty, she said, "Declan told me to bring my bow."

"Then I guess we're ready," he said.

Freesia gave him a nod before they entered the trunk. As they descended, Hope told him, "Mommy and Daddy will be unreachable. They said they'd call when they got back."

In the Reception Room, they met Edwin, Declan and Delyth. "Good morning," Delyth said with a smile. She looked at Berty with her violet eyes. "Elder Hunter says hello."

"She's still in Fairyland?" asked Berty.

"Yes," Delyth answered. "She seems to be researching something. Though she calls it knowledge gathering."

Berty laughed as he watched the Fairy pull her long, dark curls into a bun.

"Are we ready?" asked Declan. "Even on horseback, it's going to take us days to get there." He fussed with his dark cloak until Delyth's delicate hand gently touched his arm.

Outside the doors to the Empire Tree, Tenders brought horses. Berty waited until Hope was securely on hers before mounting the saddle. With Declan leading the way, they galloped out of the gates of the Sages' Grove.

Declan stuck to dirt roads that cut through the forest. When the sun reached the horizon, he chose a spot to make camp.

The flames of the campfire mesmerized Declan. "Dec," Delyth said softly, "are you okay?"

Without tearing his eyes from the dancing flames, he answered, "I've avoided these roads for so many years." His light eyes finally found his companions. "I made sure that I knew the exact way to Boudon. That way, I was assured I'd never travel back."

"And yet, here we are," said Edwin.

"Maybe in a couple of days, it will feel less surreal," Declan said. He collapsed into his bedroll, then wrapped his cloak around him. Berty could see a longing to comfort Declan in Delyth's violet eyes before she disappeared into the small tent with Hope and Freesia.

Silence overwhelmed as they packed the campsite. Declan kept them at a tree whizzing pace until Delyth insisted that they stop for a break.

Bringing Berty some food, she said quietly, "I'm worried about him."

"The faster we get there, the faster we get home. The less he has to think," he told her. "Remember, he did not take his grandfather's passing well."

They both noticed Declan staring in their direction.

Delyth quickly said, "My father's allergies are acting up. He sneezes like crazy. The morning is especially bad for him."

"Allergies?" Declan asked.

"The Healer makes extra strong honeycomb tea to help Father through the day," answered Delyth.

After a quick lunch, they resumed their maddening pace. When they stopped to camp for the night, Declan busied himself with making Hope practice her archery. The next two nights, Declan did the same as if routine would save him from his mind.

Around the campfire the fifth night, Declan finally spoke. "I apologize for my strange behavior. The village is not far. We will reach the workshop in the morning. Though they won't refuse our business, expect a less than warm reception."

Delyth gave Declan a comforting hand as they both stared into the flames.

Berty could only imagine how conflicted Declan felt. The desire to see his mother, who helped him escape, and his sister, who believed in his innocence, would contrast with the reluctance to face his brother who was angry with him, his other brother who was jealous of him, and his childhood friend who hated him. Then, there was the uncertainty of how his father would react to seeing his son after years of exile.

Laying on his bedroll, Berty stared into the still night sky. He hoped that he would be able to diffuse any volatility between Declan, his family and the village of Boudon. Trying to prepare his mind for the worst, he eventually fell asleep.

Declan took a deep breath before mounting his horse in the morning. He led them on a dirt road with Delyth riding beside him. After a couple of hours at a comfortable pace, he said, "We're here."

A timber cottage faced the road. Its windows and door gave it a friendly, welcoming appearance. A wooden sign dangled over the door, indicating a wood shop.

"Whoa," remarked Hope. Her brown eyes gazed well above the cottage's roofline.

Following her line of sight, Berty noticed a village of tree

51

houses connected by bridges situated in the high branches. The full summer foliage camouflaged the village well. From the ground, it was difficult to determine Boudon's size.

Declan's horse stopped in front of the cottage. Once they dismounted, Edwin said, "I'll stay with the horses."

Berty gave the Elf a nod, then opened the woodshop's door. A bell rang as he stepped over the threshold.

Wooden objects filled the cottage. No surface, including every wall, was devoid of something made from wood. Hope stayed close to Freesia as the five of them looked around.

"This is gorgeous," Berty heard Delyth say. "Perfect for my brother."

"Would you like me to wrap it for you?" a woman's voice said.

Turning his head, he saw a woman with long, light brown hair standing next to Delyth. She was showing the Fairy details of a box with different color inlay.

"Yes, please," said Delyth.

He caught the expression on Declan's face. The woman waiting on Delyth had to be Declan's sister, Julie.

While Delyth handed her coins across a counter, Julie asked, "Will you be needing anything else today?"

"Yes," said Declan.

Julie's light eyes found her brother.

"We are looking for a bow," he said. Declan looked as though he wanted to say more, but could not.

"For you?" she asked. She walked out from behind the counter while studying Declan.

"No." He motioned for Hope to join him.

Julie glanced at Hope. "Did you have something specific in mind?"

"She's been using a beginner's bow," Declan told her. "I

would like to try different styles to see which is the best fit for her."

Her eyes squinted momentarily as she gazed at Declan. "Obie," she called, "prepare a target."

Clutching her wrapped parcel, Delyth watched the exchange between Declan and Julie.

"Let me get a few of these down for her to try," said Julie. She walked around the cottage, pulling bows off the walls.

A side door opened. "Aunt Julie," said a boy's voice, "all ready." He entered the cottage with windswept blond hair.

"Thanks, Obie," Julie said. "Take these." She handed him the bows from the walls. Grabbing a quiver full of arrows, she said, "Come with me."

Berty followed Hope and Declan through the side door. The bows Julie gathered sat on a small table next to the cottage. A target waited in the trees. Leaning against the cottage, Obie looked to be a few years older than Hope.

Hope handed Berty the bow Declan made for her before picking another from the table. Throwing her cloak over her shoulder, she plucked an arrow from her quiver. Gracefully, she let an arrow fly.

After she shot a few arrows that hit the center dot, Declan said, "Try another."

With the next bow, her arrows continued to hit center. "She's very good," Julie remarked. "Your daughter?" she asked Declan.

"No. I'm her teacher," Declan answered. "Another," he said to Hope. Addressing Julie, he said, "She's his niece." He indicated Berty.

Julie smiled at Berty. "Obie, go get that other bow," she said.

"But Uncle Vander said—"

"Never mind what Vander said. I made the bow. I can sell

it," she said.

Obeying his aunt, Obie ran inside. When he returned, he gave Julie a beautifully carved bow.

"Try this one," she said to Hope.

Carefully taking the bow from Julie, Hope held it in her hands for a moment. She took a few shots. Smiling, she turned to Berty and Declan. "I like this one."

"Are you sure?" Declan asked.

She nodded. "It feels good." Looking at Declan, she explained, "It's comfortable. The string sings just like you said it would."

Declan smiled. "Then I guess it is the bow for you."

"We'll take it," Berty said to Julie. "How much?"

"Fifteen Vers."

"Fifteen?" said Declan. "We'll give you ten for it."

"Twelve is the lowest I can go," said Julie.

Declan nodded to Berty. "Twelve it is," said Berty who handed her twelve silver coins.

"Uncle Berty, we need to hide the horses," Hope said in a panic.

"Why?" asked Berty.

"Because if the Firewalker sees them, it'll eat them."

"A Firewalker? Hope, are you sure?" Delyth asked from the doorway.

Hope quickly nodded.

Nervous neighing reached Berty's ears. Edwin hurried through the side door. "The horses are going crazy like they're afraid of something," he said.

"You can take them around back," said Julie. Edwin ran through the cottage. "Obie, bring those bows inside. I'm going to lock up. You're all going to go someplace safer."

A bird cawed.

"The alarm," said Julie. "Hurry."

Berty magically retrieved Hope's arrows from the target. They ran inside with Edwin close on their heels.

"Obie, take them up," instructed Julie. "I'll secure the workshop."

"I'll help you," offered Declan.

Julie accepted Declan's help without question while the rest of them followed Obie inside a tree trunk. The boy led them up a dizzying spiral staircase. The staircase emptied into the main room of one of the tree houses.

"Obie, help me with the camouflage," said an older woman.

"Yes, Grandma."

When she saw who entered behind Obie, she said, "You must be customers from the store. I'm Geraldine. You are welcome to stay until the threat has passed."

"Thank you," said Berty. "Can we help with anything?"

Geraldine gave a fleeting smile. "There are bows and arrows in these trunks. If you could lay them on the table, I'd be so grateful."

As they dove into the trunks, Declan and Julie entered. "Where is everyone?" he asked.

"Gone," answered Julie. "Won't be back anytime soon. They're out being Woodsman." Her tone sounded bitter.

"So far away?" Declan asked while helping secure the leafy coverings.

"Our lifestyle depends on good quality wood," Geraldine explained. "Good quality is hard to find."

Julie rolled her eyes. "The surrounding woods don't provide for us like they used to. Not since—"

Geraldine flashed her a scolding look.

"If you know a little archery, we could use some help," Julie pleaded. She loaded two crossbows, one for each hand.

After securing a quiver to her hip, Geraldine picked a bow off the table. "You are all welcome to use one," she said.

Edwin chose a weapon. Wanting to help, Hope removed her cloak. "No," said Freesia, pulling her back.

Looking from the balcony to the group, Delyth said, "The last Firewalker was defeated with a combination of Fairy Dust and a Sethbravin. While I have Fairy Dust, I don't have a Sethbravin. This village is made of wood. Fire is the enemy."

"Do we just hope that it doesn't see us?" Julie asked.

"Delyth, how long ago was the last Firewalker seen?" asked Berty.

The Fairy slowly nodded. "Too long for its sudden appearance to be a coincidence," she said.

"Someone sent it here on purpose?" Julie asked.

"Yes," said Berty. "And we're going to have to fight it."

"How?" Declan asked.

"If I remember correctly," Delyth said, "Firewalkers have an infinite source of magical fire—different from Dragonfire. Their fire incinerates magic used against them. They conjure little Fire Beasts made of pure flames. The beasts attack with fireballs. But the most dangerous aspect of the Firewalker is the burning sting from its tail."

"What if we dumped water on it?" Geraldine asked.

"Water will spread their fire," answered Delyth. "The Fairies even tried burying it in dirt with no luck. The book said that you have to put the fire out at its source, which is within the creature."

Putting down the bow, Edwin said, "I remember you telling us that a Sethbravin is a curse breaker. It is a tool that dispels magic."

"Flocks of birds, Grandma," Obie said as he pointed beyond the vegetal screen.

56

Edwin removed his cloak. Securing his golden shield to his arm, he unsheathed his golden sword. "You have Fairy Dust. I can fight magic."

"The entire Fairy Army threw Dust at it. I am only one Fairy," pleaded Delyth.

"Two Fairies," said Freesia.

"No," said Delyth. "You have more important responsibilities."

"There's got to be a way," said Edwin. "Is there a faster way down?"

"The center counterweight lift," Julie said. "I'll show you."

Edwin said, "Cover me," then followed Julie onto a bridge.

"Positions," said Geraldine with a bow in her hand.

After watching his mother and sister take their stances, Declan uncloaked his bow. Watching him ready an arrow, Berty felt helpless.

"My Lord," Delyth whispered, "I need some advice. I don't know how to get the dust inside its body."

They walked to the edge with everyone. Peering through the cover, a reddish creature approached the village. Berty gazed upon the physical manifestation of medieval drawings of the Devil, complete with horns and a forked tail. The huge creature caught sight of Edwin as he glided to the ground.

"Why isn't its tail on fire?" Declan asked. "Is that where we should aim?"

"I don't see any fire on any part of the beast," said Julie.

Berty wondered if Julie knew or had suspicions of who Declan was.

"No one could hit that tail. It's thrashing around too much," said Julie.

Arrows rained upon the creature from all sides as it beelined towards Edwin. Berty wondered how many people were left in the village. Hope rushed between him and Declan with her new bow. The arrows burned before reaching the creature.

Declan released an arrow. When it penetrated the tail, he said, "Gotcha! Fire went out. Fairy Dust time?"

"How'd you do that?" asked Julie.

Placing a finger inside her velvet pouch, Hope placed a little Fairy Dust in the middle of her tongue. Her brown eyes darkened. "Don't worry Delyth, I've got it," Hope said. Calmly, she pulled an arrow from her quiver. Before placing it, she dipped the head in her velvet pouch of Fairy Dust.

The Firewalker had reached Edwin who was using his shield to block its fire and evading its cloven feet. When another round of arrows soared towards it, two Fire Beasts appeared. The toddler-sized, fire-people-like beasts lobbed balls of flame into the trees. The number of arrows diminished.

Hope shot her Fairy Dusted arrow. When it hit the creature, it stumbled.

"Keep that up, Hope," said Delyth. The Fairy tipped arrows with Dust before handing them to Hope.

Houses began to burn around the village. Concentrating on the fire, Berty was able to extinguish the flames, one at a time. For every fire he put out, the Fire Beasts started two more.

The Firewalker's angry roar echoed in the trees. Another Fire Beast danced to life. It threw fireballs only at Edwin. The Elf deflected the balls with both his shield and sword. He had to switch his focus between the little beast and the mother creature.

"Edwin! Look out!" screamed Declan.

The creature whipped its forked tail around its body. Edwin could not lift his shield before it lashed his shoulder. The Elf screamed in agony as he fell on his back.

Berty could not breathe.

"Edwin!" Declan cried. He ran to the lift.

Towering over Edwin, the Firewalker lunged. The creature's roar mixed with the Elf's.

Berty covered Hope's eyes.

The creature descended upon its prey. Fire Beasts disappeared in puffs of smoke. Through the red hide of the Firewalker, glittering gold poked towards the sky. As the sword retracted, the creature rolled to the side. Edwin lay on the ground, wincing in pain. His head raised slightly to see the dead beast.

Declan slid down the lift's rope. As he helped Edwin off the ground, Hope pushed Berty's hand off her eyes. Her eyes had returned to their normal shade of brown.

"Men are coming," she said. "They killed the lookout."

"How many men?" asked Berty.

"Lots."

Declan escorted Edwin into the room. In his one hand, he carried Edwin's shield. On the other, he clutched his bow. He placed both on the table next to where Edwin sat.

As Declan helped Edwin unbuckle his leather armor, Berty joined them. He saw the deep gashes in the leather where the Firewalker's tail struck. Both of them lifted the heavy armor over Edwin's head.

The Elf groaned while he carefully removed his shirt. From near the balcony, Geraldine and Julie watched Declan inspect Edwin's shoulder. Scrutinizing the leather armor, Declan said, "Never went through the leather."

"Hurts when I move my arm," said Edwin.

"It's going to bruise. I have something for the pain," Declan told him, "but it's in the saddlebag."

"What is it you need, Declan?" Geraldine asked. Her eyes glistened.

Declan faced his mother. "Hi, Mom," barely escaped his lips.

Dropping her bow, Geraldine ran to her son. She threw her

arms around him saying, "My boy, my sweet, little boy."

Julie wiped her cheek.

"Uncle Berty, they're just outside the village," said Hope.

"Who is?" Edwin asked.

Berty watched Julie join the hugging. "A small army, I'm sure," he answered.

Grimacing, Edwin touched his shoulder. "Going to need my armor."

Declan let go of his mother and sister. "You're in no condition to fight," he told Edwin.

"I didn't make Lieutenant by allowing a bruised shoulder to stop me."

"I can see them," said Obie, peeking through the vines.

Julie crouched next to her nephew. "Quietly, make sure the others are ready." Nodding, he ran.

"Let me wrap it first, so you don't hurt it more," said Declan.

Geraldine retrieved a length of cloth. "Here, this should work."

"Thanks, Mom."

As Declan wrapped Edwin's shoulder, the archers restocked their arrows.

"They're at least the size of the Fairy Guard," said Delyth looking off the balcony.

Standing next to her, Geraldine said, "We have the advantage."

"What a time for half the village to be gone," added Julie.

"Grandma!" Obie ran to her. "Men are also coming from another direction."

"They're coming to finish what the Firewalker started," said Declan.

Looking at his young niece and his injured Lieutenant, Berty realized that the attack on Boudon was a practice run. Isolated and half empty, the village was the perfect choice. "They picked Boudon on purpose," he said. "They are going to expect everyone to be archers. That's why they sent the Firewalker first. They are also going to expect the attack from the trees and not the ground. We are going to give them both.

"Geraldine, split the villagers. Arrows will reach both fronts. Delyth and Freesia, once the armies are distracted, dust them. Edwin, Declan and I will meet them on the ground."

"What do you want me to do?" Hope asked.

He looked at his niece who desperately wanted to help. "Stay here and keep your Fairy Dust handy in case you need to use it," he told her.

Addressing Julie, Delyth asked, "Is there a place from where we can fly unseen?"

Nodding, Julie said, "Obie, bring the Fairies to the back door, then you can help keep arrows stocked or whatever your grandmother needs."

Everyone scurried into position. Julie followed Declan. "Another is needed on the ground. Let me help," she said. "I've pinned my husband to the wall in under five seconds. And that was with only one crossbow."

Glancing at the crossbows in each of her hands, Berty nodded.

As they rode the lift to the ground, Berty said, "Edwin, Declan, take care of the back group. Julie, you're with me." The lift hit earth. Once they were all out, Declan sent the lift up empty.

Weapons ready, Edwin and Declan walked towards their approaching army. Berty faced the marching shielded men advancing towards him. He took a few steps past the slain creature lying on the ground.

With outstretched arms, he stilled the wind within the village. He brought his wrists together, keeping his palms facing outwards. In his mind, he summoned the power his Dragon Match, Tong, had given him.

Dragonfire erupted from his hands. The stream of fire burned the shields. Marching morphed into chaotic running. Arrows showered the shieldless men. His Dragonfire burned weapons and attackers.

The Dragonfire kept the front army at a distance. He could hear the fighting behind him. Beside him, Julie shot down those climbing trees. A sparkling shower of Fairy Dust incapacitated many men.

"Uncle Berty! Behind you!" Hope's voice cut through the fighting.

He moved his Dragonfire to one hand. Unsheathing his sword, he twisted his body. Metal clanged against metal. His sword became an extension of his right arm while his left still burned holes in the army. Automatically, he blocked his burly attacker's every move.

The man relentlessly attacked. Berty could feel his magic falter. Wind blew through cracks in his magic around the village. In his peripheral vision, magical spheres exploded. Someone was fighting a Warlock.

He had enough. With a quick swipe, his blade undercut, landing in the man's torso. The man wobbled as Berty withdrew his blade.

Covering his wound with his free hand, the man swung his sword. Berty stepped aside, then lunged. Metal crashed to the earth. The man staggered weaponless.

Blade in hand, Delyth landed beside him.

The burly man fell to his knees. "Have mercy. I surrender," he said.

Delyth blew over her open palm. The man collapsed unconscious.

"The front flank is retreating," she whispered.

Dragonfire shrunk into his hand. "You and Julie watch for stragglers," he told her.

Running to help Edwin and Declan, he saw a decimated rear flank. Both hands spewed Dragonfire. The remaining army retreated.

Sheathing his sword, Edwin grabbed his shoulder. "Whomever we captured needs to be contained," he said.

"Are you able to oversee that?" Berty asked.

Edwin nodded. "I'll be fine."

"We have a good amount of rope and some scrap wood," said Julie.

"That'll work," said Edwin. "Bring whomever can be spared."

As Julie hurried up a side lift, Declan said, "Should tend to the injured. I'll get my stuff."

"Delyth, if you could help Edwin," said Berty, "I'll go check on Hope."

Smiling, Delyth said, "She's a strong girl. I don't know if I would have been as strong at her age."

Berty rode a lift up to the village. Entering Declan's family home, he asked, "How did everyone fare?"

Hope ran to Berty, then gave him a hug.

"Better than expected," said Geraldine. "Thanks to all of you. I take it you are my son's friends. Please, honor us by staying here."

With an arm around his niece, Berty said, "That is very generous of you, Geraldine. Thank you. We are Declan's friends. This is my niece, Hope, and her Fairy Godmother, Freesia. Edwin and Delyth are still on the ground with Declan."

Chapter Five
Twisted Elf

Walking into the room, Delyth said, "Edwin sent me. The entire village seems to be helping. They'll be done in no time. My Lord," Geraldine's eyebrows raised, "Edwin wishes to know what you plan on doing with these men."

"Since we were here at the time of the attack, they can be charged with crimes against the Empire," said Berty. "There's got to be some law that deals with magical creatures like the Firewalker."

"Alfred and I will look into that when we return to the Empire Tree," Delyth said. She walked to the balcony to fly to Edwin.

Letting go of Hope, Berty said, "Looks like you were able to break in your new bow." Hope smiled. "Why don't you give it a well deserved rest." She nodded.

"My Lord," said Freesia, "do you think it is safe for me to gather our things from the horses?"

"I'd rather you not go alone," Berty said.

"I'll go with you, Freesia," said Delyth, entering the room. "Hope, do you mind if I borrow your bag of Fairy Dust?"

After carefully wrapping her new bow and quiver in her cloak, Hope handed the Fairy Princess her small, velvet pouch.

"Thank you. I'll bring it right back," she said. She and Freesia walked to the back door.

He watched Geraldine fuss around the house. "Can I help with something?" he asked.

"It is just an honor to have you in our home, Emperor," she said. "You have done so much already. Please, you and your niece sit down and be comfortable."

"Are you sure?"

Geraldine added logs to the fireplace. "My husband and two eldest sons are gone most of the time. The house gets lonely. Julie spends her days in the shop because Vander helps choose the wood. Little Obie splits his time between Julie and me. It's nice to be able to do something for someone every now and then," she said.

Giving her a warm smile, he and Hope sat at the long table.

The Fairies returned, carrying bags. As Berty relieved them of their loads, Delyth said, "We got yours and Edwin's as well, my Lord."

"I would have gone down later," he said. "Thank you."

Hope was helping Geraldine prepare dinner when Edwin, Declan, Julie, and Obie walked into the house. Grimacing and clutching his shoulder, Edwin said, "We captured a lot of men. More than what we could handle bringing to the Empire Tree alone."

Declan helped Edwin remove his armor while Berty asked, "Are there any patrols in the area?"

"None, of which I am aware at this time," said Edwin free of his leather.

"I can fly to the Sages' Grove quickly," Delyth suggested.

Edwin watched Declan unwrap his shoulder. "Too far," said Edwin. "Irmingard is closer. My Lord, we are going to need reinforcements sooner rather than later."

Agreeing with his Lieutenant, Berty said, "Delyth, fly to

Irmingard. Petition for assistance until the Empire Guards can reach us. Afterwards, fly to the Sages' Grove. Tell Alvar everything that has happened. Ask him to send guards for transport and to be stationed here in case vengeance is sought."

The Fairy secured her dark purple cloak. "When you get to Irmingard," said Edwin, "speak to my brother, Low Elf Wystan. He is in charge of day to day operations, including Warrior deployment. He needs to know that we fought Vindalf. Captain Alvar should be made aware of that as well."

She nodded. "It will take only a matter of minutes to get there once I am above the trees," said Delyth. "I'll be back soon." After giving Declan a meaningful glance, she dashed.

Turning his attention back to the Elf, Declan sighed. "Had your armor on too long. I need to get more willow bark. Luckily, there are some trees nearby." He extracted a retracting knife from his bag. "Try not to move your arm."

"Can I help, Uncle Declan?" Obie asked.

Declan looked at Julie, who nodded. "Come on," he told his nephew.

"All Obie did was follow Declan around, asking a million questions," Julie said to her mother.

Geraldine smiled.

Taking a seat closer to Edwin, Berty asked, "You mentioned fighting Vindalf. What or who is that?"

"A type of Elf we thought to be extinct," explained Edwin. "All Elves, at least in Irmingard, learn about Vindalf. We are taught to recognize their dark gray skin and colorless hair. They are soulless. Unlike a true Elf, they have no relationship with the trees. We have fought many wars against them. The Vindalf are our greatest enemy."

Berty had more questions about the Vindalf, but he felt it was time to have eyes on Delyth. After giving Edwin a nod, Berty

66

concentrated on the Fairy, then closed his eyes.

Delyth hurried into the arched tunnel through the white ramparts. Before Irmingard Warriors could tell her to halt, she said to them, "I am Princess Delyth, Advisor to the Emperor. It is imperative that I speak with Low Elf Wystan." Her voice carried a sense of urgency.

One of the Warriors called another over. After speaking in his ear, the man said, "Your escort, Princess."

She entered Irmingard with a young Warrior at her side.

Opening his eyes, he saw Declan instructing Obie to fill a pot with hot water. "Place it next to the fire," Declan said. "The bark needs to boil. Now, bring me the mortar and pestle."

As Obie helped Declan crush herbs, Berty closed his eyes. Delyth and her escort strode through massive double doors. In the large, pink and white marble room, Elves sat at tiered tables. Berty recognized Edwin's mother and father sitting in the tiers. An Elf, who looked exactly like Edwin except with dark hair, stood in front of them. The reflection of his light green robe in the marble floor made him look even taller.

"Princess, I am Low Elf Wystan," he said. "These are the Ørgranden. Please, tell us what is so urgent."

She glanced at the members of Irmingard's legislating body before saying, "I was sent by the Emperor to ask for assistance in Boudon."

"What kind of assistance?" Wystan asked.

"Military aid. We would kindly accept any Warriors you could spare until the Empire Guard arrive from the Sages' Grove," said Delyth.

"Boudon is outside Elf territory," said one of the Ørgranden. "We do not wage wars for the Emperor."

Delyth stared at the Elf. "The Emperor does not wage wars," she said in a steely tone. "We happened to be in Boudon at the time it was attacked. The attackers were defeated. We captured over a hundred men. However, we do not currently have the resources to keep them contained until the Empire Guard reaches us."

"Are you saying the Emperor travels without his guard?" asked another Ørgranden.

The Fairy took a deep breath. "The few with whom the Emperor travels are no match for an army, let alone a Firewalker."

"A Firewalker? Are you sure?" asked an Elf on the other side of the tiers.

"The creature injured the Emperor's Lieutenant."

"Edwin?" asked Femke.

Delyth nodded at Edwin's mother.

Femke covered her mouth with her fingers.

"Lieutenant Edwin is in a great deal of pain." Delyth answered Femke's unasked question.

His mother closed her eyes as if she were willing herself not to cry.

"Princess, tell the Emperor that we will—" Wystan began.

"Low Elf," said one who had spoken previously, "you are not in a position to make a decision. Lieutenant Edwin is your brother."

Wystan looked insulted. "With all due respect, Ferran, my brother is not the one asking. The Emperor is. Irmingard will not turn its back on the Emperor."

"And if we send our Warriors, who will protect us?" Ferran asked. "A woodland village is not our concern."

"If you choose to abandon the Empire, know this," said Delyth. "The Emperor suspects that Boudon was a trial run. They waged war on women, children and the aged, just to see what they could do. If it were not for the Emperor, Boudon would have been reduced to ashes and every single living soul would have been slaughtered. For whom were they practicing? The Sages' Grove? Grunnan? Fairyland? Irmingard?" The Fairy stared down the Ørgranden. "They used a Firewalker for a village in the trees. What do you suppose they have in store for the rest of us? Your moat and your tall ramparts were designed to keep something out. The Emperor will respect your decision, even if he disagrees. Before I leave you," she turned to Wystan, "Lieutenant Edwin wanted you to know that he fought Vindalf."

The Elves gasped.

"Merely a scare tactic," said a man's voice. Delyth saw the Commander of the Irmingard Warriors approach. "Vindalf are extinct."

"The Lieutenant does not use scare tactics," said Delyth. "Whatever Vindalf are cannot be extinct if he fought them."

The Commander stood near Wystan, but not close enough for the Low Elf to cast a shadow on his shining silvery armor. "Forgive me, Princess, but you do not know Lieutenant Edwin as well as I."

Raising her eyebrows, Delyth replied, "How could I when I have traveled to the ends of our world with him and fought beside him and you and he have spent so little time together?"

"The Lieutenant was mistaken. There are no Vindalf!" the Commander steamed.

Delyth watched an Elf in dark green walk towards them unnoticed by the other Elves. "Enough!" the young Elf commanded.

"Good evening, High Elf," said the Elves, hastily bowing.

"We are Elves of Irmingard. We have honor, dignity and loyalty," the High Elf said. "The Empire has been good to us. We do not repay it by dishonoring each other or ourselves. Your behavior appalls me. Ferran, I expect your resignation from the Ørgranden by sunrise tomorrow. Commander Marshall, you have forgotten your rank. If Lieutenant Edwin says there are Vindalf, then there are Vindalf. Your reluctance to believe him casts a long shadow on our loyalty, dignity and honor. You are no longer worthy of that armor."

Commander Marshall stared at the High Elf. He removed his armor, then let it drop from his fingers. The clanging metal reverberated when it hit the marble floor. He stomped from the room with Ferran following closely.

"The Vindalf are the greatest threat to the Elves and our way of life," the High Elf said. "We need a commander who takes them and every threat against the Elves seriously. Does the Ørgranden agree?"

A collective yes echoed off the marble.

"Wystan," the High Elf continued, "the people have voted you into the position of Low Elf this term. Before this, you were the finest Warrior Irmingard had seen in quite a long time. Would you give up your elected position to give Irmingard the honor of becoming the Commander of its Warriors?"

Wystan glanced at his parents before saying, "Yes."

"Then I hereby appoint you, Wystan, Commander of the Irmingard Warriors," said the High Elf. "Commander Wystan, take as many men as you need and head to Boudon as soon as possible."

"Of course, High Elf Avery," said Wystan with a nod of his head. He picked up Marshall's former armor off the floor.

"See the Dominatrix before you leave. She will give you a weapon useful against Vindalf." Avery watched Wystan leave before saying to the Ørgranden, "The candidate with the second most votes will become interim Low Elf until the next election. Princess Delyth, may I have a word before you leave?"

"You may, High Elf Avery," she said.

They entered a long, marble corridor. "Ask the Emperor if

70

he would allow any captured Vindalf to be brought to Irmingard for incarceration. We have been fighting Vindalf since before the formation of the Empire. Irmingard has a special dungeon to hold their kind."

"Their kind?" she asked.

He opened a door, then motioned for Delyth to enter. She walked into a book-lined room. The thick carpet muffled the sound of her shoes. "Please, have a seat."

Taking a seat, Delyth looked like a child sitting in her father's favorite leather chair.

"I brought you to my private study to tell you what no Elf is taught about the Vindalf," Avery said. "Vindalf means twisted Elf. They are made, not born. I am sure you are well aware of the ancient Fairy-Elf wars."

She nodded.

"Vindalf are a product of those wars. I assure you, Delyth, I am not proud of what we have done. This knowledge passes from High Elf to High Elf and I bear its burden." Avery took a deep breath. "Elf life blood relies on the trees and their magic. So much so, that even in death our souls become the breeze that rustles through their branches. Vindalf have no such connection.

"During the wars, the ancient Elves looked for ways to have an advantage over the Fairies. Some Elves discarded their very souls for this purpose.

"Beyond the forest is a cold land where trees cannot grow. When an Elf crosses the tree line and their magic no longer touches him, he transforms into a Vindalf. It changes the nature of the Elf forever. He can never return to his former self.

"Vindalf turn on their kin. They are powerfully violent. However, they are susceptible to intense fire, bright midday sun and fresh Fairy Dust. We need to know who is bringing Elves over the tree line. Someone has discovered our dark secret. I would like to know how."

Delyth's jaw dropped.

"Share what I have told you with the Emperor, but please keep it in confidence," Avery said.

"I will. Thank you, Avery."

The young High Elf gave her a half smile. "I'll take you to a balcony from where you can fly."

Opening his eyes, Berty saw Declan staring at him. "Irmingard is helping us," he said quietly.

"You woke up just in time for dinner," said Hope. She placed a wooden bowl on the table.

Declan poured amber, steaming liquid into a cup, then handed it to Edwin. "It will ease the pain and reduce the swelling. Just eat some food first. Won't be so harsh on the stomach."

Peering into the cup, Edwin nodded. As everyone noisily gathered for dinner, Declan quietly said to Berty, "That was no nap."

"I have Eagle Eye," he whispered. "Was watching. She knows."

"Will Delyth be back tonight?" Julie asked.

Berty took a seat at the table. "She should be in the Sages' Grove by now. At the speed she can fly, I expect her to return within the hour."

While they ate, Obie kept looking at Declan. Finally, he asked, "Uncle Declan, how did you learn the art of healing?"

"I apprenticed under a Wizard," Declan answered.

"Oh." Obie's voice fell.

"Why are you disappointed?" asked Julie.

"I don't know any Wizards."

"There aren't any Wizards left to know," said Declan, "but while I'm here, I can teach you some things. That is, if you are serious about learning."

A smile washed over Obie's face. "Yeah, I want to learn. Thanks, Uncle Declan."

After dinner, they sat around the table, waiting for Delyth. "Grandma," said Obie, "can I show Hope around the village?"

"It is okay with me, if you do not go on the ground, Hope takes her bow and you get the Emperor's permission," Geraldine told him.

Looking at Berty, Obie swallowed. "My Lord, may I show Hope the village?" he asked.

Berty thought that he sounded sufficiently scared. "As long as you abide by your grandmother's rules," he said.

Grabbing her bow, Hope followed Obie outside.

"Obie is a good kid, my Lord," said Julie.

Turning to his mother and sister, Declan asked, "Why doesn't Obie have a bow?"

"A bow doesn't suit him," answered Geraldine.

"He is a terrible archer," Julie said. "And an even worse woodsman. He couldn't even master simple wood crafting techniques from Grandpa."

"Cecil and Fiona discussed bringing Obie to a Matchmaker, so he can be matched with a skill," said Geraldine. "Fiona's death changed everything. Cecil hasn't been the same since."

"Surely Cecil knows the consequences," said Declan.

"He loved Fiona with everything," Julie said. "Obie reminds him of her."

Shaking his head, Declan said, "But he can't stay. There are rules."

"What rules?" asked Edwin.

"If by the ages of thirteen, you do not possess what the Village Elders deem to be a useful skill, then you must leave Boudon," Declan explained.

"And do what?" inquired Edwin.

"Many get apprenticeships elsewhere, mainly with some guild," said Julie. "Some join the Empire Guard, but usually as a last resort. No offense, Lieutenant. The skill-less are few and far between. Those who leave do so on their own."

"None taken," Edwin replied. "A good portion of new recruits leave within two years."

A weary looking Delyth walked through the opened doors. "I apologize for taking so long, my Lord."

"You must be hungry, my dear. Sit down. I'll get you something to eat," Geraldine said.

"Thank you." Wearing a tired smile, Delyth sat across from Berty. "Irmingard Warriors should arrive sometime tomorrow. I had a long conversation with Alvar. He believes that it is a good idea for Irmingard to take the Vindalf. The Empire Tree does not have any place adequate to hold them. He told me to give them a reinforcing dusting tonight for they are strongest at night. Edwin, I am going to need help identifying them."

Edwin nodded while Delyth took a quick bite of food.

"Also," she continued," Alvar is sending two waves of Empire Guards. The first will transport the prisoners and keep Boudon secure. The second will build a Boudonian Outpost. He would ultimately like it to be a joint operation between Empire Guards, Irmingard Warriors and Fairy Guards." She took another bite.

"When I was dusting earlier, I fought two Fairies in the air." After taking a sip from her cup, she continued, "Alvar is going to set up in air training for me."

"Fairies?" said Berty. "I thought your parents had dealt with the traitors."

"They did. Many were dewinged. Treachery is difficult to eradicate," she said. "These Fairies could have resided outside of Fairyland. Mother and Father will need to know about this. And I need to be the one to tell them."

"Do what you need," said Berty. He watched Hope and Obie enter, talking a mile a minute.

"Thank you, my Lord. I will leave from here after the Irmingard Warriors arrive," Delyth said.

While Freesia monitored Hope and Obie playing, Berty and Edwin walked out onto the balconies. Berty wanted to give Declan time to talk with his mother and sister.

"How is your shoulder?" he asked Edwin.

"Doing better," Edwin answered. "What Declan gave me works."

"Good. You are going to meet with the Warriors tomorrow," he said. "Get them situated, then make sure you rest."

"I can do that."

"Excuse me, my Lord," said Delyth standing behind them. "May I borrow Edwin to dust?"

Berty nodded to the Fairy. Leaning on the wooden railing, he watched villagers clear the "battlefield." In the twilight, he kept looking for a light blue figure to emerge from between the trees.

Up to that moment, there was not much he had experienced without Silvia by his side. His heart ached for her. His eyes longed to gaze into her warm, brown eyes. He yearned for her comforting smile. Knowing deep inside that she would not appear in Boudon, he waited for night to creep across the forest.

"Will they come back?" asked a young voice.

Looking beside him, he found Obie. "Let's hope not, but sense does not apply when ego is overly present," Berty told him.

"Obie, time for bed," called Geraldine.

Berty followed Obie back inside. Declan laughed with his sister at the table. "Remember, you're sharing your room with your Uncle Declan," said Geraldine as Edwin and Delyth returned.

"How are the Vindalf?" Declan asked.

"They were still unconscious," replied Delyth. "And as terrifying as Avery described."

Freesia stepped off a spiral staircase hidden in the back of the room. "My Lord, Hope is asking for you," she said.

Nodding, he followed the Fairy up the stairs. Hope was sitting up in a large bed in one of the rooms. She gave him a tired smile when he entered.

"Freesia and I are sharing this room," Hope said. She yawned while he sat on the bed. "Is it okay that I wasn't that scared today, Uncle Berty? Maybe it's because Night Golems and Frost Giants are scarier."

"Of course it's okay," he assured. "But it's not because those two are scarier. It is because you now have a way of protecting yourself."

"My bow."

"Yes. Archery has given you the means to defend yourself, if need be. And as you become more and more confident, fear will diminish and not have power over you," said Berty. "That's why Declan has you practice everyday."

She yawned again, then carefully fell into the bed. He fixed the covers around her. "Goodnight, Hope."

Closing her eyes, she said, "Night, Uncle Berty."

Outside the room, he found Freesia waiting. She smiled before entering the room with Hope.

On the stairs, Delyth's voice reached him. "Just because I am a princess does not mean I need a room to myself."

"I will stay the night at my husband's house," said Julie. "It should be checked anyway."

"Your husband's house?" asked Declan.

Her eyes searched the floor. "Owen and I are not speaking," she answered. "We had an argument the night he returned from running into you." She looked at her brother. "I may have fired

76

my crossbow at him multiple times and left him struggling to free himself from the wall."

Declan raised his eyebrows. "You *may* have?"

"I was angry with him. Very, very angry."

"And now?"

Julie slid back into her chair. "I don't know. He's never home long enough to find out." She twirled her long hair. "I'll be back before breakfast." Grabbing her crossbow, she left.

Declan watched the door with a sad look on his face. Only when his mother came down the stairs did he change his gaze.

"Declan, I hope you don't mind being in your old room with Obie," his mother said.

"Not at all," he said to his mother quietly.

"Well," said Delyth, "flying that fast takes a lot out of me. I desperately need some sleep."

"Let me show you to your room, dear," Geraldine said. "Goodnight, boys."

After his mother disappeared from view, Declan said, "The Village Elders are going to want an audience, my Lord."

"Do you see a problem with granting them one?" asked Berty.

"No, but I am wondering if I should make myself scarce."

Berty could see concern in his light eyes. "Being Empire Watcher is not a crime. Not many understand magic, and because of that, it is often feared. Magic in many forms saved this village. If they have a gripe, it should be taken with me."

Taking a deep breath, Declan looked relieved. "Thank you," he said to Berty.

Upstairs, Declan showed Berty and Edwin to Cecil's room. "Edwin," Declan said, "if the pain is too much to sleep, wake me. One flight up, door on the right."

Nodding, Edwin entered the room with Berty. They both

looked at the large bed. "I'll sleep on the floor, my Lord."

"Nonsense," said Berty. "You are injured. You need the bed more than I." He pulled a pillow and a blanket off the bed. Fixing a space on the floor, exhaustion took over, allowing him to fall asleep quickly.

He woke with sunlight spilling on his face and soreness in his back. Sitting up, he saw Edwin rubbing his shoulder. "How is it this morning?" he asked.

Grimacing, Edwin said, "Painful." He gingerly threw on his shirt. "I hope Declan's awake. He needs to give me more of that terrible tasting stuff. I want to be able to wear my armor for when the Irmingard Warriors arrive."

The aroma of food cooking over a fire found them as they descended the staircase. In the large room, Geraldine stirred the contents of a black kettle that hung over the fire. Declan poured liquid into a cup, then looked up at Edwin. He held the cup towards the Elf who gratefully took it.

After Edwin drank his medicine, he said, "Thanks. I've been too sore to check on the prisoners all night."

"Don't worry about a thing," said Geraldine bringing them bowls to the table. "Julie has it covered. You need to eat. All of you."

While they ate what Geraldine placed in front of them, Delyth, Hope, Freesia, and Obie joined them for breakfast.

"Excuse me, my Lord," said Julie approaching the table, "the Village Elders would be so honored if you and your party could join them in the treetops."

"All of us?" Declan asked.

"Yes, and me, Mom and Obie."

Geraldine stopped with dirty bowls in her hands. The frightened look on her face spoke volumes.

"You were summoned after I escaped," said Declan.

"Mom, Dad and Grandpa," Julie answered.

Declan, however, only had eyes for his mother. "Mom?"

Her light eyes found her son. "They reprimanded us. Your grandfather had a way with people, very much like how he had a way with wood. He talked them out of punishment. 'You were gone,' he told them, 'and that was punishment enough.' The forest seemed so angry that day. That was when it stopped providing for the village and our woodsmen and our archers had to travel further and further away. And now that you have returned perhaps all can be reversed."

"You know I can't stay," Declan said quietly.

She smiled warmly. "That doesn't matter. But all can be forgiven."

Chapter Six
Boudonian Battlefield

"We are not the ones who need forgiveness rained upon us," Declan said darkly. "I made a conscious effort to avoid the roads that led to Boudon. I promised Grandpa that I would come. And I have. When our business is finished here, I will leave with the intention of not returning."

Tears rolled down Geraldine's face. Closing her eyes, she nodded. She turned quickly. The dirty dishes she carried found a basin full of soapy water.

Declan stared at the table until it was time to leave. When Geraldine called everyone to follow, Declan grabbed Delyth's hand. She had become his comfort, his strength. By the time they began to walk through the village's balconies and bridges, he released her hand.

Geraldine led them inside a tree trunk into which was carved steep, narrow steps. At the end of a dizzying journey upward, they emerged onto a windswept platform hidden in the forest canopy. Three hooded figures sat on tree stumps. Their muddled brown and green cloaks blended with the trees.

They lowered their hoods. Two elderly men flanked an elderly woman. "Thank you for coming, Emperor," said the man on the left. "Your mere presence honors us."

"We are well aware that without you and your company,

Boudon would be only a memory. We are eternally grateful," the man on the right said.

"Recognizing that those who have sat on these stumps before us made a mistake, we wish to rectify it," the woman said. "My Lord, we seek forgiveness for our methods and for not correcting this sooner."

The three of them stood. The woman continued, "Declan Firth, third son of Leon and Geraldine Firth, we hereby absolve you of any wrong doing, for you were never in the wrong. The Elders were wrong. We restore the honor wrongfully stripped from your name, your family and all your descendants."

A breeze blew through the treetops. Declan's eyes followed something only he could see. "Grandpa," he said half smiling, half crying.

Through her tears, Julie gazed at her brother.

"Grandpa became a Whisper," Declan explained. "I can see, but I cannot hear. Maybe I am not listening carefully enough."

"Only a Whisperer can hear a Whisper," Hope said quietly.

Smiling, Declan hugged both his mother and sister.

"Emperor," said the Elder on the right, "we implore you. We know not how to defend ourselves against this new type of enemy."

"I understand your concerns," said Berty. "Be assured that the Empire will not abandon you. Boudon is comprised of talented archers. Allow the Empire Guards to train you to use this abundant talent in ways that can better help ensure your survival. However, I cannot guarantee Boudon's safety.

"This world is full of things we have forgotten, things we do not understand and things well out of our control. Remember that the Firewalker was only defeated because we happened to have the specialized magic to do so. We may not get so lucky again. No matter what, the Empire stands with Boudon as long as

Boudon stands with the Empire."

"These past couple of days," the woman said, "we have been reminded that we are not as alone as we may have felt. We graciously accept any help the Empire can provide, so that we may get back on our feet."

"And by accepting this help, we are recommitting ourselves and the loyalty of Boudon to the Empire," the man on the left said. "We thank you, all of you. The people of Boudon have already shown their solidarity with the Empire. We, the Elders of Boudon, have made this solidarity official. Long may be your reign, Emperor."

Berty gave the Elders a sharp nod before leaving with his party. Back in the village, Edwin stopped near a lift. "I am going to check on the prisoners," he said.

When the rest of them returned to the tree house, Declan said, "Obie, do you want to help me tend to the injured?"

The boy's eyes lit. "Of course!"

"Julie, can you do me a favor?" Declan asked. "Hope needs to practice. Can you take her?"

Julie gave her brother a wide smile. "It'll be just like we used to."

As they gathered what they needed, Delyth whispered in Berty's ear. "May I have a word?"

He led her into an upstairs bedroom for privacy. After closing the door, he waited for her to speak.

"I'm afraid the walls have ears, my Lord," she started. "I trust you know about what Avery and I spoke?"

He nodded.

"I fear for all of us. Something is not right. I will know more when I return to the Empire tree."

Berty saw the concern in her violet eyes. "Find me anytime of the day or night. We will speak then." He opened the door, allowing Delyth to enter the hall before he did.

"I must pack for my journey," she told him.

She climbed the stairs. He descended into an almost empty room. Geraldine busied herself with cleaning the nearly spotless room. She glanced at him as his feet left the bottom step.

"Delyth is packing," he said.

"Must she leave so soon?" she asked.

"I am afraid so. Dark times are coming, if they are not already here. Fairyland must be warned."

She paused mid-wipe on the large table. "What about the small villages? Some are not as well protected as we are."

"Boudon was chosen specially because of your protection," said Berty. "Outposts will be built in the far reaches of the Land of Sages, but no one should rely on the Empire Guards to protect them. The outposts will mostly be for training so that people can defend themselves."

"Are you not afraid that the trained people will join the opposition? I am sorry if I speak too frankly, my Lord," she said.

He smiled at her. "Do not be sorry, Geraldine. These are good questions. I believe that people have the right to defend themselves, their families and their villages. If someone chooses to fight for the opposition, then so be it. People must do what they feel is right in their hearts. Those who make that choice do not need to learn from us. If the Empire must teach a person self-defense, then that is because there is an opposition."

She finished wiping. "We teach archery because it is our way. We live high in the trees because our ancestors did. Those of us who are initiated into the brotherhood of the Boudonian Archers are among the best in the world. Boudon's woodsmen are second to none. People have always sought our crafts. That is the way it has always been." She hung the cloth she was using to dry. "My youngest son challenged all that the day his wand rolled out of his pocket onto the floor. I exiled him to protect all four of my children. Every day, I wonder if I did the right thing. Today, I know I did.

"My Lord," she continued, "I tell you this because I believe you to be right. You will, you must, protect no matter what. Giving someone better tools can only aid in that protection." She glanced around, then lowered her voice. "If it is not too much of a burden, can you take my grandson with you when you leave? He needs those tools and we cannot provide them here."

Before Berty could answer, Delyth emerged from the staircase. "I'm sorry. I don't mean to intrude," she said looking at them. She placed her bag on a bench, then retreated to the balcony.

He shook his head at the Fairy, letting her know that she was not intruding. "We must speak to Declan first, for he would be Declan's responsibility," he told Geraldine.

"Thank you."

"The Warriors are arriving from Irmingard," said Delyth, looking into the distance.

Joining her, Berty saw Elves galloping through the forest. Their silver breastplates gleamed in the sunlight. Edwin's tall stature walked towards them. The horses stopped. The front rider dismounted. When the rider reached Edwin, they gave each other a one armed embrace. Berty knew that the front rider was Edwin's brother—the new Commander.

A windswept Hope walked onto the balcony with Julie. Smiling, Hope said, "That was the best practice ever." She peered at the ground. "What's that big, black cage thing for?"

"Prisoners," he told her. "Now, go with Freesia and put your stuff away." He watched Edwin lead his brother to a lift. Turning his head, he asked Delyth, "Are you ready?"

"I think so." Her eyes caught Declan and Obie walking towards the house.

Staring at the Fairy, Declan stopped on the balcony. He pulled her into an embrace. "Thank you," he breathed into her dark, curly hair.

Grabbing her nephew, Julie followed Berty into the house. "Your niece has more talent than I've seen in a very long time. In a few years, she'd be able to challenge the best of the Boudonian Archers and win," Julie said. "Her other ability is just as impressive, my Lord. Does she have a form of clairvoyance? She knew exactly when the Warriors were coming."

Searching Julie's light eyes, he found the same fire in their depths as in Declan's. However, he knew secrets must be kept. "Not exactly. She is hyper aware of her surroundings."

"My Lord," announced Edwin, saving Berty from explaining further, "may I present my brother, Wystan, Commander of the Irmingard Warriors."

Berty gazed upon the brothers, one in leather armor and the other in silver. "Commander, thank you for answering our call in such a timely manner."

"My Lord," Wystan bowed. "When the Emperor calls, we answer. My men are surveying the situation and are setting up camp. We will stay until the Empire Guards take over." He glanced at Edwin.

"What is it?" Berty asked.

When Wystan did not answer right away, Edwin spoke. "Wystan believes that you are in danger. They found recent tracks running away from here."

He saw Hope listening out of the corner of his eye, then nodded. "Even with the Warriors and our high position, the Empire Tree is the safest place."

"My Lord, with my brother injured, I would like to offer Irmingard Warriors to escort you back to the Sages' Grove," said

Wystan.

"Very well, Commander. Get your men situated. We leave first thing in the morning."

Wystan bowed his head. He turned his attention to Delyth who stood off to the side. "Princess, about the Vindalf," he began.

"I will give the Vindalf an extra dose of Fairy Dust before I leave," she told them.

"Thank you, but I was wondering if it were possible," Wystan paused.

"No," Delyth said abruptly. "I know what you are going to ask and I cannot. Not because it is illegal under Irmingard law for an Elf to possess Fairy Dust, and not because I have already given Fairy Dust to a non-Fairy. Commander, Fairy Dust is ancient magic, much like the magic of the Elves. I will also not permit anyone in this room to give any Fairy Dust to anyone else. As a Fairy, I have a duty to protect our magic. Please, do not think that I do not trust you. Some things are bigger than we can fathom. I do not expect you to understand for I cannot explain it any better at this time. Know this: I must do my part to the best of my ability."

Wystan nodded. "I will admit that I do not fully understand all that is happening. The Dominatrix told me that you would most likely say no, but I had to ask anyway. I do not intend to challenge an ancient magic about which I know nothing. Irmingard thanks you for all you have done already."

Delyth gave him a sharp nod. "I have one more thing I need to do. Hope, there is something I must teach you."

All eyes watched Delyth bring Hope away from the others. The Fairy stood, facing Hope. "*Ere doe ein auk tun roe. Ere doe ein auk tun ín. On dry eck prone,*" chanted Delyth. Her opened palm tapped Hope's forehead.

"*Es newn rhyn tí*," Hope responded.

Delyth smiled. "It worked," she said. "Hope can now speak ancient Fairy. I am going to teach you how to draw a protective Fairy Ring. Use it around the camp on your way home."

Hope nodded. She took the Fairy's outstretched hand. Together, they left the house.

Edwin led Wystan through the village while Berty and Declan sat. "Do you think?" Declan asked.

"It has come to pass," answered Berty.

"The warning?"

Nodding, nine words entered his mind. *Seven Sages. Seven seals. Seven secrets. Soon sinister steals.* The words of the Pixie Priestess haunted him. He knew what had been stolen and had a rough idea who stole it. However, he had no idea how.

"These creatures," said Declan, "the Firewalker and the Fairy Eater, are not a part of our memories. How do we stop these things when we don't know what's coming next?"

Berty glanced at Geraldine and Julie having a conversation. "Knowledge, ingenuity and a little luck," he said with a wry smile.

Little feet ran to his side from the balcony. "I did magic, Uncle Berty," Hope squealed. Delight filled her brown eyes.

"The Vindalf have been dusted and transferred to the transport cages," announced Delyth. "I must go."

The men stood. "Safe travels, Delyth," said Berty.

"I should not be too long. I may return to the Empire Tree before you do," she said. She turned to the watching Geraldine and Julie. "It was wonderful meeting you both. Thank you so much for your hospitality."

"It was a pleasure having you, dear. You are welcome here anytime," Geraldine told her. She hugged Delyth. "Would you like to eat something before you go?"

Delyth gave her a smile. "Thank you, Geraldine, but I cannot. It is not wise to eat and fly. I have a long flight ahead of me, even at top speed."

When Geraldine released her, Julie gave her a hug, too. "Do you have the puzzle box for your brother?"

"I do. Telor is going to love it."

Declan held Delyth's bag for her. Taking it from him, she secured it to the front of her body. She threw her purple cloak over her shoulders. "I'll walk you out," he said.

Berty watched them leave. Wanting to give them privacy, he waited a few minutes before walking through the balconies of Boudon. He peered over the railings. Below the village, Warriors constructed two separate tent cities, one from where each army attacked. Declan joined him, then sighed.

"Miss her already?" Berty asked.

"Is it that obvious?" Declan ran his fingers through his sandy hair.

Smiling, Berty answered, "Only since you first met her." They both laughed.

When they returned to the house, Geraldine and Julie were setting the table for lunch. Watching her son, Geraldine said, "She's a lovely girl."

Declan smiled.

"But the Fairy Princess? Can you make it anymore difficult?" Julie asked with a smirk.

"I am the Duke of Fairyland, I'll have you know," Declan countered.

"Dad's home!" yelled Obie, running into the room.

"By himself?" Julie asked.

"No. Everyone is home," answered Obie. "We can see them coming through the woods."

"Julie, set extra places," instructed Geraldine. "We're all eat-

88

ing together. Your brothers can learn how to behave themselves in the Emperor's presence."

"Ger!" a man's voice called from the balcony. He rushed inside. "What's going on? Why are there Elves everywhere?"

"Leon," said Geraldine, "where are the boys?"

"One of them thought they saw a Fairy flying away," said Leon.

"They did," Declan said.

Turning, Leon glanced at Declan and Berty. He stared at his son as if he had seen a ghost. Cecil walked in with Obie strapped to his side.

"How dare you show your face here," said a voice behind Cecil. Vander pushed his blond hair out of his face.

Ignoring Vander, Geraldine said, "Leon, your son has come home."

Leon did not take his eyes off of Declan. He dropped his things on the floor. Within three steps, he held Declan in an embrace. Geraldine wiped her cheek.

"Help him," said Wystan. He entered, trying to keep Edwin upright.

Berty ran to Edwin's side. Together, they guided Edwin to the nearest seat.

"He needs his armor off," Declan said as he ran to fill a cup with willow bark infusion. Once Berty and Wystan lifted the leather over Edwin's head, Declan pressed the cup in the Elf's hand. "Drink," he instructed. After peering under Edwin's shirt at his shoulder, Declan walked to his gathered herbs.

Separating himself from his father, Obie asked, "What can I do, Uncle Declan?"

Cecil's jaw dropped slightly while watching his son crush herbs under Declan's instruction. Happy with the paste, Declan smeared it on Edwin's shoulder.

"Why not remove his shirt?" Obie asked.

"Because that could hurt his shoulder more," Declan replied. "Speaking of hurting more, what did you do?"

"Helping," Edwin said with his eyes closed.

"No more helping. We have a five day journey ahead of us," Declan told him.

"Vander, Cecil," Geraldine barked, "don't just stand there like bumps on a log. Help fill bowls. Commander, have lunch with us."

Tearing his gaze from his brother, Wystan scanned the room until he found Geraldine. "I do not wish to intrude, ma'am."

"Nonsense," said Geraldine. "He's your brother." She gave him a warm smile, then set him a place.

Almost every seat around the long table was filled. Berty sat across from Leon at the center of the table. Leon looked at the strangers sitting at his table. "Now, what has happened?" Leon asked.

Berty stared at Leon squarely, then said, "Yesterday, Boudon was attacked."

Vander dropped his spoon. "Attacked? Let me guess, dear little brother came to save the day with his little band of friends."

"Let me introduce you to my little band of friends, Vander. Lieutenant Edwin of the Empire Guard. Commander Wystan of the Irmingard Warriors. You just missed Princess Delyth of the Fairies. And sitting next to me is the Emperor of all that surrounds us." Declan watched his brother turn white.

"Uncle Declan has been teaching me about healing," Obie cheerfully told whomever would listen.

Cecil glanced at Declan before turning his attention to his son. "Has he? Do you enjoy that?"

"Yeah. We went around treating all sorts of wounds," said Obie excitedly.

Cecil gave his son a large smile. Berty caught Leon and Geraldine exchanging glances.

After lunch, Declan checked Edwin's shoulder. Geraldine and Julie told the men everything that transpired.

Berty motioned for Wystan to join him on the balcony. "Have any of the captured said anything interesting?" he asked the Elf.

"Not as yet," answered Wystan. "But many are still waking from their Fairy Dust coma."

Nodding, Berty said, "Listen carefully. What they say may give us a picture of what's to come."

A dark haired man stormed past them. "Where's my wife?" the man demanded as he entered Declan's family home.

"Yes, my Lord," was all Wystan managed to say before Julie ran towards the central bridge.

"I want all those who witnessed my union to Owen to know that our marriage was based on a lie." Julie projected her voice for all to hear.

"Julie, what are you doing?" Owen asked in a derogatory tone as he approached the bridge. Julie's family and other villagers poured onto the balconies.

"You lied to me for years, Owen," said Julie. "You pretended that you were Declan's best friend, that you actually cared about what happened to him. Every year on his birthday, you'd be at my side. In reality, you hated my brother."

"You're crazy," Owen accused. "She's so crazy that she fired her crossbow at me. Then you left me there struggling to get off the wall." He balled his fists in anger as he stepped onto the bridge towards her.

She took a small step away from him. "Are you going to hit me Owen? Just like the night I fired back at you."

Gasps echoed around the village. Leon quickly moved

through the crowd towards Owen.

"All those in favor of dissolving this union say, aye," said Julie.

"Aye," the village responded.

"All those oppose?"

Silence overtook the villagers.

Leon had reached Owen. He grabbed Owen's cloak, bringing him to the floor. A small blade rested against Owen's neck. "Touch my daughter again and it will be the last thing you do," Leon threatened.

"The union between Julie and Owen is hereby dissolved," said a cloaked Elder.

Julie gave the Elder a smile, then walked away.

"Give me a report this evening, Commander," said Berty.

"Yes, my Lord." With a bow, Wystan returned to his men.

Berty entered the house with Declan's family.

"What are you going to do now, Julie?" Cecil asked. "I know your mind has been turning."

"That depends," she answered. "My Lord, Delyth's departure has left an empty saddle. I beg your permission to fill that saddle and travel with you to the Sages' Grove. My only wish is to start a new life as a Woodsmith."

"But you can do that here," said Vander. His voice was soft.

"No, I cannot. Vander, you are the Woodsmith. Cecil is the Woodsman. Declan would have been the Boudonian Archer, had he been able to stay. I don't want to be anyone's wife. Not right now." Her light eyes implored Berty.

He knew that she would leave Boudon in search of herself with or without them. "You may join us," he said.

Smiling, she said, "Thank you, my Lord."

"Does that mean there is no room for my grandson?" Geraldine asked.

"What?" Cecil raised his voice. "You want to send Obie

92

away?"

"It's for his own good," his mother explained.

"*I* am his father. You have no right to make these decisions." He gave his mother an incredulous look. "My son is not going anywhere," he said through clenched teeth.

"Cecil," Leon said delicately, "this is his chance to learn a skill. He'll be able to come back. If not, our young Oberon will be gone for good when the time comes."

Cecil held his son close, then closed his eyes.

"What would Fiona have wanted?" Vander asked quietly.

When he opened his eyes, a tear streaked down Cecil's face. "Don't speak her name in my presence. You are all against me. My own family."

No one could speak. Declan watched his eldest brother cry while clutching his son. "Cecil?" Declan broke the silence. "To me, it sounds like everyone is with you." Cecil found his brother. "I know what it is like to be out there, alone and scared, unable to return. At least I knew how to use a bow." His brother's eyes found the top of Obie's blond head. "What do you want for his future? What does he want?"

Crouching to look his son in the eyes, Cecil asked, "Oberon Cecil Firth, what do you want?"

"I want to be a healer like Uncle Declan," Obie said softly.

Nodding, Cecil slowly stood. He walked over to Declan. Giving him a hug, he said, "Take care of my son, your nephew."

Declan's surprised look turned into a smile. "I will," he told his brother.

Geraldine's eyes glistened as Cecil clapped his son on the shoulder. "Come on, Obie. Let's go pack." Father and son ascended the stairs.

Berty's watchful eye caught Vander trying to slip through the door to the workshop unnoticed.

"Declan can you spare a few minutes?" Leon asked.

Glancing from Berty to Edwin, Declan answered, "Sure."

"Help me sort our haul," said Leon.

"I don't know if that's such a good idea," said Declan.

"Nonsense. You're my son."

With a cautious smile, Declan allowed his father to steer him out of the sanctuary of the house.

Sitting next to Edwin, Berty asked, "How's the shoulder?"

"Better. It only hurts a little when I move. Hurting it again was worth it. The Irmingard Warriors will treat me as their superior on the way back to the Empire Tree," Edwin said.

"You felt the need to prove yourself?"

"The former Commander did not like me much," explained Edwin. "I'm not exactly sure why. Wystan has only been Commander for two days. He is still earning the respect of his men, but he has the advantage of having been elected Low Elf. Commander is a more permanent job. I haven't spent much time in Irmingard. These men don't know me. In the grand scheme of things, I outrank my brother, but not in their eyes. To them, today I earned my rank." He smiled. "I'll be able to travel without my armor. It should help my shoulder."

Military politics, Berty thought. They discussed the best route to the Sages' Grove, focusing on whether or not they should stick to the roads.

"I don't want Hope as our navigator," Berty whispered. "Too dangerous. Declan could use his wand."

"Any perceived use of magic could be unwise," Edwin noted.

Declan joined them in time to give Edwin another dose of medicine. "With our Warrior escort, I think we should use magic whenever possible," he whispered. "If Wystan is right and you are in danger, my Lord, then the best route is the quickest route. Magic could help us determine that."

Nodding, Berty added, "May also be good if we passed the Empire Guards."

They paused their discussion to eat a hearty meal with Declan's family. Laughter surrounded the table although Vander did not speak to Declan.

After dinner, they prepared to leave Boudon for an early morning departure. Wystan appeared in the doorway, saying, "Excuse me, my Lord."

Berty walked with Wystan onto an empty bridge. "From what we have overheard, we are preparing for an attack to free the prisoners," Wystan reported. "I am sending seven with you tomorrow—one more than you have horses."

"Thank you, Wystan." He felt that Wystan was a lot like his younger brother in more than just looks. "If you wish to say a more private farewell to Edwin, please," he gestured towards the house.

Smiling, Wystan bowed, then entered the house.

Inside the great room, Berty overheard Wystan lamenting about missing Edwin's wedding. "I can't wait to meet Lark."

As the evening wore down, Vander allowed Hope and Freesia to sleep in his room. Cecil gave his room to Berty and Edwin. The two brothers slept in the great room.

The sun barely cast light blue across the sky as they gathered for breakfast. Edwin left to ready the horses and meet the Irmingard Warriors. Berty, Hope and Freesia stood to the side while Declan's family said their good-byes.

After the rounds of hugs, they began to walk out of the family's house. "Declan, wait," Vander called.

Stopping, Declan turned to face his brother.

Vander took a deep breath. "I'm sorry." His light eyes begged his brother to forgive him.

Dropping his bag, Declan hugged his brother. Vander picked

up Declan's bag, then accompanied them down to the horses.

With sunlight peeking over the horizon, Cecil placed Obie on the horse with Hope. They waved good-bye. Irmingard Warriors surrounded them as they rode away from Boudon.

Chapter Seven
Fairy Magic

Until they rested for the night, they stayed on the roads. They chose a campsite far from the road. After the horses were secure and the firewood was gathered, Hope began to construct a Fairy Ring around their camp.

"*Odoxa domna guidrade hín,*" Hope repeated while sprinkling sparkling Fairy Dust on the ground. When she reached the beginning of her circle, she said, "*Soltrine dayd.*"

An opalescent dome rested over their camp. The forest beyond disappeared. Berty watched the shimmering pale blues, pinks and purples swirl in the white covering.

Hope sat happily next to her uncle. "Delyth taught you this yesterday?" he asked.

Nodding her head covered in messy curly brown, she answered, "She read about it in one of her ancient books. She said that this is lost magic."

"It's so pretty," said Julie, admiring the dome.

Declan looked perplexed. "What is?"

"Delyth warned against touching it," Hope added.

"Touch what?" asked Declan.

"You can't see the glowing colors?" Julie asked her brother with her hands motioning to the dome.

His eyes followed his sister's hands. "All I see is forest."

"Delyth said that you'd probably be able to see through it, but she wasn't sure," said Hope.

Looking at Hope, Declan asked, "What do those on the outside see?"

Hope shrugged. "All she said is that it'll protect us from anything."

After eating, Declan made more bark infusion for Edwin over the dying fire. As it steeped, Declan stared at his sister. When she raised her eyebrows at him, he said, "I threatened Owen that day we met in the Dragonlands. I said that if he didn't respect you, I'd make you a widow."

"Why are you telling me?" Julie asked.

"I'm sorry that I caused him to hurt you."

Her face softened. "Declan, no. You did nothing wrong. I chose the wrong man. The signs were there. I just failed to see them. Don't blame yourself. He was a poor friend, a poor husband, a poor man."

He gave his sister a nod. Looking up at what only he could see, he said, "We should sleep."

Berty found it hard to sleep under the dome's soft glow. He wondered if Declan saw any of it.

In the morning, Hope, following Delyth's orders, would not lift the circle until the camp was fully packed and horses were mounted. She started where she ended. Going in the reverse direction, she held her hand over the dust, saying, "*Zole gurmum.*" The sparkling Fairy Dust lifted all off the ground, landing in her velvet pouch.

When the circle of dust had been collected, Hope suggested that they not take the road. Without question, Berty agreed. They rode through the forest, alive in its summer splendor. The full canopy blocked the summer sun from beating on their backs.

They stopped for a quick meal and for Edwin to drink anoth-

er measured dose. Returning to their saddles, they heard raucous-
ly wild giggling. The Warriors' gazes searched the trees. "So
many Elfies," a female voice sang from the trees before giggling
again.

"Wood Sprite," said Edwin.

Hope steered her horse away from the group. "Where are we
going?" Obie asked.

"Shh." She hushed him. The horse stopped feet away from
the outside Elves.

A young tree shook, morphing into a girlish woman. The top
of her messy, stick-infested hair reached above the heads of Elves
on horseback. Her brown skin glowed in the filtered midday sun.
When her bright green eyes found Hope, she smiled.

Within two strides of her long, slender legs, the Wood Sprite
stood next to Hope. "Hi-lo," she said to her.

"Hello, Miradelle," Hope said. Her little hand reached for
the Wood Sprite.

Miradelle closed her eyes as Hope's hand touched her cheek.
She lost her crazed look.

Recalling the Master Woodsman telling him how the last
Wood Sprite's mind had been addled, Berty wondered if Hope's
touch could bring it back.

Opening her eyes, Miradelle inhaled the warm air deeply.
She and Hope stared at each other as if they were communicating
in their own way.

Gazing at the others, Miradelle said, "The woods are filled
with malice. The way ahead will be clear. I will make sure the
forest protects you." She bowed to Hope. "Go." The Wood
Sprite disappeared into the trees.

The sun quickly approached the horizon by the time they
made camp. Hope knew the forest would protect them, so she
did not draw a Fairy Ring. After they ate, Obie sat alone, away

from the group. Declan watched him intently.

"Whatcha doing, Obie?" Declan called.

"Nothing, Uncle Declan. Just thinking," said Obie.

"Obie, come here."

"I'm not doing anything," Obie whined.

"I can see you," Declan said with a paused emphasis on each word.

Getting up, Obie slouched over to his uncle.

"Show us," said Declan.

Obie stared at Declan with a deer-in-the-headlights look, biting his lip.

"You were doing magic," Declan said calmly.

"How'd you know?" Obie asked.

Declan chuckled a little. "I'm a Watcher. I can see magic—more than most."

The boy glanced at his uncle, aunt, Berty, Hope, and Edwin. "Don't be mad," he said in a small voice. Turning his palm to the sky, Obie mumbled incoherently. A chartreuse colored sphere hovered inches above his palm.

"You battled the Warlock," said Berty. He remembered the magical collisions exploding before hitting the village.

Sheepishly, Obie nodded.

"No one is angry, Obie," Declan answered.

"Why didn't you tell any of us?" asked Julie.

His eyes found his aunt. "Because I didn't want to be sent away or... worse."

Julie opened her mouth, but no sound escaped.

"This changes everything," said Declan.

"Does this mean I have to go back?" Obie asked wide-eyed.

"No," Declan said. "You can defend yourself. I'll find a secluded place for you to practice in the Sages' Grove."

Smiling, Obie collapsed his sphere into his hands.

100

The sun barely lightened the sky as they packed the campsite. Riding through the woods, a faint giggling reached their ears. Miradelle traveled with them.

They tried to ride as far as possible before making camp for the evening. The lead Irmingard Warrior slowed, then raised his bow.

"Garik, what is it?" Edwin asked quietly.

Berty could hear rustling coming from somewhere ahead of them.

"Hold your fire, men of Irmingard," a voice called. Through the underbrush, a half dozen men wearing the leather armor of the Empire Guard emerged.

Garik lowered his weapon.

"Lieutenant, Emperor," said one of the guards. They all bowed. "We apologize for sneaking up on you. We heard the horses and came to investigate."

Edwin looked to Berty, who gave him a nod. "The Emperor expects no less," Edwin told them. "Have you made camp for the night?"

"We have, Lieutenant. We can take you to Lieutenant Noll."

They followed the Empire Guards to the expansive, woodland campsite. The Empire Guards had multiple fires and three, large, central tents. Dismounting, someone took their horses. The Irmingard Warriors stayed with them as they entered one of the tents.

In the center of the tent, an Elf studied a map. Raising his head from the makeshift table, the Elf glanced at the entrants.

"Lieutenant Noll," Edwin said right away.

"Lieutenant Edwin, I did not recognize you without your armor," said Noll. He stood board straight beside the table. His eyes caught the claret cloak in the day's dying light. "My Lord," he bowed, "I am honored that our paths have crossed."

"This is Sergeant Garik of the Irmingard Warriors," Edwin continued. "He and his men are accompanying the Emperor's party to the Sages' Grove." He glanced at Garik as if it were his turn to speak.

"Lieutenant," said Garik, "Commander Wystan has instructed me, upon our meeting, to inform you about what you will meet in Boudon."

Noll nodded sharply. "Sergeant, any information you can provide is very welcome. Speak with Sergeant Otho in the right most tent."

After the Irmingard Warriors took their leave, Noll addressed Edwin. "The Command tent is now yours."

"No," said Edwin. "I am not here to usurp your authority. We came to communicate and perhaps share the campsite."

"Of course." Noll gestured awkwardly around the tent. "I will have food brought."

The seven of them sat in a breezy corner of the tent. Noll and a few other guards brought food into the tent. "Lieutenant," Berty called to Noll. He extended his arm towards the empty spot on the ground.

Noll proudly joined them.

"Captain Alvar told you about the Vindalf?" Berty asked Noll.

"Yes, my Lord."

"Irmingard has custody of them. The rest are ours. Fill the dungeons with them."

"Yes, my Lord."

After they ate, Noll watched Edwin drink the medicine Declan gave him. "That's the last dose," Declan told Edwin. "Let me know if it hurts, but I'd advise against aggravating it."

"Be ready to leave at first light," said Berty.

"My Lord, I will ready a handful of Empire Guards to accompany you," Noll said. "The Irmingard Warriors can go back home."

Looking at Noll, he saw an eager lieutenant wanting to prove himself to the Emperor. "Thank you, Noll, but I do not wish to take any men from your task ahead. The road for us is a short one. Any Empire Guards will be better suited under your command."

"I do not understand, my Lord. Our job is to protect you," protested Noll.

"Your job is to protect the Empire. I am only one man."

"Of course, my Lord. Forgive me." Noll bowed.

"The Empire is in a state of flux, Lieutenant. Sometimes we must change in order to stay the same."

Nodding, Noll looked unsure.

"Were you looking at a map of Boudon, Lieutenant?" asked Declan.

"I am just trying to be prepared, Your Grace," Noll answered.

"As well you should be. Boudon is no ordinary village." Declan studied the Elf who was out of his element. "Would you like some inside information? Miss Firth," he gestured towards his sister, "is a Boudonian. She has spent her lifetime in the trees of Boudon."

"Yes, thank you. It would be greatly appreciated."

Julie briefly touched her brother's shoulder in thanks as she passed, following Noll to the table. Sitting on the ground, they chatted about nothing in particular. Only Edwin left the tent to have a word with Garik.

The tent was dark when they woke. Berty thanked Noll before they climbed atop their horses. Only a few Empire Guards stirred as they galloped towards the rising sun.

During a mid-morning stop, Declan extracted his wand that was hidden in his quiver. Resting on the top of his palm, the wand pointed towards the Empire Tree. "If we ride straight through, we can arrive just after nightfall," he said.

"Does anyone object?" Berty asked.

"Our torchlight will be limited, my Lord," said Garik.

"Light will not be a problem," he said.

Garik gave Berty a nod, then they continued their ride through the giggling forest.

As the woods began to darken, Berty checked on Hope and Obie. Both were still wide awake. Conjuring spheres of light, he threw them into the air. The spheres floated above them as they traveled.

When the forest ended, torches lighted the treed wall of the Sages' Grove. They slowed their pace as they approached.

"The gates are closed," said Garik.

Berty removed his light spheres. He knew the Advisory Council enacted that after Delyth's report. "Call to open them without revealing my presence," Berty told him.

"Gatekeeper! We ask you to open the gates," Garik said.

A Troll stood on the lookout. "State your business, sir," said the Troll.

"I am Sergeant Garik of Irmingard. It is unwise to linger this late in the wilderness. Please, open your gates."

"I'm sorry, Sergeant. I have my orders. These gates must remain closed," the Troll said.

Edwin positioned his horse next to Garik. "From whom? I wish to speak to the order giver!" He was annoyed.

Standing on his perch, the Troll fumbled over mumbles.

"Enough!" said Berty. "Clear the gates. They're opening now."

The Troll looked horrified as the gates opened on their own. Holding them open with magic, Berty led his party inside the Sages' Grove.

Running down the steps of the lookout, the Troll cried,

104

"You can't... How did...? I'm going to lose my job."

With a wave of his hand, the gates closed. Berty stared at the Troll. Its youthful triangular face was full of worry. Something was wrong. "Who gave you the orders?" His voice was stern.

"Uh... um." The Troll swallowed.

"Simple question. Simple answer," said Berty. He glanced at the Irmingard Warriors. They dismounted. "Fine. What is your name?"

The Troll's eyes grew wide with fear.

Unsheathing his sword, Berty pointed it at the Troll. "Who sent you?"

Turning, the Troll ran into the blades of the Irmingard Warriors.

"Seize him!" Berty ordered.

The Warriors picked the squirming Troll off the ground. Writhing, he bit on an Elf to free his hand. A sparkling substance flew towards the Elves' faces.

"*Eck oom!*" Hope shouted with her hand outstretched. The Fairy Dust froze in midair. "*Dy see trum.*" Sparkles flew into Hope's hand.

Jumping off his horse, Berty touched his blade to the Troll's throat. "Search him," he said to Hope.

She slid to the ground. Taller than the Troll, she took a velvet pouch from his belt.

"Fetch Hatcher and throw this one in a cell," said Berty, sheathing his sword.

Declan dashed inside the Empire tree. With Edwin leading, the Elves disappeared with the Troll below the ground.

"Come," he said to those remaining. Inside the tree, they ascended the steps to the reception room. "Theodore," he called.

"Yes, my Lord," said the young Dwarf.

"Declan's sister and nephew need a place to stay, but first I need a Containment Unit," he said. Running his fingers through his dark hair, he could feel it curling around his ears. The length of his hair annoyed him further.

When Declan returned, Hatcher was by his side.

Without waiting to be addressed, Berty barked, "Find out about the Troll in the dungeon."

Hatcher looked shocked. Not saying a word, he scampered down the stairs.

"Miles, my Lord," announced Theodore.

Glancing at the periwinkle clad Fairy, he said, "A Troll tried to use Fairy Dust against us. See if there are any traces."

Miles bowed his head, then quickly left.

"It has been a long day. Well, a long week. Theodore will show you to your rooms," Berty said to Julie and Obie. "Hope," he held out his hand, "confiscated Fairy Dust, please." She placed the pouch is hand. "It's past your bedtime."

He trudged up the stairs behind Hope and Freesia with Declan by his side. Feeling soft velvet between his fingers, he stopped mid-climb. "Hope," he called. When she turned, he continued, "Did Delyth teach you to stop Fairy Dust?"

She shook her head.

"Goodnight, Hope," he said with a smile.

"Goodnight, Uncle Berty."

Entering the Roundtable Room with Declan, he stared at the dark velvet.

"What does that mean?" Declan asked.

He placed the dark bag on the shiny tabletop. "It means that Delyth transferred more to her than just the ability to speak an ancient language."

Hatcher ran into the room. "My Lord, that Troll has turned. There is nothing I can get from him."

"What do you mean has turned?" he asked.

106

"With the ingestion of certain mushrooms, Trolls can turn to large Trolls. However, we lose our mental capacity. I magically sealed the cells so he can't escape," Hatcher explained. "There is an antidote. I sent for the Reducer."

"Good," said Berty, although he did not entirely know what a Reducer was. "Who was supposed to be watching the gates?"

"Jaunty," Hatcher replied. "He's missing. The Fairies will do their thing first. If they don't find him, a search party is ready."

Berty nodded. "Keep me informed."

After Hatcher left, Declan ran his hand through his sandy hair. "I thought the Sages' Grove would be the safest place for Obie," he muttered.

"The safest place is with you, learning the art of healing and using his magic freely."

Declan gave him a half smile. "Speaking of magic, if Hope took off the pendant, would she lose the Fairy magic?"

"I don't know," said Berty. "But if she starts to sprout wings, Jon and Teresa will be even angrier with me."

"I thought Delyth would be here by now," Declan said, stifling a yawn.

"Theodore," Berty asked.

"Yes, my Lord." Theodore appeared in the doorway.

"When the Containment Units have finished their sweep, bring Miles here to report." After Theodore disappeared, Berty said to Declan, "Why don't you get some sleep."

Staring at the dark blob, Declan answered, "I will stay. From where did a Troll get Fairy Dust?"

A strawberry blonde, freckle-faced Fairy popped into Berty's mind. "Millicent. Delyth believes she was hoarding Fairy Dust," he answered.

"Excuse me, my Lord," said Miles from the opened door.

Berty waived him inside.

Standing near the table, Miles reported, "No Fairy Dust any-where within the Sages' Grove."

"Thank you, Miles," he said.

As the Fairy left, Hatcher returned to the Roundtable Room. "I have started the search for Jaunty," the Troll said. "I do not know how long it will take."

"The search may take you outside the walls. If it does, have a Containment Unit accompany the party," said Berty. "I'll be in my chambers if you need me. Otherwise, we will all meet here in the morning."

Hatcher's triangular face wore a grave expression while he nodded sharply.

Rising from his seat, Berty grabbed the pouch of Fairy Dust. He bid Declan goodnight, then climbed his private staircase.

Chapter Eight
Starjen, Trolls, and a King

Wind chimes echoed through his chambers. He opened his eyes in the darkness. Sitting up in bed, lanterns flickered to life. He tied his robe as he descended his spiral staircase. The night breeze hit his face as he opened the door, reminding him of something Hope mentioned in Boudon.

Looking at the moonlit figure before him, he said, "Delyth, please come in."

A weary Delyth walked into his study. "I am sorry about the hour, my Lord. It was imperative that I came straight to you."

"It's quite all right," he told her. "Have a seat. I'll be right down."

Running up the stairs shook off any drowsiness. He quickly changed. When he returned to his study, he made a beeline for his desk. Gathering the velvet pouch, he said, "Come with me."

As Delyth followed him across the narrow bridge into the trunk, he wondered if the Sages' Grove or the Empire Tree was immune. He could not take any chances. Turning right, he led her down the dark hallway.

He stopped in front of a section of plain wall. Grabbing Delyth's arm, he pulled her through it. He thought, *light.* Candles illuminated the inner round room.

Delyth's violet eyes searched the room. "My Lord, where are

we?"

"The very center of the Empire Tree. It's called the Sorcery Room," he explained. "Nothing can reach us here."

"I do not understand."

"When we were with the Elders of Boudon, Hope said that only a Whisperer can hear a Whisper," he said. "I am not sure how it all works, but I figured this was the safest place to talk. Even you said that the walls have ears."

Berty dropped the velvet pouch on the table before they sat on the old wooden chairs.

"Is that Fairy Dust?" she asked.

"That can wait. What did you want to tell me?"

"When Avery told me about the Elves' secret—the Vindalf—being stolen, I immediately thought about the safety of the Fairies' secret—Fairy Dust," she said. "I had a long conference with my parents and my brother. I also took the time to do more research in the ancient library. Ancient creatures were my focus." She closed her eyes for a moment. When her eyes opened, she stared at the pouch. "What about that Fairy Dust?"

When he told her about the Troll, she gasped. "Can you examine this Dust?" he asked.

"Of course, I can." She took the bag from Berty. "Was anyone affected?"

"No. Thanks to Hope." He explained how his niece stopped the Dust.

"What?" she breathed.

"How will this affect her?"

She let out a deep breath. "I was going to return to Fairyland tonight. I will see to her in the morning. Her pendant will be removed."

Berty nodded.

"My Lord, there's something else you need to know," said

Delyth. "My father has taken ill again. Elder Hunter blames herself." Her eyes started to well. "She says that she must have allowed some of the poison from the Faematask to fall to the ground when that man attacked her in the Dragonlands. I looked it up. The only thing that can save him now is a Witch."

He stared at her in disbelief. "Are there any Witches left? Unless... Alina."

"I mentioned her to Elder Hunter," said Delyth. "She said Estelle can find a Witch."

"Then, we wake Estelle," he told her.

Magically extinguishing the candles, he brought her back into the dark, narrow hall. He led her further down the hall. When he faced the hall-ending door, he grabbed her arm again. They walked through the door into the wide hall on the other side.

"Emperor, Delyth, I thought I was alone in my nighttime wanderings," said Estelle. The silver thread in her Navy dress twinkled in the sconce light.

"You're just the person we were coming to see," he said.

"My father needs a Witch," said Delyth. "Elder Hunter says you can find one."

Estelle smiled. "Let's see what starjen say." She approached the steps that led to the Stargazing Platform. "Come," she said.

They followed her up the stairs. The sky opened before them. "Stand there," she instructed, indicating near the railing. As she walked towards the center of the platform, her light blonde hair glowed in the moonlight.

She opened her arms towards the sky. "*Starjen, talat meg,*" she told the heavens.

As if in a trance, she danced around the platform. Her feet deliberately touched certain places on the wood. Ending her dance in the center, she looked at the path her feet made on the wood. Berty thought that she could see lines drawn on the platform. All he saw was moonlit darkness.

"The poison that afflicts King Elrick," Estelle began, "will gnaw at him until the first leaves well to the North turn." She spun. "The Witch you seek will be found in the Outlands. Let the trees be your guide."

She walked towards them. Her light eyes reflected the star-light. "So, not Alina?" Delyth asked her.

"It's not yet her time," said Estelle.

"Thank you, Estelle," Berty said.

Smiling, she accompanied them back inside the tree. "I'm glad I could help. Your father has time to be healed. When you see Ellri, tell her hello from me and all will be right. She will understand," she said to Delyth.

He watched Estelle walk down the curved hall. She missed Silvia as well. "We will leave today," said Berty.

Delyth's eyes looked wet. "Thank you. I'll examine this Fairy Dust, then try to sleep."

Giving her a one-armed squeeze, Berty stepped through the wall, leaving the Fairy alone to succumb to her tears.

Morning arrived earlier than Berty had wanted. He could have used a couple of extra hours of sleep, but duty called. When he reached the Roundtable Room, he found Alfred sitting at the table.

"Good morning, my Lord," said the aged Elf. "I spoke with Delyth."

"Then you know that my niece's lessons must wait even longer," he said.

Colvin entered behind Declan and Estelle. "Hatcher and Alvar are on their way," said the Dwarf.

Once they were seated, Hatcher entered with Alvar. The Troll's eyes were red and puffy. Berty's heart dropped.

"We found Jaunty just before sunrise," said Hatcher barely in

112

the seat. His head began to shake from side to side as if he were not believing what was going to escape his lips. "Stabbed in the trees just beyond the clearing. They found Fairy Dust. Said it was probably used to lure him there." He closed his eyes. After taking a deep breath, he looked at Berty. "The Reducer will be here today. She will keep that Troll normal size. Alvar has agreed to interrogate."

The Advisory Council sat silent for a moment until Delyth opened the door. Before taking her seat, she placed a dark velvet pouch on the table. All eyes found her.

"The Fairy Dust confiscated from the Troll is from this cycle," Delyth said. "It could have been given to the Troll or stolen from any Fairy anywhere. Given that Fairies fought in Boudon, my suspicion is that this little bit was given to him to use here."

"What is the punishment for murder?" Berty asked.

"Death," answered Alvar.

"Who determines whether a man is innocent or guilty?" he asked.

"You do, unless you appoint a judge," said Alfred.

Berty's eyes found Alvar. "I need evidence that the Troll in the dungeon committed murder," he said. "For there is a possibility that Jaunty was lured into the woods by the prisoner, then killed by another." He glanced at the dark bag's reflection in the tabletop. "I do not want to condemn an innocent man to death."

"Innocent?" asked Hatcher.

"Of murder, not treachery. Of that, he is guilty beyond doubt."

Looking relieved, Hatcher inquired, "My Lord, may Jaunty's body be returned to Bridgetown, so that his family may mourn, and he be given a proper Troll burial?"

"Has the murder weapon been found?" Berty asked in return.

"No," replied Alvar.

"Scour that section of woods," he said. "Then, he may go home."

"Thank you, my Lord," said Hatcher.

"My Lord, if I may," said Alfred, "perhaps Hope would expedite the search."

He did not wish for Hope's abilities to be used on a whim. She was only a child. To how much should she be exposed? "No," said Berty. "I do not know how her gift works exactly. I cannot expose her to the murder of an innocent person. I will not subject her to gruesome details well beyond her comprehension. She is much too young. The Empire Guards can use their skills. You may go. Delyth and Declan stay."

When the door closed on just the three of them, Berty said, "About Hope."

"Knowledge of the language of the ancient Fairies has allowed her to use the ancient magic. She is able to call forth the language, and hence, the magic without the pendant. However, she loses control over the Fairy Dust. She needs the pendant to use it. Since I cannot go with you, I recommend she wear the pendant in case of," Delyth did not finish. "I need to be with my father."

"We will leave this afternoon," said Berty. "Thank you, Delyth. Go. Be with him."

As she rose, Declan said, "Wait. Take this." He placed his gold Watcher's Locket in her hand.

She hung the gold chain around her neck. After giving him a quick peck, she hurried to the Stargazing Platform.

"We are heading to the Outlands," said Berty. "Do you think Edwin can make it?"

"Yes."

"Good. He and Sean will come with us."

"What do I do with Obie?" Declan asked.

"Take him with us," said Berty.

"This time, he'll get his own horse," said Declan.

"No horses. I want to be as inconspicuous as possible," said Berty.

Descending into the Reception Room, they found Julie, Obie, Hope, and Freesia eating breakfast. With plates of food, Berty and Declan joined them at the table.

"Thank you for allowing me to stay the night, my Lord," said Julie. "I will seek lodging in the village today."

"You're welcome," Berty said.

"Where will I go?" asked Obie.

"With me," Declan told him. "You know, Julie, Fairyland has need of a good Woodsmith. I'll recommend you to the King and Queen once I return."

Julie almost choked on her juice. "Thanks. Return from where?"

"Running an errand for King Elrick," Declan answered.

"Am I going, too?" Obie asked.

Nodding, Declan said, "Go through your stuff. Anything you want to leave, goes in my chambers. Hope, after breakfast, collect your arrows. I need to know how many you have left."

"We leave today, so be packed," Berty added. "Theodore will make sure everyone has provisions."

"My Lord, how long will we be gone?" asked Freesia.

"Depends on how long it takes us to get to the Outlands."

"Just the five of you?" Julie asked.

"No," replied Declan. "Two others."

Julie's eyebrows raised.

"Three," said Berty. "Elder Hunter will join us before we enter the Dragonlands."

"So eight of you, two of which are children?" Julie remarked.

Pointing to Hope, Declan said, "She has her bow," moving to Obie, "and he has magic."

"Magic that he hasn't yet developed," Julie argued.

Berty saw her point. Extra Empire Guards were brought for Hope's and Freesia's protection last time. However, no guards could be spared. "Come with us," he said to her.

"Me?" Julie pointed to her chest.

"You are an expert with the crossbow," said Berty. "Plus, it will work in your favor with Fairyland."

Her gaze shifted from Berty to Declan.

"It'll be the adventure we always talked about having. Remember?" Declan said to his sister.

A nostalgic smile swept across her face. "I'll go."

Everyone except Berty left to pack. He spoke to Theodore about having supplies ready. Climbing the steps to his private staircase, he returned to his chambers. He sat at his desk, penning more chapters of *the Adventures of Leigh and Marcus* while it was still fresh in his mind.

When he heard his wind chimes, he put down his pen. "Come in."

"My Lord," said Alfred, entering, "they found the blade."

Rising from his desk, Berty motioned for Alfred to sit. "And?" he asked while joining the Elf.

"They found it easily in the light. It was covered in blood and the blade matches the wound." Alfred's blue eyes were heavy with sadness. "There was no sign of anyone else nearby. The blade's handle had traces of Fairy Dust."

"Then the one in the dungeon committed murder," said Berty.

"It looks that way, my Lord. Alvar is interrogating him as we speak. There is one other thing," said Alfred. "The blade is a Goblin's dagger."

"A Goblin's dagger," he repeated.

"The blades are curved and a matte gray. Every Goblin carries one," Alfred explained. "The question is how did a Troll get a hold of a Goblin's dagger."

Berty wished he had an answer. "Alert Lord Darnell. Perhaps the Goblins themselves can shed some light on this. If need be, remind them of the treaty they signed with the Trolls. We don't need another war breaking out between them. Have Jaunty's body returned home to Bridgetown when you see fit."

"I will," said Alfred. "Good luck on your journey, my Lord. I hope you find the Witch in time."

"Me, too, Alfred."

After Alfred left, he made sure everything was in order. Donning his cloak, he crossed the short bridge to Hope's chambers. Entering, he asked, "Are you ready?"

"Yes," both Freesia and Hope answered.

In the Reception Room, Theodore had supplies waiting for them. As they distributed provisions, Hatcher came running up the stairs.

Hyperventilating, Hatcher said, "He killed himself."

"In the dungeon?" Berty asked.

Hatcher nodded. "He ate something sewn into his garments. He told us nothing."

"Find out who he was," said Berty.

Hatcher could not hide his feelings of disbelief. "I will inform Chief Miercia about the interloper," he said.

Berty watched his Advisor descend below the floor. His whole body felt heavy. Looking at his handpicked group of seven, he knew he had to muddle through for Elrick's sake.

Chapter Nine
A Woodland Journey

The Sages' Grove bustled on the bright, summer day. They slipped out of the opened gates with the people going about their business. Their cloaks swished over the lush underbrush as the cool forest welcomed them.

They walked for hours before stopping for a break. Searching the sky beyond the canopy, Edwin said, "We won't make it to Perimeter Road before nightfall."

"We can still walk a ways," Declan began.

Turning out the conversation, Berty closed his eyes. A light blue cloaked figure moved quickly through the woods. Her large staff did not hinder her speed. Opening his eyes, he smiled slightly. Silvia was coming to join them.

While they continued their trek to the Dragonlands, Berty's eyes swept the forest. He expected to see her around every tree. A gentle tug on his cloak caused him to focus on his niece.

"Silvia is close, but she's losing the ability to find us," she said.

"Then, we will find her," said Berty. She placed her little hand in his. They broke away from the group.

"My Lord, where you going?" Sean asked meekly.

He had forgotten that because of Sean's punishment, the crystals do not allow Sean to be far from him outside of the Sages' Grove. "You should come with us, Sean," he said. To the rest of them, he said, "Continue. We will be able to find you."

Sean did not ask any questions, nor did he complain as he followed Berty and Hope. Happy that Sean seemed to be learning respect, Berty had Hope lead the way.

When he heard the rustling of someone walking in the woods, his eyes began to search. Finally, he spotted light blue shining between the trees.

"Silvia," he called.

She stopped. Turning, her brown eyes found him. Smiling, she sighed in relief. "I knew you were here somewhere," she said. She almost ran towards him. "Hi, Hope, Sean."

He wanted to dive into her warm, brown eyes. "Long trek from Fairyland," he said to her. "Let's get back to the others."

Silvia stayed beside him while Hope navigated the darkening forest. She said nothing. He could tell her mind turned.

A roaring fire pierced through the dusky woods like a lighthouse calling boats safely to the harbor. As they ate, Declan introduced Silvia to his sister and nephew.

"I heard about what happened in Boudon," said Silvia. "I am glad you are okay."

"How's Elrick?" Declan asked.

Silvia stared into the dancing flames. "He gets worse every day. It's as if the poison is re-entering his body gradually." She buried her lips into her knuckles. "It's all my fault." Her eyes closed.

"It is not your fault," said Berty. "That man tackled you to the ground." He placed a hand on her arm. "We will find the Witch and bring her back to heal him."

She nodded her head slightly.

He wished he could comfort her, that all it would take would be to hold her close and tell her it would be all right. However, he knew he could not. She would not feel comfort until Elrick was healed.

Night passed quickly. At first light, they began walking on a small footpath taking them to Perimeter Road. The forest kept them cool as the sun climbed higher in the sky.

"People," whispered Hope. She and Obie walked with Freesia.

Under his cloak, Berty kept a hand on the hilt of his sword. He saw Edwin and Sean do the same. Declan and Julie had their readied bows, keeping them hidden under their cloaks.

"Halt in the name of the Emperor!" said a man who wore what looked to be an Empire Guard's uniform. He stood on the path in front of them, holding up his hand. The leather body armor did not look right to Berty. A second man, wearing the same, joined him.

Edwin stepped towards them. He unleashed his golden hued blade, slashing their leather body armor across their stomachs. The leather cut easily in two.

The two men stood frozen, gawking at the true Empire Guard.

"Impersonating an Empire Guard is a crime," said Edwin.

Looking at Hope, Berty whispered, "Where's the nearest patrol?"

Hope touched a tree, then closed her eyes. Her shut eyelids moved rapidly. Opening her eyes, her hand released the tree. "Perimeter Road, just over that hill."

"Arrest them," Berty ordered.

Splitting, the men bolted for the trees.

Looking at one of the men, Berty magically made him trip. Using magic, he dragged him across the forest floor to Edwin's feet.

Declan launched an arrow towards the other man. The arrow caught his clothes, pinning him to a tree. As Edwin tied up the first man, Berty magically bound the second.

With the prisoners in tow, they arrived at Perimeter Road. The wide road looked less derelict to Berty. The vegetation was receding to the confines of the forest. Edwin met the patrol. After transferring the prisoners to the patrol, they crossed the wide road.

A border Troll informed them of entering the Dragonlands. Once over the border, they stopped for a midday break.

"I want to find the tanner who agreed to make fake guard armor," said Edwin.

"What would you do? Instill the fear of the Empire in him?" Declan asked.

"Yes." Taking a deep breath, Edwin sighed. "There needs to be more patrols. We just don't have enough men."

"I'm sorry, Edwin," said Silvia. He threw her a puzzled look. "At one time, manned outposts dotted the Empire. Now, they are ruins, forgotten and lost to time. I allowed the Empire Guard to shrink and the patrols to lapse, under Leif's guidance." She glanced at Berty. "I followed what previous Empresses did, thinking that it was the right thing to do. I was keeping with tradition."

"No one can prevent everything," said Berty. "Edwin, I know you're angry. Fine the tanner for the first offense. If he does it again, he spends some time in the dungeon. We will do the best we can with the men we have. A war may be coming, but new recruits to the Empire Guard should want to be there, not be forced to join. Let's keep going. We've rested long enough."

The canopy in the Dragonlands was much denser than in the Land of Sages. Walking was cooler, although the breezes seemed still. An unnatural calmness settled in the forest. Darkness approached quickly. They decided against using light to help them traverse, because Dragons could attack the light source. Instead, they made camp earlier than they wanted.

"It's awfully quiet," remarked Declan. "Is it just the time of year, or what?"

"I don't know. I have yet to smell smoke, so they aren't fighting," said Berty.

"Maybe the First Dragon Council has chosen a new ruling clan," Silvia suggested.

"Maybe we just haven't gotten in far enough yet," Sean said darkly.

"The clans are voting," said Hope, "far from where we are." Gazing at Sean, she cocked her head to the side. "Why don't you like the Dragonlands?"

"I never said that I don't like the Dragonlands," Sean answered.

Seeing Hope's eyebrows rise, Berty silently laughed.

"It's a weird place. That's all," said Sean.

"What's that?" asked Obie. His finger pointed well beyond their camp. A swarm of multicolor diffused dots raced through the forest.

"Knownots. Lots of them," replied Edwin.

A muffled roar reached their ears. "Sounds like the Dragons are chasing them out," Edwin commented. The last of the colored dots flew out of sight. "They must have caused a lot of trouble." Edwin chuckled.

"Those things are menaces," said Sean. "They hide one shoe, and after you go crazy looking for it, they put it next to the other one. All you hear is squeaky giggles. Or they loosen the scabbard from your belt so your sword falls off as you're walking."

Everyone started to laugh.

"It's not funny," Sean whined. "If I had the Staff of Lightning, they'd leave me alone."

"Sure they would," said Declan, laughing.

Sean's cheek rested on his wrist. "Not funny," he muttered. He sat, sulking for the rest of the evening.

Berty awoke with the feeling that he was being watched. He hated that feeling.

Before they began their trek, a disembodied voice said, "Nice to see you again, Emperor. What is your quest?"

"We're heading to the Outlands, Tong," Berty answered the voice.

Obie's eyes searched for the source of the voice. Scootching closer to his aunt, Obie mumbled, "What is a tong?"

"Shh," Julie shushed him. She kept her eyes on Berty.

"Allow me to escort you through," said Tong. His long, black body and boxy head materialized near the branches.

Obie jumped. He stared at the Dragon's sleek body. Tong's tiny black feathers shimmered in the filtered, morning sunlight.

Chuckling, Berty let the Dragon guide them. Tong glided just under the forest canopy as they walked.

"Where are the other Fairies?" Tong asked.

"With their sick father," Berty answered.

"Oh." Tong's golden mustache drooped sadly.

Tong landed while they took a break. His short legs kept his sleek, long body close to the ground. His golden, globe like eyes watched over everything. Gracefully, he took to the air when they began walking.

Once again, when evening came, the dark forest impeded their ability to navigate. "Tong, may we use light to continue to walk?" Berty asked.

"Moving sources of light are banned in the Dragonlands while the voting takes place," Tong answered. "Just last night, Known-ots had to be forced elsewhere. Dragons cannot even shoot fire."

"Then we make camp," said Berty.

As they sat by the campfire, Tong curled around the campsite. "How long does the voting take?" asked Berty.

"Until they make a decision," Tong answered.

"Don't you get a vote?" asked Silvia.

"Only each of the thirteen clans have a vote. Since, I am not in a clan, I am not even part of the process," explained Tong. "The members of each clan vote for which clan they wish to be the ruling clan. No member can vote for his or her own clan. The votes within the clan are tallied. Whichever outside clan gets the most votes becomes the clan's vote. Each clan submits their clan vote. If one clan does not receive two-thirds of the clan votes, then the process starts over."

"How long can this last?" Declan asked. "Do they only have a certain amount of time?"

"Thirteen moons, one for each clan. If the decision is not reached by the thirteenth moon, then the clan who ruled before the vote stays as ruling clan."

"When was the last time the clans voted?" asked Silvia.

"When they carved the lands into the thirteen districts. Well before the age of men," replied Tong.

The Clan of Cian had been the top clan for a very long time, thought Berty. It was no wonder that they were not taking losing power very well. He fell asleep, relieved that the quiet forest was not a result of something sinister.

They continued walking as soon as the morning light allowed. The large distance between trees and the relative lack of under-brush eased their passage.

Walking next to his sister, Declan said, "You've been quiet."

"I knew we had to go through the Dragonlands, but I didn't think it would be quite like this," Julie said. She glanced at the Dragon flying above them.

"What were you expecting?"

124

"I don't know. More resistance, I guess," answered Julie. "Our brothers made it sound like the adventure of a lifetime."

Chuckling, Declan said, "I highly doubt that their first journey into the Dragonlands was anything like mine." Tousling Obie's hair, Declan said nothing more.

When it was too dark to travel, they made camp. "Uncle Declan, what happened on your first journey to the Dragonlands?" Obie asked.

"We met Tong," Declan said with a sly smile.

Knowing that it was not a good time to talk about Tong's fiery greeting, Berty asked, "How's the journey for you, Obie?"

"Awesome," Obie replied. "Would like to practice my magic though. Aunt Julie said it would be too much like light."

Silvia's eyes snapped to Obie. "She's right," said Berty. "You'll probably get a chance when we get to God Mountain."

"When will that be?" Julie asked.

"Another day or so," said Silvia. "I'm not sure how long it will take us to cross God Mountain."

Berty watched Silvia and Julie have a conversation without hearing it, although he was not far away. His eyes were mesmerized by the dancing reds in her almost shoulder length hair. The fire, however, did not reflect well in her gold dress. The shining gold dress she wore since she became Elder Hunter had dulled. He was not sure if it was from wear, dirt or magic.

Wanting to ask about the dress, he bit his tongue. She had asked him to give her time. He did as she requested and was not going to mention the Elder's Curse.

Chapter Ten
Broken

Silvia looked weary while they traveled through the Dragon-lands. Walking next to her, Berty asked, "How are you?"

Her eyes met his for a moment. "A little tired. I didn't sleep well," she said. "I kept replaying the moment from when that man grabbed me, to when I fell, in my mind. I have been trying to figure out why I did not realize that any of it dropped out of my possession. I know I shouldn't torture myself like that."

"You'd rather torture yourself in other ways?"

"Berty," she said with a roll of her eyes. She watched a small, brown bird fly between them and the Dragon. When the bird landed on Edwin's shoulder, she said, "Must be from Lark."

Reading the note that was attached to the lark's leg, Edwin stopped walking. "My Lord," he said. He turned to face Berty. "It is a message from Alfred. That rogue Troll, Flanders, was assigned to border duty. He should have never been anywhere near the gates. Chief Miercia is deeply concerned. The Goblins say that the stab wound is not indicative of how Goblins use their daggers. Goblin daggers have insignias on the ends of their handles that mark to which house the dagger belongs. The Goblins are investigating. Lord Darnell will not allow anyone to undermine the treaty. He wants to know if you wish to be informed when the prisoners from Boudon arrive."

"Only if there is a problem," Berty said. "I want to know what the Goblins find. Thank Alfred and your wife."

Edwin held the bird gently in his hand. The lark listened intently as the Elf whispered. Holding his hand towards the sky, the lark flew back to the Empire Tree where Lark, Edwin's wife, would interpret the message for Alfred.

They had almost reached the border of God Mountain when they made camp. Per Berty's instructions, Edwin burned the letter from Alfred in the campfire.

In the morning, they thanked Tong and bade him farewell before they began their ascent into God Mountain. Reaching the rolling mountain summit, they gazed at the lush, green tree-covered mountain range.

"Which one is God Mountain?" Julie asked.

"All of them," said Berty. "Hope, which way to the Outlands?"

Hope stood on the mountaintop, overlooking God Mountain. The wind straightened her brown curls. Her cloak whipped behind her as if she were flying. "There are two ways," she said. "One is more direct. The other will take longer, but keeps us out of more dangerous areas."

"How much longer?" Silvia asked.

"The direct way will take about two days. The other will take at least five days, weather permitting," Hope answered.

"I opt for the shorter route," said Silvia. "From what Estelle said, Elrick may have a little over a month left. We do not know how long we will be in the Outlands."

Her brown eyes pleaded with Berty. Time was not on their side. "Does anyone object?" Berty asked.

His group said, "No."

"We don't know what we are going to face," Berty told them. "Be ready for anything. Hope, use your bow if you feel

127

you need to. Obie, you can use whatever magic comes to you. Freesia, Fairy Dust if need be."

"I hate this place," Sean mumbled.

"Let's get through here as quickly as possible. Please, lead the way, Hope."

Filled with trepidation, they followed Hope's path that cut through the woods, going down the mountain.

"I remember Estelle saying to stay out of the valley," Sean complained in his mousy voice.

Berty regretted taking Sean with them. He would have rather had one of the former Roman soldiers that they rescued from there. Unfortunately, they were busy with Empire Guard duties. Sean acted, for the most part, as if he were still an adolescent. Like Declan, Berty found it hard to believe that Sean was descended from one of the Seven High Sages.

They followed a path that ran along the small river cutting into the valley floor. Berty thought the ground pulsated with each touch of Silvia's staff. Sparse trees kept the valley warm under the summer sun.

Hope would only stop for short breaks. She made every move more quickly than in the Dragonlands and forbade anyone from touching the river when Sean wanted to wet a cloth for his head. "Because I said so," she exasperated as Sean sniveled about why.

"But I won't be touching the water," whined Sean.

Spinning around, Hope placed her hands on her hips. She looked like a mini Teresa. "Don't break the water's surface with anything unless you want to die a horrible death. Now, stop it!"

Sean took a few steps away from the river. When everyone started walking again, he asked, "What's in there?" He sounded like an excited child.

"Things," Hope dismissed.

Berty felt so proud. He was impressed with her ability to handle Sean.

Before sundown, Hope chose a spot next to the path to make camp. She did not allow anyone to leave to collect firewood. Immediately after stopping, she formed a Fairy Dust dome to protect them. They made a fire using whatever wood they found within the dome.

After studying the dome, Silvia said, "This is some impressive magic you're doing, Hope."

Hope's smile reached from ear to ear. "Thank you."

When the fire died, the opalescent glow softly illuminated the campsite.

"Does it ever stop glowing?" Sean asked.

"Only for me," said Declan. "Go to sleep."

Berty's shoulder shook. "Wake up," Declan whispered. When Berty opened his eyes, Declan motioned for him not to speak. He watched Declan wake each person quietly.

"What's wrong?" Berty mouthed.

"We're surrounded," breathed Declan. "Some sort of creatures are circling the dome and trying to break it."

Crouching next to Hope, Berty whispered, "What's out there?"

"I don't know," she whispered.

"Ask the trees."

"I can't. When I use Fairy Dust, I can't hear the trees," Hope whispered.

He almost fell over. One magic canceled out the other. Over his niece's shoulder, he saw Silvia twisting her staff into the ground. When it stood on its own, she gestured for Hope to come to her.

After Silvia whispered in her ear, Hope nodded. The girl clasped both hands around the staff. She closed her eyes. Inhaling

129

audibly, Hope's eyes opened. Without saying a word, she strode to the center of the dome.

"*Krak dom on. Krak dom twine. Krak dom thrine,*" said Hope. Her little hands pushed outwards with great force. The dome burst into opalescent shards. Dome pieces flew into the valley. Brown hairy creatures dominoed from the epicenter.

"Hurry! Before they wake," said Hope.

Sprinting serpentine to avoid mounds of brown fur, they followed the path Hope chose. They swapped running for brisk walking when the path's grade got too steep leading out of the valley.

Two thirds of the way up the mountain, Hope stopped in a treed area. They sat on the ground to catch their breath. "I'm tired, Uncle Berty," Hope said.

"We can sit for awhile," Berty said.

Hope shook her head. "The vibrations fade," she said. "Have to keep going. They'll find us."

"What do you mean by vibrations?" asked Silvia.

"Every time your staff hits the ground, it sends out vibrations," explained Hope. "The vibrations keep them away." She looked up the path. "We're almost there."

"Want me to carry you?" Berty asked.

Standing, Hope said, "I'm okay." She led them towards the mountain summit. Reaching the crest, she paused to gaze upon the winding mountain pass before them. "The Outlands are down there," she said.

The setting sun cast long shadows on the path. Finding a secluded spot, they camped for the night.

Declan jumped out of a tree to have breakfast. He took last watch. Edwin and Sean took the first two. Berty thought the three of them needed more sleep, but no winks could be spared.

Sparse vegetation covered the leeward side of the mountain.

The path gave no respite from the intense afternoon sun. They stopped under rare, path-side trees for shade.

At the bottom of the mountain, the path emptied into vast waves of chartreuse amber. Large trees punctuated the grasslands, football fields apart from each other.

"This must be the Outlands," said Declan. He had stuffed his dark cloak into his bag while coming down the mountain.

"Where do we find the Witch?" Berty asked.

Hope's eyes searched the grasslands. "The Witch will be found within the Ghost Tribe," she stated.

"Ghosts?" asked Sean.

Ignoring him, Hope led them through the tall grass. When the top of the grasses reached her neck, Berty placed her on his shoulders.

"Do you think we could get out of the sun for a little while? That tree is certainly big enough," said Julie, wiping her brow.

"No," said Hope as she pulled on Berty's hair. "Big spotted cats in the trees."

"Great," said Sean. "If the heat doesn't kill us, then we can always be mauled to death."

"You make it sound as if there are only two options. I'm sure there are plenty ways to die in a place like this," Declan said.

Berty heard the ringing of Edwin sword being unsheathed. He sliced something in the grass. "Like by snake," Edwin added.

Julie pulled Obie closer to her as she loaded her crossbow. They continued to wade through the tall grass until they reached a dusty clearing. Berty placed Hope on the ground. Trying to conserve water, he merely let some moisten his mouth. As soon as he swallowed, dryness returned. "We need to find some water," he told Hope.

The sun was falling towards the flat horizon, but the decreasing angle did not decrease its intensity. He felt dizzy, stumbling a few times over the parched earth. Barren sticks, as dry as the earth below, longed for a rainy day. He would settle for just one cloud to eclipse the sun.

Obie walked next to Hope as if he were her protector. The clearing became a forest of short, barren sticks. Berty did not know what kind of vegetation they could possibly bear. He thought he saw one of the sticks move, but he felt no breeze. Squinting, he saw nothing but dry, brown, pointy rods piercing the dry, brown flatness.

The earth shook beneath his feet. He fell into Declan. Four sticks rose out of the ground. Attached to the sticks was a car-sized head of a serpent. Its dirt colored body grew out of the dead earth. A forked tongue flicked before retracting into its scaly head.

Standing between Hope and the serpent, Obie pushed her away. Scaly lips parted, revealing long, pointy teeth. Its opened mouth snapped forward. It stopped inches from Obie as if it hit an invisible barrier.

With her one hand on her staff, Silvia stood with her arm outstretched. She held the barrier between them and the serpent. The large head kept hitting the barrier with great force. It was angry that it could not taste its prey.

Through a haze, Berty saw movement behind the giant head. He thought the movement was person-esque. Perhaps it was a ghost.

Light pink blurred in front of him. Both Obie and Hope were wrapped in the color. The pink whisked them to safety.

Berty's clear vision returned. The serpent crashed lifeless to the hard ground. A tall, dark figure stood on it, retrieving a long, white spear from the scaly body. Turning his head, he found Silvia collapsed on the ground, still clutching her staff.

He dove to her side. "Silvia!"

Weakly, her eyes found his. "The Curse is breaking," she breathed.

"You must be from over the mountain," said a voice with a thick accent. Looking up, Berty saw a man standing beside him. White paint streaked across his dark skin. "It is not safe here and she needs attention."

"Who are you?" Berty asked.

"Forgive me. I am Ojore, Hunter of the Ghost Tribe," he said. "Our Shaman can see to her."

Nodding, Berty said, "Thank you." He gently lifted Silvia off the ground. She kept hold of her staff.

"I should thank you," said Ojore. "You made my job easier. It is hard to kill a Cerastes while it senses you. Because of you, I was able to collect all four of its horns."

As they followed the Outlander, Declan asked, "Why do you need its horns?"

"The Shaman needs them," Ojore answered. "You have come far?"

"The Land of Sages. What is a Shaman?" said Declan.

"The healer who knows the old ways," said Ojore.

"They are also called Witch Doctors," Berty added. He looked at Silvia in his arms. She appeared so weak. Silvia's crystal caught the setting sun. The blue faded.

Ojore led them to a bone spiked wall. A piece of wall lifted in front of them. Inside the spiked enclosure was a small village of woven grass topped huts. The bone structure closed behind them.

"Bring her this way," Ojore said.

Woven grass mats covered the walkways, filtering the intense sunlight. As they walked through the village, villagers stared at them. It was obvious to Berty that they had never seen outsiders. Ojore led them into a large hut. He motioned for them to wait, then disappeared behind a curtain covered doorway.

An older man entered the room with Ojore. The bone piercings in his nose and ears intimidated. The man's dark eyes glanced at Silvia. "Put her there," the man instructed, pointing at a table in the middle of the room.

Berty laid her on the person sized table. She held her staff across her body. Berty watched as the man studied her. When the man looked at Berty, he noticed that his bone necklace matched the bones in his nose and ears.

"She must return to the Empire Tree. Only the Scepter can save her. All the Sage Stone wearers must be present," the man said in his thick accent. "I will make a poultice to reserve her strength." He gazed at Silvia. "No more using magic," he told her.

Weakly, she nodded.

"She is in good hands with the Shaman," said Ojore. "Come. I'll take you to the Chief."

Reluctant to leave Silvia's side, Berty placed a hand on her arm. "Go," she breathed. "Goblins hold the answer to Elder's Curse. Hope use trees to send the message."

"Okay," he said. With a squeeze of her arm, he left her in the Shaman's care.

Ojore brought them into an open walled hut that resembled a longhouse. Sitting at the far end of the hut had to be the Chief of the Ghost Tribe. His bone necklace had many strands that reached to his navel.

"Welcome, guests," said the Chief.

"Father, they killed the Cerastes with me. They hail from the Land of Sages," said Ojore.

The Chief smiled. "Then we feast with our new friends," he said. "How would our new friends like to be addressed?"

A healthy amount of gray salted his black hair. The lines around his eyes indicated many years of laughing. Looking at the

Chief in the eyes, Berty said, "I am the Emperor of all that surrounds us. With me, I have brought a chosen circle—Advisor, Lieutenant and skilled specialists."

"My Lord," said the Chief with a low bow. "You have brought great honor upon my house and this tribe." He rose from his chair. "Come. We feast."

Grass mats were placed in the center of the long hut. Berty sat on a mat across from the Chief in the center of the eating area. Tribal leaders and Berty's traveling companions sat on either side, filling the long hut. Food was brought on woven trays. The trays sat on mats that formed the table like area. Toasts were made to everyone's health, then they began to eat.

The food was spicier than what Berty was used to eating and the meats were a little chewier. However, he paid more attention to the Chief's conversation than to the food.

"We haven't had visitors such as yourselves in generations," said the Chief. "One man even stayed with us for a while. He possessed a staff that could harness the power of great storms."

Sean stopped eating. "What happened to him?" He asked.

"He left the village one day and was never seen again," said the Chief.

"And the Staff of Lightning?" Sean asked.

"You are familiar?"

"He was my great-grandfather," said Sean.

The Chief smiled at him. "Everything he left was kept. You will see it."

"Thank you," Sean said.

After the food was cleared, the Chief asked, "Emperor, your journey was not easy. What brings you all this way?"

"We are in need of your Shaman," said Berty.

"Other than the one who is with him now?"

"She was injured fighting the Cerastes, Father," said Ojore.

"There is one back home who is gravely ill and needs his help," Berty explained.

The Chief asked someone to fetch the Shaman. When the Shaman arrived, he sat, waiting for someone to speak to him.

"How is the woman?" asked the Chief.

"She has been given nourishment and is resting," the Shaman answered.

"Good. The Emperor needs your help in another matter."

Trying to ignore the bone sticking through his nose, Berty said, "The Fairy King was attacked by a Faematask. The beast's magical poison is killing him. You are his last hope. We beg you to come with us to Fairyland."

"I am not as young as I once was, my Lord. I cannot go."

Berty's heart sank.

"However, I can give you a potion that will push out the poison," the Shaman said. "Cerastes horns have anti-poison properties. The fresh horns will make a very good potion. I need to get started right away."

"Thank you," said Berty. The Shaman hurried back to his hut.

"My son will show you where you will be sleeping," the Chief said.

"We greatly appreciate your hospitality," said Berty. "How can we repay you?"

"You will journey tomorrow back to the Land of Sages. Allow my son to experience life beyond the mountain," said the Chief.

"It would be an honor to have your son join us, but I must warn you that we are on the brink of war," said Berty.

"Then Ojore will learn much," said the Chief. "He will make a great chief."

Walking proudly, Ojore led them to a hammock filled hut.

"This is where the unmarried women sleep." The men walked across the village to an open hut, also filled with hammocks. "For the unmarried men, of which I am one."

Sean was whisked away to see his great-grandfather's belongings. The rest of them chose hammocks. They were discussing the journey back when Sean entered the hut. His flat nose was red and gray eyes were puffy.

"Everything okay?" Edwin asked him.

Sean nodded. Silently, he climbed into a hammock. Giving Sean space, Berty continued their discussion until it was time to sleep.

When Berty woke, he found his way to the Shaman's hut. Silvia sat on the table, securing a small bag around her neck. Seeing him in the doorway, she smiled.

"I do not have enough strength to get to Fairyland," she said. "Perhaps Elrick can be brought to the Empire Tree?"

He removed his gold locket from his pocket. "I'll ask Delyth," he said. With the rod portion of the clasp in his hand, he wrote on the inside of the locket. "Made it to the Outlands. Returning today with help. Imperative all with crystals be at the Empire Tree. Can Elrick be healed there?"

"Can you walk?" he asked her.

"Slowly."

The locket vibrated in his hand. Opening it, he read Delyth's message to Silvia. "Mother, Father and I will leave soon. Carrying Father will make a slow trip. We will alert Goscislaw."

"Thank you," wrote Berty. "All will be explained when we arrive."

He helped her off the table. Holding onto him and her staff, she stood.

From behind a curtain, the Shaman entered. "The potion is almost ready," he said. "I will bring it out to you."

After thanking the Shaman, he helped Silvia through the village. They gathered in the Chief's long hut for a small meal and to replenish their supplies. The Shaman hurried into the hut to hand Declan a small bottle and give him specific instructions.

Ojore stood proudly in front of his father. White warpaint was absent from his face and body. He wore what reminded Berty of a one-shouldered, colored toga that reached to his knees. His father checked the bone armband and bone necklace before handing him a long wooden spear with a bone top. To Berty, it resembled two stacked arrowheads.

"I will honor Mother's memory and I will not let you down, Father," Ojore said.

"Go not for me, nor for the memory of your mother," his father said. "Go for yourself. If you are proud of all you do, then you know that we are, too." The Chief pulled his son into a hug.

Behind the Chief, the whole village accompanied them to the bone gate. Friendly hands waived until the bone gate lowered, leaving them in the wilderness.

Berty helped Silvia walk through the grasslands. "I sent a message to the goblins," Hope said. "One will meet us at the base of the mountain."

"I wonder why," Silvia mumbled.

At the foot of the mountain, a small, gray skinned Goblin stood near a crack in the rock. His black, beady eyes looked at every one of them. "Emperor," the Goblin said in his squeaky voice. "Lord Darnell wishes for you to join him in the Hidden Chamber."

The Goblin led them into the mountain. The little amount of light that seeped through the crack barely lit the small cave. In the darkness, Berty thought he saw what looked like dog sleds.

"Two in each chariot," said the Goblin. Other Goblins emerged from the shadows to guide them to the chariots.

"Could we light a torch to see?" Sean asked.

"Sorry," squeaked one of the Goblins. "The moles prefer it dark."

"Moles?" said Sean.

"You can't see them, but each chariot is pulled by a team of eight moles," the Goblin answered.

Berty and Silvia sat in the first chariot. The Goblins could see well in the dark. After each of the other four Goblins squeaked, "Ready!" the chariots began to move.

The mole-pulled chariots raced through the dark underground. A bumpy ride kept their shoulders constantly colliding. Silvia slid her hand in his. Berty gave her fingers a gentle squeeze. They moved with the bumps as one instead of into each other.

When the chariots slowed, he was not sure how far or for how long they had traveled. The chariot stopped. "Follow me," said the squeaky voice of the lead Goblin. Somewhere in the distance, a light came to life.

They followed the Goblin towards the light source. The lights came from torches resting on the walls of a large underground room hewn out of the rock. Multiple dark tunnels lead somewhere from the empty central room.

From one of the many tunnels entered Lord Darnell. "Thank you for coming," he squeaked. "Please, everyone, have a seat."

Berty thought that Darnell would go somewhere more private, as the room seemed to be some sort of crossway. Looking closer, he saw rocks that were probably places to sit. He allowed Darnell to sit first on one of the rocks. After helping Silvia to a rock, he sat next to her. After the rest of the group had found rocks, Darnell addressed them.

"We found the dagger's owner," said Darnell. "He was bludgeoned to death by a Troll carrying Fairy Dust. Both Miercia and I think that these deaths are an attempt to sour Goblin-Troll relations. She is appalled at the Troll's betrayal. We Goblins may be highly territorial, but we have always stayed neutral when it comes to the affairs of men.

"However, as Guardians of the Hidden, I am taking precautions. I do not want to distrust my own, but ancient magic is being resurrected. I, therefore, have implemented the ancient security measures. Note that what I have done cannot be undone, not by me anyhow.

"My Lord, I have been carrying this with me." He extracted a scroll from inside his vest. "I took it before I sealed everything. It is the Elder Scroll. To banish the Elder's Curse, you must read from it in the place of origin. All that was present then, must be present now." Darnell slid off his rock. He placed the scroll in Berty's hands.

"There isn't much time," squeaked Darnell. "The chariots will take you as close as they can go."

"Thank you, Darnell," said Berty.

The Goblin Lord nodded sharply. As Darnell disappeared into a tunnel, the chariot drivers returned to collect them.

The chariots rode in complete darkness. Seeing nothing, Berty focused on the way Silvia's hand felt in his. Her soft, slender fingers rested gently on the back of his hand. In the dark, he smiled.

She was coming back with him to the Empire Tree. The Elder's Curse was about to be broken. Elrick was going to be healed. Silvia could travel through the portal and meet his parents and brother. She could even be with him when Hope goes home. And if the coming war allowed, just for one evening, take her on a real date—have dinner, go dancing, see art, something. He squeezed her hand as his heart rejoiced.

Berty's muscles stiffened when the chariot stopped. The Goblins led them out of the cave into moonlit woods. "The Sages'

Grove is about a day's walk that way," said the Goblin, pointing.

"Thank you for bringing us so close," said Berty.

Freesia carried Hope as Edwin found a suitable campsite. Staying close to Silvia, Berty brought her food and drink. "I am very grateful that the Goblins brought us here," said Silvia. "I do not think I could have walked all that way."

"Just a little further," said Berty.

"I know," she said. Her brown eyes searched into his. "Thank you for being patient and understanding. You're a phenomenal Emperor." She smiled briefly. "I don't know what's going to happen when the curse fully breaks, but I know you will be there for me."

"Of course, I will." He took her hand in his.

At first light, they began walking towards the Sages' Grove. Silvia's arm was locked in his as he helped her walk.

Hope gasped. "What is it?" asked Julie as Berty and Silvia turned.

"Nothing. Bug," she said. For a moment, Berty thought he saw a glimpse of terror on her young face.

"Are you sure?" Berty asked.

Nodding, Hope walked closer to Freesia.

Once Silvia began to stumble, they stopped to rest. "My legs can't seem to hold my weight," Silvia mentioned.

"I'll carry you," said Berty. Before she could answer, he swept her into his arms. She clutched her staff, trying to keep it out of the way.

Resting her head on his shoulder, she whispered, "I'm sorry to place this burden on you. I owe you my life."

"For that, we're even," he whispered back. "Martin may have introduced us, but *you* changed everything."

Smiling up at him, she said quietly, "I guess I did."

Chapter Eleven
Black Recharge the Veil

The sun began to set as they spied the treed wall of the Sages' Grove. Once inside the gates, Berty said, "Declan, go to Elrick. Sean, get the Sages' descendants together in the Scepter Room. Edwin, make sure everyone gets food and that Ojore has a room." He let the group go ahead of him. Walking through the doors of the Empire Tree, he said to Silvia, "Welcome home."

She made a small sound that let him know that she was glad to return.

In the Reception Room, Edwin spoke with Theodore. The Dwarf drew silent as he watched Berty pass with the last Empress draped in his arms.

The other descendants waited in the Scepter Room, except Elrick, when Berty entered. Only a small gasp escaped Lida's lips as Berty lowered Silvia to the floor. She leaned against a column. Declan helped Elrick walk into the Scepter Room while Berty extracted the Elder Scroll. Sean relieved Declan, who promptly left the room.

The scroll was written in the ancient tongue, but Berty could understand every word. He instructed, "You must be touching the column from which you collected your crystal." Sean helped Elrick to his column before moving to his own. The carved wood felt smooth under Berty's fingers. He gave Silvia a soft smile. "I have to recite this, then I don't know what, but the Elder Cycle will be finished."

Reading ancient words, his brain automatically translated them. The first line read, "Break the bonds." He forced his mind to see the old language and willed his tongue to pronounce the words properly.

With a quick glance at the claret crystal of the Scepter, he said, "*Deil inn brand. Koma hunt var eigna. Sløk inn seiðr. Ellri létta. Fyllan hring.*"

He could feel the words reverberate off of the smooth, wooden walls. Nothing more was written on the scroll. He waited.

The crystal glowed brightly, slightly beyond its facets. Almost as if it were an optical illusion, the deep red shrank away from the outer edges. The color formed a single point in the center of the crystal. In a flash of red, the crystal's inner color filled the round room, knocking Berty to the floor.

Berty opened his eyes in darkness. "Hello?" he asked tentatively.

A sconce flickered light into the Scepter Room from the hall. He saw the outlines of the others lying on the floor. Standing, he let his pupils widen. The large, multifaceted crystal of the Scepter had gone dark. Berty blinked. No, it was not dark. The crystal was black.

Figures in the circle stirred. "Is anyone hurt?" Berty asked.

"I am fine," said Lida. "Elrick?"

The Fairy King groaned in response.

"It's okay, Your Majesty," said Sean. "I've got you."

Berty heard heavy footsteps run out of the room. He could see a faint silhouette trying to stand. "Alfred?"

"These old bones will be all right," Alfred said.

He knelt next to Silvia, who was still slumped on the floor.

"Silvia?" His fingers grasped her wrists. They felt the steady beat of blood pumping through her veins. "She's unconscious," he told the others. "I'm taking her to her chambers." As he lifted her off the ground, he noticed that the staff to which she clutched had become a mere stick.

Goscislaw arrived in the doorway, carrying a torch with Declan by his side. "Elrick!" said Declan, rushing to the Fairy's side. "We're going to take you to your room. You need some rest."

Goscislaw stepped into the Scepter Room with the lighted torch. The brightly burning fire was snuffed out by an invisible hand. "This cannot be good," growled Goscislaw.

Not being able to see his private entrance, he carried Silvia into the main staircase. In the sconce light, he noticed that Silvia's blue crystal was clear. "What color are your crystals?" he asked Alfred and Goscislaw. They followed him across the bridge that led to Hope's chambers.

"No color," answered Alfred. "My crystal is clear."

"Mine is as well," said Goscislaw. "What do you suppose it means?"

"I don't know," said Berty. He crossed the bridge to his chambers. A few steps later, he entered Silvia's chambers with Alfred and Goscislaw.

"We will wait here," Goscislaw said. The Dwarf and the Elf sat on the yellow couches while Berty disappeared behind the wall-filling Sages' Seal.

Carefully, he laid her on her bed. He sat on a small bench that he pulled next to her. Buff eyelids covered her warm, brown eyes. Her lips rested slightly parted. Dark red hair softly framed her face. Her gold dress shimmered in the lantern light with each rhythmic breath.

Berty's eyelids began to feel heavy when her eyelashes fluttered. Brown irises found him. He smiled. "How are you

144

feeling?" he asked her.

"My head hurts a little," she said.

"Can I get you anything? Food? Drink? Medicine?"

She smiled at the offer. "No, thank you." Attempting to sit up, she said, "Ooh, I did not know my body could ache so much."

"I'll have Declan look at you and make sure everything is okay," said Berty.

Squinting momentarily, she asked, "Declan?" Her brown eyes searched the air. "I do not believe I know a Declan."

His lungs stopped the intake of air for a moment. Trying to preserve his smile, he said, "Declan is learned in the art of healing."

"Oh," she said. Her eyes roved around the room. "That would be very good. I am going to change. I am still wearing my cloak. Did I fall?"

"Yes," he answered. "I will be downstairs if you need anything."

"Thank you," she said with her warm smile.

He turned to leave. Her warmth could not stop the sick feeling in his stomach.

"Wait," she called. He stopped. "I do not know your name."

Gazing at her kind face, he replied, "Berty."

"Thank you, Berty," she said, smiling.

With a nod, he descended the steps. It was the first time his heart did not leap when she said his nickname. His insides did not bubble with excitement. He could not shake the queasiness. When he entered her study, Alfred and Goscislaw stood.

"My Lord, what's wrong?" said Alfred.

"She doesn't know me," Berty answered. "I will be right outside." Walking out her door, he called for Theodore.

The young Dwarf appeared on the platform. "The Outlander has been given chambers, my Lord, and everyone is being tended."

"Very good, Theodore," said Berty. His voice had no feeling. Even his lips and tongue felt numb. He did not know how he could speak to anyone. Words had to be forced out of his mouth. "When Declan is satisfied with King Elrick, he needs to see to Miss Hunter."

He barely noticed Theodore bow. On their own accord, his feet brought him back inside Silvia's study. He wanted to resist his feet, but he could not. His ears knew that Alfred and Goscislaw conversed, but they could not discern what the men said.

Wind chimes made him focus on the door. "Come in," he said.

Declan entered Silvia's study. "Elrick is doing well. He needs to rest," he told the room. "How is she?"

Leaning against her desk, Berty answered, "Achy." Movement in the back of the room made him turn his head.

Silvia stood in front of the Sages' Seal. She wore a sapphire blue dress like the ones she wore when she was Empress, except her dress lacked gold trim. In her hand, she held paper with many creases. Her brown eyes filled with sadness as she looked at the men in her study.

"High Elf Alfred, Prince Goscislaw," she said. "I wish I remembered why you are here. Emperor, I apologize for having no memory of you." She glanced at the papers in her hand. "Apparently, I suspected that I might lose my memory. I wrote myself a letter." She read from the papers. "Your name is Silvia Hunter. Do not remove the crystal that hangs around your neck." Looking up, she continued, "It goes on, explaining how I got here and goes through my entire life. The last thing I remember is learning

146

of the Pixie Priestess arriving on our shores."

"That was a long time ago," said Goscislaw.

"So I have read," Silvia said.

"I wonder if your memory loss has anything to do with the Scepter's crystal turning black," said Alfred.

Her eyes snapped to the aged Elf. "Black?" Silvia said, sounding alarmed. "The crystal is black?"

"What do you know about it?" asked Alfred.

"There is a piece of scroll," Silvia began.

He remembered coming across a torn piece of yellowed parchment in the Sorcery Room. "Black recharge the veil," he said.

"Yes." She looked at Berty. "My mother told me that section was part of larger writings about the Scepter. They locked them away, but I know not where."

A rock wall with a picture of a scroll popped into Berty's mind. "I do."

"The Goblins?" asked Declan.

"No. Could you please step to the side?" he asked Silvia. When she obliged, he touched the bottom circle on the Sages' Seal. A trapdoor in the wood floor opened. "The ladder takes you through a portal to the vaults."

He climbed into the hole. "Are you coming?" he asked them.

Silvia folded her papers, then waited her turn. At the bottom of the ladder, the rock wall opened to the Emperor's Vault antechamber. In the torch lit rock room, he waited.

"I have never been in here," said Silvia, "of that I know. I was not aware of the door in my floor. How did you know of it, my Lord?"

"Chance," said Berty. When they all gathered, Berty touched the picture of the scroll on the stone wall. A plain piece of rock

147

wall opened, revealing the library.

Examining the books on the shelves, Declan said, "Is this all in the ancient tongue?"

"It looks that way," said Alfred.

"We will need everyone who can read the ancient tongue," said Berty. "The more people, the faster we can find something."

"That leaves me out," said Declan. "I'm useless when it comes to the ancient tongue. I believe Delyth can read it."

"And Estelle," Alfred nodded. "Perhaps Lida will help as well."

"Count me in, my Lord," said Goscislaw.

"Good," said Berty. "Ask the others if they will help. We will start in the morning."

When they returned to Silvia's study, Berty closed the trapdoor. "Would it be all right if we use this entrance?" he asked.

"Yes, of course," she said.

"Thank you. We will bid you goodnight," said Berty.

"Before I forget," said Declan. He retrieved two small bottles from inside his cloak. "Willow bark infusion for any aches or pains you may have." Handing a bottle to Silvia, he said, "One dose for tonight. I'll have more at breakfast if you need it." He handed the second bottle to Alfred. "I had to make some for Edwin, the chariot bounced his shoulder too much."

"Declan, thank you. How did you know that I could use some?" Alfred asked.

"Lida suggested it." Declan followed the Elf and the Dwarf through the door.

Realizing that he was left alone with Silvia, Berty gave her a nod. "I'm the next branch over if you need anything," he said. "Or you can call for Theodore. He is the Head Tender."

She gave him a faint, polite smile. Tearing his eyes away from her, he quickly escaped into the summer night. He crossed to his platform to find Declan waiting for him.

"How are you doing?" Declan asked.

"I'm not sure," Berty replied. "Between the black crystal, her amnesia, impending war…." He did not finish his thought.

"Restoring the Scepter will bring her memory back," said Declan.

Nodding, Berty thought about the Scepter. "Has much changed now that the Scepter is black?"

Declan looked from the tree towards the wall. "No. The magic protecting the Sages' Grove doesn't seem to stem from the Scepter. But, I could be wrong. It could be too early to tell."

"Keep an eye on it," said Berty.

Getting ready for bed, Berty kept telling himself that Silvia would regain her memory soon. He stared at his room's intricate wood ceiling, trying to clear his mind. He had needed sleep since Boudon. Closing his eyes, he focused on his comfortable bed.

"Your Highness, wake up!" said a man's voice. "Telor!"

Opening his eyes, the Fairy Prince gazed at his intruder. The man wore the shimmering periwinkle armor of the Fairy Guards. "Colonel Gwron, what is it?" Telor asked.

"Fairyland is being attacked," said Gwron.

Telor jumped out of bed. Rushing towards the window, he saw his colorful city aflame. "What are our options?" he asked.

"I do not know, Your Highness," replied Gwron. "They are using magic and beasts no one has ever seen."

"It's like Delyth said." Telor began getting dressed. "Colonel," a glow outside his window caught his eye. He watched as a green dome crept across the sky. "They're trapping us here. Evacuate as many as possible. Barricade the castle."

"What about you, Your Highness?"

"My duties lie elsewhere. Anyone who cannot escape retreat

to the Throne Room," Telor instructed.

Gwron ran out of the room as Telor laced up his boots. Grabbing his bow and quiver, he secured them to his back. Quickly, Telor removed velvet bags of Fairy Dust from their hiding places throughout his bedroom. He picked up the carved wooden box that Delyth bought for him in Boudon, then stashed it in a black velvet bag. In one fluid motion, he secured his dark purple cloak around his shoulders.

The sounds of Fairies scrambling in the castle reached his ears as he zipped down the hall. Arriving at a plain wooden door, he touched the handle, saying, "*Bachtum.*" The door swung open. He slipped inside.

With one look at the stone steps of the Tower's spiral staircase, Telor flew above them at blurring speed. At the top, he stopped at the periwinkle metal door. "*Oganda,*" he said. The door opened before him.

He stepped inside the small, circular room. Reaching inside the dark bag, he extracted the box. He knelt beside the center octagonal stone on the floor. "*Gune.*" The stone rose above its resting place. Stretching his arm into the void, he removed a hand-filling, radiant stone. Carefully, he placed the stone inside the box. The floor lowered into place as he slid the box into the bag.

Outside the metal door, he said, "*Clonganda.*" The door closed. He flew down the Tower steps with his great speed.

A small group of citizens and Fairy Guards gathered in the Throne Room with supplies. "We are trapped inside the magical green dome," said Gwron. "The castle walls will not hold them out for long."

Five glowing figures popped out of the Throne Room's golden walls. "The Fairy Guardian Spirits," Telor said. They spoke to Telor in the language of the ancient Fairies. All he could do was look at them blankly.

"I don't know this tongue beyond the few words Delyth taught me," he pleaded.

One of the Fairy Guardians stood in front of Telor. "*Ere doe ein auk tun roe. Ere doe ein auk tun ín. On dry eck prone*," said the ghostly Fairy. His translucent hand went through Telor's forehead.

"*Es newn rhyn tí*," Telor said in return.

The spirit and Telor had a quick conversation in the ancient Fairy language. "Take what you can carry," Telor told his people. "We can escape, going under their magic."

Approaching a section of wall, Telor reached out his hand and said, "*Tome dyme*." The wall faded to translucence. Turning to the other Fairies, he said, "The Fairy Guardians will guide you through the bowels of the castle. Go!"

"We are abandoning Fairyland, Your Highness?" Gwron asked.

"Look around you, Gwron. It is only stone," said Telor. He pointed to the Fairies escaping into the wall. "*They* are Fairyland. We must protect Fairydom itself. Wherever Fairydom makes its home is Fairyland."

The enemy pounding on the doors of Fairyland Castle echoed off the walls of the Throne Room. Telor extended his hands towards the massive wooden double doors. "*Lapsa*," he said. The doors shimmered with an opalescent glow. "That will not keep them out indefinitely, but it will buy us time."

Inside the wall, Telor solidified the doorway to the Throne Room. He ran through the black stone corridors of the ancient ruins upon which Fairyland Castle was built. Finally, he caught up to his people who waited near a weathered stone door. A Fairy Spirit spoke with him.

He nodded. "This leads to the woods outside of Fairyland,"

said Telor. "You are to run as far into the Dragonlands as you can. We will use only the light of the moon and stars to guide us out there. Are we ready?"

"Yes," the group murmured.

"Extinguish all your torches," he ordered. "When I open the door, you will leave in groups. A Fairy Guard will accompany each group."

The corridor slipped into black. The five Fairy Guardians became mere dim ghosts. "*Ogan loo,*" Telor said quietly.

Stone moved aside, letting the night wind slap their faces. Telor and Gwron orchestrated the Fairies' escape into the wilderness.

When the last of the Fairies were set to go, Telor thanked the Fairy Guardians. In the faint moonlight, Telor whispered, "*Clogandoo.*" The stone sealed shut. They were exposed to the night.

Chapter Twelve
Unravelings

Telor could see the green glow that ensnared to the walled city of Fairyland. Branches above his head exploded.

"Run!" he told the others.

Weapon carrying men ran towards them. Gwron unsheathed a periwinkle metal sword. The Colonel stood his ground. A Fairy Guard readied his bow.

"Go, Your Highness," said Gwron.

Telor froze. A dark shape slithered over his head. Looking up, he saw a light shape speeding through the trees.

A glowing sphere hit Gwron's armor, knocking him to the ground. Telor lobbed an arrow at the Warlock. The shapes in the trees opened their large, boxy mouths. Dragonfire rained upon their enemies. The Dragons barricaded the Fairies from their attackers.

"Gwron!" shouted Telor.

The Colonel groaned.

"Let's get him out of here," said Telor. With the help of a Fairy Guard, they lifted Gwron away from the inferno.

The yellow Dragon roared ferociously.

"Fairy Prince, this way," said Tong.

The Fairies followed Tong into the depths of the Dragonlands while the yellow Long Dragon kept the invaders at bay.

Berty sat up in the darkness. Sweat drenched his entire body. He felt as though he had just been running through the woods. A hand ran through his wet, dark hair. He was unsure of what had just played behind his eyelids. Was it real or a dream, a warning or a premonition?

Cool breezes caressed his torso. His body shivered as goose-bumps covered his skin in waves. Closing his eyes, his head fell back onto its pillow.

He woke in a groggy haze. A shower cured his grogginess, but an uneasy haze remained while he dressed. Stepping out of his chambers, he met Silvia, who was crossing onto his platform from hers.

"Good morning," he said. "How are you feeling?"

"Better, thank you," she smiled. "Hungry."

Silvia followed Berty across the narrow bridge to the trunk. He stopped in front of the entrance to the tree. The doorway was darker than usual. Instinctively, his hand reached towards the opening. It could not pass the black barricade.

Standing beside him, Silvia examined the entranceway. "I have never heard of this before," she said.

Returning to Berty's platform, he led her across the down-ward sloping bridge to Hope's chambers.

She glanced at the bundle of green leafy branches. "Your child?" Silvia inquired.

"Uncle Berty!" said Hope, running out onto the platform. "How is," her big brown eyes saw, "Silvia!" Before Berty could answer, Hope threw her arms around Silvia's waist.

Silvia gazed at the loose, brown curls resting against her pink dress. Tears collected in the bottom of her eyes.

Hope looked up at Silvia. The smile faded from her little face. "What's wrong?" she asked.

"She doesn't remember," said Berty.

"Oh," Hope said sadly. She unlatched herself from Silvia.

"I wish I did," said Silvia. She caught a glimpse of Freesia leaving the bundle. "Until my memory returns, we can get to know each other again. How does that sound?"

"Good," said Hope, giving her a smile.

The four of them crossed the bridge. No dark barrier impeded the path inside the trunk of the Empire Tree. Silvia peeked through the doorway of the dark Scepter Room.

"What happened?" Hope asked.

"That's what we're going to find out," said Berty.

"Can I help?" Hope said.

Turning away from the darkened doorway, they descended the steps. "Not until after archery," Berty told her. "And I don't want to keep you from seeing Alina."

"She's studying Witchery in the mornings. I can only see her in the afternoon," said Hope.

"Witchery? Don't you mean Witchcraft?" asked Berty.

"Don't be silly, Uncle Berty. Witches *practice* Witchcraft, but they *study* Witchery," said Hope like it was the most obvious thing in the world.

He allowed Hope to enter the Reception Room before him to get her breakfast. Filling a plate with food, she sat at the table across from Obie.

Declan helped Elrick to a seat while Delyth placed a plate of food in front of her father. Berty approached the breakfast table with Silvia close behind. She seemed hesitant to interact with people she did not remember.

"Elrick, how are you doing?" Berty asked as he took a seat.

"Well, my Lord. Weak, but well," the Fairy answered. "I deeply appreciate all you have done."

"He insisted on having breakfast with everyone to thank all of you," said Lida.

155

Berty gave her a smile. Noticing that every seat around the breakfast table was filled, Berty announced, "I wish to officially welcome our new friend, Ojore, Hunter for the Ghost Tribe of the Outlands, to the Empire Tree. You honor us."

Theodore scurried into the room. "Pardon the interruption, my Lord," he said. "A Goblin has arrived. He says he has urgent news."

"Bring him here," Berty told him.

The gray skinned Goblin followed Theodore to the table. His dark, beady eyes scanned the table before saying, "Fairyland has fallen."

Gasps echoed throughout the room.

"They attacked in the dark of night," the Goblin squeaked.

"What of my son?" Lida implored. "Crown Prince Telor?"

"I know not, Queen Lida," said the Goblin. "I am sorry." The Goblin exited, leaving the room in a shocked silence.

The memory of Berty's vision returned to him. He had to speak with the Fairies privately. "Silvia... Do you mind if I call you Silvia?"

She shook her head.

"Bring Estelle, Alfred and Goscislaw to your study," he continued. "Lida, Elrick and Delyth, please come with me."

With Declan's help, the Fairies followed Berty into the Roundtable Room.

"You know about Telor," Delyth said before taking her seat.

"Among other things," Berty answered.

"I'll close the door on my way out," said Declan.

"Nonsense," said Elrick. "You are the Duke of Fairyland. Stay."

Berty magically closed the door while Declan took his seat at the Roundtable. "Please forgive me," he said. "I was unaware of what I was seeing at the time. Telor escaped Fairyland with

156

something from the Tower."

Delyth breathed a sigh of relief.

"He and other Fairies who were in the castle, as well as Fairy Guards took refuge in the Dragonlands. Two Dragons aided their escape—Tong and the yellow Dragon who Delyth helped," he said.

"Where are they now? Is my son all right?" Lida asked.

Closing his eyes, Berty focused on Telor. The Fairy Prince walked among black stone ruins. When he opened his eyes, four pairs of eyes stared at him. "Telor is fine. They are in the protection of ancient Fairy ruins deep within the Dragonlands. Different ruins than the ones we visited. Both Dragons guard its location. Colonel Gwron was injured by a Warlock. His armor shielded him. He is recovering."

"We must go to him," said Lida. "Bring him here."

"No," said Berty.

"My son is out there!" cried Lida.

"He is well hidden," Berty reasoned. "If you go to him, you could expose him and yourselves. He is under the protection of the Fairy Guardian Spirits. Two Dragons are risking their lives for your son. The scattered Fairies will find this place. The ruins will become their sanctuary."

Elrick placed his hand on top of Lida's. She nodded reluctantly.

"When the time is right, we will drive them out of Fairyland," Berty said. "But, we cannot do anything until we discover what to do about the black crystal. We do not know how it could hinder us."

"Do not worry, Lida. Telor is strong," Elrick assured. "The Emperor is right. We can only make things worse for him and for whatever remains of Fairydom. You and Delyth take care of the crystal. Declan will be with me."

Rising from his chair, Berty noticed that his private entrance was impassable there as well. He led the women to Silvia's chambers. Inside her study, they found the others waiting.

"No one else has the authority to open it, my Lord," Silvia said.

Without saying a word, he pressed the bottom circle on the Sages' Seal. The floor opened. He stepped inside. "Let's leave this open so we can come and go as we need."

He did not wait for the others in the antechamber to open the library. The seven of them rifled through the shelves, looking for information about the Scepter.

"Telor did the right thing," Berty overheard Delyth say in the next aisle.

"It has no protection," Lida said. "The Tower was the safest place."

"I disagree. The Tower was modern construction. It needs ancient protection. The ruins can provide that," said Delyth.

No one said anything as Berty removed the book from a shelf.

"I think you are right," said Lida. "The stone has been the target all along. If the legends are correct, then its power is second only to the Scepter."

"I am sure they are trying to break into the Tower as we speak," said Delyth.

"We cannot worry about that now," Lida said. "Your father must regain his strength. We may have to fight for the very survival of the Empire, let alone Fairyland."

Berty brought his chosen book to the table where others had already begun reading. Flipping through the pages, he noticed that every so often, Estelle would look up from the pages before her to stare at Silvia. After a moment, her icy blue eyes would return to the page.

Reaching the last page, he found nothing about the Scepter.

He closed the book as his pocket vibrated. Extracting the glowing Watcher's Locket, he opened it. Declan had sent a message about Hope wanting to talk with him.

Berty replied, "Bring her down."

He was carrying a new book to the table when Declan and Hope arrived in the antechamber. "Look at all those books," Hope said.

As Berty walked out of the library to meet them, Declan addressed him. "She and Obie bickered all morning until she told me that she needed to see you."

"What's the matter?" Berty asked.

She twisted her fingers together. "I didn't wanna bother you, Uncle Berty, but Obie made me," she started. "When we were walking back to the Sages' Grove, the trees told me something." Her big, brown eyes looked up at him. She took a deep breath. "They're hunting for me," she said in a small voice.

Crouching to be eye level with her, he placed his hands on hers. "Who is?"

"The anti-Imperialists," she answered.

He felt the color leave his face. "Why didn't you tell me then?" he asked.

"The Whispers would have found me and told them," she said. "The trees told me that I am only safe from the Whispers in the Sages' Grove. Its magic keeps them out. Also, um, Whispers can't go through portals."

Placing his knee on the ground, he hugged his niece. "When you're on this side of the portal, you have to stay within the Sages' Grove. Okay?"

She nodded.

He gazed at her from arm's-length. "Don't worry about anything. You're safe here," he assured. "Go sit at the table. We will look at some books together."

She scampered into the library as he stood. "Find out about Whispers," he told Declan. "Do it discreetly. Are they just an Elf thing?"

"I will," said Declan. "I left Elrick with Obie and Julie. She's fashioning him a cane to help him walk. Obie is impressing him with his magic. Am I leaving Hope with you?"

"Yes. Tell Freesia she'll be back for lunch."

Declan gave Berty a nod, then glanced at the group in the library before climbing the ladder.

"Want to pick out a book?" Berty asked Hope.

Her eyes widened and loose curls bounced as she nodded. Together, they strolled between the shelves. Her head cranked to see the rows of books that towered over her. "What are we looking for, Uncle Berty?" she asked.

"Something that tells us why the Scepter's crystal has turned black."

"Okay." Hope quickened the pace as if she knew how to navigate the sea of books.

Berty followed her to the back the Library Vault. A door-sized section of wall was free of shelves and old tomes. "I think we need to look in there," she said, standing in front of the wall.

Looking at Hope, he wondered how she knew about the door. His niece and her gifts were a complete mystery to him. Yet, he did not want them explained. He found solace in his ignorance. "How do you propose we open the door?" he asked.

She studied the rock. Cocking her head to one side, she said, "Magic."

"Magic it is," he said. Focusing on the smooth rock, he thought, *I am a Sage; open for me.* The door sank into the floor.

"Cool," she said.

Flames burst onto the wicks of the many candles throughout the room. The candles illuminated scrolls, boxes, earthen con-

160

tainers, and strange objects. "Only those with crystals can enter," he told Hope. He was not sure how he knew it to be true. "Can you bring Silvia, Alfred, Queen Lida, and Prince Goscislaw?"

"Yup." He watched her run through the aisles.

Taking a step inside, Berty guessed that the room held all the stuff that did not make it into the Sorcery Room. He glanced at the items that had not been touched for generations.

"Just when I thought the Empire Tree could not have anymore secrets," growled Goscislaw. His eyes scanned the room with awe.

"I think we have only begun to scratch the surface as far as secrets are concerned," said Alfred.

Lida peered at a glittery Fairy figurine. "Elrick is going to be upset that he missed this," she said.

Silvia was the first to remove a scroll from the diamond shaped shelves.

"Uncle Berty, what can I do now?" Hope asked from just beyond the doorway.

"Go help Delyth and Estelle," he said from the door.

"Okay." She almost skipped through the library.

Turning, he caught Silvia staring at him with a scroll in her hand. She gave him a little smile, then opened the scroll.

"This is it," she said. "Well, almost," she added as her eyes moved further down the paper.

"What does it say?" Lida asked.

"It talks about the Scepter magnifying magic and how it retains magic," Silvia said. "Crystalline structure... Conductor for magic... Captures magic... The transfer of magic...."

Removing another scroll from the same diamond, Alfred said, "This one is about choosing the Empire's steward."

Silvia picked a scroll from the middle of the pile in the diamond. As she read, her eyes opened wide. "The color of the crystal will change when the balance of magic has been disturbed," she translated. "The crystal will vary from white to a chosen color that it feels will return the balance." Her eyes skimmed. "Black is the absence of magic."

"How do we fix it?" Goscislaw asked.

"It does not say," Silvia answered. "The bottom of the scroll has been torn."

"Then it matches the scroll in the Sorcery Room," said Berty. "Black recharge the veil."

"But what does that mean?" said Goscislaw.

"If magic is absent, then we need to give it magic," Berty deduced.

"The Scepter holds the veil in place between the worlds," said Alfred. He was reading from another scroll. "Without its magic, anyone can find the portals." The Elf looked up. "The Empire would be exposed. The world on the other side has changed. Magic and our way of life would be in grave danger."

"Re-instill a healthy fear of Troll," Goscislaw growled.

"People don't believe in Trolls or Elves or Fairies or magic," said Berty. "Those who do are usually children or considered insane." He looked at each one of them. "The modern world as a whole, we are better without."

"Yet, you are from that very world," said Lida.

"Am I?" Berty asked.

Silvia reached for a small folded piece of paper stuck on the side of the wooden diamond. Unfolding it, she read, "The scroll about the Scepter's origins have been entrusted to the Goblins. Only the Goblin Lord knows how to reach the Origin Scroll."

"Extend an invitation to Lord Darnell," said Berty.

"There is more on the scroll," said Alfred. "The Scepter cannot be black during the Hallows. That is the time when the magic of the Scepter must be at its strongest."

"The Hallows," repeated Berty.

"Halloween," Silvia explained. "Actually, it is four days. One day prior and two days after."

"Gives us some time," said Goscislaw.

Rolling scrolls, Lida said, "Not as much as you would think. We are on the short side of Midsummer."

Once all the scrolls had been returned to the diamond, they entered the library proper. At the table, Hope was helping put the books away.

"Did you find it?" Delyth asked.

"Yes," answered Lida. "Let's go tell your father."

Estelle glanced at Silvia before exiting the library with Hope. The Fairies climbed the ladder first with Silvia following. As Berty made sure the stone door closed securely, he overheard Hope telling Estelle, "Don't be sad. She doesn't remember me either."

Grabbing Hope's hand, Estelle said, "I miss my friend. That's all. She'll return and remember us both."

"How do you know?" Hope asked.

"Starjen," Estelle said with a smile. "Come. It's our turn up the ladder."

Chapter Thirteen
The Mad Mage

Estelle's words uplifted Berty's spirits. Reaching Silvia's study, he closed the trapdoor. He saw Silvia waiting beside her desk.

As he walked away from the Sages' Seal, Silvia stated, "I have been thinking." His insides froze, not knowing what she was going to say next. "I'm going to ask the Head Tender for new chambers. I do not feel right being here."

"Why not?" He gazed into her warm, brown eyes, searching for an answer.

"You should be in here. Not me," she said.

"I have my own chambers," he answered. "These have always been yours and always will be yours."

She smiled briefly. "I take it that you own the house." He nodded. "What about the access to the portal? Or the access to the vault?"

He understood her concern. She felt as if she were intruding. "Hope's chambers have a portal to the house," he said.

"I am no longer Empress. I have no place here. I do not belong on these high branches."

"When you brought me through the portal, my chambers were constructed next to yours. Just as it is now," he said. "Who was I, but just a man your brother sent?" He could not read her expression. "If you feel you would be more comfortable some-where else, then speak with Theodore about a transfer. But please, do not leave because of me."

Her head tilted slightly to the right. He wondered if she were seeing him in a new way. "I will think about it," she told him.

"Good," he said. "Darnell should be arriving at any moment. Let's hear what he says."

"You want me to be there as well?" she asked.

"As former Empress, your input is invaluable," he said. "And you are the descendent of a Sage."

She walked with him to the Reception Room. "What of the seventh?" she asked.

Berty sighed. "Did your letter tell you how you became an Elder? How I became Emperor?"

"Yes, of course."

"Then you know that *he* is responsible for all of this," Berty replied. "While he is improving, he is not quite capable."

"I see."

When they stepped off the staircase into the Reception Room, the Goblin Lord entered from the staircase across the room.

"Emperor! I came as quickly as I could," squeaked Lord Dar-nell.

While Silvia slipped away, Berty waited for Darnell to reach him. "Thank you for making haste. Come this way." He led the Goblin up the steps to the dark Scepter Room. With an intake of breath, the Goblin's jaw dropped.

Peeling Darnell away from the dark doorway, Berty brought him to the Roundtable. "I do not think that I need to explain the problem," said Berty. "To fix it, we need the Origin Scroll."

Darnell's beady gaze rested on the reflective tabletop. "The Origin Scroll," he repeated in his high, squeaky voice. He ran a long, knobby thumb along his jawbone. His eyes snapped to look at Berty. "Halls of Enchantment."

"What are the Halls of Enchantment?" Berty asked.

"The most dangerous place in the Empire," answered Darnell. "You will need a neutral, non-Goblin Guide to lead you there. No one on the Advisory Council nor a Sage can be a Guide. Once inside, expect challenges. This is a journey for which you need to be well prepared. I know of this place only by reputation. The magic is ancient and perhaps forgotten. Your best ally is knowledge."

He ingested the Goblin's words for a moment.

"You will not be able to remove the Scroll from the inner sanctum. It may be wise to take the Advisory Council with you," Darnell advised.

"Darnell, thank you for your wisdom and your advice," said Berty.

Standing, the Goblin said, "Good luck, my Lord." He hesitated to walk away from the table. Berty thought the Goblin had more to say. Darnell bowed, then left the room.

"Theodore," said Berty. The Dwarf was quick to appear at Berty's side. "Bring the Advisory Council, King Elrick, Queen Lida, Prince Goscislaw, and Miss Hunter."

Magically, Berty added four more chairs around the table. He stayed seated as the others filed into the room. Once everyone had found seats, he said, "I have just spoken with Lord Darnell. What we seek lies within the Halls of Enchantment. The entire Advisory Council plus Miss Hunter will journey with me. We leave tomorrow. Take the rest of the day to prepare yourselves. You should be armed with knowledge and a weapon. I know not what we will face, but I expect anything to be ancient in nature. We will need a neutral Guide."

"My Lord, I will provide you with the best Guide," offered

Goscislaw.

"Thank you, Goscislaw," he said.

"With all of you absent, who will steward the Empire?" asked Lida.

"I was hoping you and Elrick would take that charge," said Berty.

"It would be a great honor," said Elrick.

"Edwin will be Acting Captain of the Empire Guard," Berty said. "Hatcher will tell you who he puts in charge of the gates. All of you, do what you need to do. Elrick, Lida, if you would please stay a few moments longer."

The room emptied quickly. Berty informed them of Hope's predicament.

"The walls keep her safe," said Lida.

"To an extent. I do not want her gift being advertised. Beside yourselves, the only ones who will know anything about her secret is her Fairy Godmother, Sean, Julie, and Obie," said Berty.

"I like Declan's family and that Ojore is an interesting fellow," said Elrick. "If we need non-Empire Guard help, can we ask them?"

"Of course," he said. "Theodore is a very capable Head Tender with magic of his own. Whoever is loyal to the tree, will also be loyal to the both of you."

Parting with the Fairies, Berty walked to his chambers via Hope's. On his platform, stood Silvia. Her dark red hair kissed her face in the gentle summer breeze. Her warm eyes invited him. He had to remind himself that she was not the same woman he knew.

"I was wondering," she said, sounding the way she used to sound, "if the vault had any information about the Halls of Enchantment."

"Let's find out," he said. Together, they entered her study, then climbed down into the vault.

Entering the Library Vault, Berty realized that it could take all afternoon just to find something. "I have an idea," he said. Standing near the table, he announced, "Halls of Enchantment." His eyes searched the shelves for movement. Nothing.

"It might work better using the ancient tongue," Silvia suggested.

"I don't really know it," confessed Berty.

Her eyebrows scrunched. "But you can read it," she said.

"Because of this." He showed her his red stoned pinky ring. "It allows me to translate into English."

"If you can go one way, then you can go the other way with language," she said. "Try."

He knew that she could just say the words and spare him the trouble. He also knew that she would not. She was beginning to feel like the old Silvia to him. He relaxed his mind and closed his eyes, hoping the words would come to him.

His lips parted. With his tongue, they formed, "*Seihǫllen.*"

The rustling of paper reached his ears. Opening his eyes, he saw a few books land on the table. They opened to the correct pages.

"I knew you could do it," said Silvia. She placed her hand on his arm. Too quickly, it slipped away.

They each took a book to read. Berty's book described the Halls of Enchantment as a place of changing magic.

The Halls of Enchantment belonged to a Mage named Ede. In his time, the Halls served as his palace. Each hall was imbued with different kinds of enchantments. The Halls impressed, wowed and intimidated visitors. Ede enjoyed the spectacle as it brought business his way. Every so often, he would add new enchantments to showcase his magical range and abilities. A magical explosion caused the ground to swallow Ede and his palace. Over the course of a single day and night, the flora regrew as

168

though nothing had ever been there.

Explorers searched for the palace. Many entered, never to return. Those who survived spoke of uncontrolled magic as if from the mind of a mad Mage. The Dwarves sealed the passage.

After he finished reading, he looked across the table at Silvia.

Noticing his head move, she said, "According to this, there are seven halls, all with different magic. At the request of the Empress, the Goblins sealed the magic inside the halls so that it could not escape. The Goblin Lord gave the Empress a key in case it ever needed to be opened again. There is no mention of the Origin Scroll. Where would we find the key?" Her brown eyes searched his.

"Darnell never mentioned a key."

"Perhaps it is in the other room where we found the scrolls earlier," Silvia suggested.

"I don't think an Empress would have kept it there," he said. Staring into the antechamber, pictures on the wall popped out at him. "Does it describe the key?"

Her eyes scanned the pages. "No."

"Help me look," he said, rising from his seat. She followed him out of the library. His hand grazed the picture of the trunk. Another section of the rock slid away.

They stepped through the rocky opening. Sconces illuminated a large room that reminded Berty of a museum. Resting on pedestals, items on display had descriptive plaques in either the ancient or modern tongue.

"Look at all this," exclaimed Silvia. She read an inscription beneath a jeweled dagger. "Gift from the Magi of Calcutta." Meandering through the room, she said, "Gifts from important people. Artifacts from all over. Why would they be kept locked in a vault?"

"So nobody steals them?" he speculated. He studied the items as he moved around the room.

"This is it!" he said. "Key to the Palace of Ede." The metal
key had a pear shaped mother of pearl handle. Picking up the
handle, he studied the octagonal metal key part. Inside the hollow
octagon was the outline of a heptagon in which was a hexagon.
Following the metal shapes, he found in descending order, a
pentagon, a square, a triangle, and a line. On the line, the center
point was indented. A different Rune was embossed on each of
the eight metal sides.

Showing Silvia, he turned the key over in his hand. "I wonder what these mean," he said.

"Where are we going to find someone who knows Runes?"
she asked.

"Alina." Wrapping the key in the soft cloth on which it laid,
he tucked it into his pocket.

"Who is Alina?" Silvia asked.

"I'll explain on the way," he said. The books returned to
their shelves and both doorways sealed.

When they reached Hope's platform, he began to cross the
bridge. "Why are you going that way?" she asked.

"To get to the village."

"There is a better way to get to the house of Rowan," she
said.

Returning to her side, he said, "Lead the way."

She tugged on a rope, raising a bridge to Hope's platform.
They walked along the bridge until Silvia tugged on another rope.
They stepped onto a crossing bridge. The bridges eventually
brought them to the far side of the Sages' Grove.

Leaving the bridge, they entered a lookout tower attached to
the wall. After descending the ramp, their feet found earth. A
few steps later, Berty's knuckles rapped on the Rowan's door.

The wooden door swung open. "Emperor, what can we do

for you?" Cal asked.

"We do not wish to intrude, but we need Alina's help," said Berty.

Cal ushered them inside. Alina hovered over the cauldron, adding herbs to whatever her mother had cooking. Obeying her father's call, she walked over to Berty and Silvia.

"Hope says that you can read Runes," Berty said.

She nodded.

He extracted the cloth wrapped key. "What do these mean?" he asked.

Alina hesitated to touch the metal and mother of pearl key. After studying it for a minute, she said, "They're Elemental Runes. At the top is Wind. Bottom—Fire. The right side is Earth. The left is Water. On the angles, Winter and Summer are opposite each other. Winter lies between Wind and Water while Summer is between Earth and Fire. Spring is between Fire and Water. And between Earth and Wind lies Autumn." She placed the key back on the cloth in Berty's palm.

"Why are the seasons considered Elemental Runes?" Berty asked.

"The seasons represent Secondary Elements. Together with the four Primary Elements, they represent the Magical Elements," Alina explained. She stared at the key, tilting her head to the side.

"What is it?" asked Silvia.

"It's missing the third group—the Cardinal Elements," Alina said. "North, South, East, and West. Each one corresponds with one of each of the other two." She grabbed a piece of paper and drew four Runic symbols. She labeled each symbol with a Cardinal Direction. "You may need this," she said, handing Berty the paper.

"Thank you very much, Alina," said Berty.

As they retraced their steps through the bridge system, Silvia said, "She is learning her Witchery well."

"Does everyone know it was called Witchery, but me?" he muttered.

She laughed a little. Hesitating to tug on a rope, she asked, "Did you want to go straight to dinner or stop at your study first?"

The key pressed into his flesh with only a few layers of material as separation. Although it would be safe in his study, he did not feel as though he and the key should part. "Dinner," he answered.

She brought him to the bridges he knew. They entered the Reception Room from a side entrance. Goscislaw was absent from the dinner table. The Dwarf had returned to Grunnan to prepare a Guide. After dinner, Berty spoke with Julie and Ojore.

Julie agreed to be an extra pair of eyes on Hope under the guise of keeping up her practices while Declan was away. Ojore was honored to work with and learn from the Fairy King and Queen. He also took a shine to Obie, teaching him the ways of hunting.

Before packing, Berty stopped in to see Hope. "Why can't I come with you?" she asked. "I should never have told you they were after me."

"Yes, you should have," Berty told her as he looked into her disappointed face. "That's not the reason you are not going. This is something that the Advisory Council has to do. While we're gone, you can introduce Obie to your friends and practice your archery. You do want to impress your parents and grandparents with your expert skills?" She nodded. "Then, in a couple of weeks, I'll have Declan set up an elaborate archery range in the backyard of my house. You'll be able to show everyone how good you are."

"Okay, Uncle Berty," she said. "How long will you be gone?"

"I'm not sure," he answered. "But, since Alfred has to come, Lida and Elrick have agreed to teach you the ancient tongue."

Her face looked happier.

"Want to see something cool?" he asked.

Her curls bounced eagerly. He pulled the cloth wrapped key out of his pocket. Slowly, he peeled away the cloth.

"Ooh. That's so pretty. What's it for?"

"You have to promise not to tell anyone," he said.

"I promise."

"We're thinking that it may unlock something where we're going," he told her in hushed tones.

"Oh." Her widened brown eyes stared at it.

Covering the key, he placed it back in his pocket.

"Are you going to fix the Scepter?" she asked.

"We are going to try," he said with a small smile.

She looked at him pensively. "What happens if you can't?"

"We'll cross that bridge when we come to it," he replied. "I'm not going to worry about that now." He gave her a reassuring smile. "I don't want you to worry about that either."

Nodding, she leaned back in the puffy seat. "Will I see you before you leave?" she asked quietly.

"Of course."

She smiled.

After giving her a big hug, he stepped onto her platform. He gazed at the sinking sun through the tree's upper branches. He let out a deep breath.

"Everything all right?" Silvia asked. She walked onto the platform from the bridge. The orangish sky gave her an ethereal glow.

"With the exception of a few hours here and there, Hope has been with me everywhere I have gone," he said. He walked with her slowly up the bridge to his chambers. "All her family is

173

elsewhere right now. I don't know how long we will be gone."
Reaching his platform, they stopped. "I don't want her to feel
like I'm leaving her, too."

Her hand touched his arm. The way she rubbed his soft cot-
ton sleeve comforted him. "Hope probably feels as though she is
missing out on a great adventure. That's all."

"Maybe. I just feel guilty leaving her with relative strangers.
Pretty much everyone with whom she has formed a bond is
leaving."

"Do not worry so much," she said. "Her Fairy Godmother
will make sure that she does not notice any of that." She smiled
her warm smile that Berty adored. "Both Martin and I had our
own Fairy Godmothers. When we were going to school on the
other side of the portal, they would wait for us at the bus stop or
at home with a snack. Our parents were there, too, but we did
not see them until later in the afternoon sometimes. And when
our parents were busy with Empire business or when my father
took Martin on one of their expeditions, my Fairy Godmother
always made it seem like I did not miss out on anything."

Moving his hand on top of hers, he said, "Thank you. I
needed that." He smiled. Wanting to keep his hand on hers, his
hand returned to his side. Hers quickly slid off his arm.

The silence felt slightly awkward. He longed to hug her, perhaps kiss her, but he did not dare. To her, he was still an un-
known. He felt creepy knowing more about her than she knew
about him.

Adding to his creepy feeling, he asked, "Can you come in for
a moment?" He quickly followed with, "I need to talk to you
more privately." The words sounded terrible when they flew out
of his lips. His creepiness kept building.

"Of course," she answered. Her calmness did not spill onto
him.

He led her into his study. Her eyes roved around the room, taking in the club chairs, the nearly empty shelves, the Sages' Seal carved into his desk, and the table in the back of the room.

Extracting a piece of paper from his pocket, he held it towards her. "This should be kept separate from the key," he said.

"The corresponding Runes," she breathed. Her fingers hesitated to touch the folded paper. "Why me?" she asked. "I'm not one of your Advisors. Alfred would be a better choice. Or Delyth."

"They both would be good choices, but not better ones," he told her. "Just because you have lost your memory does not mean that I have lost my trust in you. You are the same woman regardless of what you remember."

Her eyes glistened slightly. "Thank you," she said, taking the paper. She had stopped using the moniker, my Lord, but she still did not call him Berty either. Half turning to go, she said, "I've decided to stay in those chambers." She gave him a quick smile, then averted her eyes.

Berty thought that he saw her blush as she turned away from him. He smiled, watching her leave his study.

Chapter Fourteen
Seihǫllen

After packing what he thought he might need, he climbed his spiral staircase. He carefully placed the cloth wrapped key on his nightstand. As he readied for bed, he wondered if Silvia's memory would return in time and not be tied to the restoration of the Scepter.

Guilt weighed heavily on Berty while he trudged through his morning routine. All the comfort Silvia gave him the night before escaped in his sleep.

Donning his claret cloak, he stepped out of his chambers. Cloaked in light blue, Silvia crossed the short bridge to join him. "How are you this morning?" she asked.

"I'll let you know after I speak with Hope," he said as they walked down the bridge to Hope's platform. She gave him a smile, then turned onto the bridge leading into the trunk.

He rang Hope's wind chimes to announce his presence. Entering her chambers, he saw Hope trotting down the steps in her nightgown. Her robe trailed on the floor. By the time she reached her uncle, she had tied her robe around her. "Will you promise to tell me all about it?" she asked.

"Of course I will," he told her. "Listen to Freesia and don't leave the Sages' Grove." Remembering how scared she looked in the woods, he added, "Come with me."

He led her to the top of her stairs. Facing the tapestry between the doors, he said, "This tapestry is a portal."

Her eyes widened.

He jerked his head towards the tapestry.

She nodded eagerly.

He whispered, "One."

"Two," she said quietly.

"Three," they said together. With one step, they passed through the tapestry. The dark paneled wood in the upstairs hall dampened the bright summer sun.

Hope turned to gaze at the tapestry hanging on the wall behind her. She smiled. "Very cool, Uncle Berty."

He crouched to be eye level. "First, it may not be the same time on both sides of the portal. Second, the house has magic. If you need anything, ask the house. Third, the house will protect you as long as you stay within the property. So, if you are ever feeling scared or threatened in any way, you can come here. Fourth, only you, me and Freesia have unrestricted access to this portal. No one else can come through without an attachment like holding hands. Fifth, you can enter the house when I'm gone, but you cannot come here alone, you cannot answer the door, you cannot leave the property, and my car and cell phone are off limits. Okay?"

"Okay." She looked happy.

Standing, he said, "After you."

Returning to Hope's chambers, she walked with him down the steps. "I'll see you soon," he said.

She gave him a big hug. "Bye, Uncle Berty. Don't have too much fun without me," she said.

Laughing a little, he said, "I'll try not to." He gave her a big squeeze, then kissed her on the head.

He entered the trunk lighter. In the Reception Room,

breakfast was being served on one table while provisions waited on another. Fixing a plate, he sat with his Advisory Council.

"Our Guide should be here soon," said Colvin.

"Miss Hunter," said Alvar, "you did not get a weapon from me yesterday. Do you want me to have a selection brought before we leave?"

"Thank you, Alvar, but that will not be necessary," Silvia said. "I am carrying my family's rapier."

"Very well," said Alvar. "Alfred, do you have enough arrows?"

"Plenty. Thank you," answered the aged Elf.

Alvar distributed provisions.

"You seem happier," a familiar voice said in Berty's ear.

Turning his head, he saw Silvia standing beside him. "You were right," he said. "She told me not to have too much fun without her." He smiled.

A Tender escorted a Dwarf into the Reception Room. "You must be our Guide," said Alvar.

"Yes. Prince Goscislaw sent me. My name is Baldur," he answered. "When everyone is ready, we will be heading to the tunnels."

Berty examined his group. Colored cloaks adorned his Advisory Council. With the exception of Colvin's muted tan cloak, the rest may have well been jewels dripping from their shoulders. Their Guide wore a rich brown cloak that could never blend into a crowd.

They squeezed into the small, wooden room that dropped them into the tunnels below the tree. Baldur led them to two waiting mine carts.

"Colvin, sir, if you would please take the second mine cart," said Baldur. "Emperor, you and two others can come with me."

Berty had Alfred and Silvia sit on the back bench. As he took

178

his seat on the middle bench, he watched his Advisors take seats in the second cart. Alvar and Declan took the back bench, the women sat on the middle bench, while Colvin and Hatcher sat riding backwards on the final bench.

Baldur closed both mine carts. Sitting on the bench with Berty, he moved a lever. Both carts rolled on the tracks. Gaining speed, they plunged into a dark tunnel. Expecting complete darkness, Berty's eyes detected light under the seats. He leaned forward to see a pierced metal lantern behind his legs.

The lantern illuminated a large pack under the bench in front of them. Baldur was very well prepared. The Dwarf's dark eyes roved in their sockets. He watched the tunnel pass as if he were taking a quick inventory. Berty imagined that tunnels were more interesting to a Dwarf.

Taking the lantern from underneath the seat, Baldur crossed to the front bench. He lowered the lantern in front of the speeding cart. Quickly resting the light on the mine cart floor, the Dwarf grabbed the top of the cart. He muttered something under his breath over and over.

The vibrations of the cart rolling on its track left Berty's feet. His stomach felt as if he were in a free fall. After two gentle thuds, the vibrations returned. Baldur watched the second cart behind them before taking his seat next to Berty.

Wooden mine supports whizzed by his peripheral vision. The tunnel beyond the cart was dark. Every so often, a twinkle in the rock walls or ceiling caught Berty's eye. The twinkles disappeared quickly like the short blink of summer lightning bugs before they blended in with the grass.

Baldur leaned forward. His eyes squinted. Picking up the lantern, he held it out, slightly above his head. The Dwarf pulled a lever. With a gentle lurch, the mine cart slowed.

They stopped in front of a rock barricade. Baldur raised a

shepherd's hook that was attached to the cart. Hanging the lantern on it, he unfolded a map. His finger followed a line. He glanced at the rocks covering the tracks, then studied the map.

"What's wrong?" asked Berty.

"This cave-in is not on my map," said Baldur. He placed the map on the bench in front of them. His hands reached into his pack. Extracting a small device, he turned a few of its knobs. "Stay here," he said as he got out of the cart.

The Dwarf placed the device on different sections of the blockage. Taking a step back, he studied the ceiling. Both hands rested on top of his thin, light hair.

Alvar stood near the first cart. "What's the problem?" he asked.

"I'm trying to determine the best way through," said Baldur, without tearing his eyes from the rock. Using a small hammer, he tapped the rocks. After tapping roughly each rock at least twice, he said, "The rocks are fairly settled. I should be able to clear a small area through which we can climb."

"Do you need help?" asked Colvin.

Baldur retrieved his pack from the mine cart. "It is always helpful to have an extra pair of eyes. Watch for movement as I remove rocks," he replied.

He extracted specialized equipment from his pack. Colvin lit a few more lanterns. Everyone watched Baldur remove rocks with surgical precision. Once the hole could swallow his torso, he recalibrated his device, then stuck it on the rock above the opening.

His feet disappeared into the dark hole a few times. Eventually, he stood, saying, "We're through." He looked at Berty. "Heat from the lantern could disrupt the rocks. We're going to have to go dark. And one at a time. Who wants to go first?"

"I'll go," said Delyth.

Turning, Berty gave the Fairy a nod. He knew her wings glowed in the dark. She climbed out of the mine cart, he said, "Declan is next. Then, Estelle, Alfred, Silvia, Alvar, Hatcher, me, and Colvin."

"I would like to wait until the end with Colvin, my Lord," said Hatcher.

"Very well," said Berty.

As the line formed, Baldur had Colvin and Hatcher remove everything from the mine carts. The numbers dwindled on Berty's side of the cave-in.

Hearing Alvar say, "Out," Baldur allowed Berty to climb through the hole.

The hole was more of a dark tunnel. His eyes detected a diffused lavender light. He knew Delyth's wings emitted the soft glow. His belly slithered towards the light. He heard a soft beep as dirt trickled onto his head. The glow brightened. Strong hands pulled him to his feet. "Out," he said into the tunnel.

Berty waited to the side while Declan and Alvar pulled Hatcher and Colvin out of the hole. Poking his head through the hole, Baldur said, "Start running. The whole thing is unstable."

Quickly, Declan and Alvar grabbed the Dwarf by his arms. They pulled Baldur and the pack tied to his leg out of the crawl space.

The light from Delyth's wings did not spread far from her body. Rumbling reached their ears. They stumbled over the old metal and wooden tracks. Berty released two spheres of light.

Trying to outrun the cloud of dust, Baldur yelled, "Cover your faces!"

Berty scrambled to throw his cloak over his head. Small stones pelted his back. The rumbling silenced.

"It's over," said Baldur. "Is everyone all right?"

When he uncovered his face, his spheres showed a wall of

rock blocking the passage through which they crawled. Silt covered colored cloaks.

"Guess we're not going back that way," said Colvin.

"This way," said Baldur. He lit a few lanterns, then handed one to Alvar and one to Hatcher. "The entrance is close."

The old mineshaft descended deeper into the Earth. At the outer wall of a bend, Baldur stopped. "Here it is," he said.

He touched the rough rock wall between timber supports. The rock melted, revealing a large, dark, metal door. "This door was designed to barricade magic," Baldur explained. "Only a Guide knows it's here. Emperor, if you could please extinguish your light."

Berty's palms absorbed the spheres.

"On the other side of this door lies a corridor which leads to the Halls of Enchantment. This door must close once you pass through. I will await your return," said Baldur. "Knock three times and I will open the door for you."

"Thank you, Baldur," said Berty.

At the Dwarf's touch, a wheel popped from the smooth door. He turned it until he heard a soft hiss. The large, metal door creaked outward. Mustiness escaped the dark tunnel.

Alvar lifted his lantern high. He stepped inside the downward sloping tunnel first. Berty's hands groped his pocket to feel the small lump of metal and mother of pearl. He entered the tunnel with Declan and Silvia.

The door crunched closed behind them. A faint sulfur stench reached his nose. He began to feel like Dante. Each step confirmed his descent into the seven levels of Hell. He exhaled audibly. Feeling pressure on his arm, his eyes found a delicate hand. They followed the arm to Silvia's face. Her warm, brown eyes calmed him. Latin made everything sound more ominous. He decided on Milton instead.

182

An unassuming, massive, circular piece of wood met them at the bottom of the tunnel. In the lantern light, Berty examined its concentric rings. The cross-section of trunk did not reveal a place to insert a key.

"How do we get inside?" asked Colvin.

"Look for a place to insert an octagonal key," Berty answered.

"Is that a Rune?" Silvia asked. She pointed to a mark on the upper left of the circle near the bark.

Scrutinizing the mark, he said, "I think so." His eyes roved to the upper right. "There is another one."

"Two more on the bottom," said Hatcher. "They form a square inside the circle."

Silvia extracted the piece of paper Alina gave them. She examined all four Runes, matching them with those on the paper. "Upper left is North. Upper right is South. Lower left is East, and lower right is West."

Taking a step back, Berty stared at the wooden circle. His eyes relaxed. The Runes moved to different places on the wood. He blinked. The Runes had not moved at all. "Oh," he said. With his hands, he magically coaxed the Cardinal Directions to the correct locations. North on the top. South to the bottom. East moved to the right and West to the left.

With the Runes in place, a nine sided hole appeared in the center of the wood. He pulled the key out of his pocket. Turning the key so that the Runes for Winter and Wind faced North, he fitted the metal into the wood.

The concentric rings on the wood spiraled into the key, then pulsed out to the bark. The round wood door broke into eighths, like an inverted star. All eight swung inward, making a circular entrance to the Halls of Enchantment.

Bowls of fire roared to life as they entered the large, glittery room. "Now what?" asked Colvin, looking around.

"I have a feeling the room will tell us," said Alfred.

The glitter from the walls and ceilings converged on the far end of the room.

"Is that the exit?" asked Hatcher.

"No," said Alfred, watching the glitter form into a tree. It then morphed into a bow. "It's the beginning of an Elf legend. Before we adopted the ancient tongue, the ancient Elf language was written as pictographs." He watched the forms carefully as they changed shape. Lines and squiggles with leaves and animals made no sense to Berty.

He noticed a mural on the floor. Each corner of a central square had a chubby cherub face blowing towards what looked like a pine branch depicted in mosaic tiles. Berty knew he had seen the picture before, but he could not place where.

When the glittery pictographic language disappeared, five possible exits glowed. Each had a different pictogram emblazoned on the door—a tree trunk, a bow, a leaf, a horn, and a star.

"The legend states that the trees are our brethren," Alfred explained. "They gave us the bow and the arrow. When the leaves could no longer protect the Elves, the trees showed us the way. They pointed to a star under which we would build our city of Irmingard to keep all of Elfdom safe."

"So we go through the star," said Colvin.

"The correct door is the horn," Alfred said. "Albrecht the Collector used a ram's horn to call the Elves to Irmingard. The horn still sits in the heart of Irmingard. The fifth High Elf removed it from its wooden pillar on which it proudly rested. Since then, it has been buried under the city."

"But there was no horn in the pictographs," Colvin protested.

"Precisely. You need to know the rest of the story," said Alfred.

"Are you sure?" asked Berty.

"Very," said Alfred.

"Then, we go," Berty said.

Alfred led them through the door with the horn. Brass bowls of fire illuminated large cages dotted around the second room.

"Who keeps animals in cages?" Delyth asked.

In their respective cages, leopards and panthers prowled as monkeys jumped from bar to bar. Colorful parrots squawked when they passed. "How is this kept?" Silvia asked.

"Magic," said Declan. "I don't think they're real."

"A magical menagerie," Estelle said, peering at a zebra through bars. "I wonder why?" She looked at Silvia.

Berty gazed at a red panda. "Exotic animals have always been a zoo's biggest draw," he said.

"Ede dazzled his visitors," said Silvia. "The path to the door will take us past every animal."

They meandered around the cages. With the door insight, Declan readied an arrow on his bow. The floor trembled. Alvar unsheathed his sword.

A towering creature thundered towards them with a battle-axe poised over its head.

"Troll?" asked Colvin.

"That's no Troll," said Hatcher.

Berty stared at its one large eye in the center of its forehead. "Cyclops," he whispered.

An arrow flew past the cages, striking its target. The beast exploded into dust.

"Is anything real?" asked Delyth.

Without answering, they walked through the door.

The next room was cold and dark. Little dots of white light twinkled while suspended in the darkness. Standing next to Berty, Estelle gawked at the floor to ceiling twinkles.

"They're stars," remarked Estelle. Her hand reached, then

paused. "I think it's supposed to be the summer sky, but... Oh." She smiled. "We are looking at the stars' position in the sky thousands of years ago. Fascinating."

"What's the catch?" Colvin said.

"Stay here," she instructed. "I'm going to have a closer look." Estelle walked carefully around the stars. Her steps were deliberate as if she were avoiding stepping in certain places. Standing in the center of the room, the stars reflected on the silver thread in her Navy dress where her dark cloak parted. She turned on the spot, surveying the celestial puzzle around her.

Returning, she smiled. "It is a star map. Our path is written in the stars. All we need to do is follow it."

"And if we don't?" asked Alvar.

"Uncertain outcome," said Estelle. "I saw multiple doors. And certain stars and constellations point to different triggers. I think the trigger has something to do with the constellation. Taurus may release a bull. Orion or Sagittarius could set off arrows. Aries a ram."

"Or a battering ram," inserted Alvar.

"Exactly. I'd hate to see what Aquarius would unleash," said Estelle. "Follow me exactly. Step where I step. Do not cut through a constellation or touch a star."

Berty allowed Delyth, Silvia and Alfred ahead of him. They walked in single file behind Estelle. Her every move was copied. She held open the door at the end of the path for her fellow Advisors and Berty.

The room they entered reminded Berty of a fun house—full of mirrors and creepy.

"Colvin!" Alvar shouted from the doorway. The Elf fell to his knees. "He needs rope!"

Peering through the doorway, Berty saw the star room's floor gone. Alvar hung over the edge, asking, "Are you okay?"

"I'm hanging here," answered Colvin.

Using a spoken enchantment, Alfred conjured rope. With Berty and Declan holding one end, Alvar threw it down the large hole.

Colvin latched onto the handle of his pickax embedded into the rock wall. "Can you grab the rope?" Alvar asked.

"Got it!" said Colvin. He climbed the rope with his pickax keeping him stable. When he reached the floor, Berty and Declan pulled him through the door.

"What happened?" Hatcher asked. "One second you are right behind me, the next," his arm made a downward motion.

"Hit a star," Colvin said quietly.

"Can't you follow simple directions?" asked Hatcher.

"I slipped, all right?" said Colvin. "What's with all the mirrors?"

Closing the door behind them, they stared at their many reflections filling the room. "They're portals," said Declan.

"How do you know?" Silvia asked.

"All I see is separate blue discs, like every other normal portal," he explained.

"A simple incantation will reveal everything," said Hatcher. The Troll walked around the room, muttering under his breath. Coming full circle, he said, "Most of the portals just go to another part of the room. Others travel back to the first room. That one," he pointed to a mirror near them, "will take us to the next room."

"Any traps?" asked Alfred.

Hatcher shook his head. "Nothing like the star room."

One by one, they crossed through the mirrored portal. Colvin would not go last. Hatcher assured him that he would make sure everyone went through the correct portal.

The portal brought them to an army's training room. Fully

armored soldiers sparred around the room. Sounds of fighting filled their ears as they waited for everyone. Berty eyed the door on the opposite end of the room.

Once Hatcher came through the portal, they walked towards the door. The sparring soldiers did not notice them. When they crossed about a third of the room, silence found them.

Weapons drawn, the soldiers stared at them through the slits in their helmets.

"Why do I get the feeling that they're not going to let us pass?" said Declan.

As soon as they drew their weapons, the armored soldiers charged. Clanging metal echoed against the smooth walls.

"Declan! Stop!" cried Delyth. "For each soldier you hit, three more materialize. We can't use magic against them."

Lowering his bow, the color drained from Declan's face. "I'm weaponless."

"Catch," yelled Alvar. He threw his spare bow and quiver to Declan.

Securing the Bow of the Moon, Declan hung the quiver from his belt, then began using the non-magical bow.

Both being archers, Declan and Alfred picked off soldiers. Delyth fought with her sword near Estelle, who used a pair of sais. With a swipe of Berty's sword against the armor, the soldier disintegrated into dust.

Silvia's long, thin blade was much faster than the soldier's. She never told him that she knew how to use a sword. Fighting his way across the room, he realized that he did not know many details about Silvia. He knew the woman she was—intelligent, wise, compassionate, strong, and kind. That was all that mattered to him.

When the last of the soldiers had turned to dust, they took a quick breath before rushing through the door.

"Duck!" yelled Estelle. A candelabra crashed into the wall above their heads. Items flew across the room. A glowing yellow sphere collided with a large table, reducing it to splinters.

"What's this room supposed to be?" asked Colvin.

"I don't think it knows," said Delyth.

"At least the door is clearly indicated," Hatcher said.

"We just have to get there," said Alvar, staring into the room. "It's a battlefield."

The stoic Elf was right. Magic exploded everywhere.

"Look out!" Delyth shouted. A chair spiraled towards them. They scattered. The chair crashed into the floor where they were standing.

Alvar knocked items aside with his sword. Using the Bow of the Moon, Declan shot spheres of magic. Berty and Silvia magically pushed obstacles out of the way. As they approached, a fireplace in the center of the room began shooting flames.

Berty watched a small table race through the room. Following its trajectory, it would crash where Silvia was standing. She magically stopped debris from hitting Estelle and Alfred.

Her magic blocked his from moving the table. "Silvia, move!" he shouted. She could not hear him over the explosions and smashes.

Darting around obstacles, he sprinted towards her. His arms grabbed her waist. He pulled her to the floor as the table shattered at their feet. "Are you okay?" he asked.

Her brown eyes found his. She smiled. "I am now," she said softly.

He could feel her hand on his back. His fingers brushed her dark red hair off her face. He inhaled the berry pie intoxication. His head lowered. Their noses grazed each other's. Her lips pressed softly against his.

"Berty," she breathed.

He raised his head enough so that her eyes came into focus.

She smiled. "What a good way to get my memory back." Her cheeks flushed.

Something crashed above them.

"Let's stop this insanity," she said.

He helped her to her feet.

"Enough." Silvia's voice reverberated throughout the room. All the magic ceased. Chairs, tables and candlesticks froze in midair. The room morphed into a forest. When the forest disappeared, the room had order. A dining table and chairs sat on one side of the fireplace while a seating area gathered on the other.

Her eyes scanned the room. She nodded, then led them to the door.

Walking with her, he watched her touch Estelle's arm. His Silvia—the one who knew him—returned to him. Estelle smiled at her friend before they entered the next room.

No chaotic magic greeted them. No soldiers, no stars or animals filled the long room. Studying his surroundings, Berty thought that he had stepped inside a baroque palace. Gaudy ostentatiousness oozed from ceiling to floor. On the far side of the room sat a deep purple and gold throne high on a dais.

"I don't see a door," said Colvin.

"What we seek is behind the throne," said Berty.

The wide, central, red carpet muffled their footsteps. Alvar and Declan constantly watched for surprises.

Almost reaching the carpeted steps, Berty glimpsed at a man walking across the dais. His long, silver robe dragged along the carpet. As the man reached the throne, he noticed them approach while stroking his long, white beard. "Halt," he said. "I was not informed about visitors. Who dares come unannounced?"

They stopped just before the dais. Berty wondered if they gazed upon the ghost of a Mage. "You must be Ede," he said.

"I am," said the man.

"We were not formally announced for there was no one to announce us," Berty said.

"What have you done with my men? How did you get in here? You are not welcome in my palace!" scolded Ede.

Berty kept his eyes on Ede, who held onto his throne for support. "You have no men. We entered using the key."

"The key?" Ede patted his robe. "How did you obtain the key?" He squinted as he studied Berty. "Mage or Sorcerer?"

"Sorcerer."

Ede sat on his throne. "I do not share my secrets. And I only take on young apprentices."

"We have not come for your secrets. Nor is anyone seeking an apprenticeship," said Berty. "I am the Emperor of all that surrounds us. We have come for something that is hidden in these halls."

Ede laughed. "There is no Emperor because there is no Empire. Not here."

"Indeed there is. How long have you been underground, Ede?" he asked.

Ede threw him a quizzical look. "Underground? My palace is not underground." He stared at his floor to ceiling windows. "Am I?" He stood.

"In a single day and night, the Earth swallowed your palace and you within it, and above grew the forest where nothing dies," Berty stated.

Ede descended. "That would explain the lack of visitors," he said. "Consumed by my own magic." A little laugh escaped from behind his white facial hair. "Something valuable hidden here?"

"Only to the Sages," Berty replied. "A Goblin hid it here."

"Goblin," Ede repeated. He turned around as if the surrounding air was interesting. "I remember a Goblin. Come."

191

The Mage led them onto the dais. Behind the throne, he magically opened a hidden door. "What you seek is in there."

His Advisory Council entered the hidden room. He looked at Ede's color changing eyes. In them, he saw no malice, only the desire to be the best Mage.

Inside the small room, Silvia magically lit candles. They huddled around a single small table as Silvia and Alfred read the Scroll.

"The crystal and the metal of the Scepter were mined from a cavern where magic thrives. The Fellowship of the Keepers guards the Cavern," translated Silvia. "In the hollow of the Empire Tree, we, the Seven High Sages, created the Scepter, in secret, using each of our unique magic. The magic needs to be recharged every five hundred years. Our Sage Stones must pass from generation to generation, so that they may remind us of this task. The enchantment lies within the stones." She looked at Berty.

"Our unique magic," repeated Delyth. "So, Sean needs the Staff of Lightning?"

"I feel the Scepter is overdue for its five hundred year recharge," said Alfred. "Delyth is right. He needs that staff."

"What happens if he can't find it?" asked Declan.

Pairs of eyes glanced at one another. No one could utter a word.

"The Trolls will do what they must to secure the portals," said Berty. "And the Goblins will steer outsiders away."

"Come the Hallows, the magic will fade. We must prepare now," Alfred said.

"Can he find it after the Hallows?" asked Hatcher. "Can the magic be brought back?"

Alfred's blue eyes scanned the Scroll through his glasses. "Maybe, but it may need a boost from recently gathered crystal or ore from the Cavern," he answered.

"Add that to the list of things we don't know," said Colvin.

Declan shifted his weight. Biting his lower lip, he glanced at Berty.

"Is there anything more the Origin Scroll can tell us?" asked Berty.

"No," answered Silvia.

"Yes," said Estelle. "Well, not that Scroll. This one." She held a small scroll open in her hands. "The Empress and her Advisory Council used the Scepter's magic to lock away magical creatures that plagued the land. If the Scepter's magic weakens, then the prisons will be opened."

Delyth's small hand covered her mouth. Her violet eyes stared at the table. "That's how the creatures...," she looked at Berty. "They used old Fairy Dust to unlock the prisons," she said. "It would be the only way without the Scepter itself." Closing her eyes, she shook her head. "Leif and Millicent know exactly what they are doing."

"I fear they also had help from within the Watchers' Guild," Silvia added. "That's why they were so against me having a Watcher."

They searched the small room for more scrolls, but found none.

Ede waited for them on the dais. "Did you find for which you came?" he asked.

"Yes," said Berty. "Can we get through the palace without issue?"

The old Mage smiled. "There is a quicker way." He showed them through a door off to the side of the throne. A narrow corridor brought them to the door to the outside.

Eyeing the opening with trepidation, Ede would not approach. "Lock the door and keep the key, Emperor," he said. "Someday, I will figure out how to re-emerge on the surface.

When I do, may I call upon the Emperor?"

"You may," said Berty. "Good luck to you."

The inverted star closed to a round disk of solid wood behind them. Berty removed the key, then placed in his pocket.

They climbed out of the tunnel. Reaching the door, Alvar knocked three times. When the heavy door opened, Baldur greeted them. The Dwarf made camp just beyond the door.

"How long did you think we would be?" asked Colvin.

"You've been gone a little over a week," said Baldur.

"Can't be. It was just a few hours," Colvin responded.

"In the Halls of Enchantment, anything is possible," said Berty. "How are we getting out of here?"

Baldur started packing. "This leads to an old salt mine. We will take one of the other tunnels. If we can find another couple of carts, it will make it easier," said the Guide.

With Baldur leading the way, they followed the mineshaft. It emptied into a large cave. Salt glistened in the lantern light.

"Perhaps we can rest for a bit," said Alfred.

Baldur chose an area where they sat and ate. While the Dwarves searched for spare carts, Silvia sat next to Berty.

"How did you know that above was the forest where nothing dies?" she asked.

"It just clicked in my head," he said. He gazed into her warm, brown eyes. "How did... Your memory?"

Blushing a little, she answered, "Magic has rules. The Scepter acted as a conduit to bond us. When it was severed, the pieces remained. The kiss transformed those pieces."

"Does that mean you would lose your memory if we kissed again?" he asked quietly.

She rested her hand on his. "No. We're safe."

Holding her hand, he said, "Good."

Chapter Fifteen
Home

Colvin and Baldur rode into the cave in mine carts. "All we could find were utility carts," said Colvin. "They don't have benches for seats, but it's better than walking up the mineshaft."

"Shouldn't we use more than two?" asked Alvar.

"We are only two Dwarves," Baldur answered. "Only a Foreman can move more than one of these carts at a time." He and Colvin readied the carts for travel.

"Same as last time, except Estelle will ride with us," said Berty. They climbed into the doorless carts while Baldur showed Colvin the map.

Salt stuck to the corners of the beat up old mine cart. Baldur's large pack sat in the front corner of the cart. When Colvin yelled, "Ready," the carts began to move.

Rocking, the cart felt as if it were not secure on its track. Baldur kept watch of the tunnel. Berty caught Alfred close his eyes. He wondered if the Elf was getting motion sickness. His feet bumped into Silvia's. They smiled at each other.

Closing his eyes, he focused on Hope. She ran around with the children of the Sages' Grove. Alina and Obie laughed with her. From the bench, Freesia watched.

The Fairy turned her head sharply. A couple of hooded men

studied the children. She turned to focus onto the children.

Hope caught Freesia's gaze. Grabbing Obie's hand, they ran between the buildings with the other children. She gave Alina a little nod, then she and Obie kept running. They sneaked into the guard tower. She led Obie across the bridge system over the village. Pausing, she watched Alina reach Freesia. They continued to the platform in front of her chambers.

Entering her chambers, she grabbed her bow and quiver. She led Obie up the stairs. Holding his hand, she pulled him through the tapestry.

Berty opened his eyes. Staring at Silvia, he said, "She went through the portal."

"Is she okay?" Silvia asked.

He closed his eyes. Hope and Obie leaned against the paneling, catching their breath.

"Where are we?" asked Obie.

"My uncle's house. We will be safe here," Hope answered.

"Then why did you bring your bow?" Obie asked.

"Because *your* uncle told me to."

After hanging their cloaks, Obie followed Hope to her room. "How long are we staying?" he asked her.

"Until my uncle returns," she said. "Whispers can't cross portals."

Opening his eyes, he nodded. "She just got scared."

"You'll see her soon," Silvia said. His arms pushed against the cart floor to stop himself from crushing into Alfred.

As they ascended out of the mine, Baldur checked the map a few times. Taking the lantern, he inched up the sides of the mine cart. Berty watched the Dwarf lean half over the top. His feet lost contact with the inside.

Baldur screamed. Jumping off the cart floor, Berty grabbed the Dwarf's ankles. The lantern fell from Baldur's hand. Landing on its side, it burnt out. Berty pulled Baldur back inside the cart.

"Are you okay?" he asked in the darkness.

"Yes, thank you," Baldur answered. "Just need to get another lamp."

He could hear the Dwarf fumbling in his pack. After lighting another lantern, Baldur checked the map.

"Good thing I carry spares," said Baldur. "Only one more lever to move and we'll be on the direct route to the Empire Tree."

"Why not use magic to move them?" asked Berty.

"Only Foremen can do that," the Dwarf explained. "The other one will not be as difficult. It's been used within the century."

The cart leaned as the track rounded a bend. Metal squealed against metal. They entered a brightly lit cavern. Looking up, he saw carts racing along bridges.

Baldur leaned over the side of the cart. The Dwarf's feet returned to the floor. He exhaled.

Berty could feel the cart shift. Sounds of busy carts faded as they entered another tunnel.

The mine cart stopped, but Berty's body still shook. They climbed out of the carts. The shaking subsided as he followed Baldur through the tunnel.

When they reached the box that took them back to the surface, Baldur said, "My Lord, it has been a pleasure to serve you." The Dwarf bowed.

"Thank you, Baldur," said Berty. He squeezed into the box with his Advisors and Silvia. Baldur proudly stood as the doors to the tunnel closed.

An empty Receiving Room greeted them when the doors opened. Wearily, they climbed the stairs. The setting sun cast an orange glow onto the Sages' Seal.

"Get some rest," he told his Council. "We will have a joint meeting with the Sages' descendants in the morning."

They trudged more steps. While the others crossed the bridge to Council Circle, Berty and Silvia battled another flight.

"Will you come with me to check on Hope?" he asked as they stepped off the bridge.

"I'd love to," she said with a smile.

He led Silvia into Hope's chambers. After climbing the stairs in the back of the room, he took her hand. Together, they entered the house.

Sunlight gently spilled through the open windows. He glanced at the maroon and brown cloaks hanging on the wall. Glancing at Silvia, he realized that it was the first time she had been inside her old home since she became Elder. He gave her hand a gentle squeeze.

"Hope," he called as he peered into bedrooms. "Hope?" He and Silvia descended the steps.

"Uncle Berty?" Hope ran into the foyer from the hall. She squeezed him around his waist. Obie stood near the phone, watching with a smile. "How was it? What happened? Did you fix the Scepter?"

"All in good time," said Berty. "What happened in the Sages' Grove?"

"They were looking for me," Hope answered. "The trees warned me. When I told Freesia, she told King Elrick and Queen Lida. With Julie, they made a plan. But I didn't come alone, I brought Obie."

"I see that." Obie was not who Berty meant, but he did not tell her.

"The kitchen is making us macaroni and cheese," said Hope. "Obie's never had it before."

His eyes found Silvia who stood near the stairs.

198

"I could go for some mac and cheese," said Silvia. "Why don't we all have some and your Uncle Berty and I will tell you all about the Halls of Enchantment."

Hope smiled. "Okay."

Ringing filled the room. Startled, Obie moved away from the wall.

"Mommy and Daddy!" squealed Hope.

Picking up the brass receiver off the white rotary phone, Berty said, "Hello?"

"Berty," said Kate's voice. "You're home from saving the world." She chuckled.

"Mom?"

"Were you expecting someone else?" his mother asked.

"Jon and Teresa," he said.

"We haven't heard from them either. Their busy getting everything done, I'm sure. John did say it may take them longer than expected," Kate said. "Anyway, I am just calling to remind you that your father and I will be picking Hope up tomorrow."

"Tomorrow? What time?"

"Around ten," Kate answered. "We're meeting Robert and Lillian at the mall. Shopping should take hours, plus lunch."

"Sounds good, Mom. See you tomorrow."

When he hung up the phone, he asked, "Hope, why was your grandmother reminding me that you have a shopping trip with them tomorrow?"

"I was supposed to tell you that they called," she said.

"I see. Anything else you were supposed to tell me?" he asked her.

She shook her head.

The four of them entered the kitchen to find dinner waiting for them. As they ate, Berty and Silvia shared their stories.

"So, what's going to happen to the Scepter?" Hope asked.

"We don't know," answered Berty.

Obie watched the kitchen clean while Hope only had eyes for her uncle. After a moment of silence, Hope asked, "Do you think they are still looking for me in the Sages' Grove?"

"It's possible," he replied. Fear shimmered in her brown eyes. "I'll tell you what. We will all go back to the Empire Tree tonight. In the morning, you and I will bring Freesia and Julie back here. You can practice your archery in the backyard before your grandparents come. Okay?"

"Okay." Relief carried in her voice.

Freesia waited in Hope's chambers for them to return. Berty said goodnight to his niece. He and Silvia took the bridge to their chambers as Obie ran into the trunk.

"Would you come to the house with me tomorrow?" he asked Silvia as they walked onto his platform. "After the meeting. Meet my parents?"

A wide smile spread across her face. "I'd be so honored."

He walked her to her chambers. Being with her in the moonless summer night, he could not make his feet move. His one hand found her waist. The other caressed her soft cheek. She closed her eyes as he inched closer. His lips tenderly found hers. Seconds, minutes, hours could have passed, and he would not have noticed.

Inhaling, they put air between their faces. They laughed a little. When his hands slid to hold hers, his thumbs rubbed the backs of her hands.

He did not want to let her go, not after being apart for so long. "We'll leave straight from the meeting," he told her.

Giving him a nod, she said, "Goodnight, Berty."

He smiled. "Goodnight, Silvia." Her hands slipped out of his. He watched her enter her chambers, then he left her platform.

Lying in bed, his smile did not fade. The Scepter could stay black forever. With Silvia by his side, all was right with the world.

In the morning, he greeted Silvia with a quick kiss. Smiling, she asked, "Breakfast at the Roundtable?"

"Yes." Reaching Hope's platform, he noticed Julie approach. "I'll be there soon," he said. Silvia touched his arm, then left him waiting for Julie.

"Thank you for doing this," he told Julie.

"My Lord, it is an honor," she said.

They entered Hope's chambers to find Hope waiting with her bow in hand. "Are we ready?" Berty asked.

"Can I show Grandma and Grandpa my bow?" Hope asked in return.

"If you're good," he said. "Take Julie through the portal."

"Okay," Hope squealed. Tugging Julie's hand, she said, "Come on, Julie."

Berty peeked inside his dual pocket watch. It told him that it was five in the morning on the other side of the portal. He stepped through the tapestry after Freesia.

The house's gas lights wooshed to life. Birds' morning songs played just outside the open windows. The sun would soon rise.

He gave them a quick tour of the house, ending in the kitchen. Leaving Freesia and Hope to choose breakfast, he took Julie to the garage. She marveled at the old tools and weaponry. "You can set up targets anywhere in the backyard," he said.

Opening the back door to the house, the smoky aroma of bacon cooking hit his nostrils. "I'll be back before your grandparents arrive," he said to Hope. "Start getting ready about nine. Wear clothes from this side. See you soon and remember my rules."

Leaving them to eat breakfast, he returned to the Roundtable

Room. Tenders had covered the reflective tabletop with food. Everyone except Goscislaw and Sean were in the room, eating and chatting. Upon seeing Berty, they stood quietly. He motioned for them to sit. He sat in his chair next to Silvia, then took some food for himself.

Sean wandered into the room. His gray eyes scanned the table. Berty indicated that he sit in one of the two empty chairs. Sean lowered onto one chair as if it were made of nails.

"Sorry for keeping you waiting," growled Goscislaw as he entered. He sat in the last seat.

Magically, the door closed. A hush fell onto the table. "We all know the problem at hand," said Berty. "In order to restore the Scepter, Sean must find the Staff of Lightning. Have you made any progress, Sean?"

"No, my Lord," Sean replied. His head stayed low.

"Then, we must prepare for the inevitable," he said. "When the magic stops flowing through the Scepter, creatures from our past will roam freely. Sageans will be in danger of more than just bands of thieves."

"The anti-Imperialists have completely taken over Fairyland," said Lida. "Who is next?"

He stared into Lida's green eyes. "The Sages' Grove."

"Then we must centralize. Bring fighters and resources from the South here," said Elrick.

"No," said Berty. "They will not advance on us, not yet. The power of the Scepter is still too strong. Plus, we have the magic of the trees protecting us. That gives us time to learn about the creatures and build outposts to help protect the people."

"We don't have enough men," said Alvar. "We would spread ourselves too thinly."

"Leave the construction to the Dwarves," growled Goscislaw. "We will start with the outpost near Boudon."

"Good. Colvin and Alvar will coordinate outpost construction," said Berty. "Alfred and Delyth will study magical creatures. Elrick and Lida are Empire liaisons. Your jobs will be to inform communities of possible creatures and attacks. I believe it to be wise to not mention the state of the Scepter. Is there anything else?"

"Yes, my Lord," said Alvar. ""I would like permission to recruit young Oberon as the Empire Guard's first Warlock."

Berty's focus changed from Alvar to Declan. "I see no problem in having those who can use magic in the Empire Guard. However, Oberon is Declan's charge," he said.

Declan hesitated, then said, "I promised to teach him the art of healing."

"He can still learn that as well," said Alvar.

"You may speak with him. He will decide his fate," said Declan.

Glancing around the table, Berty said, "Do what you need. Sean, keep searching. Do not give up, even after the Hallows."

Sean bowed his head.

With nothing more to be said, Berty rose. He returned with Silvia to Hope's chambers.

"You run a good Roundtable," she said, taking his hand.

"Thanks." He pulled her through the tapestry.

Placing her hand on a crystal doorknob, she said, "I'm going to find my old clothes. Martin put them in the attic for me."

He watched the hem of her pale blue gown disappear up the back stairs. Little feet clomped up the main steps.

"Softer," said Julie. "If you were hunting, the animal would hear you coming. It would run and you'd have no dinner."

"But I'm inside the house," Hope argued. "There aren't any animals here."

"No," said Julie, reaching the hall. "Practice everywhere

there aren't animals, so when there are, you'll be successful." Seeing Berty, she smiled, then bowed her head.

Hope ran down the hall towards Berty on her tiptoes. "How was that?" she asked.

Laughing, Julie said, "Better."

"I had a great practice, Uncle Berty," said Hope. "We left out a target so I can show Grandma and Grandpa."

"Great," said Berty. He noticed Freesia by the top of the stairs. "Hurry back. You want to be ready for when they get here."

After Hope took Julie through the portal, Berty showed Freesia where Hope kept her clothes. "She never unpacked, so I'm sure everything is really wrinkled," he told the Fairy.

"Don't worry," Freesia assured.

Hope passed Berty in the hall on the way to her room. Entering his, he changed into modern clothes. He walked out into the hall to find Silvia emerging from the back staircase. She glowed in her flowery outfit.

"Silvia!" said Hope. Her once neat curls bounced as she ran to hug her.

They walked down the steps. Hope babbled to Silvia who listened intently. He walked behind them, noticing that Silvia had legs. The backs of her knees mesmerized him until the doorbell rang.

A metal pineapple doorstop held the stained glass door open. His parents stood on his porch. "Come in," he told them.

The wooden screen door slapped its doorframe behind his parents. He allowed Hope to hug her grandparents before greeting them with a hug of his own.

His mother's brown eyes found Silvia standing at the base of the stairs. "Mom, Dad," said Berty. "I would like you to meet Silvia."

When Silvia approached, Kate extended her hand. "So nice to finally meet you, Silvia." They shook hands warmly.

"It's nice to meet you, too, Mrs. Chase," said Silvia. Shaking his father's hand, she said, "Mister Chase."

"Are you finished with your teaching?" Kate asked.

"I am."

"What is next?" Kate inquired further.

"I am not sure. All I know is that it feels good to be home," answered Silvia.

Kate smiled. Glancing from Silvia to Berty, she gave her son a look that he did not understand. A tug on his mother's hand saved him.

"Grandma, Grandpa, I wanna show you," said Hope, bursting with excitement. "Follow me." She ran through the swinging kitchen door.

Chuckling, George said, "We better hurry or we'll miss out."

Berty ushered his parents through the kitchen out onto the back porch. Hope was already waiting in the grass with her quiver slung on her back. "Can you see me?" Hope asked.

They leaned against the white wooden rail. "We can see," said George.

Picking up her bow, Hope took her stance. Berty thought he heard his mother hold her breath. Gracefully, Hope chose an arrow from her quiver. After setting it, she let it fly. The arrow hit the center of the target. She shot two more times before running onto the porch, bow in hand.

Looking at her stunned grandparents, her excitement melted.

"You're a natural, Hope," George said. "I wonder where you get all your talent."

Hope smiled.

"Collect your arrows, then put it away," said Berty. "I'll take care of the target."

Jumping off the porch, she ran through the backyard.

"Don't you think she's a little young?" said Kate.

Berty kept his mouth shut as Hope returned.

"I'll help you put it away," said George. "Where does it go?" He entered the house with his granddaughter.

Hope's voice carried through the screens. "In my room."

Kate's eyebrows raised. "Her room? A weapon? Berty, what's wrong with you?"

"Jon and Teresa didn't tell you."

"How long have they known?" Kate asked.

"Since the beginning," said Berty.

With a sigh, Kate frowned.

"Archery teaches discipline, balance and hand-eye coordination," Silvia interjected. "I started fencing at the age of four. My parents said it taught grace and focus and developed the mind."

Kate's face softened. Nodding, she said, "It seems to make her happy."

"Very," Berty answered.

They returned to the foyer where George and Hope waited.

"Ready for some back-to-school shopping?" Kate asked Hope.

"Do I have to go back to school?" groaned Hope.

"Don't be silly," said Kate. "You want to be ready when your mother and father come back from Africa."

A smile returned to Hope's face. "When are they coming home?"

"Soon," answered George.

"Bye, Uncle Berty! Bye, Silvia!" Hope waved.

Berty and Silvia watched Hope leave with his parents from the front porch. "Guess I should put that target away," he said.

"Already done," said Silvia. "I was wondering if the house had any information about the Sages or whatever."

He followed Silvia up the back stairs until they ended in a hall of sorts. It was more of a round room with many doors. "At one time, the house had Tenders. They would live up here," she explained. "Now, it is just bedrooms for Fairy Godmothers and storage."

They entered a room full of trunks and cabinets. Pouring over forgotten items, Berty asked, "For what are we looking?"

"Scrolls or books taken from the tree," Silvia suggested. "Or maybe transcriptions."

Trunks and cabinets were neatly organized without a speck of dust. No cobwebs lurked in the corners or above their heads. "Where does the house get its magic?" he asked.

Silvia sat on the floor in front of a trunk. With her hands on its lid, she said, "I don't know. If it were tied to the Scepter, wouldn't it be black, too?" Opening the trunk, she said, "Berty, come here."

Approaching Silvia, he saw leather bindings filling the trunk. She plucked one from the top. Cracking a spine, she perused a few pages. After choosing a book for himself, he sat down next to her.

"The Empire Tree used to have a Sage's Circle where each Sage had chambers," Silvia recited from the pages. "The Sorcery Room was the Sage's study. The Watching Rooms housed the Library. The Sages would have regular meetings once a decade. At the last meeting, the Seven High Sages decided to hide their identities and scatter."

"Why?" asked Berty.

Her eyes scanned the pages. "It seems that they were in constant danger of being forced to do others' bidding. Kidnappings and other atrocities would happen to either them or their families. They deposited the crystals into the pillars of the Scepter Room.

"The Empress, the one writing this, moved the Library and

other things to the Vaults. She closed the door, making everything private."

As she skimmed more of the diary, he opened the leather bound book in his hands. He began to read. "Did you know that the Goblins used to be the only Tenders the Empire Tree had?" he asked.

"No."

"Once the Sage's Circle began disappearing from the branches, the Goblins would no longer provide Tenders. They complained about the balance being off," he said. "To still serve the Empire, they became in charge of all that is hidden. The Goblins refused Advisory Council positions, but agreed to come when summoned." He skimmed the rest as she took another from the trunk.

"It's empty," she said, leafing through an identical journal. Grabbing one more, she did the same thing. "This one is, too."

"Are you sure?" asked Berty. "Perhaps it's hidden."

She clasped the book in her hands. Her eyes unfocused. Blinking, she opened the journal. Flipping through the pages, she said, "Nothing. Why have a trunk full of nothing?"

He turned to the last page of the journal in his hands. "I think I know. She writes, 'Whoever finds these and cannot read them, keep them for the one who can.'" After closing the book, he looked at Silvia.

"You try," she said, placing the book in his hands.

Holding the book in both hands, he thought, *reveal your words to me.* He opened the book. Blank pages stared up at him.

"Oh well," she said. Silvia carefully placed the books back in the trunk. "The house does hold answers. Just not for us right now."

Closing the lid, she stayed on the floor. "Hope's a talented archer," she said. "Declan has done a good job teaching her."

208

She smiled. "Estelle has taken to tree life well."

"She has."

"I'm not sure how I found her exactly. I just followed my feet," she said. "It's funny how things work." Placing a hand on his, she continued, "Your mom will accept the bow by the time they return."

He laughed. "I hope so. Hope will never give it up."

After lunch, they sat on the wooden swing hiding in the corner of the front porch. Silvia rested her head on his shoulder while he placed his arm around her. They talked about their childhoods. Both Silvia and her brother, Martin, each had their own Fairy Godmother. They both attended the same private school.

"I also had private tutors and had to read everything my mother gave me," she said. "I needed to learn about the Empire and how to be Empress. After Martin married Martha, the love of his life, he stayed on this side of the portal. For the most part, I stayed on the other. Each time I crossed the portal, Martin had aged years while I did not."

His parents' burgundy sedan pulled into the driveway. Berty and Silvia sat up on the swing. While Hope and her grandparents dove into the trunk, they approached the car. "Need some help?" he asked.

"Sure," said George. He passed a couple of shopping bags to his son. Silvia took a couple as well.

"I got a new book bag," Hope informed him. "It's maroon to match my cloak."

"Can't wait to see it," said Berty. They brought all the new purchases to Hope's bedroom.

After Hope showed off her new backpack, Kate said, "Mommy and Daddy will be home in a couple of days. Keep everything in the bags until you get home."

"Lillian and Robert are getting your brother's house ready for them," said George. "We'll be joining them later after we take you kids out to dinner."

"Can I wear my cloak?" Hope asked.

"Not to go to the restaurant. You'll get it dirty," Kate replied.

Hope sat between Silvia and Berty in the backseat of his parents' car. The city passed by the window out of which Silvia stared.

"Is everything okay, Silvia?" Kate asked from the front seat.

She turned her head, then smiled. "Yes. I'm just... Things change when you're away."

He wondered when Silvia had been outside her house last. Inside the dark restaurant's waiting area, Silvia glanced at all the Western paraphernalia plastered on the walls. They did not wait long before the hostess sat them in a large, dark, wooden booth.

Right after ordering, Kate began her questioning. "How did you two meet?"

"The editor," said Berty.

"I'm related," Silvia interjected.

"Did you grow up here, Silvia?"

"Between here and there," she answered.

"Where Berty goes for his story?" George asked.

"Yes. I went to school here, but spent most of my time there."

The questions paused when their food arrived. Between bites, Kate asked about Estelle, although she did not know her name.

"Estelle blossomed once she was out of her abusive father's reach," explained Silvia. "With her improved social skills, she secured a career in astronomy."

Kate smiled warmly. "You must be so proud."

210

"It makes me happy to know that she has found her place," said Silvia.

The subject changed often throughout dinner. After returning to the house, Berty's parents got out of the car to say goodbye. Both Kate and George hugged Silvia.

"I hope we will get to see you again soon," Kate told her. Hugging her son, she said, "Jon and Teresa will be stopping here first from the airport. Their plane touches down in the morning some time."

"Two days. We'll be waiting for them," said Berty.

The three of them waved from the porch until the burgundy car drove out of sight. Before crossing through the portal, Berty and Silvia reassured Hope that she would be safe inside the Sages' Grove.

Freesia waited for Hope in her chambers. "Goodnight, Hope," said Berty with a hug. "We'll walk with you to breakfast."

"I'd like to continue her lessons in the ancient tongue since Alfred cannot," Silvia said while they crossed the bridge.

"She'll be thrilled," said Berty.

They stopped on his platform. "What happens when her parents return?" Silvia asked.

"What do you mean?"

"Will she only be here summers and some weekends?" she asked him. "Will her Fairy Godmother stay here until she returns? Not that she can return to the Guild."

He looked into her brown eyes. "I don't know. I guess I haven't thought that far ahead. Hope will return here," he said. "Do you think Jon and Teresa should be told?"

Her fingers massaged his temple, then followed his jaw line to his chin. "Probably someday. You'll have to figure out how and when." She kissed his cheek. "See you in the morning."

He watched her cross the bridge to her chambers. When she disappeared from view, he pushed aside all thoughts in exchange for a good night's sleep.

Walking with Silvia through the tree felt natural to him. Her dresses were no longer trimmed in gold, but that did not matter. The best part was greeting her with a hug and a kiss in the morning.

Hope practiced skipping to breakfast without making a sound. After eating, Silvia and Berty accompanied Hope and Declan across the bridges spanning over the Sages' Grove to the practice area. When archery finished, Hope watched Obie's hunting lessons with Ojore.

"He wants to join the Empire Guard," Declan told Berty. "I have two years to immerse him in the art of healing before he becomes a full recruit."

"She leaves the day after tomorrow," said Berty.

"Obie is going to miss her. They have become good friends," said Declan.

Chapter Sixteen
Changes

The men stood shoulder to shoulder watching their charges. Hope's laugh bounced off of every surface. Ojore gave her a spear, which she threw like a javelin. Watching her and Obie throw reminded him of his high school track and field days. She left the Outlander and his pupil to join Silvia and him.

"That was fun," said Hope. She led Berty and Silvia across the bridges into the Empire Tree.

Hope and Silvia entered Hope's chambers while Berty continued on to his own. Inside his study, he extracted his trusty notebook. He filled its pages with more of *the Adventures of Leigh and Marcus*.

Retrieving him for lunch, Hope said, "Silvia told me what a great archer I was and how I learned so much from Alfred." Her eyes sparkled. Silvia and Freesia met them on Hope's platform.

After they ate, Freesia took Hope outside to play with her friends. Berty gave Silvia his arm as they strode away from the Reception Room.

"Could you open the Library Vault for me?" she asked. "It is only a matter of time before Alfred and Delyth exhaust their resources. Declan is doing research at the Watchers' Guild. All those books that Empress hid should tell us something."

"Sure." Berty wanted to spend time with Silvia. He also wanted to finish writing, so he could give a good chunk to Martin. "I'll be right out," he told her as they stopped in front of his chambers.

Grabbing his notebook and pen, he rushed back to Silvia's side. "After Hope goes home, I was going to bring this to Martin," he explained. "Would you like to come?"

She squeezed Berty's arm. "Go to the newspaper to see my brother?" Elation took over her face. "That sounds fun. He'll be so surprised." She surprised him with a lingering kiss. "Thank you."

With a smile, he opened the trapdoor. In the vault, Silvia chose a book while Berty sat at the table, writing.

"Hungry?" Silvia asked after a few hours.

He looked up to see piles of books occupying the table. "Probably should eat. Those are a lot of books."

"The ones I have yet to read," she said.

Gathering his notebook, he stood. "I'll leave this open for you."

They returned to the branches, then headed to dinner. "Did you find anything?" he asked.

"Interesting, just not useful." When they entered the Reception Room, she eyed Hope and Obie sitting next to each other. "I've been reading a lot of the stories I learned as a child. The differences are slight, but noticeable."

While they ate, Declan entered the room from the stairs below. He looked weary. Plopping onto a chair across from Berty, he mindlessly scooped food onto his plate.

"You look beat," Delyth said.

"Who knew reading could be so exhausting?" said Declan.

Delyth laughed.

"Spiral staircases should never be that long," he said, spearing a piece of meat. "You're fine going down, but coming back up," he shook his head.

No one spoke about what they read. Subjects were kept light. Elrick pined for Fairyland's late summer flowers. Although Berty knew Elrick missed more than just vegetation, he also knew that the King would not mention his son. Silvia retired to her study after dinner to give Berty time with his niece.

Sitting at her table, Hope painted. She looked up from her artwork. "I'm making a welcome home present for Mommy and Daddy," she told him.

He smiled.

"My Lord, may I have word?" Freesia asked quietly.

"Of course."

"When your niece returns to her parents' care, I was to fly to the Godmother Guild to wait for her return," said Freesia. "However, with the current state of Fairyland, I cannot. I am asking your permission to stay in these chambers. Perhaps while I wait for Hope, I can help Obie with his education."

"Of course you may stay," said Berty. "I am sure Declan would welcome your assistance."

"Thank you, my Lord. Hope will say her farewells tomorrow," Freesia said.

He nodded. Sitting at the table with Hope, he asked, "Whatcha painting?"

"The Empire Tree with all its levels," she answered. "I'm working on the Roundtable now. Then, the Scepter, the mystery floor, and the star place."

"The mystery floor?"

"There's nothing up there, but a hallway."

Laughing, he said, "Off the hallway are the Watching Rooms. I'll show you tomorrow."

"Okay," she said. "I'll finish that floor after."

"Goodnight, Hope." He kissed her on her head. Freesia had her put all her paints away before she was allowed to go to bed.

A whiff of wetness greeted Berty when he stepped outside his chambers in the morning. "Smells like rain," Silvia said with a smile.

"Any progress?" he asked as they strolled to breakfast.

"I am emptying the ocean with a thimble," she answered.

After breakfast, Declan carried a large bag to the practice area. Setting it in front of Hope, he said, "Inside this bag, you'll find everything to make arrows. I'd like for you to make two."

Hope dove into the bag. Watching her carefully, Declan gave no indication if she were constructing the arrows correctly or not. Once she had finished making two, she held them out for Declan's inspection.

Taking one, Declan said, "Let's see how they work." He raised his bow, motioning for her to do the same.

Her handmade arrows touched their bows. Pulling the strings, they released her arrows. Both hit their targets, but hers landed off center.

"Not bad," said Declan said. "You have to make sure that everything is even or it wobbles in the air, making it go off target. I compensated for the wobble."

Hope nodded.

"The important thing is they didn't fall apart," he told her. "We'll focus on arrow making next time." He smiled, then pulled a piece of cloth from a side pocket of his bag. Giving it to Hope, he said, "A cloth target, so can you practice anywhere."

She stared at the wad of beige cloth in her hands. With a glance at Declan, she gave him a hug that knocked him backwards.

"Start your lesson with Miss Hunter," Freesia told Hope. "I will be right up after I speak with His Grace." The Fairy stayed while Hope skipped ahead of Berty and Silvia.

Berty got a lot of writing done before Hope rang his wind

chimes. "It's lunch time, Uncle Berty!" she said, running over to his desk. She looked at his open notebook. "Am I in there?" she asked.

"Of course you are," he answered.

"If Silvia is Leigh and you are Marcus, what name did you give me?"

In his story, fictitious Hope arrived via boat from a faraway land. "Olivia," he told her.

"Ooh," she said with a smile.

Resting his pen on the notebook, he rose from his chair. "Ready?" She took his hand as they walked into the tree.

On the landing just inside the trunk, Berty told Freesia and Silvia, "Go head down. We'll be right there." While the two women descended, he took Hope up the next flight.

When he opened an arched wooden door, he said, "Take a peek. This is where I practice my swordsmanship." She gawked at the weapons on the wall and the dummy heaped on the floor. He closed the door.

Bringing her to another door, he opened it. He ushered her into the curved, nearly empty room.

"What's that?" She pointed to the table holding a miniature Sages' Grove.

He dragged a chair over to the table. Lifting her onto the chair, he asked, "What does it look like?"

"The village!"

He blew into the center of the tree. The village came alive.

"Cool."

"This is very complex magic," he said. "I want you to," he paused. A dripping of dark liquid oozed from the base of the tree. Quickly, he blew into the trunk again. All movement stopped.

"What happened?" Hope asked.

"I don't know." The dark seeped back inside the tree. "I

think this magic hinges on the Scepter. It's not working properly. Keep this room to yourself. Okay?"

"Okay." She stared at him. "Don't worry. It will all work again soon."

"If you say so." He brought her to lunch.

When Freesia took Hope outside to play, Berty accompanied Silvia to the vault.

Sitting at the table, he waited for her to join him. "What's the matter?" she asked.

He told her about the incident in the Watching Room.

"I want to say the Scepter caused it, but I don't think that's the case," she said. "The dark liquid disturbs me." Silvia would not say more.

Berty pushed to get his writing done before dinner. When he finished his story, he asked Silvia, "Ready to eat something?"

She held up her index finger. A couple of moments later, she lifted her head out of the book. "I could really use a break," she said.

Back in her study, she asked, "How did you enter the Sages' study place in the back of the library?"

"Magically announced myself as a Sage," he replied.

At dinner, Hope ate quietly. Her melancholic mood troubled Berty. When she caught him staring, she asked, "Do I have to go back to school?"

"Yes, you do."

She pushed food around with her fork. "I hate school," she muttered.

"I'm sure your mom and dad will let you come back some weekends," he said trying to lift her spirits.

"I know," she said. "I just didn't wanna have to…"

"I have a feeling this year is going to be different," he told her with a little smile.

She sighed, then returned Berty's smile. When she finished eating, she climbed the staircase with Freesia.

He did not know what to do. All the magic in the world would not make her like school or make the children within it not tease her. His heart broke. She wanted to stay as much as she wanted to see her parents. When he finally tore his eyes from the stairs, he noticed Obie's eyes were still glued to them.

Silvia was a wonderful woman. She understood or at least empathized. He liked her suggestion of sparring in the training room.

After changing his clothes, he took his stance. He held his sword while focusing on the dummy on the floor. "Begin," he said. The dummy did not move. "Begin," he commanded. Nothing stirred. "Begin!" he shouted. The dummy remained a lifeless lump.

He screamed in frustration. Disappointed that he did not get a sort of live sparring partner, he turned the crank on the wall. A dummy hanging from the ceiling swung into the center of the room.

Unsatisfactorily, Berty released his frustrations on the defense-less form. After removing his padding, he walked through the tree. As he crossed the bridge, he saw Obie leaving Hope's chambers. "Goodnight, my Lord," the boy said as he passed.

When Berty entered, Hope was coming down the steps. Melancholy had been washed away. "I finished my painting for Mommy and Daddy," she announced. "It has to dry overnight."

He peeked at the colorful two-dimensional Empire Tree diorama. "They are going to love it," he told her.

She smiled. As she pushed an errant brown curl out of her face, Berty noticed something on her thumb.

"What's that?" he asked.

"A ring." Hope held it out for her uncle to see. "Obie made

it." The light wood had reddish and dark wood petal-esque inlays that made it look like a flower. "Declan helped him." Gazing at it, she smiled.

Berty made a mental note to speak with Declan later. "That's nice," he said. "Do you have everything you're bringing with you ready to go?"

"Almost," said Hope. "Can I bring my Fairy Dust?"

Staring at his niece, he did not know how to answer. "I wouldn't show your parents. They won't understand Fairy Dust." He thought that Teresa would make her leave her bow at his house. "Ask Delyth at breakfast if it will even work on the other side of the portal."

"Oh. I didn't think of that. Okay, Uncle Berty, I will." Hugging him, she said goodnight.

Silvia's smile was the sunshine in the morning rain. Warm raindrops pelted his hood while they walked to breakfast.

"Obie gave Hope a wooden ring he made," he mentioned to Silvia. "Should I be concerned?"

Laughing, Silvia replied, "They're kids. And they have become good friends. If it were ten years from now, I'd be concerned that he did not ask you first. It's a lovely token of friendship."

Hope and Obie had been through plenty together. She was not the only one experiencing changes in life. Silvia always gave the proper perspective.

At the breakfast table, Hope laughed. He was going to miss the jovial environment that she brought to the Empire Tree. Fun Uncle Berty who came and went was not going to cut it after her summer with him.

He waited while Hope hugged everyone, saying good-bye. "This was the best summer ever, Uncle Berty," she said as they climbed the stairs.

"I'm glad you could spend it with me," he said, smiling. She latched onto his waist when they entered her leafy green bundle. Silvia and Freesia followed them into her chambers.

"Are you ready?" Berty asked. Hope's curls bounced as she nodded. "Freesia, you could meet her parents. Do you have something that will disguise your folded Fairy wings? Besides your cloak."

"Yes, my Lord."

Both Freesia and Hope hurried upstairs. Giving Silvia a smile, he climbed the steps with her.

Freesia emerged from her room, wearing a soft pink vest over her blouse. Entering Hope's, she said, "I'll carry your bag."

With a bow and quiver attached to her body, Hope walked into the hall with the box Delyth gave her. In her other hand, she carried the painting for her parents. Behind her, Freesia held a small bag.

"After you," Berty said. Hope and her Fairy Godmother stepped into the tapestry. With Silvia's hand in his, they crossed through the portal.

Silvia escaped to the third floor to change while Berty knocked on Hope's open bedroom door. Lightning flashed through the windows. Thunder rumbled shortly after.

"I can't show them in a thunderstorm," said Hope. She sounded disappointed.

"As soon as the rain clears," said Berty. "I'm going to change, then I'll help you bring all your stuff to the foyer."

Freesia kept all of Hope's things organized. Clothes stayed in one area while school supplies were confined to another. When the last of Hope's belongings rested in the foyer, the four of them headed to the kitchen for lunch.

Silvia was instructing the kitchen when the doorbell rang. "Mommy and Daddy!" Hope jumped off the kitchen chair.

Following his niece, he reminded her not to answer the door. Reaching the stained glass front door, he turned its brass handle. Berty came face-to-face with a man who was not his brother.

He quickly studied the man's crisp pinstripe suit and neat, black, tight, curly hair. "Can I help you?" Hope stood behind Berty, holding onto his shirt.

"Mister Hubert Chase?" the man said.

Berty nodded.

"I am Lawrence Trane from Silverman and Trane." He handed Berty his card.

Berty glanced at the business card. "You're a lawyer."

"We represent Chase Technologies as well as Jonathan and Teresa Chase," said Lawrence.

His stomach dropped. Opening his mouth, he could not get it to form words.

"Is there somewhere private we can talk?" Lawrence asked.

"Yes. I'm sorry. Come in." Berty stepped aside so the man could enter. "Hope, go back in the kitchen and stay there."

Berty led Lawrence into the sitting room. "Please, have a seat." He closed the pocket door, then sat across from the stranger in his home.

"Mister Chase, there is no good way to tell you this," Lawrence began. "Your brother and sister-in-law did not make their flight today. It seems as though they are lost in Africa."

"Lost?"

"They never returned from their safari," answered Lawrence.

"What?"

"Mister Silverman is with your parents, George and Kate Chase, and Teresa's parents, Robert and Lillian Regnik. They are meeting with an official from the State Department," Lawrence explained. "They are following all the proper procedures to find Jon and Teresa."

"I see."

"Which leads me to why I am here. Teresa set up a contingency plan." Lawrence opened his briefcase. "In the event they did not return in time, you get legal temporary custody of their daughter, Hope." He placed a stack of papers on the coffee table. "So she can go to school, the doctor, things like that."

Staring at the papers, he rubbed his eyebrow. "School," he swallowed, "of course."

"You also have temporary control of Chase Technologies with your father, George."

"I know nothing about the business," he admitted.

Lawrence continued, "Temporary means six months. After that time, if they are not found, you get full guardianship of your niece. All of their assets would be put in trust for Hope of which you would manage until she turns twenty-one." Berty looked blankly into his dark eyes. "Mister Chase, I need you to sign these papers." He placed the pen on the table.

Picking up the pen, Berty asked, "Can they be found?"

Lawrence's steely exterior softened. "I don't know. Your brother is a good man. I've known him for years. Be assured that we are exploring all avenues open to us."

Nodding, Berty asked, "Where do I sign?" He scribbled his name everywhere Lawrence indicated.

After Berty received his copies, he walked the man to the door. "I hope we don't meet like this again," said Lawrence. "You will know when we know."

Berty shook his hand. Opening the door, he could barely see the tree lined street through the deluge. Thunder cracked as he closed the door.

When he walked into the kitchen, Hope asked, "Will Mommy and Daddy be here soon?" Lightning flashed in the windows.

How could he tell her in the best possible way? "Hope," he

sat down, "Mommy and Daddy won't be back for a while."

"Why not?"

"They are missing, but people are looking for them," he answered. "Until they come home, you'll stay here. And you will go to a new school."

Tears wanted to burst from her eyes at any moment. "How long until they find them?"

"I don't know."

She ran to him. As he comforted her, he did not want to think about the horrors of what might have happened to them. The responsibility he now had weighed heavily on him.

Sitting in the living room with his cell phone, he dialed the number for the local grade school. When a woman answered, he said, "I would like to enroll my niece in second grade. Do I need to come in or can we do this over the phone?"

"We can start it over the phone. All her records can be faxed later. We'll mail you all the necessary forms, if you cannot come in beforehand," the woman answered.

"Great."

"Her name and current address, please."

"Hope Katherine Chase. Seven two seven Oak Street."

"Okay. I need to let you know that we have just merged with another grade school in the district. Class sizes have doubled and we may not have enough materials for all students in all classes," she said. "You still have time to enroll your daughter in a private school."

"Excuse me?" Berty said.

"Oak Street is in a more well-to-do area. If you can afford to send her elsewhere, I would. You do not want to send your daughter here. She will not get what she needs to prepare her for a brighter future. Did you still want to enroll her here?"

Berty could not believe what some school administrator was

telling him. "No," his mouth uttered. When the call ended, he stared at his dark phone, not knowing what to do.

"Berty?" Silvia peeked between the sliding doors. "Are you okay?"

"The school told me not to enroll her there—a public school."

She slipped into the sitting room. "There's a desk in the study in which you can file those," she said as she pointed to the legal papers. "May I borrow your phone?"

He placed it in her hand, then showed her how to make a call. Picking up the papers, he left her on the settee. In the hall, he could hear Hope and Freesia gathering all of Hope's things from the foyer. The wooden rolltop desk knew exactly what Berty needed. A filing drawer opened as he approached.

Returning to the sitting room, he saw Silvia close his phone. "I just spoke with Martin," she said. "He's going to give Hope a recommendation for the Whingham Academy." He sat next to her. "It's a good school. Martin and I went there. His sons went there and his grandson goes there."

"How am I going to afford to send her there?" he asked.

She tucked his phone in his hand, then stood. "Come with me."

He followed her to the back stairs. She led him down into the basement. Gaslight illuminated a packed earth floor and massive foundation rock. They walked into a back room.

"Touch the wall," she instructed.

When he touched the wall, a rock section moved away. Metal boxes lined a secret room.

"There should be one labeled education fund," she said.

Finding it, he swung open the metal door. A drawer full of paper bills slid towards him. He closed the drawer, then he left the security deposit box vault. "Where did that come from?" he

225

asked.

"Probably best if you don't think about these things," she replied.

Taking Silvia's advice, he followed her up the stairs. They started to help Hope with her bags when his cell phone rang.

"May I speak with Mister Chase?" said the woman caller.

"This is he."

"Mister Chase, I am Miriam calling from the Whingham Academy. Your child, Hope, has gotten a recommendation from a Mister Martin Hunter. Since school will be starting in a few days, we need to set up an all-day appointment as soon as possible. Does tomorrow work?" she said.

"Yes, that will be fine."

"Great. We will expect you and Hope at nine. Have a good day."

When he hung up, he took the remaining few bags back to Hope's bedroom. Freesia organized all of Hope's things in the closets and drawers. Watching Freesia hang clothes according to color, he realized that they would have to retrieve items from Jon and Teresa's house in order for her to go to school. Not tonight, he thought.

"Berty," Silvia called softly from the hall. He met her in the wood paneled hallway. "I can show Freesia the ins and outs of the house, if you like. She's going to have to stay here with Hope while you travel between here and there."

Nodding, he said, "Thank you."

He walked into Hope's room. Everything had been put in its proper place. "Freesia, why don't you take the time to get your things from the Empire Tree. Hope is going to need you here."

She smiled, then gave Berty a nod.

When she left, Berty sat on the spare bed. "We have an appointment with a new school tomorrow," he told Hope.

"I don't have to go back to my old school?" she asked.

"Nope." He watched her smile. "Let's see if there are any games in the study."

After finding a deck of cards, Hope sprawled out on the rug. The rain had finally ended when Silvia and Freesia entered the study. "Is everything suitable?" Berty asked.

"Very, my Lord, thank you," said Freesia.

Berty beckoned Freesia into the hall. "On this side of the portal, it is best to call me or to refer to me as Mister Chase."

"Like on the telephone."

"Yes. I do not wish to advertise life on the other side." Behind her brown eyes, she understood. "On this side, you would be known as Hope's nanny."

The ringing doorbell ended their conversation. Freesia entered the study while Berty answered the door. His parents and Teresa's parents stood on his front porch. Worry replaced their usual pleasantness.

"Come in," was all that Berty could say.

"How's Hope?" Lillian asked as soon as she crossed the threshold.

"We had a good hug," Berty said. "She's in the study." He led them down the hall.

"We just came from our meeting," said George.

"I don't know who annoys me more, lawyers or government officials," Robert muttered. "Maybe it's a tie. They're both—"

"Robert!" Lillian scolded.

Berty stopped in the doorway to the study. "Did it not go well?" he asked.

The women entered the room. "Nana! Grandma!" Hope said.

"Things aren't as quick as we'd like them to be," said George.

Grumbling, Robert added, "Red tape and protocols. I don't

care about any of that. I just want the kids."

The men followed their wives into the room. After lots of hugging, Hope introduced her grandparents to Freesia. Kate introduced Silvia to Robert and Lillian.

A cell phone began to ring. "That's me," said Robert. Pulling a phone from his pocket, he said, "It's Matt. Lily?"

"You tell him," Lillian said.

"Matt," said Robert while he walked out of the room. Lillian slowly fell into a chair.

Standing next to Berty, Silvia said, "Let me do dinner. You spend time with your family."

He squeezed her hand. "Thank you." She and Freesia left the room.

Looking at her son, Kate smiled. He knew she caught their exchange. "She's a lovely woman," Kate said. "She's good for you."

Feeling pleased, Berty answered, "She is." When Robert entered, he continued, "Stay for dinner."

"Matt's going to put in for his vacation time," said Robert. "He'll be home soon."

Berty saw frustration on both sets of parents' faces. "Hope, Silvia and Freesia could use some help," he said.

"Okay," said Hope before running out of the room.

"So? What happened?" asked Berty.

"First, we had to meet with the lawyers. Sign papers and all that," George said.

"Then, we had to wait for the State Department," Lillian added.

"We had to give them their itinerary, passport information, cell phone numbers, and information on the company," said Kate.

"And do you know what they said?" said Robert. "'We'll look into it.' They couldn't give us an idea of how long it would take. It didn't even sound like they'd get to it right away." He shook his head in disgust.

"There's nothing more we can do," George said. "We can't even hire private investigators because it could compromise whatever the government is going to do."

"'This is a volatile situation and must be handled delicately,'" Robert said in a high voice as if he were imitating someone. "What a waste." He walked out of the room.

Lillian stared at the doorway. "Perhaps Silvia needs a hand setting the table or something," said Kate. Rising from her chair, Lillian followed Kate out of the room.

His father placed a hand on his shoulder. "We'll get them back," George said. "Do you need any help with Hope?"

"Freesia is staying here, so I should be okay."

"We're only a phone call away if you need us."

"Thanks, Dad."

Lillian poked her head into the room. "Dinner is ready. Have you seen Rob?" she asked.

"He didn't come back here," said George.

"I'm sure he didn't go far," Lillian said, then walked away.

Berty and his father entered the dining room through the beveled glass pocket doors. The table was set simply. The plain stoneware plates accompanied the white tablecloth and matching cloth napkins. His mother and Silvia sat a big bowl of spaghetti, a salad and cut bread on the table.

Robert entered the room with his wife. She sat him in a chair, then poured iced tea in glasses.

A hand touched Berty's arm. "Berty, sit down," his mother said. Her brown eyes told him that all would be all right, just like they would when he was a child. However, he could see fear and uncertainty dwelling in her pools of brown.

The only chair available was at the head of the table. When

he sat, he saw Silvia at the other end. Food passed from hands to hands. He had never remembered sitting at the head of the table before. Dining room dinners were always at someone else's house.

Robert did not contribute to the conversation during dinner. His spaghetti suffered from excess twirling. Freesia would not eat until others had begun to eat. Berty noticed her watching how everyone ate. Spaghetti was not a common dish in the Land of Sages.

After dinner, Robert found scotch in the liquor cabinet. Berty poured cordials for everyone else. "We need to discuss the business," said George.

Feeling like a deer in headlights, Berty sat with his small glass of dark amber liqueur.

"I know you don't know much about the business," said George. "Other people run the day-to-day, but you should make an appearance at the office, so people know a Chase is still at the helm."

"Dad, I'm not... Everyone will know that I don't have a clue," he protested.

"Exactly."

Berty slowly placed his glass on the table. "Are you saying what I think you're saying?"

"There is a possibility that someone inside the company had a hand in their disappearance," said George.

Kate downed her drink.

"I'll go in to make sure everything hasn't exploded into chaos until you get Hope situated," said George.

He nodded, then took a healthy sip of his drink. The warm alcohol burned all the way down his throat. He was not sure how he was supposed to root out the traitor in a company about which he knew nothing, even if it was his family's.

Chapter Seventeen
Atrophy

His and Teresa's parents left after tucking Hope into bed. When the door closed, Silvia asked, "How are you doing?"

"None of it seems real right now," he answered. "I didn't get a chance to ask earlier. How was talking with Martin?"

"He was so surprised that I called. He can't wait to see me," Silvia said. She smiled at the prospect. "I've moved some of my things into one of the bedrooms."

They climbed the stairs. "I've been thinking," she said when they reached the top. Entering Berty's bedroom, they sat in the wing chairs near the fireplace. "We should destroy the miniature."

"In the Watching Room? Why? How?"

"I do not believe that it was created for a pure purpose," she said. "The Scepter, I believe, contained any malice or impurity within the miniature. Now that its magic is waning, using the miniature could spread," she paused, "bad things." She stared into the dormant fireplace. "I don't know how to destroy it. Perhaps until we do, we hide it in the vault." Her eyes found his.

"Do you think it would fit down the trapdoor?" he asked.

"Probably not. We'd have to take it the normal way."

He nodded in agreement.

"Nighttime, when there aren't as many people walking through the tree. We'll do it after Hope's meeting," she said, then left him sitting in the chair.

Wondering what else would need to change inside the Empire Tree, he readied for bed. The cool night breeze made him fall asleep quickly.

The four of them ate breakfast in the kitchen. Berty told Freesia that they would be back later. She was free to go through the portal if she chose.

Berty plugged in his phone when he got into his car. After making sure Hope wore her seatbelt, he pulled out of the driveway.

"Once I finished school, I rarely left the house," Silvia mentioned. "It's amazing how so much has changed."

A fifteen minute drive brought them to the Whingham Academy. The front of the school resembled a grand Federal style castle. After parking in visitors' parking, the three of them walked under the portico to the massive solid wood doors.

Inside, rich wood paneled walls dampened the bright summer sunlight. Red carpet cushioned their feet. A woman sat at a large, wooden desk that faced the door. "Can I help you?" she asked.

"I have an appointment," he said.

She smiled. "Chase?"

He nodded.

"First door on your right."

"Thank you."

"I'll wait here," Silvia said.

He handed her his phone. "In case my parents call."

Nodding, she sat on the padded bench that lined the wall. He and Hope found the door. The plaque said, "Lower School Director." Just beyond the door, a woman greeted them.

"I am Berty Chase. This is Hope Chase."

"Go ahead in. Ms. Stapleton is waiting for you."

On the next door, the plaque read, "Jane Stapleton, Director."

Sitting behind the desk was a woman with perfect posture. "Mister Chase, thank you for coming today. My name is Jane Stapleton. Please, have a seat." Berty sat in one of the not too comfortable chairs across from Jane. When a woman knocked on the door, Jane said, "This is Miss Napp. She will be conducting Hope's placement testing."

Miss Napp smiled at Hope. "We are going into a classroom to have a chat," she said. Hope left the room with her.

"I need to ask you a few questions, if you do not mind," Jane said.

"Not at all."

"Did you just move to the area?" she asked.

Berty smiled. "Hope is my niece. She spent the summer with me while her parents were on a business trip. Yesterday, they were supposed to come home. Instead, I signed guardianship papers." Jane gasped softly. "Officially, they are missing. You can understand that I want the best for my niece. I know that this is probably a unique situation."

"Do not worry. We deal with all sorts of parental situations here. You can be assured that our faculty will be sensitive to her needs. Tell me, what are her interests and hobbies?"

"Hope likes to learn. Over the summer, she has taken up archery and horseback riding," he answered. The interview continued about her previous school and her personality. He filled out forms for enrollment. Afterwards, Jane took him on a tour of the school.

"The school is K through twelve, divided into Lower and Upper Schools," Jane explained. "On our over one hundred acres, we have stables where she can find a horse to ride. We also have an archery club as well as fencing, lacrosse, field hockey, and crew, to name a few. Beneath the gym is an indoor pool where we teach swimming. In the greenhouses, children get their first taste of botany. Our curriculum is different from most schools. We believe in a well-rounded education. Children will be exposed to as much as possible. That way, they can make informed decisions about their futures."

The tour ended back at her office. "Everything you need will be mailed to you soon," Jane said. "We look forward to having Hope with us. Miriam will assist you with uniform information and other items."

While Jane walked into her office, Miriam handed Berty a piece of paper. "This is the dress code," she said. "Below, you'll see the stores that carry our uniforms. She'll wear a jumper through sixth grade. After that, girls wear kilts and blazers." She gave him a second piece of paper that listed the school supplies she needed.

Hope entered with Ms. Napp. "She's all done."

"We are as well," said Miriam. "You will need to go to the business office in the center hall about tuition."

Leaving Hope with Silvia, Berty received the tuition bill from the business office. He was surprised that they took cash—no questions asked. As they walked to the car, he wondered who else sent their kids there.

Berty drove to the closest store that sold uniforms. They bought two plaid jumpers, a bunch of matching shirts and a pair of school approved shoes. Hope was so excited.

On the drive home, Hope's smile gradually faded. Berty and Silvia exchanged glances. There was nothing they could do. They tried to have light conversation at dinner. Finally, Hope said, "What does impede mean?"

"To stop," answered Berty.

"Oh." Disappointment filled her small voice.

"What's wrong?" asked Silvia.

"The ocean impedes the trees' communication, so they can't tell me where Mommy and Daddy are," Hope replied.

Silvia's eyes glistened. Placing an arm around her, she said, "Don't worry, Hope. They will be found."

Hope's head rested on Silvia. Perhaps Berty could do something after all. Closing his eyes, he focused on his brother.

Brown muslin shrouded anything beyond the back of a cargo truck. Jon and Teresa sat next to each other. Their backs rested against the side of the crate. Colored cloth covered the faces of men, who kept large guns as companions. A couple of teenage girls were also being jostled in the back of the truck. Tears streaked down the younger one's face while the other sat like a regal warrior, paused between battles.

The passengers stopped bumping into each other, but the engine still hummed. Men's voices conversed in a foreign tongue. Jon tried to adjust his glasses. The bent wire frames caused his cracked lenses to sit askew on his face. Teresa squeezed his hand as the truck began moving again.

Opening his eyes, Berty looked at Hope who still attached herself to Silvia. "They're in transit in the back of a covered truck."

Hope's brown eyes widened. "You saw Mommy and Daddy?" She lifted her head.

"Yes. I know they are all right, but not where they are."

Smiling, Hope said, "Thanks, Uncle Berty." She ran out of the kitchen with Freesia on her heels.

"What is it?" Silvia asked.

"I'm not sure if they're being protected or held captive," he told her.

With a wave of her hand, she cleaned the table. "You'll know in time," she said.

He held her hand across the table. Her mere presence gave him strength. He needed strength to believe that his brother and sister-in-law would be found.

Silvia spoke with Freesia as Berty tucked Hope into bed. Once Hope had fallen asleep, Berty and Silvia donned their cloaks, then slipped through the portal.

They crossed into the trunk of the Empire Tree in the still night. After climbing the central steps, they entered the Watching Room. Silvia covered the miniature of the Sages' Grove with a cloth. Taking hold of either side, they lifted. It tilted towards her.

"It's too heavy," said Silvia.

"Why don't we use magic?" said Berty.

"Too dangerous. I don't want to take a chance that anything could escape," Silvia said.

Understanding, Berty said, "I'll get help."

Quietly, Berty ran down the stairs, then onto Council Circle. When he found the bundle of green branches he wanted, he rang the wind chimes.

"Come in," said Declan's voice.

Berty entered to find Declan seated at his table with an open book. Looking up, Declan said, "I smuggled a couple of books out of the Watchers' Guild."

"Can I tear you away for a little while?" Berty asked.

"My eyes could use the break," Declan answered. "Everything all right?" He rose out of his seat.

"We're moving something." On the way to the Watching Room, he informed Declan about the situation with his brother.

"Do you suspect Leif had anything to do with their disappearance?"

He had not thought about that. Could Leif have the resources to wreak havoc on both sides of the portal? He wanted to think that the answer was no, but his mind would not allow it. Fortunately, concentrating on not dropping the miniature pushed every other thought out of his head.

Declan carried without question. He helped Berty while Silvia guided. After reaching the Reception Room, it rested on the table as the men caught their breath.

The steps to the Receiving Room were narrower. One had to descend backwards. Silvia told Declan when to step down. In the magical elevator, Silvia helped to hold the large tabletop Sages' Grove.

Choosing a large mine cart, they placed it on the middle bench with the edges resting on their knees. When they reached the vaults, Silvia said, "I can't open it."

As she held the one corner, Berty freed a hand to touch the Sages' Seal. The three of them entered the antechamber.

Finagling, Berty touched the picture of the trunk. He and Declan placed it on top of an empty pedestal.

"Magical item storage," remarked Declan, looking around.

"More like the Island of Misfit Toys," Berty muttered. Both Silvia and Declan gave him a strange look.

"It would be nice to know why these things are down here," said Silvia. She magically crafted a plaque that said, "Sages' Grove model. Do not use. Destroy."

They returned to the tree using the ladder leading to Silvia's study. As they walked to Hope's chambers, Berty said, "Thanks, Declan. How is everything going?"

"We're compiling information. I have other Watchers helping me research. The Guild Master is deeply concerned about the use of banished beasts," answered Declan.

"I have to spend some time on the other side," Berty told

him. "You know how to reach me."

Declan nodded. "If you need any help," he said.

Berty and Silvia entered Hope's chambers. "You and Declan have become pretty good friends," Silvia observed.

Before they crossed, he told her Declan's suspicions. Kissing Berty on the cheek, Silvia said, "Goodnight." The gentle touch of her lips lingered on his cheek while he watched her walk down the dark hall to her new room.

After showering in the morning, he peered at his Empire Mark in the mirror. The colored Sages' Seal still graced his left shoulder blade. He tried to see if the fading Scepter would cause it to fade as well. Knocking on his bedroom door curtailed his contortionistic scrutinizing.

He realized that he had yet to dress. "Hold on," he said. He quickly pulled on a pair of shorts, then said, "Come in."

Silvia opened the door. "Oh," she said. Her eyes quickly looked somewhere else.

"I was just checking my Empire Mark," he explained. He slipped a shirt over his bare torso.

Leaning against the edge of the bed, she said, "It took me a while to deal with Leif's betrayal. I thought that I had come to terms and accepted his deception. He has hurt me deeply. Pondering whether or not he had a hand in hurting your family on this side… I could not sleep. Can he hate you that much?"

"Yes." He leaned on the bed next to her. "Or Leif could have discovered who Hope is. They want the Wood Listener." Sliding his arms around her, he squeezed her tightly.

"I don't think we should go alone," she said softly.

Loosening his embrace, he said, "I can only fit one other in the car."

"Declan," she said.

He messaged Declan, asking him to join them. Declan replied, "Hatcher needs to speak with you."

In front of Hope's chambers, he met Declan and Hatcher. He led them both into Hope's playroom.

"Thank you for seeing me right away, my Lord," Hatcher began. "As the Scepter's magic weakens, whatever magic it has is receding into the crystal. The portals inside the tree—such as the ones that lead to your base on the other side—will soon no longer be protected. Anyone can use them from either side."

"How soon?"

"Nightfall."

"Thank you, Hatcher," said Berty. When Hatcher left, Berty brought Declan through the portal.

Berty had Declan carry his bow and quiver in a bag. During the car ride, Hope asked Declan about everyone she missed.

Jon and Teresa's house had a lifelessness that Berty had never seen. When she got out of the car, Hope touched the trunk of the young tree in the front yard. Reaching the front door, Berty realized that he did not have a key. He pretended that he did, unlocking the deadbolt, then turning the knob.

Even though Teresa's parents were there only days prior, a stale smell permeated the foyer. He left the front door open, so that fresh air could rush through the screen door. Hope brought Freesia and Silvia upstairs while Berty and Declan searched from room to room.

Each room was pristine. When they reached the kitchen, Berty's eyes searched the fenced in backyard through the window. Berty's cell phone vibrated in his pocket. "Hello?"

"Berty, it's Lillian, Teresa's mom. I just wanted to make sure Hope had everything. If you need anything."

"Thanks, Lillian," he said. "We're over at Jon and Teresa's now, picking up her stuff."

"Oh, good. Robert and I put some food in the fridge. Take

239

it." He could hear her take a deep breath. "Berty, if you need any help, someone to watch Hope, anything, you can reach us at this number. Okay?"

He thought Lillian would start crying at any moment. Tears were probably already forming in her eyes. "Thank you. I will," he told her.

When he hung up, he found Declan staring at him. He opened the fridge. Nothing inside could help fill the emptiness deep in his heart. He could not remember a time before his little brother. Although they had their differences growing up, he did not want to imagine a time without him.

"Why is it cold in that thing?" Declan asked.

Seeing milk, eggs and juice, Berty closed the door. "Uncle Berty, can I bring some toys?" Hope asked, standing in the doorway.

"A few. There is only so much room in the car," he said.

He heard her open a door in the hall. "Wait," he ordered. Declan followed him to the basement steps. After flipping the switch, they descended. The mostly finished basement had four rooms. Hope and Freesia chose games and toys in the large, open playroom. He and Declan checked the laundry room and the storage room. The third door was locked.

"Hope, what's in the other room?" Berty asked her.

She shrugged. "I dunno. Daddy goes in there. I'm not allowed to disturb him." She placed a doll in the box of toys she was taking. "Mommy says it's work stuff."

Wanting to respect his brother's privacy, he left the door locked. He found a small cooler in the storage room. In it, he put the perishables from the fridge.

"Declan, is there any ice in the freezer?" Berty asked. Declan gave him a blank look. He had forgotten that Declan knew little of his world. Showing Declan the freezer, they covered the food with ice.

Silvia neatly arranged everything in the trunk of his car. After making sure the lights were off and the doors were locked, they drove away from the vacant house.

As he emptied the trunk of his car, he felt as though he was stealing a chunk of his brother's life. "You are only helping him," Silvia whispered in his ear. How did she always know what to say? "Because of you, his world won't fall apart." Agreeing that all of it was only temporary, he wondered how long he should give the "proper channels" to find Jon and Teresa.

He brought the mail onto the back porch so he could watch Hope and Declan practice. The Whingham Academy sent Hope's test scores. She tested well. Her teacher was Rebecca Minor. He glanced at the bus schedule and the welcome letter.

Silvia sat in the wicker chair next to him. "I can't believe school starts in a few days," he told her. "Do you think she can spend it on the other side of the portal?"

"Her grandparents can stop over at any moment," Silvia said. "It may be better to have others come here or she not leave the tree."

"I don't want to keep her from the life she has made there," he argued.

"She has to learn to balance. For the rest of her life, hers will be a world in between here and there." Silvia always made a lot of sense.

"How do you know everything?" Berty asked.

Chuckling, she said, "I don't know everything." She gazed in Hope's direction. "But I do understand what it is like to be her age and to have a secret life." Focusing on Berty, she said, "I'm going to start using the other portal—the one in the fireplace—during the day only. Could you open the vault for me?"

"I may not need to. Portal restrictions will be null in a couple of hours. But I will, if need be," he said.

After staying for dinner, Declan returned to the Empire Tree. Berty found Hope in her room, arranging items on her desk.

"Are you all ready for school in a couple of days?" he asked.

"Yup. I'm just organizing," she said.

He sat on the spare bed. She sat down next to him, asking, "No one is going to believe me about the Land of Sages and the Empire Tree and all that, are they?"

"No, I'm afraid not."

"Is that why you don't tell anybody?"

"Mainly, but I don't think that anyone from here would understand or even like life over there," he said. "That's why it's important to keep the portal locations secret."

"What's not to like about magic?" Hope looked up at him with her innocent, brown eyes.

"Not everyone uses magic the way we do. And magical creatures can be dangerous."

Hope nodded. "Okay, Uncle Berty."

Smiling, he said, "Until school starts, you sleep here, but you can visit the Empire Tree during the day. You cannot leave the tree and you must stay with Freesia. Once school starts, we will see how your schedule is. Okay?"

She squeezed him tightly. "Thanks, Uncle Berty."

Hope ate breakfast enthusiastically. Afterwards, she and Freesia headed through the portal. In the basement, Berty carefully counted his discounted tuition rate from the horde of green bills. Feeling uneasy carrying around tens of thousands of dollars in cash, he and Silvia stopped at the school.

"She did not even count it," Berty told Silvia when they returned to the car. "Ready?"

Excitement filled the car. "I've never seen his office," she said. She peered at the buildings as they drove through the city.

"The glass buildings are sleek, but there is just something about the old stone architecture."

Berty smiled. He loved how she saw beauty in everything. When he found a parking space, they entered the tall building that housed the newspaper. Reaching the fourteenth floor, Berty led Silvia to the reception desk.

The woman behind the desk gave him a smile that quickly faded. "Hi, Cheryl. We are here to see Mister Hunter."

"He's expecting you," she said. Her voice was flat.

Out of earshot of the desk, Silvia said softly, "She does not like me." Berty threw her a puzzled look. "If looks could kill." She laughed a little.

A man wearing a light gray suit walked towards the corner office. His silver hair reflected the fluorescent lighting. He turned to bark at someone sitting at an open desk. Looking in their direction, he stopped. In slow motion, he straightened, and a smile crept into his face. "Come in, both of you," he said.

When they entered the corner office, he closed the door. "Silvia," he said, "you haven't changed." He opened his arms.

"Hi, Martin," Silvia said. She gave her brother a long hug. "It's been awhile."

Martin studied his sister at arm's length with a smile on his face. "I'm so glad you're here," he said. Glancing at Berty, he said to him, "I knew you'd take good care of her." He motioned for them to sit. "What do you have?" Martin asked.

Extracting his notebook, he handed it to Martin, who quickly fetched someone to photocopy the pages. "Thank you for recommending Hope to the school," Berty said.

"You're welcome," said Martin. "My grandson, Mike, will be starting third grade this year."

"Mike? I thought his name was Martin as well," said Silvia.

"Martin Michael Hunter, the third," said Martin. "Marty, my

oldest," he told Berty, "decided that calling the child, Mike, would be less confusing. And it was what *she* wanted."

"She?" asked Berty.

"Tamera," Silvia answered. "Junior's—Marty's—ex-wife. Martin didn't like her."

"She was completely wrong for him," Martin said. "When Mike was turning three, Marty and Tamera planned a big party at their house. We, Martha and I, wanted to help. Tamera said that she could handle it. All she needed was someone to watch Mike. She brought him over that morning before running the last of her errands. Martha kept Mike entertained all day as she waited for her phone call. When the phone rang, it was Marty. He had just come home from work to find Tamera gone. She only left a note. Broke his heart. It took a few years for Mike to stop asking about Mommy." He took a breath. "Anyway, Mike's a good kid. Have they found your brother and sister-in-law yet?"

Berty shook his head. His mouth did not want to form the word no. The return of his notebook saved him from saying anything.

"It's only a matter of time," Silvia said to him. "Speaking of which, we should go. Our world, as we know it, is ending. We only have so long to prepare."

Martin nodded. "There's a magical change, isn't there?" Silvia did not answer her brother. "You can feel it," he said. "Guess you never really lose your ties."

Although no crystal hung around Martin's neck, he, too, descended from one of the Seven High Sages. Berty wondered what kind of bond Martin had with the Scepter. He also wondered if his brother had a similar bond. Perhaps, he thought, one had to be in the Scepter's presence to form any type of bond.

After giving his sister a hug good-bye, Martin shook Berty's hand. "I better get an invitation," Martin whispered, "even if I have to cross the portal to attend."

"Don't worry," Berty whispered back.

Martin walked them to the elevator. "Good luck," he said before the doors closed.

"Thank you," Silvia said to Berty. She squeezed his hand.

The house was full of warm summer breezes. Freesia left a note saying that she and Hope were visiting the Empire Tree. Grabbing their cloaks, Silvia and Berty stepped through the portal leading to Silvia's chambers. Arm in arm, they strolled on the bridges of the Empire Tree.

On Hope's platform, Theodore appeared. "My Lord, may I have a minute of your time?" the young Dwarf asked.

"Of course. What's the problem?"

"Locks are not staying locked," Theodore answered.

"Locks to what?" asked Berty.

"Everything. People's chambers, the kitchens, the tree itself."

He and Silvia exchanged glances. "Have Hatcher, Alvar, Edwin, and Colvin meet me in the Roundtable Room," said Berty.

"Yes, my Lord." Theodore disappeared.

"I'll check on Hope for you," Silvia said.

"I want you there as well," said Berty. "This could affect the house." They hastened their pace through the tree.

When the men entered the Roundtable Room, Berty asked, "Where is Theodore?"

"I am here, my Lord," Theodore said in the doorway.

"Good," said Berty. "Close the door and have a seat." Once the Head Tender joined the table, Berty began, "Is this just in the Empire Tree or is this elsewhere?"

"We are having magical problems at the gates as well," said Hatcher.

"Everything is locked magically," Theodore explained. "After a little while, all the magic is undone. I relock everything, then it unlocks again."

"Can we lock things manually—without magic?" Berty asked.

"Some things. The doors to the Empire Tree have a heavy bar for fortification that can be used," Theodore said. "However, chambers can only be locked from the inside."

"What about the vaults and the dungeons?"

"The dungeons are fine. Those have keys," said Alvar.

"The vaults are not," said Colvin. "There is no way to keep them closed without magic. Declan said he can see the magic surrounding us oscillate. The Scepter is affecting all magic."

"Where is Declan?" Berty asked.

"Watchers' Guild," replied Edwin.

Berty turned to Silvia. "After the Hallows, what will happen to magic? Will the portals disappear?" He looked at Hatcher.

"Portals existed before the Scepter," said Hatcher.

"We cannot assume that life and magic will revert to a pre-scepter time," reasoned Berty. "The Scepter has had a magical hold on many things in this world. We must prepare for a less magical life." His stomach dropped as the words left his mouth.

"Are you saying the portals will close?" Hatcher asked.

Staring at the Troll, Berty did not answer. He took a deep breath. "Silvia, are there keys to the house?"

"Yes."

"Then, we'll start using them," he said. "Also, can you and Alfred do Scepter research?" She nodded. "Colvin, is there anyway we can limit access to the vaults?"

"I believe so."

"Theodore, we need locks with keys on all doors. Alvar and Edwin, increase security in and around the tree. Pretend magic protects nothing. Hatcher, do what you feel you need at the gate. Also, check on the portal status."

When the room emptied, only Silvia remained with him. He

never thought he would have to make a choice between one side of the portal or the other. When he closed his eyes, he could see Hope laughing. How would he tell his family?

"We have time to prepare," he told Silvia.

"In case the portals close," she said.

He nodded. "If I stay here, will you stay, too?"

Placing her hand on his, she said, "Yes."

The warm brown of her eyes welcomed him. His fingers caressed her soft hand. "I was hoping to court you," he said. He held his bottom lip between his teeth.

Her delicate fingers pressed against his lips. Her smile radiated a growing warmth. As her fingers released his lips, his hand found her wavy, dark red hair. Their lips met. Troubles melted from his mind. The vacancy they left filled with hopes and dreams of a better life.

With their foreheads touching, he focused on searching into her eyes. Her two eyes merged to become one brown eye. He chuckled under his breath. Pulling back just enough for her eyes to separate, he said, "I love you, Silvia Hunter."

She smiled. Her hand gently touched his cheek. "I love you, too, Berty Chase," she said.

Smiling, he kissed her again. "I don't want to live without you," he whispered.

"Nor I you," she said quietly in his ear.

He grabbed both her hands. Sliding off his seat, he pushed the chair away. His right knee dropped to the floor. "Marry me?" he asked.

Silvia squeezed his hands. "Yes," she answered.

Rising from his kneeled position, he coaxed her off the chair. He embraced her as they sealed their promise with the kiss.

A throat cleared behind Berty. Not letting go of Silvia, he turned to see Declan standing in the doorway. "Sorry to interrupt," said Declan, "but I was told you wanted to see me."

"I'll go find Alfred," Silvia said. He watched her saunter away until she closed the door behind her.

"I need a ring," he said, still staring at the door. "Then, I'll propose properly." He looked at Declan. "That's not why I wanted to see you. Tell me about the magic."

Chapter Eighteen
Forever and Ever

Declan sat in his chair. "I've been watching," he said. "There's these disruptions in the flow of the magic. It will then stop. When it comes back, there is a burst of magic that sort of kills all the other magic."

"It's short-circuiting," said Berty, who also sat. "Then it surges and blows everything."

"I don't understand."

"What electricity does when it's not working properly," he explained. "My dad would do demonstrations in the basement for Jon and me. He invented machines that ended up building the business. Wood is inert, but I wonder if we were able to ground the Scepter, would it stabilize the flow of magic."

Declan looked like he was digesting Berty's words. "How?"

"I don't know." Staring at the ceiling, he said, "Maybe I'll ask my dad if he has any ideas." He tore his eyes away from the Scepter Room above them. "In the meantime, we need to prepare for no magic to protect the Sages' Grove and for the portals to close, at least for a little while. I have made the choice to stay on this side of the portal. Hope on the other hand…"

"Will live with her parents on the other side," Declan finished.

Berty nodded.

"What about," Declan found the reflective tabletop very interesting. "Remember when Estelle said something about Hope saving us all?"

"Total annihilation," said Berty.

"Yeah." He looked at Berty. "What if she needs to be on this side of the portal to do that? What if we can't reopen the portals?"

Berty understood what Declan was saying. "How do I take a child away from her parents? They're not going to be apart for just the summer. We're talking forever. No communication. I can sacrifice myself, but I will not sacrifice my brother for the greater good." He rubbed his chin. "Maybe Estelle," he wanted to say was wrong, but he knew she was not, "maybe we're misinterpreting. Maybe Hope has already done what she needed to do. When I discovered Hope's gift, I always thought that she belonged here, that she would end up here—eventually. Perhaps it's," he sighed. "Who am I to talk about the future?" Running a hand through his dark hair, he muttered, "I need a drink."

The two of them left their discussion at the Roundtable and joined the rest of the tree. In the Reception Room, seeing Silvia brought a smile to his face. He watched her talk with Alfred.

"Congratulations," said Declan quietly.

"Thanks," he said, looking at his friend. "When my brother and sister-in-law come home, we will have a small ceremony at the house. I want you to be there."

Declan smiled. "I will."

Berty allowed Hope to play in the village with her friends. He watched his happy niece run with the other children. Her laughter bounced between the white cob buildings.

After dinner, he accompanied Hope and Freesia to the house. Silvia would return later when she and Alfred finished for the evening.

As Hope ran down the hall, Berty checked his cell phone that he left on his dresser. His father left a message for Berty to call. Thinking there was news about Jon and Teresa, he called. When his father answered, he said, "Dad, what's up?"

"Your mother and I want to come over tomorrow," said George. "I want to talk about Monday with you. We were thinking morning, in case you and Silvia had evening plans."

"Okay," he said. "Any news?"

"Not yet."

"Hope likes to get up early. See you in the morning, Dad."

He found Hope and Freesia in the study. "Grandma and Grandpa are coming over in the morning," he announced.

Taking a seat, he said, "Hope, come sit over here." Once Hope sat near him, he continued, "You know the Scepter is broken." Hope nodded. "Well, it is messing up the magic. Anyone can enter the chambers or pass through the portals to this house and from this house. The Scepter will continue to deteriorate until Halloween. Freesia, you know it as the Hallows. We are not sure what will happen with the portals. Either they will be exposed for everyone to find or they may close."

Hope gasped. "Forever and ever, Uncle Berty?"

"I do not know," he replied. "Freesia, Obie is welcome to come here, so that you may fulfill your promise to Declan. Hope, you can go over there if you have finished your homework and on the weekends. It might be best to either have Declan or Julie come here for your archery lessons."

"If the portals close, what happens after Halloween?" Hope asked.

His stomach dropped while he looked at his niece. "I'm going to live in the Land of Sages. So is Silvia."

"What about me?" she asked.

"You will stay here with your parents," he told her.

Her eyes began to well. "So, I'll never see anyone again?

You, Silvia, Declan, Delyth, Alina, Obie?" Tears streaked down her little face. "Fairy Dust?" She sobbed into her hands. "How will I hear the call of the Mother Wood Sprite?"

Berty did not have an answer for her. She peeked at him through her fingers. He could barely see her red eyes. "We're going to try to stop the Scepter's effect on other magic," he said.

Her hands freed her face. Tears stopped streaming down her cheeks, but the tip of her nose was red. He opened his arms. She ran to him, hugging him tightly. "What happens if Mommy and Daddy don't come home?"

"They will," he told her. He kissed her on the top of her head. Out of the corner of his eye, he saw Silvia standing just beyond the doorway.

When Hope finally let go, Freesia brought her upstairs to get ready for bed. Berty dropped his head into his hands. Sitting next to him, Silvia placed a hand on his back. Throwing his arms around her, they sat on the couch.

Berty heard Hope scampering down the stairs. "My mom and dad are coming in the morning," he told Silvia. "Dad wants to talk about me going into the office, I think."

"I told Alfred that we would go into the Library Vault tomorrow," she said.

"Go. Mom will keep Hope occupied," he said. "We'll join you when they leave."

When Hope entered the room, she said, "I'm all ready." Her mood had lightened.

"Are you okay, Hope?" Silvia asked.

"Yeah," she said. "The portals won't close. You guys will fix it."

After tucking in Hope, he returned to Silvia's side. "I hope we can," she told him.

He poured them both amber colored drinks. "Me, too," he

said. Taking a sip, the warm alcohol burned all the doubt in his throat.

Morning arrived earlier than he wanted. Silvia and Freesia left after breakfast. While Berty monitored Hope's archery practice, the doorbell rang. Carrying her bow, she ran onto the back porch. "Grandma and Grandpa are here!" she shouted.

He made her leave her bow and quiver in the kitchen before they answered the door. Hope gave both her grandparents hugs when they crossed the threshold.

Berty led his father into the sitting room as Hope said to Kate, "Come on, Grandma, you can watch me practice," while pulling her towards the kitchen.

"First, I want to give you something," George said to Berty. From his pocket, he extracted something small and shiny. A ring rested on his open palm. "Your great-grandfather gave it to your great-grandmother. A single flawless diamond set in platinum. For Silvia, when you're ready."

Smiling, he took it from his father. "Thanks, Dad." He studied the clear stone surrounded by intricately designed white metal. A fire erupted in its depths as he turned the ring in his fingers. He placed it in his pocket for safekeeping.

"About Monday," his father continued. "You can go in after Hope starts school. I was there all week. Something's not right. You have to figure out what it is."

"George?" Kate screamed from the hall. She dragged Hope into the sitting room with her. "The kitchen!" was all she could say.

Berty and George raced into the kitchen. Flour, sugar and butter measured themselves into bowls. Vanilla and eggs flew across the room. Horrified, Kate stood in the doorway, clutching Hope close. Hope kept trying to tell her that it was okay. George watched the magic beat ingredients together. His father looked delighted.

"Berty, explain to me, right now, what is going on," Kate demanded.

"It's magic, Grandma," Hope said. "That's what happens when you read from the cookbook. I tried to tell you."

"Magic?" Kate's eyes followed the flying objects across the room. She could not utter a word as teaspoons dropped batter onto a baking pan.

George smiled. Looking at his son, he said, "Show me?"

Berty glanced from one parent to another. "Show you?"

"The world about which you write," George expounded. "You've been there. I would like to see it."

He could not believe his ears. His mother was always the supportive one when it came to his creative endeavors. But, it was his father who was asking.

George nodded. "I owe you an explanation, Berty. I told you a little about this, Kate. All my life, I've dreamed of this place—a wondrous place, full of magic and different peoples. When you were young, Berty, you would write about it. I tried to discourage it. But I didn't really understand. My father, I found out as an adult, drew pictures of this same place. He told me that his father went searching for the entrance to this world. He never found it, but *you* have. Please, Berty."

Berty could not say a word. He only nodded.

Tearing her eyes from the pan flying into the oven, Kate stared at her husband. "I remember seeing your father's draw-ings," she said. "I had always thought Berty had seen them, too." She stepped further into the kitchen as she unlatched Hope from her side. "Are you telling me this is all real? I never thought you believed in such things."

"It has to be real," said George. "There is no other logical explanation." He held his hand out towards his wife.

254

Taking a deep breath, she placed her hand in his.

"Will you take us, Berty?" George asked.

He nodded. "Hope, grab your bow and quiver, then bring your grandparents upstairs. I need to lock the house."

After locking the doors with the key Silvia gave him, he joined them in the upstairs hall. Hope already wore her maroon cloak. Throwing his cloak over his arm, he said to his parents, "Ready?"

George smiled while Kate barely nodded.

He gave Hope a nod. She took Kate's hand, then pulled her through the tapestry.

George jumped a little when they disappeared. Giving his father a smile, he guided him through the portal.

"Where are we?" Kate said.

"This is my room," said Hope.

"Hope's chambers within the Empire Tree," Berty said.

They descended into Hope's playroom. Kate looked around approvingly. "Where is your room?" she asked her son.

"My chambers are close," he answered.

When they exited, George stopped. He gaped at the massive tree trunk. Hope tugged her grandfather's hand to cross the bridge. Peering into the dark doorway, George asked, "What's in there?"

"The Scepter," Berty said.

"Why is it so dark?" said Kate.

"It's broken," Hope offered.

"I'll explain later," said Berty, who kept them moving. They peeked inside the Roundtable Room, then continued down the staircase.

In the Reception Room, Berty's father froze in front of the dais. He examined the Sages' Seal. "It is just as I pictured in my dreams. Your grandfather drew it like that, too, only his was in

255

color."

Berty lifted the back of his shirt. "Like this?"

His mother gasped. "Berty, where did you get that ghastly thing?" she scolded.

"Yes," his father answered.

"The Scepter," he said to his mother while lowering his shirt. "It's my Empire Mark." He threw his cloak around his shoulders. "Theodore," he called.

Kate jumped when the Dwarf suddenly appeared. "Yes, my Lord?" he said.

"How is the lock installation coming?"

"Slow, but well."

"Good. Do we happen to have two extra cloaks for my mother and father?"

"Of course," Theodore replied. "I will fetch them."

"Why are you installing locks?" his father asked.

Berty scanned the room. Seeing no one, he said, "The Scepter, as I understand it, is short-circuiting the magic that keeps everything secure."

His father's eyebrows raised. He knew his father's mind turned. When Theodore returned with cloaks, Berty helped his mother fasten hers. George, on the other hand, donned one with ease.

"Why do we need these? It's summer," said Kate.

"You'll see," he told her. "I was going to ask for your help, Dad, to stop the short-circuiting. Declan can explain what is happening better than I."

He and Hope led his parents down the stairs into the Receiving Room. The room was busy with people conducting Empire business. They walked out of the large, wooden doors of the Empire Tree.

"Isn't this quaint," Kate remarked as her head turned in every direction.

Smiling, Berty said, "This way." He brought them past the barracks to the Guard's practice area. In his usual spot, Declan was still shooting arrows.

Hope ran towards him. "Be careful," Kate called. Reaching Declan, Hope began to send arrows flying through the air. Declan turned his head, searching. Seeing Berty approach, he raised a hand in greeting.

Not too far from Declan, Ojore watched Obie throw a spear at different targets. Declan lowered his bow to greet Berty's parents.

"We're going to take a walk around the village," he told Declan. "After, my dad wants to talk to you about what we discussed yesterday." Declan nodded. "Collect your arrows, Hope. We're going."

"Can't I stay out here with Obie?" she pleaded.

"No," Berty said firmly. "Not without an adult."

"But there are adults everywhere," Hope argued.

"Arrows. Now." His voice was stern. She ran to the target to pickup her arrows.

His mother placed a hand on his arm. "You'll make a good father someday, Berty," she said with a smile.

Running back, Hope said, "Declan, some of my arrows broke. Can they be fixed?"

"When the shaft breaks, they will never fly right," Declan told her. "But, you can reuse the tips and the wood can be used for something else."

"Okay." Hope secured her bow to her back, and covered her quiver with her cloak.

They strolled through the village around the tree. "That is one massive tree," said George. In the marketplace, his mother browsed the stalls. She could not hide the smile on her face.

When Kate saw something she liked, George asked the merchant, "How much?"

The merchant replied, "Ten rons."

"Six rons," George offered.

Berty stood back and watched his father enjoy haggling. They reached a price of eight rons. Having the money in his cloak, Berty magically transferred it to his father's pocket.

George extracted the dull gray coins from his pocket. He looked at his son before placing them in the man's hand. Carefully wrapped, he carried the trinket for his wife. As they meandered back to the Empire Tree's main entrance, George asked, "How did you? Nevermind."

Reaching the Reception Room, they found Declan, Obie and Freesia. Berty allowed Hope to go with Obie and Freesia. The four of them watched the children run up the steps ahead of the Fairy.

"What's on her back?" George asked about the almost rectangular purplish blue.

"Her wings," answered Berty. "Folded. She's a Fairy. Why don't the two of you use the Roundtable Room. Mom and I will be here."

Whilst George followed Declan upstairs, Berty and his mother sat at the large table. A Tender brought a tea service. Berty placed a cup of tea in front of his mother. "I'm sorry," Kate said. "I didn't understand. Is this where you met Silvia?"

"Actually, the house used to be hers," he explained. "Silvia brought me here. I obtained the house when I succeeded her."

"This place is incredible. I can understand why you are here all the time."

He placed his teacup on its saucer. "Mom," he began, "in a couple of months, I might be spending all my time here permanently."

""Why?" she asked. "I hope I didn't give you the impression that I disliked Silvia, because that can't be further from the truth."

"Mom, no." He swallowed. "The portals may close." Looking in her brown eyes, he answered her unasked question. "By Halloween."

Staring at her son, she said nothing.

"Can I see it?" George asked as he approached.

Rising, Berty said, "Mom, are you coming?" Silently, she followed her son up the stairs.

They stood outside the dark Scepter Room. George pulled a palm-sized flashlight out of his pocket. With the press of a button, bright light cut through the darkness. Roving around the room, the beam of light found the seven columns and the pillar holding the black crystal attached to its white metal staff. Declan only had eyes for the fat, blue flashlight in George's hand.

Berty followed his father into the darkness. When they reached the center of the room, he warned, "Don't touch it." Cautiously, George walked around the pillar, keeping the light on the Scepter.

When they emerged, George crossed to the bridge. He looked over the side. Returning to his family and Declan, he said, "You were right, Berty. It does sound like it is short-circuiting. Our only option is to try to ground it. If we don't, when it finally blows, it could send a surge so forceful that it knocks out everything."

"Which would close the portals," Kate connected. She looked from her son to her husband. "What do you need, George?"

"My tools." George's eyes sparkled with excitement. "I wonder if I'll get a voltage reading."

Kate smiled. She turned to Berty. "We will do whatever we can to not lose our son." Closing her eyes, she covered her mouth with her hand. Her body began to shake as she sobbed.

"Mom." Berty threw his arms around her.

"I need both my sons," she said into Berty's shoulder.

Realizing that the possibility of never seeing him or Jon again ate at his mother, he walked them across the bridge, then up to his chambers. In his study, Kate collapsed into a chair.

Chapter Nineteen
Modern Magic

George dragged a club chair in front of his wife. The chairs almost touched. Sitting in it, he held her hands. He leaned across to her, saying, "We won't lose either of them. Remember, they said that kidnapping for ransom is common. We will find a way to pay the ransom when they contact us."

"Why haven't they contacted us?" Kate asked through her sobs.

A little color drained from George's face. "I'll make a few calls on Monday," he said.

Pulling a tissue from her pocket, Kate wiped her eyes. "How long will it take to get your tools?"

"They're in the car," George said.

Kate laughed a little. "Tried to take them to work again?"

George smiled. "I know, fruitless." After his eyes examined Kate, he said, "I'll be right back." He looked up at Berty. "Right?"

Nodding, he said, "Declan, take my dad through Hope's portal. Make sure you lock the deadbolt on the front door when you come in."

George gave Kate a quick peck before leaving with Declan. Alone with her son, Kate asked, "Where can I freshen up?"

"Upstairs, off the bedroom." Once his mother disappeared up the spiral staircase, he leaned against his desk and closed his eyes.

In the darkness, he could hear the hum of a truck. The hum died. "We stopped," whispered Jon. The back opened, flooding the inside with dim light.

Armed men motioned for the riders to get out. Jon tried to help Teresa and the two young women off the truck, but he was pulled away. They glimpsed at the corrugated metal shack barely lighted with one floodlight that could have fallen at any moment. A rusted door opened. Their armed chaperones marched them inside.

A huff and a puff could have blown the shack down. The men inside did not cover their faces. They spoke to the incoming men in a language Berty could not understand. A door in the floor opened. Jon, Teresa and the two girls were pushed down the steps under the door.

"Berty, are you okay?" his mother asked. Her voice sounded far away.

Opening his eyes, he saw his mother walking towards him. He decided that total honesty would be best. "I saw Jon and Teresa. They're being taken somewhere. To be detained, I think," he told her.

She cocked her head to the side. He knew she was wondering how he was able to see them. "You saw them? Are they hurt?"

"They seem fine," he said. "Jon's glasses are broken."

A breath of relief escaped her mouth. "How do you see them? Do you know where they are?"

"Magic, when I close my eyes. I don't know where they are. Under some shack."

His wind chimes rang. "Come in," he said. Declan and George entered his study. George's tool bag hung from his shoul-

262

der.

"They're alive, George," Kate said.

"How do you know?" George asked.

"Berty said so," she answered. "Let's go fix that Scepter." Her mood had lifted some.

When he left his chambers, Berty called for Theodore. "Have Colvin meet us at the Scepter's Room entrance," he told the Dwarf.

Fiery hair and beard shined in the stairway. "My Advisor, Colvin, specializes in Mining and Construction," Berty said to his parents. "Colvin, I would like you to meet my mother and father. We're going to limit the Scepter's magical interference."

"An honor to meet you both, ma'am and sir," said Colvin.

"Call me George," his father said. He placed his bag on the landing. Digging inside, he handed Colvin a regular sized flashlight and Kate a yellow voltmeter. He gave Declan the small flashlight from his pocket. "Okay. Declan, you keep yours on the Scepter. Colvin, yours is to light the room better."

Colvin stared at the metal stick in his hand. "How do you work it?" Declan asked.

"You don't have flashlights here," said George. After showing them how to turn flashlights on and off, Kate handed him the digital reader.

"Is this magic?" Colvin asked. He kept pressing the button creating a strobe effect.

"Modern magic," said George. "Let's see how similar magic and electricity really are."

The three men entered the room. Berty heard his father say, "Interesting." When George returned to his bag, he said, "It's messing with the digital readout. Have to breakout the old tools." Excitement peppered his voice. When he pulled something red out of his bag, he reentered the room.

A couple of minutes later, the three men exited the Scepter Room. As George packed his bag, he said, "Magic can be measured in volts. The Scepter fluctuates. We are going to need to stabilize it. Lots of well insulated copper wiring and a busbar of some sort."

"Copper wire is easy," said Colvin. "But what do you use for insulation?"

"How pure is the copper?" George asked. "What's the metal mix?"

"No other metals. Just copper," answered Colvin.

"We're going to need to draw up a plan. Take some measurements," said George.

Hearing footsteps on the bridge, Berty turned. Hope and Obie ran to the trunk. "You and Colvin can start after lunch," he said.

After leaving George's bag in the Roundtable Room, they headed to the Reception Room where his parents met the other inhabitants of the Empire Tree.

As Kate and Lida bonded over their unreachable sons, Silvia asked quietly, "What made you decide to bring them through?"

"The kitchen," answered Berty.

Silvia laughed. The ring in his pocket pressed into his leg. He wanted to propose properly. All he needed was the perfect plan to surprise her.

When lunch ended, his father left with Colvin while his mother accompanied Hope and Freesia outside. "Julie," he called. They stood amongst the chaos of people going about their business. "Would it be too much for you to come through the portal maybe a couple of times a week to make sure Hope is practicing well?"

"I would love to, my Lord," Julie said with a smile. "While I am on that side of the portal, would I be permitted to collect

264

wood?"

An idea popped into Berty's mind. "Absolutely. We would have to show you how to get there," he said.

Bowing her head, Julie said, "Thank you."

Outside, he saw his father and Colvin inspecting the base of the Empire Tree and the surrounding earth. He approached his mother who was watching Hope play with her friends. "She's going to miss this," he said.

"It is nice to see children just being children," Kate mentioned. "Your father will do everything he can."

"I know, Mom." He glimpsed at Alina whispering in Hope's ear. The girls giggled. "I'm glad that I was able to share this with you, even if only for a little while."

His mother smiled. "Your father and I read your story faithfully. Now, I realize that it was not completely fiction," she said.

In the evening, Berty's parents returned to the house. While Freesia got Hope ready for bed, he, his parents and Silvia conversed in the family room.

"I have all the measurements I need. Tomorrow, I will draw a plan for the Scepter," said George. "I'd like to go back on Monday to see what Colvin thinks. I know you won't be home so how...?"

"Freesia will be here," he said.

"I can accompany you through the tree, if you'd like," offered Silvia.

Smiling, George said, "Yes, thank you."

"If I hear anything," said Kate, "can I call the number Teresa gave me to talk to Hope?"

"You're staying home?" Berty asked.

"I don't want to be too far from the phone," said Kate.

Berty nodded. "Yes. The phone rings both here and there."

After kissing their granddaughter goodnight, his parents left.

Berty gave Hope the gift of spending the morning in the Sages' Grove. He helped Silvia and Alfred research in the vaults. When morning turned to afternoon, Hope begged to stay just a little longer. Saying no, Berty and Hope crossed the portal after lunch.

"How come Silvia gets to stay?" Hope asked.

"She's not starting school in the morning," Berty answered. "We'll get your book bag packed and uniform ready. I have to make sure my suit isn't wrinkled and search for a tie."

He made sure Hope packed everything on her school supply list while Freesia laid out her clothes on the extra bed. Hope then helped him pick a tie as he aired out his navy blue suit that he usually kept in the dry cleaner's bag.

Freesia and Berty walked Hope to the bus stop after dinner, so there were no surprises in the morning. Silvia was waiting for them at the house when they returned.

Berty and Silvia watched Hope play in the yard from the porch. "This should expend some of her nervous energy," Silvia said. Lowering her voice, she continued, "You were right. The portals can close because of the malfunctioning Scepter. Until now, the Scepter has been acting as a conduit, boosting magic. Hatcher has confirmed that the Scepter was connected to the portals to increase their security. The Scepter's boost cloaked the portals so they could not be found by those who have not used them at least once before. Their magic has been intricately linked for a very long time. Once the Scepter goes, there may not be enough magic left to keep them open."

He kept his eyes on Hope while asking, "Will stabilizing the Scepter even help?"

"To an extent. The Scepter is also connected to the Empire Tree and the wall surrounding the Sages' Grove," she explained. "We will not know if it worked until a day or two after Halloween."

His eyes focused on Silvia. "You can use my cell to call Martin tomorrow morning."

While Hope changed for bed, Berty filled her pink plastic lunchbox. "Mine was metal," Silvia reminisced.

"So was mine when I was really young," said Berty. "It was covered with the characters from Sesame Street. I was partial to the Cookie Monster. Probably because my mom always made the best cookies." He smiled, but he felt a touch of sadness inside. Silvia listened and smiled. He knew that she did not have the faintest idea about what he spoke. She just let him bask in his memories.

He programmed the house's phone number into his cell. Fascinated, Silvia watched. He wrote down the phone numbers for his cell, his parents, Teresa's parents, and Martin's office. Before they went to sleep, he taught Freesia how to dial. They practiced a few times, calling Berty's cell phone.

When Berty's eyes opened in the morning, he wanted to groan. The last time he had to get up for work, he interviewed Silvia. Going to work for his brother motivated him to jump out of bed.

Buttoning his suit jacket, he caught himself in the long mirror. He glimpsed at his father standing in the suit and tie.

As he entered the kitchen, Hope looked at him. "Uncle Berty, you're dressed like Daddy."

He smiled at her, then poured himself some coffee. Silvia retrieved Hope's lunchbox from the icebox.

Before they left, Silvia made sure Hope had everything. Giving Hope a hug, she said, "Have a great day. I want to hear all about it when you come home. Okay?"

"Okay, Silvia," Hope said excitedly.

Silvia stayed in the house to call Martin while Berty and Freesia took Hope to the bus stop. Berty was not sure how Freesia would react to seeing a school bus.

A few other children, ranging in age, waited on the corner of Oak and Pine, wearing the Whingham Academy uniform. All the adults exchanged polite hellos.

A half-sized, yellow, school bus roared towards their corner. Reading the numbers, he knew it was the bus that would take Hope away from him, if only for six hours or so.

Red and yellow lights flashed. Big tires stopped turning. Mostly glass bi-fold doors cranked open. The older children boarded first while the younger children received hugs and kisses.

"You have fun, and don't be afraid to make new friends," he told Hope while hugging.

Detaching from him, she said, "Bye, Uncle Berty."

Was she happy? Was she sad? Was she nervous? Was she scared? He did not know. Her little feet climbed the big black steps. He could barely see the top of her head past the seatbacks. She chose a seat near the window. When she looked at him, he smiled and waved. She waved back with a little smile.

The tires began to move. He watched the little bus drive off, removing her from his protective care. Leaving him, she was defenseless—no Fairy Dust, no bow. Involuntarily, he sighed.

"Don't worry, Daddy, she'll be fine," a woman said to him.

"I'm not... I'm her uncle," he said, still watching the last vestiges of yellow disappear down the tree-lined streets.

The woman gave him a smile. "The first time is always the hardest. For you, not her," she said.

"I hope so," he said. With nods to each other, the adults dispersed.

"I should be home in time to pick her up from the bus stop. In case I'm late, don't wait for me," he said to Freesia on their way home.

Silvia greeted him at the door. "Was it difficult?"

"Very."

Scooping her into his arms, they kissed. She gave him the strength for the next leg of his journey.

Chapter Twenty
Chase Technologies

Chase Technologies resided on the outskirts of the city. Berty had only visited the large complex a few times. He was grateful for his father's directions. They led him straight to his brother's parking space. After taking a deep breath, he turned off the engine. He got out of the car with his father's paper in his hand.

A green golf cart with a yellow rotating light on the white roof stopped behind his car. The hood read *Chase Technologies Security*. The older man behind the wheel said, "I'm sorry, sir. You can't park there. That space is reserved for Mister Chase."

"I am Mister Chase," Berty informed him.

"I know there are two sons. I'll need to see some ID," he said.

Berty handed the man his driver's license.

"You're the writer!" Smiling, the man gave back the little plastic card. "Your father always speaks very highly of you every time I see him. I'm Bill, senior head of security." They shook hands. "I've been working for your father since before moving to this larger location. Nice to finally meet you as an adult, Mister Hubert Chase."

"Berty, please," he said.

"I wish you were here because of better circumstances, Berty," Bill said. "They'll find your brother soon. Well, if there is anything you need, let me know."

"I will, Bill. Thank you." Reaching the Executive private entrance, he entered the security code his father gave him on the keypad. The steel door beeped open.

Cream walls welcomed him. Finding his way to Jon's office, black and white prints of machines, parts and plans punctuated the cream.

The hallway led to an empty desk in front of a smooth wooden door. He glanced at the plaque on the desk, reading, *Thomas Wesnicki*. Walking past, he opened the door that said, *Jonathan Chase, President*.

The office held a commanding view of the industrial complex nestled in the surrounding woods. He drank in the clean, modern steel and glass juxtaposed with wild nature.

"Excuse me," said a man's voice behind him. "Do you have an appointment with Mister Chase?"

Turning, he spied the slender, young man standing near the large desk. He took note that he was wearing a three-piece suit without the jacket, then said, "I am Mister Chase." He wondered how many times he would have to repeat himself.

"Oh my God, *you're* the brother. You are so gorgeous!" The man quickly covered his mouth with his hands. "I'm sorry. That was so inappropriate."

Highly uncomfortable, Berty said, "You must be Thomas."

"Actually, it's pronounced *Toe-mah*," corrected Thomas.

"Wesnicki?" he said with raised eyebrows.

Speaking with his hands, Thomas explained, "That's how I pronounce my name. Thomas is just so ordinary. But you can call me whatever."

Berty half smiled. "That's all right, *Toe-mah*."

Thomas let out a breath.

271

Opening his jacket button, Berty sat in one of the sleek, brown leather couches. He motioned for Thomas to sit, then said, "Tell me, how long have you worked for my brother?"

"Mister Chase hired me about three years ago. When he went from VP to P, I went, too. Dolores, your father's secretary, stayed on for about a month to train me to be the P's assistant. Last week, big Mister C was very impressed that I kept her system. If it ain't broken, you know?"

Berty nodded. "I can see why Jon hired you." Thomas smiled. "Who has been running things while he has been over-seas?"

"Mister C chose Director of Operations, Victoria Dunne, to essentially run the company. Once a week, big Mister C would come in for a status report," Thomas replied. "However," he said in a low voice. He paused to close the door. When he returned to the couch, he continued, "According to Eunice, Kirk Duncan, VP, felt that both he and his position were marginalized."

"Did you say any of this to my dad?" asked Berty.

The door opened before Thomas could answer. A stocky man entered with a brown folder in his pudgy hands. After placing it on the desk, he noticed Berty and Thomas. "Sorry to intrude. I did not think anyone was here," he said.

Berty stood to greet the intruder. The light caught the sheen on the man's dark suit as he approached Berty. "Berty Chase," he said, extending a hand.

"Kirk Duncan," the man said, shaking Berty's hand.

"Vice President," said Berty. "Nice to meet you."

"Likewise," Kirk said. "I hope you don't mind, I placed the report George asked for on the desk."

"Not at all. Thank you," said Berty.

Kirk flashed a disingenuous smile, then left.

Standing beside him, Thomas said, "He does not like you."

272

"All I have is a name," he confessed. "My being here is pure nepotism. I know nothing of the business and he knows it." He buttoned the top button of his suit jacket. "Any chance of getting a tour?"

"Absolutely," said Thomas. "I'd be delighted to show you around."

As Berty closed the office door behind him, he locked it magically. Touring the offices, he met Victoria Dunne, who handed him a brown folder enclosed report. When he met Maggie Lin, Director of Sales, she said, "I want to apologize to you. I feel personally responsible for your brother's disappearance. My work opened the lines for the African expansion."

"The ones I hold responsible are the people who took Jon and his wife," he said. Before leaving her office, Maggie handed him her sales report.

While he carried brown folders, Thomas brought him to the catwalks above the machines that manufactured all sorts of parts. Many of the machines were his father's patented designs.

The trip around the complex fascinated Berty. Thomas knew everything about the business and the people—more than Berty really wanted to know.

When Berty returned to the office, he sat at the desk, not knowing what he should do. The three brown folders stared at him. Opening one, he began reading jargon to which he was not privy. His red stoned pinky ring did nothing to help him understand. He kept reading anyway.

A knock on the door gave him a welcomed break. "Come in," he said.

Thomas opened the office door. "I am going to head to lunch. Is there anything I can do for you before I go?"

"I noticed a coffee machine over there. Where do I put the water and where's the best place to get water for it?"

Eyeing the reports on the desk, Thomas smiled. He walked past the large glass topped table to the wall with a small, sleek counter. "Your brother keeps a special coffee for reading reports," he said.

Berty joined him by the stainless coffee maker.

"The water is already connected in the wall," Thomas explained. He grabbed a small box from the cabinet. "This tray pulls out here." A coffee grounds basket ejected from the machine. Thomas plunked a pillow of coffee grounds into the tray. "Make sure it clicks when you push it in, then press this button." Within seconds, hot brown liquid dripped into the glass carafe. "Here is a mug. Cream. Sugar. Stirrers. Also, Teresa makes him keep cereal and granola bars in here. But, he always keeps a stash of Snickers and peanut butter cups somewhere down there."

"Thanks, *Toe-mah*. Have a good lunch." Berty heard the door close. While waiting impatiently for the coffee to finish, he took a Snickers bar from the near empty box. He used to have one with his coffee when he worked at the newspaper. Noticing the other boxes only had one or two missing, he chuckled. He never knew Jon did that as well.

He heard a soft knock on the door while he collected the reports from the desk. "Come in," he said. A woman entered. "Victoria, what can I do for you?"

"Oh, um, I'm just dropping off some additional figures for my report," said Victoria. Cautiously, she stepped towards the desk. "These are actually projections I put together. Kirk usually doesn't want them included in the reports, but I thought maybe you'd like them."

"I want the business to run well into the future," he told her. "I will look at them. Thank you."

Victoria smiled, then handed him another brown folder.

Alone with four brown folders, he understood why his father

274

wanted him there. Office politics were playing out and only Berty could be objective.

He sat at the table to finish his candy before reading the next report. The next sales report was mostly written in plain English. It was easier to read, plus he skimmed over most of the numbers. As he opened the third report, the alarm on his cell phone chimed.

Opening the office door, he peeked his head out to see Thomas at his desk. "*Toe-mah*, I have to leave. I don't want to miss Hope getting off the bus on her first day of school. Do we have something in which I can take the reports home?"

"I have just the thing," said Thomas.

Berty was tidying the office when Thomas handed him a brown accordion folder. "Thanks," he said as he placed the reports inside. "Lock the office. I'll see you tomorrow."

During the drive home, he hoped that his father could help him make sense of the reports. He pulled into the driveway minutes before he had to walk to the bus stop. Only stopping to bring the reports in the house, he and Freesia left through the front door.

They arrived on the corner in time to see the half-bus arrive. The smell of diesel fuel reached them before the bus stopped.

Hope jumped off the bus, wearing a smile. Berty felt relieved. Taking her small hand, they strolled down the sidewalk. "How was your first day?" he asked.

"I didn't think school could be fun," she said. She rambled about her teacher, the kids in her class, what they did, lunch, and recess. Inside the house, Hope repeated her stories for Silvia, who listened intently.

"Why don't you change out of your uniform and I'll change out of my suit, then we can go through the portal," he told Hope.

"Okay!" she said. "I'll tell you all the rest later, Silvia." She ran upstairs.

"How was your day?" Silvia asked Berty.

"I have no idea what I'm doing and my tie is going to choke me when I least expect it," he said, then picked up the reports. She gave him a quick calming kiss before he climbed the stairs to change.

Berty brought the reports with him to the Empire Tree. "Is my dad here?" he asked Silvia as they crossed the bridge from Hope's chambers. "I didn't see his car."

"He's somewhere with Colvin right now," Silvia answered. "Your mother dropped him off this morning."

Passing the Scepter Room, he found it empty. No one was in the Roundtable Room either. The Reception Room was filled only with light. He turned to climb back up the stairs.

"Where are you going?" Silvia asked.

He stood beside her. His fingers slipped to her short, dark red hair. "You cut your hair," he said. "Like when we first met."

"I was wondering how long it would take you to notice," she teased.

Laughing, he said, "I like your hair short. Tomorrow, Julie is coming over after school for Hope's archery. Julie asked if she could pick up some wood from over there. No one knows the woods like you."

"I could go for a walk in the woods," Silvia said. "Do you need to discuss whatever it is you are carrying with your father?"

"When he's ready," he said. They climbed the steps. "Did you tell Martin?"

Silvia sighed. "Yes. He wanted me to ask you to write a happy ending before," she did not finish. "He's going to come over and say his good-byes." She blinked back her misty eyes.

He squeezed her tightly.

"Oh, Berty," she managed to say. They walked slowly

through the tree. "I failed him—my brother. Actually, *we* failed the Empire. And by we, I do not include you. I was the last in a long line of Empresses. Not because I failed to produce an heir, but because we were poor stewards of the Empire we were chosen to serve." She paused for a few steps. "Perhaps, it is not too late to right the wrongs of my foremothers. There is still time. The path can still present itself. Maybe that is why my Empire Mark has not faded, it is only motionless. We still have a chance. The Sages built all of this. I am convinced that their secrets lie in the vault beneath the tree. The secrets of the Sages can save us. I'm going to read every piece of paper in there if I have to." She kissed him on the cheek. "See you at dinner, Berty."

He watched her cross the bridge to her chambers, then entered his study. Placing reports on the table in the back, he called for Theodore.

When the Dwarf entered his study, Berty's stomach grumbled. "Could you have my father come to my study when he is able?"

"That may be awhile," said Theodore. "Colvin took him to Grunnan."

"When he returns then. In the meantime, could you bring me something to eat? Just to tide me over until dinner. I skipped lunch."

"Of course, my Lord."

While he waited for his food, he spread the reports across the table. He was reading the third report when he heard his wind chimes.

Theodore brought him a small tray. He set it on the table as Berty ran his fingers through his dark hair. "Something wrong, my Lord?"

"This business report is so convoluted. You would think three months of transactions would be more straightforward," he answered. "I'm not familiar with this, so I'm not sure at what I am looking." He glanced at Theodore. "These should be three of the same reports, but they don't feel the same. Something is not right and I cannot pinpoint it."

"I deal with all the Empire's business," Theodore said timidly. "I can look at them for you while your father is in Grunnan, if you wish."

Looking at the Empire's business manager, he smiled. "Have a seat, Theodore."

Theodore leafed through the three reports while Berty took time for a snack. The Dwarf's head snapped back and forth as his fingers shuffled papers. "The numbers don't add up," he said finally.

"Where?"

Showing Berty the papers, he said, "Here. Each report has a slightly different number. More than one, actually." Berty circled the numbers to which Theodore pointed.

"What do you think?" Berty asked. "Mathematical errors or theft?"

The Dwarf rubbed his chin. "On the surface, it looks like one or more cannot add. However, my gut is telling me that someone is stealing. From what is before me, I cannot determine who."

"My dad suspected. I wonder if Jon did, too," he said. "Thank you, Theodore. I'm going to need previous reports." He stared at the brown folder containing the projections Victoria gave him. "I also need a plan."

He skimmed Victoria's projections before heading to dinner. When he entered the Reception Room, he saw his father and mother sitting at the table. George glowed. The Land of Sages agreed with his father. He convinced Kate to have them both stay for dinner in the Empire Tree.

Berty told his father about Theodore's findings. After crossing through the portal, George said, "Trust no one in the company. It might be wise to get outside help to go through all the numbers."

Climbing into bed, Berty knew exactly what he had to do.

He made sure Hope safely boarded the school bus before heading to work. Seeing Thomas in the hallway, he said "*Toemah*, my office." Berty stood by the large windows as Thomas entered. "Close the door," he ordered.

Thomas slowly approached him. Berty could feel his trepidation.

"I have no intentions of making my being here permanent," Berty told him. "While I am here, I want Chase Technologies to be the best it can. Jon chose me for this and I do not want to let him down. I want him to be able to take back the reins as if he were never gone." Turning his head to Thomas, he asked, "I need to know where you stand. Are you with me?"

Thomas smiled. "Of course, I am."

"Good," he said. "In order to make this an even more successful company, I need to know my leaders. Can you get background information, resumes, HR files, and the like on Duncan, Dunne and Lin? I want to know at what they excel, strengths and weaknesses. Anything you can find. This is just for me."

"Doing your homework?"

"Exactly. Speaking of, I also want a list of our contracts, who supplies us, whom we supply, and what we sell."

"Yes, boss," Thomas said with a smile.

Chapter Twenty-one
The Collide

Taking a breath, Berty left the office. He knocked on the door of another office. A woman's voice told him to enter. "Victoria," he said, "I have had a chance to look over your projections. To see whether or not we can go forward this way, I think it is important to know from where we came. Could you provide me with the reports from this past year and last year? That should give a good foundation on which we can springboard."

"When would you like them?" she asked. She looked pleasantly surprised.

"I know it's a lot of paper," he said. "End of the day. If it will take longer, just let me know."

Disappearing down the corridors, he found the next office door on which he knocked. When he entered, he said, "Maggie, I hope this isn't a bad time."

She stared at him. "Is something wrong, Mister Chase?"

"No," he answered as he sat in a chair. "I'm here to ask you to put together sales projections for me. I like to see projections from now till the end of the year, and then how you see sales going for the next five years." She sat up straighter. "Make sure you also give me your reports from this year and the previous year, so I have a little background from which to work."

"I can have it on your desk tomorrow," she said.

"Sounds good, Maggie. Have a good day."

One more office, he thought. He knew he would get a less than warm reception. His feet brought him to an empty desk with the name, Eunice Watkins on it. He knocked on the door behind it. "Come in," said a man's voice.

"Kirk, a minute of your time," said Berty. Kirk wore an expression that read, please do not make me explain my report to you. Sitting on a chair, he said, "Jon's trip to Africa was to expand this business. Right now, my job is to follow his lead. Which brings me to why I am here. With your knowledge and expertise, I would like for you to put together projections for the end of the year, plus the next five. I would like you to include your analysis, recommendations and your overall thoughts about where we can go from here. In your plan, tack on your reports from this year and the last. That way, I can see a base. Make it as detailed as you can in a day or two."

From across the desk, Kirk stared at him for a few seconds. "Allow me to apologize for not thinking that you have any business acumen. You are more like your old man. I'll get a plan to you as soon as I can."

After shaking hands, Berty left. He returned to the office unsure of Kirk's sincerity. Sitting at Jon's desk, he had nothing to do, but wait. While he waited, he began to pen a happy ending for *the Adventures of Leigh and Marcus*.

The only distraction was Thomas entering to bring him the reports that Victoria prepared and company information. "I'll have the other stuff ready tomorrow," Thomas said.

Pleased with what he had, Berty returned home. He pulled into the driveway as Hope and Freesia entered the house. Carrying his increasing pile of papers into the house, he asked Hope how her second day of school was.

"Great!" Hope said.

"Any homework?"

"No. Are we going over there now?" she asked.

"After archery. Julie is coming over, so go get changed."

She ran upstairs with her book bag on her back. When he reached the top of the stairs, Silvia and Julie had stepped through the tapestry. All he managed was a, "Hi," before Hope sprinted out of her room.

"See you in the backyard," Hope said. Laughing, Julie followed.

"Another long evening?" Silvia asked him.

Setting the folders on his dresser, he said, "Looks that way. I could use a good walk in the woods."

She smiled. Placing her hand in his, she said, "I'll let you change. I'm going to do the same."

He had just pulled a T-shirt over his head when the doorbell rang. As he descended the steps, he heard a man say, "I think I may have the wrong house."

Peering through the screen door from the steps, Berty said, "Matt?"

Matt watched him cross the foyer. "Berty. I do have the right house."

Berty smiled at Silvia who answered the door. "Silvia, this is Teresa's brother, Matt. Come in. I didn't know that you would be home from Japan so soon."

"Hi," said Matt as he crossed the threshold. "They understand family. They gave me a couple of weeks. I brought Hope a little gift. How is she doing?" He carried a small, pink, Hello Kitty gift bag.

"Well, considering." Although he had probably showered and changed since landing, Matt still looked as if he had spent numerous hours in a plane. "See for yourself. She's out back."

282

Berty led Matt through the kitchen to the back porch. Seeing Hope and Julie shooting arrows, Matt stopped. "Whoa," Matt muttered.

Silvia stayed on the porch as Berty ushered Matt into the yard. "Hope! You have a visitor," Berty called.

Both Hope and Julie turned. "Wow," Matt breathed.

"Uncle Matt!" squealed Hope. She ran to him.

Matt swept her into his arms. "Hey there, munchkin. You're getting really big. I'm going to have to find a new nickname for you," he teased. "Whatcha been doing?"

"Archery. Watch me!" She wriggled out of his arms. Running towards Julie, she grabbed her bow.

With a smile, Berty watched Hope show off for her other uncle. A small part of him envied Matt. Matt still got to be fun and quirky Uncle Matt. And, the hardest part, Matt would still get to see her after Halloween.

As Hope and Julie approached, Matt's fingers quickly combed his dark hair and smoothed his checkered, button-down shirt. "Did you see me, Uncle Matt?" Hope asked.

"I did. You are some archer," answered Matt.

Hope beamed. "Thanks. Uncle Matt, this is Julie. Julie, my Uncle Matt," she introduced.

Smiling, Matt said, "Nice to meet you, Julie."

"And you," said Julie with a small smile.

"Hope, why don't you put your bow away and show Uncle Matt your room," Berty suggested.

"Okay!" Tugging on Matt's hand, she pulled him inside.

"Another brother?" Julie asked. She watched them enter the house.

"Her mother's brother," replied Berty. "I only have the one." He caught a glimpse of Silvia on the porch. "We're going to the woods in a minute." He could feel the ring in his pocket as he returned to the porch.

Berty, Silvia and Julie entered the foyer as Matt and Hope came downstairs. "Can Uncle Matt come on the walk with us?" Hope asked upon seeing Berty.

Looking at her face, he could not deny her time with Matt. "If Matt's up for a walk in the woods," he said.

"Come with us. Pleeeeease, Uncle Matt," Hope begged.

"I'll come," said Matt.

Walking through the front door, Berty noticed Matt's BMW parked on the street. "Retrieved your car?" he said.

"Yeah. I'm staying at their house at my mother's insistence," Matt answered.

"So, Matt, what do you do?" asked Silvia as they walked down the sidewalk.

"I'm a corporate financial analyst. Just by looking at a company's financial records, I can see everything that is going on in a company and key employees," said Matt.

Berty remembered the stack of reports on his dresser. "Would you mind helping me out while you're here, Matt? I was given reports yesterday and the numbers aren't right."

"For Chase Technologies?"

Berty nodded.

"I can do that. Just give me what you have and I'll work my magic," said Matt.

Julie looked from Matt to Berty. He could not tell her that Matt's choice of words was just a euphemism.

The sidewalk ended. Entering the woods, Silvia led the pack. "Young forest," Julie remarked.

Listening for a summer rain fed brook, Berty guided Silvia away from the others. "You're doing well walking light footed, Hope," Berty overheard Julie say. "Now, you have to learn to compensate for the forest rustle. Don't worry, that can take years to master. True Boudonians are said to be able to walk on the wind. My brother, Declan, can be that light on his feet."

They reached the brook that cut through the forest. "We're awfully close to the portal," Silvia whispered.

Smiling, Berty took both of her hands. He gazed into her warm, brown eyes. "This is where my life changed forever," he told her. "You gave me a cloak." Letting go of one of her hands, he fetched the ring from his pocket. "Silvia, whatever the future holds, I want to hold it with you." He dropped to one knee, then presented her with the ring his father gave him. "Will you marry me?"

She merely glanced at the ring before saying, "Yes."

He slipped the ring onto her finger. Not letting go of her hands, he kissed her. "Now, that I proposed properly, we can return to the others," he breathed.

They giggled. He stole a kiss, then they began to walk back to where they left Hope, Julie and Matt. A rustling nearby made them stop. After exchanging nervous glances, Berty closed his eyes.

"Julie, someone's coming," Hope whispered nervously.

Julie said to Matt, "Get her back to the house, now!"

"What about you?" Matt argued.

"Go!"

"Too late," said Hope. A half-dozen men in cloaks emerged from the trees.

Opening his eyes, Berty said, "Trouble." He pulled the Watcher's Locket from his pocket. His finger encircled the Watcher's Symbol counterclockwise. "Declan," he said into the closed locket, "we need help. Hope's in trouble." He squeezed the gold locket until it had a blue cast.

Silvia took a step backwards when Declan and Edwin appeared next to Berty. Dropping the chain of Declan's locket,

Edwin studied the unfamiliar forest.

"Hope, Julie and Matt are surrounded by six men," Berty said, pointing. "Julie may have a crossbow. The rest of us are unarmed."

The four of them wove through the trees.

"Give us the girl," said a man's voice.

"You'll have to get through me," warned Julie.

A man laughed. "A woman with a crossbow."

Touching a tree, Edwin became invisible. Declan raised his bow. Silently, he disappeared between the trees. Silvia and Berty crept forward. From around the tree, Berty could see the backs of the hooded men. The men formed a semi-circle across from Hope and her protectors.

Matt clutched Hope tightly. Huddled next to them, Julie pointed her crossbow at the men. The three of them inched backwards.

Finding a clear spot, Silvia stood firmly, facing the men's backs. Wind blew through their semi-circle. The men stopped advancing.

From the branches, Edwin materialized as he landed between the men and their prey. He raised his golden shield when a stream of magic erupted from a man's hand.

An arrow from nowhere hit one man, forcing him back a few steps. Julie shot her crossbow while Matt grabbed a staff sized branch off the ground. Pushing Hope behind him, Matt skillfully attacked one of the men with his branch.

Another man chased after Hope. Running through the me-lee, Berty swiped his hand in the air. The man flew through the forest.

When Berty reached Hope, he grabbed her hand. "Over there," pointed Hope.

Turning his head, Berty thought, *no.* A man ran into an invisible wall.

Berty could not use Dragonfire for fear it would attract unwanted attention. He watched the man fall to the ground with two arrows in his back. Keeping Hope in his grasp, he disguised them as a bush.

He watched Silvia magically manipulate the forest to keep the remaining men in the range of Edwin and Declan. His hand shielded Hope's eyes as Edwin brutally slashed the Warlock. Together, Declan and Julie brought down two more men. Matt knocked another into Edwin's waiting blade.

When the men were defeated, Berty removed their camouflage. Carnage surrounded them.

Surveying the forest floor, Matt asked, "Why were these men after Hope?"

"Long story," replied Berty. "I want to know how they found her."

"We can't leave them here," said Silvia.

Silvia was right. No one could find Empire spillover. Berty had half a mind to impale them on the side of Perimeter Road. "We must take them through. Make sure their bodies are seen. I want to send a message," he said.

"Berty? What is this about?" said Matt.

"I only see five," said Edwin. "Where's number six?"

Berty closed his eyes. The sixth man lay in the underbrush. Focusing on him, he magically dragged the man across the forest floor.

"How...?" Matt began.

Staring at Matt, Berty said, "All questions will be answered back at the house. We're going to lose daylight soon."

"Ready?" Silvia asked.

Nodding, Berty said, "We all stick together. Matt, keep your branch thingy. You may need it." He looked at Hope. "Is anyone coming?"

Her hand touched the nearest tree. She shook her head.

Magically, Berty lifted the six bodies off the ground. Matt gasped. Silvia conjured wind that erased evidence of their battle.

They marched the bodies to the invisible portal. Matt walked, holding Hope's hand without saying a word. "Going to have to carry them through," said Silvia. "Can't use magic through magic."

"How do we know someone isn't waiting on the other side?" asked Edwin.

"One Warlock, three swordsman and a bowman," Declan counted. "What's the other one?" He searched the body. Pulling a wand off the man, he said, "A Watcher."

Berty knew that only Watchers could see portals. "To find their way back," he said.

"I'll scout," Edwin offered.

"No," said Berty. "I'll do it." He closed his eyes. A pine grove encased him. He heard the eagle call. A Troll hid, frozen in the bushes. His bird's eye view followed the path to the road. Encircling a wide swath of the forest, he saw nothing. When he opened his eyes, he said, "All clear."

Silvia crossed with Declan and Edwin as they carried a body. Hope and Julie stayed while Berty and Matt carried another through the portal. Before he and Matt brought the last one, Berty made Hope and Julie step through the portal.

Berty magically mobilized all six. As a group, they walked the bodies to Perimeter Road. On one side of the road, he carefully piled one on top of the other. After taking one last look around the surrounding forest, they walked back to the portal.

In the grove, the Portal Troll waited for them. Bowing his triangular head, he said, "I'm sorry. They attacked me."

Staring at the dark blond curls covering the Troll's head, Berty said, "Guardian Trolls. Let Hatcher know when it's done."

Slowly, the Troll's light brown eyes looked at Berty. "Instead of me, my Lord?" he asked softly.

"To protect you," Berty replied. "You cannot ask your riddle if you are attacked."

The Troll stood to his full two and a half foot height. "It will be done."

Once everyone crossed the portal, Silvia led them through the woods. "We can station guards at the portal entrance," said Edwin.

"We must allow the Trolls to do their job," said Berty. "Guardian Trolls are impervious to almost all magic. Empire Guards are not." He was not sure how he knew about the Trolls, but his mind did not dwell on it. All he wanted to do was to get Hope back to the house quickly. He was glad that Matt was not asking any more questions.

When their feet found the sidewalk, Edwin's head moved like a pendulum. He watched a car turn into a driveway until Declan nudged him.

Berty's parents' car was parked in the driveway. He did not want to speak to his mother just yet. Opening the screen door, he let the others into the house before him.

Freesia greeted them in the hall. "I brought your mother upstairs," she began. Noticing Edwin and Declan, she asked, "What happened?"

"We were attacked," Berty answered. "Bring Hope to see Delyth." Crouching in front of Hope, he said, "Get your bow and your quiver. Go straight to Delyth. Tell her what happened. Ask her to teach you ancient Fairy defense."

Hope nodded, then ran up the steps with Freesia.

"Would you like to have Empire Guards stationed here?" Edwin asked.

"Why don't we continue this in the dining room," said Silvia. Once the six of them entered the dining room, Silvia closed the pocket doors.

"The magic protecting the house is strong," Declan said. He took a seat at the cloth-covered dining table.

"But what about outside the house?" argued Edwin. "Hope needs protection when she leaves."

"Why?" said Matt. "Why does Hope need protection? Who is trying to abduct her?"

"Hope has something so special that people are willing to kill to get it," Berty answered.

Matt stared at Berty as if he were waiting for Berty to expound. "That's it? I feel that you're only giving me half the story, Berty. Who's Delyth? What is ancient Fairy defense? And what do you mean by Trolls, Empire Guards and magic?"

"I don't expect you to understand, Matt," said Berty. "It's my problem. Besides, in a couple of weeks, you're going back to your life in Japan."

"That's not fair! She's my niece, too," said Matt, raising his voice.

"You may be her uncle, but I'm her legal guardian." He tried to keep his voice calm.

"That doesn't mean you know best. You got guardianship because you're here."

"Not all of us run away halfway across the world."

"At least I could make a commitment," Matt retaliated.

"Marrying one of the worst women in the entire world is not an accomplishment under commitment." Berty's blood began to boil. He asked, "What does this have to do with Hope?"

"I don't know, Berty! You won't tell me!" Matt screamed.

He could see Matt's frustration all over his face. "You're right," he conceded. "I am reluctant to tell you." He took a breath as Matt calmed some. "You have to promise me that what I say does not leave this room. Hope's safety depends on it."

Matt nodded.

"After Thanksgiving, I discovered that Hope has a rare gift. She has the ability to communicate with trees. She is what's known as a Listener—a Wood Listener to be exact. Up until recently, this knowledge has been secret."

Laughing, Matt said, "You want me to believe that people are after Hope because she can talk to trees?"

Berty stood. "Come with me," he said to Matt. "We'll be back."

He brought Matt upstairs to the tapestry in the hallway. "I don't understand," Matt said.

"You will." Taking his arm, Berty pulled Matt through the portal. Without saying a word, he marched Matt down the steps and through Hope's empty chambers. When they reached the platform, they stopped.

The Empire Tree shone greatly in the setting sun. Matt's eyes did not rest on one spot. "Holy... That's one massive tree," he said. He peered over the side of the platform before studying the green leafy bundle through which they came.

Berty ushered Matt back into Hope's chambers. After stepping through the tapestry, he and Matt returned to the dining room. Silently, Matt sat on his chair.

"Julie, I want you to work with Hope every day, here," said Berty. She nodded. "Edwin, we need increased security within the tree, especially on the upper levels. I am fairly certain that Leif compromised the location of the portal. He is probably also aware of the other one." He looked at Silvia.

"He knows it exists, but no one is supposed to know where it is," Silvia said.

"All it takes is a Watcher," said Declan. "If you know what

you are looking for."

Staring at the tablecloth, Silvia shook her head.

"If I may," said Julie. Berty gave her a nod. "How did they know we would be in the woods? Or did they just get lucky?"

"The Watcher would have found the house," said Declan. "The Warlock would've combated its magic."

"That's not enough," Julie said. "We were unarmed. I only had a small crossbow on me. It seems to be more than just coincidence."

Berty addressed Declan, "Could the magic that protects the Sages' Grove have become so unstable that Whispers could overhear us?"

Fear glimmered behind Declan's light eyes. "Yes."

"Important conversations need to happen underground from now on," said Berty. "Declan, Edwin, thanks for coming."

"Berty?" said Matt. "Do you think Teresa and Jon were taken to get to Hope?"

Berty could not pretend that thought did not cross his mind. "They're being held in a secure, high tech, underground facility," he blurted. Realizing what escaped his lips, he said, "The dilapidated shack is a ruse. They were taken by professionals. I don't think it has anything to do with Hope."

"How are we going to get them back?" Matt asked.

Glad that Matt said *we*, Berty answered, "My dad thinks someone in the company had a hand in it."

Matt scowled. "Let me look at the financials. I'll find them."

"Let's go check on Hope," said Berty.

As they rose from the table, he overheard Matt telling Julie, "I'm sorry you didn't get any wood. Why don't you take this and see what you can do with it." He handed her the branch with which he fought.

She smiled. "Thank you."

Matt watched her walk out of the room with her brother. "Those were some pretty cool moves you did out there," Berty said to him.

"Thanks. A co-worker introduced me to jōjutsu," said Matt. "Japanese stick fighting. It's so much more than just hitting with sticks."

As they climbed the stairs, Silvia said, "Matt, join us for dinner."

"I wish I could," Matt said with a glance at Julie, "but I'm having dinner with my parents tonight." He followed Julie through the portal.

Alone with Silvia, Berty held out his hand. When she slid her hand in his, they stepped through the tapestry.

Outside of Hope's chambers, Declan watched something move above the Sages' Grove. "I left Obie with Ojore," he told his sister without taking his eyes off the air.

"It was nice meeting you, Matt," Julie said. Branch in hand, she followed Edwin across the bridge.

Matt jumped when Theodore appeared on the platform. "Princess Delyth wanted me to tell you that she is in the vaults," he said.

"Edwin needs you to take him down there to discuss security," Berty said cryptically.

Looking a little confused, Theodore did not question. He gave Berty a bow, then disappeared.

Matt's head turned in every direction while they crossed the bridge to Silvia's chambers. Silvia led the men down the ladder to the vaults.

Freesia sat at the table in the Library Vault doing her needlework. Looking up, she said, "Princess Delyth brought Hope to her vault. King Elrick and Alfred are in the back of the library."

After squeezing Berty's arm lightly, Silvia entered the library.

He opened the main stone entrance to his vault. Declan touched the Sages' Seal that led to the Advisors' vaults.

"Delyth's vault is down here," said Declan. Torches erupted to life, lighting sections as they walked down the long, stone corridor. Light spilled into the corridor from an open vault. "Delyth?" called Declan.

"In here," said Delyth's voice.

They entered a book filled room. Upon seeing Declan, Delyth smiled warmly. Hope stood under a dummy frozen in mid-air. "We borrowed it from the training room," Delyth said.

"Hope, your Uncle Matt has to go," said Berty.

Her brown curls bounced as she ran to Matt. "You're leaving already? But you just got here."

"I know. It's been a long day," Matt told her. "I'll be back tomorrow. Okay?"

She smiled. "Okay, Uncle Matt." Giving him a hug, she said, "See you tomorrow."

"When you're done here, meet us in the library," Berty said to Delyth. "Declan, gather everyone." He walked Matt back the way they came.

After returning to the house, Matt said, "I'm sorry for getting angry with you. That's a crazy life I do not even begin to understand."

"It's all right. We both have a lot going on," said Berty. He stopped in his bedroom. Placing personnel files aside, he gave Matt all the financial folders. "I should be getting more in the next couple of days. If you need anything else, let me know."

"I will," said Matt.

After seeing Matt out, Berty rushed back to the library. Seeing his parents and Ojore, almost everyone was there. "Where's Estelle?" he asked.

"She's receiving a message from the stars and cannot be disturbed," said Declan.

"She'll have to be informed later," he said.

The library's long table had only one seat left. Keeping it open for Estelle, Berty stood at the end of the table. "You're probably wondering why I have gathered you here. We just discovered that what we say can be overheard by Leif's men. Use caution when speaking. You never know who is listening. Just because you do not see anyone does not mean no one can hear you."

"Even inside, my Lord?" asked Hedda.

"Yes. By all means, go about your lives normally. However, Hedda and Lark, I need the two of you to guide loved ones into refraining from talking about where the Empire Guards are. Knowledge of where, who and how many in the wrong hands can get guards killed. Be on the lookout for treachery and those who try to coerce information from the families."

Lark and Hedda exchanged glances. "Lark and I are up to the task, my Lord," said Hedda.

"Very good," he said. "You two may go." After the Elf women left, he continued, "For those of you who may not know, we were attacked today on the other side of the portal." Berty heard gasps. "There may be retaliation of some sort. And, it may spill into the Sages' Grove. Do not leave the tree unarmed in one form or another. The house of Rowan must be protected. As the next Witch of Rowan, Alina and her family are viable targets. All of you, and Estelle, are also targets for being aligned with the Empire. Do what you need to do to protect yourselves and each other. If the Advisory Council and Silvia will stay, the rest of you can go to dinner."

When the table emptied, Berty took a seat. "Hatcher, you know the portal is no longer secret."

"Yes," answered Hatcher. "Chief Miercia is personally selecting Guardians to protect that portal."

"Good," said Berty. "Declan saw something on the platform earlier. What was it?"

"A tear in the magic surrounding the Sages' Grove," Declan replied. "The tear swims in the magic, leaving a long hole for anything to enter or escape."

"I thought the magic comes and goes," said Colvin.

"It does, but when it's there, it is not whole."

"Can any Watcher see this?" Berty asked.

He could see Declan thinking. "I'm not sure. I don't ask. I do not want to draw attention to it, nor do I want to let anyone know there's something wrong if they cannot see it. There has to be other Watchers like me. It may be best to assume that every Watcher can."

A strange silence surrounded the dinner table. Light conversation felt strained. Finally, Berty said, "Matt offered to look over the numbers, Dad."

"Good," said George. "We're going to need some solid evidence to convict the person who set this up."

Chapter Twenty-two
Safe Keeping

Kate studied her husband, then addressed her son. "I'm glad that Matt is home. Maybe he can distract his father. Robert is beside himself. He feels so powerless. Lawyers and government officials have tied his hands. He's on the phone and the internet desperately trying to seek someone who can help him bring his little girl home." Her brown eyes glistened.

"The parents of your daughter-in-law?" Lida asked.

Kate nodded.

"He needs a project to get him through," said Elrick.

George laughed. "Robert was a stockbroker. When he retired, day trading and collecting rare items became his projects."

Confused, Elrick said, "I don't understand."

George spent the rest of the dinner explaining stocks. No other conversations mattered at the table. They all listened intently to a small slice of life on the other side of the portal.

"Do people not make things over there?" Julie asked.

"Sure they do," said George. "Expertly crafted handmade items are well sought after."

After dinner, Berty returned to his house with Silvia and his family. With Silvia by his side, he said, "Mom, Dad, Silvia and I are engaged."

His mother smiled. "That's wonderful," she said, hugging

them both. "It's nice to hear good news." She gazed at Silvia's ring. "It belongs on your finger. What about the wedding?"

"We were thinking about a small ceremony in the backyard when Jon and Teresa come home," said Silvia.

"That sounds lovely," Kate said. "If you need help with anything, you let me know."

Smiling, Silvia said, "Thanks."

His parents insisted on tucking Hope into bed. Before falling asleep, Berty stared at the untouched personnel files on his dresser. He would have to read them in the privacy of Jon's office.

He woke to the rhythmic falling of raindrops. In the kitchen, Freesia and Hope ate breakfast. While sipping his coffee, he noticed the Fairy Stone pendant hanging from Hope's neck. "Are you planning on bringing Fairy Dust to school?" he asked.

Hope shook her head. When she swallowed, she said, "Delyth thought that I should wear it, just in case."

"Perhaps you should wear it inside your shirt to keep it safe," Freesia suggested.

As she tucked it behind her collared shirt, Berty said, "I'll be driving her to school today and picking her up."

"Can I ride in the front?" Hope asked.

"No."

"Are you and Silvia really getting married?" she asked.

"Yes."

Entering the room, Silvia asked, "Do you have your lunch, Hope?"

"Yes. When do I call you Aunt Silvia?"

Silvia laughed. "Technically, I don't become your aunt until after your uncle and I are married. Have a good day and be safe." After giving Hope a hug, she kissed Berty. She watched them get into the car, then waved as the car rolled out of the driveway.

At the school, Berty scanned the parking lot before allowing

Hope to get out of the car. He clutched onto her hand while they walked through the front door. Reluctantly, he let go of her hand. He walked behind her, watching her every step.

"Sir, all visitors need a pass from the front desk," said a woman walking towards him.

"I'm just making sure she gets to her classroom," Berty told her.

"Sir, you can't be here," she said sternly. "It's school policy."

Putting a hand on Hope's shoulder, he made her stop. "And you are?"

"Colleen Adstrom. I teach fourth grade."

"My tuition dollars help pay your salary," said Berty. "I don't care about your policy. Come on, Hope."

"Even parents are not allowed in the hallways without a pass," Colleen scolded.

He stared straight into her hazel eyes. "What are you going to do about it, Colleen? Report me? Call security?" After a few seconds, he ripped his stare away, then ushered Hope down the hall. Once she safely entered her classroom, he turned to find the Lower School Director standing behind him.

"Good morning, Mister Chase. A word in my office, please?" she said.

"Excellent idea," he told her. He followed her into the office.

They sat on opposite sides of her desk. "Mister Chase," she began, "school policies are for everyone. You cannot pick and choose by which ones you wish to abide. These policies are to keep every child safe."

"Safe. That is an interesting word. First, don't chastise me. Second, don't patronize me. You claim that the school cares about the children's safety, yet I see no security."

"Our security measures keep children safe."

He laughed. "Measures. Do you remember me telling you about Hope's parents?"

"Yes, of course."

"Yesterday evening, when Hope was playing not far from my home, people attempted to abduct her."

"Oh my God."

"The men were armed. I'm thinking of having her carry her bow and quiver on her, everywhere, at all times."

"I understand, but we do not condone violence."

"When it comes to Hope's safety, Ms. Stapleton, I could not care less about what you do and do not condone. If Hope cannot be safe at this school, then I am afraid I will have to ask for a refund—in cash—and place her elsewhere."

Jane sat forward in her chair. "That will not be necessary. The school has state of the art surveillance and bulletproof glass."

"Neither of those can stop predators from entering school grounds," Berty said. "Visitor passes and a teacher telling me that I am not allowed beyond a certain point does not reassure me. Until you have patrolling armed guards, I am sending her to school with her bow. Actually, since she has to ride the school bus, she's going to do it anyway." He gave her a quick smile. "Thank you for your time, Jane. I must get to work." Rising from the chair, he added, "By the way, I am picking her up today, too. Just so you know." He walked out of the office, wondering if homeschooling would have been a better choice.

A pile of brown folders waited on the desk in Jon's office. "Good morning," Thomas chirped.

"What do we have here?" Berty asked.

"Maggie Lin's and Kirk Duncan's projections," answered Thomas. "I should have everything else for you in about an hour. I had to use, like, five different printers."

"Thanks, *Toe-mah*." Closing the office door, Berty placed the

300

personnel files on the glass top table.

Kirk graduated with an engineering degree from a top university. He worked for them for twelve years. Victoria also obtained an engineering degree, but from a less prestigious university. She worked for the company for six years, three of which as Director of Operations. Maggie, however, had a liberal arts degree. Her previous employer sent her to get her MBA, but she never finished. She began working for them three years ago and recently was promoted to Sales Director.

Thomas knocked on the door, interrupting Berty shuffling papers. "Here is everything," said Thomas. "And I do mean everything. Jim in accounting wanted me to make a good impression, so he added a financial summary for the last fifteen years. I wonder if he has a crush on me."

Berty's cell phone rang. It was a local number he did not recognize. "Could be Hope's school. I have to get this," he told Thomas. Thomas closed the door on his way out. "Hello?" he answered.

"Berty, it's Matt. I've been pouring over the reports you gave me. We need to talk."

"Good. I have more stuff for you. I'll be over soon. I'm leaving right now," Berty said.

He threw all the brown folders in his messenger bag. Stopping at Thomas' desk, he said, "I have to go."

"Is everything okay?" Thomas asked.

"Should be. I won't be back, so you can lock up."

Berty drove to Jon and Teresa's house. Matt led him into the kitchen. Papers were strewn all over the table.

"There are two separate issues," said Matt. "Over compensation and slow embezzlement."

Placing his bag on a chair, he retrieved all the folders. "Explain."

"Slow embezzlement is self explanatory. Someone has been skimming over many years. Just enough to stay under the radar," Matt explained. "Over compensation is a bit trickier. Someone is trying to make themselves look better or become indispensable. And there are a multitude of reasons why a person does that." He began leafing through the folders Berty brought. "I remember a while back Jon telling me that he wanted me to look at some stuff. He didn't tell me why. All he said is that when he was done, he would mail me a flash drive. I'm beginning to wonder if he knew something was wrong."

Loosening his tie, Berty waited for Matt to continue.

"I've been searching the house for the information Jon wanted to send me. I couldn't find anything. Do you think it's in Africa?"

"Did you check the basement office?" Berty asked.

"There's a basement office? I know of the one upstairs."

He led Matt into the basement. Seeing the closed door, Matt tried to turn the knob. "It's locked. I only have the key to the front door," Matt said.

"Hope told me about this room," said Berty. He magically opened the locked door.

Filing cabinets littered the cramped room. On an old, small, formica table sat a piecemeal desktop computer. Turning it on, Matt said, "Looks like he put this together himself out of spare parts."

Berty examined the old filing cabinets. None of the drawers had labels. Trying to open a drawer, it would not budge.

"The computer is password-protected," said Matt.

"The filing cabinets are locked," Berty added.

"I never knew Jon was so paranoid."

"Neither did I." He magically unlocked the filing cabinet.

Matt leaned back in the old computer chair. Looking around

the room, he said, "If I were Jon, where would I put a flash drive?"

Perusing one of the folders, Berty said, "Hey, Matt, come look at this."

Matt looked at the folder. "Detailed financial records by department. Jon, Jon, Jon. This is great if I had a month or two, or a team."

"Maybe the stuff I brought can help narrow," said Berty.

Bringing the folders to the dining room, Matt spread papers all over the table. Not being much help, Berty made lunch. They ate at the kitchen island.

"So far, all I can tell is that both problems started prior to last year," Matt told Berty. "But, I think I see a pattern emerging. It gives me some direction for downstairs."

"Good. You think you can obtain solid proof?"

"I'm hoping. We'd have to show a lawyer."

Berty helped Matt sort through the filing cabinets. Matt had him place the collected files on the floor in the playroom. When both of their cell phones rang, they froze Matt's organizational process.

Answering their phones, both said, "Mom?"

"I'm on my way to pick up your father, Kate said. "There's been contact. We are heading over to meet with the lawyers and our State Department liaison now. I'll call you when I know more."

"Okay, Mom. After I pick Hope up from school, I'll be waiting at the house for your call."

Hanging up, Berty and Matt stared at each other. They knew they both received the same phone call. Silently, Matt took notes while Berty placed files on the floor.

When Berty's alarm beeped, he said, "I need to go." Matt nodded. He left Matt sitting on the basement floor.

Hope waited for him in the school lobby with a watchful teacher by her side. He was glad his words did not fall on deaf ears. On the drive home, Hope jabbered about her day.

Berty kept his cell phone on him while he watched Hope and Julie, wearing cloaks, practice archery in the rain. *The Adventures of Leigh and Marcus* sat on the table next to him in an attempt to finish. The words could not come.

A delicate hand touched his shoulder, then ran through his dark hair. His eyes closed. When they opened, Silvia was sitting next to him. She tenderly held his hand. "Your mom told me. Have you heard yet?"

"No." His eyes pleaded with her for distraction.

"Martin came over today," she said. He asked me to bring him through the portal. We strolled through the Empire Tree and the Sages' Grove." Her eyes welled. "It was a wonderful day." Tears rolled down her cheek.

He squeezed her hand.

With a handkerchief, she dried her eyes and face. "Your dad is making progress. He spends a good portion of his time underground with the Dwarves."

His cell phone rang. Without looking at the caller ID, he said, "Hello?"

"Hey, it's Matt. I found them. I'm coming over with some things to show you. That door in the basement won't lock."

"I'll be here. Don't worry, I'll fix it." Hanging up, Berty closed his eyes. Focusing on Jon's basement office door, he locked it magically.

He told Silvia about Matt. "Guess I shouldn't pretend that I'm going to get any writing done," he said. Swiping his hand over his notebook, it returned to his bedroom.

When the doorbell rang, he reluctantly left Silvia's side to answer it. Matt stood on the front porch, holding a box. He and

Matt entered the dining room. After digging through the box, Matt pulled two brown folders. He placed them on the table in front of Berty.

"Kirk Duncan has been embezzling money for the last nine and a half years. It started out small, virtually undetectable. The amount jumped when he became Director of Operations, and then again when he became Vice President," said Matt.

Tapping the other folder, Matt began, "Victoria Dunne has been overshooting her numbers for a while. Kirk Duncan exploited those numbers. No, they are not cohorts. In April of this year, her overcompensating spiked. That was right after Jon was talking about Africa. This woman is guilty of something. I would like to take a closer look at her."

Stunned, Berty stared at the folders. "And Maggie Lin?"

"Should get promoted."

Their cell phones rang. "Mom?" they both answered.

"We're coming over," Kate said.

"I'm at Berty's," said Matt.

"So are Teresa's parents," Kate added.

"Okay. We'll be waiting," said Berty.

He looked from the box to Matt. "Come, say hi to Hope."

"Is Julie here?" Matt asked.

"They're outside."

"In the rain?"

When they walked out onto the back porch, Silvia greeted Matt. Watching Hope and Julie, Matt said, "You know, archery suits Hope."

"Our parents called. They're coming over," Berty told Silvia.

"Freesia and I will keep Hope upstairs," said Silvia.

"Hope!" Berty called. "Time to come in."

Hope and Julie joined them on the porch. "Your cloaks are soaking wet," said Silvia. "Why don't you both hang them here to dry. Julie, if you need to borrow a cloak, I have a spare one upstairs."

Inside the house, Silvia and Freesia ushered Hope to her room. "Julie, do you have a moment?" said Matt. "Sorry you had to see my outburst yesterday. It was not my best moment."

"That's okay. I understand. I have a nephew," Julie said. "Why isn't your wife here?"

"I am no longer married. I've been divorced for a little over six months," Matt answered.

Julie smiled. Rolling his eyes, Berty checked to see if the sitting room had enough seats for all of them.

The doorbell rang. When Berty entered the foyer, Matt was staring up the empty staircase. He gave Matt a nudge before answering the door. When both sets of parents crossed the threshold, Lillian asked quietly, "Where's Hope?"

"In her room," said Berty. He led them to the sitting room.

After everyone was seated, Kate said, "The good news is that they're okay."

"The bad news," said Robert, "is the ransom."

"Fifteen million for Jon. Ten for Teresa," George said.

"Dollars?" Matt asked.

George nodded. "We have seventy-two hours to get the money together."

"And if we can't?" said Matt.

"We don't know," said Lillian.

"Where are we going to get twenty-five million dollars?" asked Matt.

"We have some money saved," said Robert, "but it won't be nearly enough to even pay for one ransom."

"Do we know where they are?" Berty said.

"What are you thinking, Berty?" Kate asked.

"Twenty-five million comes from Chase Technologies.

There is no other way to get the money. And the liquidation process would destroy the company," said Berty. "If we knew where they were, we could," he glanced at Matt's parents, "send a team."

"To extract them?" Robert asked.

"I know people," said Berty.

"Whatever the price, I'll pay it," said Robert.

Kate looked at her son softly. "We can let the company go, Berty."

"It will take longer than three days to liquidize, Kate," said George.

"Especially when your VP is embezzling money," Matt said.

"What?" said George.

Nodding, Matt continued, "And your Director of Operations is no saint either. I'll show you." George left the room with Matt.

Lillian took one look at her husband, then said, "We should see Hope."

Berty called for Hope. After she entered the back sitting room with her maternal grandparents, Kate said quietly to Berty, "You don't have to do this."

"Yes, I do. Dad built this company and Jon is taking it further," said Berty. "Let me, Mom. Before they close."

Giving him a hug, she said, "Okay."

"Excuse me," said Silvia from the stairs. "Berty, Estelle needs to see you. She says it's urgent."

"Go," said Kate.

Berty found Estelle staring out the window of his bedroom. "Estelle," he said, announcing his presence.

She turned. "My Lord, starjen told me about your family. They gave me a map." She held out a folded piece of paper.

"Show me."

Estelle unfolded the paper on top of the round coffee table between the two wooden chairs. To Berty, the map looked like a bunch of dots. "Your brother's things are here," she pointed to a dot. "He and his wife are here," she indicated another dot.

The dots she touched glowed different colors—the first red, the second blue. "Estelle, I don't know how to read a star map."

"Silvia does," she said. "The items are in an inn. Your parents know where."

"Estelle, thank you and the stars. Stay here. I'm going to have Silvia come up. Show her what you showed me," he said.

Running down the steps, he had only eyes for Silvia. "Go see Estelle. She has a star map for you."

As Silvia climbed the stairs, Kate threw Berty a puzzled look. "Once Robert and Lillian leave, I'll explain."

Walking out of the dining room, George said, "Just got off the phone with Silverman and Trane. Matt and I have a meeting in the morning."

Kate gave George a strong smile. "You're bringing criminal charges against him."

"I like to be there when they arrest Duncan," said George.

"Don't worry, Thomas will give you the play-by-play," Berty said.

Seeing Silvia descend, he allowed his parents to enter the other sitting room without him. "All we need to know is where they were staying last," she said. "We can find them from there."

"You'll be able to read the map?" he asked.

"Yes."

"What map?" Matt asked as he approached.

"The map that will lead us to Jon and Teresa," Berty told him quietly.

Lillian entered the hall. "We're going to get going," she told her son. "Do what you need to do here."

Following her, Robert said, "Berty, whatever the price. Let me know." Saying good-bye, they left.

"We don't have much time," he said. "Mom, Dad, I need the location of their last hotel. Silvia, could you please bring Hatcher, Declan and Edwin."

Standing between her grandparents, Hope looked up at him. "What are you doing, Uncle Berty?"

"Going to get your parents."

"Can I help?" she asked.

"You can help me by giving me a hug before I go," said Matt.

She smiled, then ran to her uncle. When Matt's car drove away, Freesia collected Hope and brought her upstairs.

Kate carried Jon and Teresa's travel itinerary in her purse. In the dining room, Silvia and Hatcher studied it.

At the other end of the table, Berty sat with Declan and Edwin. Kate and George bounced between the two groups. "I say we leave as soon as possible," Berty said.

"Who all is going?" Declan asked.

"Us and Silvia."

"Just the four of you cannot go," said George.

"We could use Sean," Edwin said.

"Ojore would make a good addition," suggested Declan.

Berty nodded. "Fine. We will bring them both. Have Theodore prepare provisions for not just us, but Jon and Teresa as well."

Silvia and Hatcher finally lifted their heads out of the map. "The portal that will take you closest is half a day's walk from the portal near here. I will take you myself," said Hatcher.

"We will all meet here while the morning is still dark," Berty said. His cell phone rang. Edwin and Hatcher watched curiously as he answered. "Matt?" said Berty, recognizing the number.

"Somebody broke in," Matt said.

"To Jon and Teresa's?" he asked.

"The police are here," Matt continued. "The house is a wreck. They tore this place apart."

"Is anything missing?"

"Any of the files you brought that I did not put in the box and the upstairs computer."

"What about the basement office?" Berty inquired.

"Hold on." Berty heard Matt moving through the house. "No one got in there, but it looks like they tried."

"Bring your things. You can stay here," he said. "In Hope's bedroom is the wooden doll I gave her. Bring that, too. It will tell her who broke in."

"I'll be there as soon as I can," said Matt.

A horrified look froze on Kate's face. "Matt and the files will be safest here," said Berty.

"And who will protect Hope?" his mother asked.

"Freesia. Mom, Hope will be fine."

"How will we get in touch with you?" she asked.

He looked at Declan to answer. "Through Delyth. She will be holding my Watcher's Locket."

"I'll make you a pot of tea," Silvia said to Kate.

"Show me?" Kate asked her.

Silvia brought Kate through the swinging door to the kitchen.

"Go. Prepare yourselves," said Berty. "I'll wait for Matt."

Wandering into the kitchen, he found his mother talking with Silvia. A flowery porcelain teapot sat between them on the table. "I don't see why you have to go, too," said Kate. She placed her matching cup on its saucer.

"I'm the only one, besides Estelle, who can read that map," Silvia reasoned. "And Estelle... Let's just say she is not well equipped to protect herself."

Noticing Berty, Kate asked, "Is Matt here?"

"Not yet."

"Where's your father?" his mother inquired further.

"I don't know. I thought he came in here with you."

When the doorbell rang, Berty let Matt in with his box. Matt dragged his suitcases upstairs. He gave Matt the last empty bedroom.

"Thanks for letting me stay," Matt said. "I was afraid that going to my parents' would lead to their house being broken into and ransacked."

"You're welcome to stay until you go back to Tokyo. Silvia and I will be gone by the time you get up tomorrow. Hope will show you how the house works. Freesia's room is upstairs. Oh, and there's no electricity." Matt looked at him in disbelief. "You are welcome to go through the portal. There is one thing you should know about the portals. We expect them to close by Halloween."

"So, asking Julie out would be a bad idea?"

Berty let out a laugh. "Just know that time is limited. I'm going over. You coming?"

Leaving his suitcases, Matt followed Berty through the tapestry. "This place is even cool at night," Matt said.

Chapter Twenty-three
The Ghost and the Snake

Chuckling, Berty led him into his chambers. While Matt looked at everything, Berty headed up the spiral staircase. Thinking about traveling clothes, he opened his wardrobe. He magically sent the plain shirt, pants and boots to his bedroom in the house. Downstairs, he grabbed his sheathed sword. Matt watched him secure it to his belt.

"Are you scared?" Matt asked.

"You fought a swordsman with a stick," Berty reminded him. "Were you scared?"

"All I thought about was protecting Hope," said Matt.

Berty gave him a look that said, *there's your answer.*

Taking Matt through the tree, he said, "All I can think about is how dare someone do that to my little brother. I want to rip the person limb from limb. Merely going to jail doesn't seem to be enough."

"Hope's wooden doll had a little rag type doll with it," said Matt. "I dropped the rag doll on her dresser by accident. A flash drive fell out of it."

"Are you taking it to the lawyers' tomorrow?"

"Yeah. I'm beginning to suspect corporate espionage," Matt said. "And I believe Victoria Dunne has a hand in it." He stopped talking when Julie entered the Reception Room. She smiled at him briefly as she crossed the room.

"Julie, have you seen Hope?" Berty asked.

"She and Obie are listening to Ojore's stories. I believe your father is there as well," Julie answered. "Freesia is keeping watch. They should be back soon."

He said to Matt, "Hope should be able to tell you all about that flash drive."

When they returned to the house, Berty knocked on Hope's bedroom door. "Have you spoken with Uncle Matt?" he asked.

She nodded. "Uncle Berty, can Mommy and Daddy come through the portal once before they close?"

Her brown eyes pierced into his. He could feel her underlying sadness. She was much too young to be so sad. "That's a good idea," he said. He gave her a big hug. "You be good. Listen to Freesia. If you need to contact me, talk to Delyth."

"Okay, Uncle Berty. I love you."

"I love you, too, Hope." With a final squeeze, they let go. "Get ready for bed, then I'll tuck you in."

On his way back to Hope's room, he saw Silvia emerge. Smiling, she said, "She's all ready for you."

He grabbed her hand as they passed. Sitting on the edge of Hope's bed, he smoothed her covers. "We will all be home before you know it," he said.

"I know," she said with a yawn.

He kissed her goodnight on her forehead, then turned off her light.

In the hall, Matt waited for him. He followed Matt into his bedroom. Matt said quietly, "I've seen her talk to that doll, Ashley, before, but I never knew it talked to her. Anyway, the people who broke in were professionals. The trees told the doll that they've been watching the house for days. Ashley overheard them talking about the files and the flash drive. Your father and I discussed having their house searched for bugs.

"She also told me about the other doll. After the Superbowl party debacle, Jon gave Ashley a rag doll. It seems that Jon has been keeping that flash drive in the rag doll for months. He would regularly update it. After tonight's break-in, I understand Jon's paranoia."

Berty shook his head. "Why didn't Jon tell anyone?"

"I don't think he had enough proof. Hopefully, we will. I'll try to keep you updated."

"Thanks, Matt, for everything," Berty said. "See you when we get back." After leaving Matt's room, he tried to sleep.

The drive to rescue his brother and sister-in-law forced him out of bed in complete darkness. After his shower, he dressed in his Empire clothes, which were better suited for traveling. Sword and cloak in hand, he tiptoed downstairs.

Seeing a light in the kitchen, he entered. Silvia was orchestrating the kitchen to make breakfast. "Good morning," she said, then gave him a lingering kiss. "I found large knapsacks in which we can fit our weapons and cloaks. There is one at everyone's place in the dining room."

He entered the dining room. Laying his cloak over the back of his chair, he began to pack the bag.

Bringing him a mug of coffee, Silvia said, "The others should be here soon. I instructed Declan on where to go."

Declan arrived with everyone in tow. Theodore handed out provisions, which they packed in the bags on the table. After sliding his sword inside the full knapsack, he tucked his cloak on top.

Once Theodore left, Berty quietly addressed the group. "We're going somewhere I have never been. We will be on this side of the portal where people, as a whole, do not wear cloaks or carry swords or bows. Expect anything. Be vigilant. Stay together."

The sky was just beginning to lighten when they ventured onto the sidewalk. The mature trees shaded them from the flooding light of the street lamps. Lights began to illuminate windows as the houses' occupants stirred. Stepping off the sidewalk into the forest, darkness swallowed them.

Approaching the portal, Hatcher said, "We are staying off of Portal Road. We would attract too much attention."

Berty agreed. Even without Edwin's armor, his towering height advertised that he was an Empire Guard accompanying a Sages' Grove party.

One at a time, they crossed the portal. In the pine grove, grunting startled them. "Guardian Trolls," Hatcher whispered. Following Hatcher, they passed gruesomely tall, brutally ugly, club wielding variations of the Trolls Berty came to know. Their quick glare gave Berty fearsome shivers.

Traveling on wide, Portal Road would have shaved a few minutes off their trek. The sun was high when they reached their chosen portal.

"Thank you," Berty told Hatcher.

"Good luck," Hatcher said.

The portal brought them to a grassy knoll. The setting sun did not lift the heat. After looking at the star map, Silvia said, "This way." She led them through a busy town. Vendors were setting up their food stalls for evening sale. The map brought them to a large resort at the edge of town.

Through the automatic sliding doors, air conditioning instantly cooled them. A smiling face greeted Berty at the reception desk.

Berty plastered a smile on his face. "I believe you are holding something for Chase."

"Ah, yes," the woman said. "I need to see your passport, please."

Magically, he produced a passport inside his bag. He gave her the small, dark blue, magical creation. She glanced at it. Handing it back to him, she said, "Right this way, Mister Chase."

Behind the reception desk was a holding room. The woman asked the security guard for the bags for Chase. The bags rolled out of a back room on a luggage trolley. "Did you and the missus enjoy your safari?" the security guard asked.

"It was like nothing else," Berty said, smiling.

"That is good." The man watched Berty roll the trolley into the lobby.

Silvia talked to the woman at the front desk. The woman handed her a map and a keycard. Smiling, Silvia approached Berty. "We're in a villa named Giraffe."

The six of them walked through the resort until they found the detached stucco villa with a giraffe on it. Once inside, she explained, "I asked about renting a car. She said that no one would rent us anything during the night. We will have to wait until morning. It will take too long to get there on foot."

"Couldn't we have gotten horses?" Sean asked.

Ignoring him, Berty focused on his foyer. Concentrating on Jon and Teresa's luggage, he sent them to his house.

Edwin and Declan inspected the villa. They exchanged glances. Edwin walked through the sliding glass doors onto the stone patio. Declan crept out the front.

"What is the meaning of this?" said a man's voice with a distinctly British accent. "Sneaking up on me like that. I'm lost."

"Sure you are," said Edwin.

Edwin and Declan forced the man inside the villa. The man's light colored pants and shirt were wrinkled and dusty. "I'm just trying to find my way back to Elephant," said the man.

"He's been following us since we entered town," Edwin told Berty.

"You must have me mistaken for someone else," the man said.

"Have a seat," said Berty. "Getting lost is tiresome."

Reluctantly, the man sat on a chair Declan placed in the center of the room.

"I'm sure your, ah, employer has better things for you to do than follow us," Berty said.

"I have not been following you. My name is Nigel Burns. I am just a guest at the resort, staying in Elephant villa."

Smiling, Berty said, "How about a little honesty, Nigel."

Nigel chuckled. "Honesty? I am not the one masquerading as Jonathan Chase." He looked at Silvia. "*You* are not Teresa Chase."

"I never claimed to be," said Berty. "Tell me, Nigel, what is your interest in Jon and Teresa Chase?"

Leering at Berty, he said, "I could ask you the same question. After all, I don't believe I caught your name. I told you who I am."

"Did you now?" Berty placed a chair a few feet in front of Nigel, then sat, facing him. "Do you work for a government or a private agency?"

Nigel said nothing.

Shrugging, Berty said, "I don't care either way. As for who I am, you don't really want to know."

Nigel leaned forward a little. "You know where they are?"

Studying Nigel, Berty decided not to answer.

Nigel nodded slightly. He stared at Berty. "I'll make a deal with you. Give me their location and I'll tell you my interest."

Berty leaned back in the chair. "If you can't find that information with all your resources and contacts, then how do you know you can trust us to give you that information?"

Taking a breath, Nigel said, "They have yet to pay the ransom. Are Jon's and Teresa's lives not worth twenty-five million US dollars? Or does the family have other plans?"

"That amount of money is tough to acquire on such short notice," said Berty.

Nigel squinted for a moment. "Here you sit." His scrutinizing stare examined Berty. "Family resemblance. Yet, no one with a family name passed through customs. How did you get here?"

"I'll keep my secrets, thank you."

"That was quite a feat, considering the fact that you do not have a passport. You never even applied for one."

Berty asked, "What does your government want with Jon and Teresa?"

"Nothing," Nigel admitted. "It is the people with whom your brother was doing business. The part of the company with which he dealt is legitimate. However, they also smuggle for the people we believe took your brother and his wife."

Swallowing, Berty said, "And who is that?"

"They are know as the Nyoka." Ojore raised his eyebrows. "They are dealers—arms, drugs, ivory, antiquities, people, but mainly young girls," Nigel said with disgust. "There has been a multinational effort to eradicate them for decades, but no one can ever find their headquarters. Monitoring the Chases has been the closest we have come, then we lost them. I have told you what I know. Will you tell me?"

Berty glanced at Silvia for support. She gave him a little nod. "I'll tell you what," he said to Nigel. "You arrange transportation and we'll take you to where we believe they are. It is quite a ways from here."

"You'll take me? Am I to believe that the six of you are going to infiltrate a dangerous arms dealer?" Nigel shook his head. "Why would I tag along with such a hodgepodge crew? You're a writer for God's sake."

Standing, Berty said, "It's your choice. We're going with or without you. Sean, see Nigel out."

"Give me an hour," said Nigel.

After Sean closed the door, he said, "I don't trust him."

"We don't have to," said Berty. "He would have followed us anyway. If he comes with us, at least we know where he is."

"My Lord," said Ojore, "I know of the Nyoka. That tribe has a reputation of being vile and lacking honor. We've always been forbidden to marry any of them. They are poison. If what that man said is true, it is a sad day."

"I'm sure he gave us the watered-down version. They are probably a lot worse than what he said," Berty said.

A knocking at the door froze their conversation. Answering the door, Declan allowed Nigel to enter.

"I got approval to join your suicide expedition," Nigel announced. "We will leave in a few minutes to pick up our vehicle." He dropped a bag on the floor.

"I must prepare for war, excuse me," said Ojore. Grabbing his knapsack, he left through the sliding glass doors.

"So, who are you people, really?" Nigel asked. He tried to peek at Silvia's two maps.

"People you will never see again," answered Berty. "I don't care what you do with the Nyoka or their complex as long as I get my brother and sister-in-law."

"If this pans out, there will be international backup," Nigel admitted. He opened his mouth to say more, but did not.

Nigel stared at Ojore as he entered the villa. White war paint strategically covered his body. Leather protected more delicate body parts. He almost had a whitish glow when he said, "I am ready to face Nyoka."

Picking up their bags, they left the villa. The only way out of the resort was through the main entrance. Tourists who lingered in the lobby stared at Ojore. Resort employees would not make eye contact with him or any of them. One word floated around the lobby. "Kivuli," people breathed.

They were not charged for the villa and practically rushed out of the hotel.

"About time, Nigel. It's got everything you asked," said a man with a local accent, getting out of an SUV. After taking a good look at Ojore, he quickly averted his eyes.

Ojore said something to the man in another language. The man looked up, saying something in return.

Nigel thanked the man, then said, "I drive."

Not contesting, Berty had Silvia sit in the passenger seat, Sean and Declan in the third row, while he sat between Ojore and Edwin.

Finally seeing the star map, Nigel said, "What kind of bloody map is that?"

"Don't worry about the map. You just drive where I tell you," Silvia answered.

Outside of town, the headlights pierced the dark expanse of nothing. "So, what was that in there? The not looking at any of us and whispering something?" Nigel said.

Ojore smiled. "They called me Kivuli, meaning ghost. Their legends state that if a person looks at Kivuli in the eye, someone they know will die."

"What rubbish," Nigel muttered.

"Your friend believes it as well," Ojore stated. "To ease his mind, I told him his people were blessed. In return, he wished me a good hunt. It is nice to see we are remembered."

The SUV bounced over the rough roads. Berty felt his sword hitting against his legs through the knapsack. He did not want to have to use it, but his family's life took precedent. Closing his eyes, he focused on his family.

Dressed in suits, George and Matt entered the house. "Kate?" George called.

Kate entered the hall. "How'd it go?"

"There is enough evidence to arrest both Kirk Duncan and Victoria Dunne," said George. "Kirk for being a lousy, good-for-nothing thief, and it turns out that Victoria has been working for two companies—us and a competitor—for the better part of two years."

"The police picked her up this morning," said Matt, opening his jacket. "She said that she had nothing to do with Teresa's and Jon's disappearance. All she did was pass along information about the company, their trip to Africa, et cetera. The company, who was paying her, arranged the abduction for enough ransom money to destroy Chase Technologies. The police believe that this same company hired the people to break into their house."

"Have you heard from Berty?" George asked.

Shaking her head, Kate replied, "Not yet."

Berty opened his eyes. Pulling out the locket, he wrote, "On route. Will message again once we have Jon and Teresa." He hoped that it would ease some of their anxiety.

Silvia had Nigel turn onto another dark road. After getting used to the bumpy ride, Berty had lost track of how far or long they traveled.

A lone light ahead made Nigel slow down. "Border crossing," said Nigel.

A uniformed man wearing a large gun held out a hand to stop them. Another man emerged from the small building on the side of the road. Walking around the SUV, they spoke in anxious tones. Quickly moving the barricade, they waved them through.

"You strike fear in these people, Kivuli," Nigel said. "That was an easy border crossing."

Berty jostled into Edwin and Ojore. Each turn led them onto a bumpier road.

"We're close. Turn off the headlights," Silvia instructed.

Closing his eyes, he could see the area ahead of them. Berty said, "Pull off to the right. We can hide the SUV there. We will walk the rest of the way."

Nigel drove expertly into the bushes. Outside the SUV, Berty removed his sword from his bag. He motioned for the others to do the same. Watching, Nigel shook his head, then opened the back of the SUV.

Nigel slung guns over his shoulder while looking at them fastening cloaks around theirs. "Who are you people?" he whispered.

Silently, they approached the shack that Berty saw Jon and Teresa enter. "It's a rusty shack," Nigel mumbled.

"Hiding an underground complex," Berty whispered.

Looking through small binoculars, Nigel said, "I don't see anyone. We should take out the light." He lifted a rifle.

Berty pushed down the barrel. "Too noisy. Declan," he said. He watched Nigel's horrified expression as Declan raised his bow.

His arrow severed the wire. The shack's exterior darkened. The door opened, spilling light onto the dirt. A man holding a flashlight stood in the doorway. Holding out his hand, Declan recalled his arrow.

Berty held his breath. The man swung the flashlight around the shack. He returned to the door. Darkness enveloped the ground.

They tiptoed closer. Holding a short, bone tipped spear, Ojore knocked on the door. When the door opened, the man let out a high-pitched scream. They followed Ojore through the shack's doorway.

The man scrambled into the corner. Pointing to the floor,

Ojore spoke to the man in what Berty guessed was his native language. Trembling, the man could barely speak.

"Under the boards, there is a two man latch that opens a hatch," Ojore said.

With pleading eyes, the man spoke to Ojore. Ojore took a step back. Shaking his head, he said, "No."

Edwin and Sean found the latch.

"What?" asked Berty.

"He wants me to kill him," Ojore answered. "So they won't kill his family."

"We can protect him and his family if he cooperates," said Nigel.

"All he knows is the shack. He is not Nyoka, not directly," Ojore said. He spoke to the man in his language.

The man murmured something. His eyes glazed. Ojore translated, "No one can save me from the Thunder Stick."

A loud bang shook the shack. The man's head slumped against the wall. His eyes stared nowhere. Blood oozed from his temple. A black gun slipped from his slack grip.

Nigel shook his head. The rest of them stood in shock. Finally, Berty said, "We're losing night. Let's go."

Declan stood ready with his arrow while Edwin and Sean opened the hatch. Peering into the hole, Declan waived them forward.

The stairs led them into a dim corridor. At the base of the stairs, Declan looked in all directions. "There is either a lot of magic or a lot of electricity down here," said Declan. "George is right about them being similar. It flows everywhere."

Closing his eyes, Berty saw his brother sitting in a dark cell. He brought his sight through the corridors. "This way," he said, raising his hood.

"They're going to see us on surveillance eventually," said Nigel. "I'm going to find their control room." He disappeared down a different corridor.

They arrived at a steel door with an electronic keypad. Berty looked from the keypad to Declan. "Use your wand. Draw some out, then push it back quickly to overload it."

Fetching his wand from his quiver, Declan pointed it at the keypad. Within seconds, the keypad flashed, then went dark. Berty opened the door.

On the other side of the door, a small nook held a surveillance desk. "Why isn't there a guard?" mumbled Edwin.

They ran past empty cells until they saw the form of a person inside one. "Jon?" said Berty.

"Berty?" Jon sat up, looking through the bars with his cracked glasses.

They heard a scream. "No," sobbed a young female voice.

"I hear that every night," said Jon. "And every night, I pray it's not Teresa."

Declan, Edwin and Sean ran in the direction of the screams. Opening Jon's cell with magic, Berty said, "Let's get Teresa and get out of here."

Jon stumbled out of his cell. "I'm fine," he said. The four of them rushed towards the sounds of the struggle.

They arrived at another group of cells to see Sean pulling his bloody blade from the lifeless guard on the floor. Silvia entered the opened cell. A young, barely teenage, girl cowered against the wall.

Three more cells held girls. Two were a little older than Hope. The other, Berty saw on the truck with Jon and Teresa. Finally, he saw Teresa. "Stand back," said Berty. With a small swipe of his hand, the cells opened.

Jon ran to Teresa. He held her close. The older teenager pried the gun off the dead guard. "Come," she said to the others, "no need to fear Kivuli. He is not hunting us."

"Hurry, they're coming," said Nigel, running into the hall. Ammo dripped down his body. "I found their guns, but we need to find another way out."

Discovering another door, Declan overloaded the keypad with his wand. "Handy," said Nigel, opening the door. He released a round of gunfire. "Clear," he said.

They ran from corridor to corridor, shooting their way through Nyoka. The corridors emptied into a room where a man stood, holding a crystal topped staff. Pelts, feathers and small, shining objects adorned the wood.

"They've desecrated my great-grandfather's staff," Sean said through gritted teeth.

"Tell me, Kivuli," taunted the man, "what good is a lone ghost in the den of the snake?"

"Nyoka," said Ojore. He laughed. The ground shook. "Today, you die."

"Kill them," the man told his men. Raising their guns, not one pulled the trigger. The man slammed the staff on the ground.

Declan and Edwin lobbed arrows while Nigel and the oldest girl fired stolen weapons. Amidst the firefight, Ojore hurled his bone tipped spear. Letting go of the staff, the man fell to the ground.

Sean ran to grab the staff before it crashed to the floor. Barrels lowered as he removed everything but a single feather. He held the staff high, then quickly slammed the bottom on the ground.

Streaks of lightning emitted out of the crystal in every direction. Bursting light bulbs showered them with glass. In the darkness, the feather glowed.

Berty immediately conjured a sphere of light to guide their way. "On second thought, I don't want to know," said Nigel, following them.

Explosions and gunfire echoed through the corridors behind them. "That will be back up," said Nigel.

They found stairs that ended at a hatch. Nigel removed a grenade from his belt. He motioned for the others to stay. Opening the hatch, he threw the grenade. He joined them at the bottom of the stairs. The explosion above rocked them. Following Nigel, they climbed through the hatch.

The remnants of the shack were scattered in the dirt. Emerging into morning sunlight, Berty absorbed his sphere.

Escaping Nyoka ran out of other shacks that dotted the grasslands. There was no place to hide. They ran in the opposite direction, hoping they would be ignored.

Nigel spoke to someone on his cell phone. "Triangulate my location. There's more of them out here." Looking behind him, he said, "We've been seen."

He threw a grenade. As it was about to land short of its target, the wind carried it further. It exploded. The Nyoka opened fire.

"No!" Silvia shrieked. With both of her hands in front of her, the barrage of bullets struck an invisible barrier.

"Do not hold any metal," said Sean. "Miss Hunter, let down your barrier." As Silvia lowered her hands, Sean's staff tapped the ground.

The Staff of Lightning shot a constant stream of white lightning. The hot sparks ignited the gunpowder, causing a series of explosions.

Berty could hear the rotating blades of the helicopter. "Sean, that's enough."

The lightning ceased. "A portal!" said Declan.

Nigel caught the black helicopter in his binoculars. "That's my ride," he said. "Go!"

Berty and Nigel gave each other a nod. Turning, Berty said,

"Lead the way."

"Grab hands," said Silvia.

Berty held on to Silvia's and Teresa's hands as Declan pulled the group through the portal only he could see.

Chapter Twenty-four
The Science of Magic

The grasslands looked the same, but Berty no longer heard helicopters, explosions and gunfire. "Are we in the Outlands?" he asked Ojore.

"I believe so," Ojore answered. "We are far from my village." He stared at the sky. "We should make camp. We will need a large fire that will last throughout the night. A good meal would not go amiss either."

"This is your land, Ojore. We will do as you suggest," said Berty.

Ojore chose a campsite, then delegated duties. Over the fire, they roasted an antelope. With some food in their stomachs, Jon and Teresa finally relaxed.

"Thank you," said Jon. "It's been awhile since we've seen the light of day. Berty, that was crazy."

Studying his brother and sister-in-law, he asked, "How are you feeling? Does anything hurt?"

"How's Hope?" Teresa asked.

"She's fine," said Berty.

"You didn't happen to bring a spare pair of glasses?" Jon asked.

Berty held out his hand. Jon placed his glasses in his brother's open palm. "She likes her new school," Berty said. Teresa smiled. He placed his other hand on top of Jon's glasses. Fixed, he handed them back to Jon.

"How'd you do that?" Jon asked.

"Matt's home," Berty said. "I have a lot to tell you guys, but first I need to message Mom and Dad." He pulled out the large, gold Watcher's Locket.

With its rod, he wrote, "Got Jon and Teresa. Everyone is fine. In Outlands. On our way home. Found Staff of Lightning."

Declan dressed wounds while Berty made introductions. He discussed what was going on with the company and Matt's findings.

"I knew something was wrong," said Jon, "but I never suspected both."

The locket vibrated in Berty's hand. When he opened it, it said, "Glad to know everyone is safe. Magic is becoming more erratic. George and Colvin are finishing the countermeasures. Safe travels."

"Get some sleep. We will journey when dawn breaks," Ojore told them. "Cannot let the fire die. Edwin, if you will take first watch, I will take last."

A scream pierced the night. Berty sat up. The older girl crouched over the other teenager, saying, "Shh, shh. It was only a nightmare. No one here will hurt you. You are safe now."

The girl sobbed, "I want to go home."

"We must make a new home," the older girl said. "We may come from different places, but we are sisters now."

Declan handed the sobbing girl a cup. "Drink this. It will help you sleep. No more nightmares," he said.

As the girl raised the cup to her mouth, Berty lowered his body and closed his eyes.

When Berty woke, Ojore held sacks cut from the antelope hide. "For carrying water," Ojore said. "Call me Ojore," he said to the girls. "What are your names?"

One of the young girls said, "Fana."

Taking the bag, the other young girl barely whispered, "Kafi."

The young teen, who had the difficult night, said, "Rabia."

"I'm Akia," said the oldest. She gave him a hard stare as she took her water canteen.

"Let's go before the sun gets too high," said Ojore, breaking his gaze with her. He led them through the grasslands.

"Is Hope making friends? Is she happy?" Teresa asked Berty.

"Talk only when we rest. Save your strength," instructed Ojore.

"Yes," Berty breathed. They walked the rest of the morning in silence.

During the heat of the day, they sat in the shade. Teresa bombarded Berty with questions about Hope.

"Shouldn't we be walking?" Sean finally asked.

"Only if you wish to die," said Ojore.

"And we need to reach water first," Akia added.

"Yes," said Ojore with a glance in her direction.

"What's with the staff thing?" Jon quietly asked Berty. "Our captors called it the Thunder Stick and claimed it as a source of all their power."

"The Staff of Lightning is Sean's rightful inheritance," Berty answered. "He's been searching for so long. Funny, I thought that finding it would have changed him a little." He remembered how Estelle transformed when she found her amulet.

"How does it work?" his brother asked.

"The staff? Must be magic in the crystal only Sean can unlock," Berty said. He then realized that he was talking to his brother about magic. Looking at Jon, he waited for a reaction.

Jon adjusted his glasses. "When you say magic, you mean?"

Magic. What else could magic mean, but magic? Berty did

not know how to answer. Of all the questions he had ever asked, he never questioned what magic was. He had just accepted its existence. Glancing at Silvia, he smiled to himself. "Empty your mind of all preconceived notions and just observe," he told his brother.

Jon laughed a little. "You sound like Dad. That's something he would say."

Berty always thought he was different from his father. He did not follow in his footsteps. He did not take over the business. Jon did all of that. Perhaps he was more like his dad. He just took a different path to get there. Not responding, he watched Silvia converse with Teresa.

"They're getting along well," Jon mentioned. "Think they are talking about us?"

"Among other things," said Berty.

"How long do you think it will take to get to civilization?" Jon asked.

He looked at his brother. "Depends on your definition of civilization."

Raising his eyebrows, Jon said nothing.

Conversations and naps ended when Ojore decided it was a good time to move. They continued walking until the sun dove under the horizon. Dinner consisted of leftover antelope.

"So, Declan," Teresa began. "Berty tells me you are teaching my daughter archery."

"She is a natural—very talented," said Declan.

Teresa flashed a smile. "I would have preferred her to be older before learning something like archery. When Berty coaxed Hope into telling him about her difficulties with the children at school, he thought archery would help her. I believe it has. When I spoke with her last, she sounded so happy. Do you normally teach ones so young?"

331

Cocking his head to the side, Declan said, "My siblings and I could shoot arrows before we could walk."

"Why, though?" Teresa asked. "Help me understand her fascination."

"It's more than a fascination to her," Declan said. His expression softened. "Her bow is simply an extension of who she is. There's a partnership an archer has with his bow. I can't explain it."

Edwin nodded in agreement. "Nothing will protect her as well as her own bow. Proper self-defense has to be instinctual. She gets that comfort from her bow."

"Defense? From what does she need defending?" Looking from Edwin to Declan, Teresa's eyes fell onto Berty.

Berty swallowed to keep down the bubbling guilt. "Just in case," he said.

"Everyone should have the ability to defend themselves, even children—especially children," Edwin offered.

Teresa studied the Elf in the firelight. "Do you have children?" she asked him.

"Not yet."

Nodding, Teresa stared into the fire. Tears began to streak down her face. "I miss my little girl. Being in there, I... I never thought I'd see her again." Her hands covered her face. She cried into Jon's chest as his arms enveloped her.

Sleep was short. They continued their silent journey as the blue just began to lighten its hue. Rays of sunlight reached the tan grasslands, revealing Teresa hunching while she walked. Her one hand grabbed her stomach while the other halfway covered her mouth.

"Teresa, are you all right?" Jon asked.

"Last night's antelope isn't settling well," she said.

Lightly rubbing her back, Jon said, "I think it might be food

332

in general. It's not like we ate much while we were in there."
He turned to Declan. "Do you have any of the pink stuff in your
bag?"

Seeing the confused look on Declan's face, Berty translated.
"Do you have anything for an upset stomach?"

Declan nodded. He pulled a tan, withered something from
his bag. "If we could stop to make a fire, I can make a tea," he
said.

"We do not have a good spot here for fire," said Ojore.

"I have an idea," said Berty. "Get it all ready."

Declan extracted a cup and a knife from his bag. With Jon
holding the cup, Declan scraped spicy powder off the dried root
into the cup. He poured a measure of water over the spice.

"Have your wand ready," Berty told him. Once Declan's
wand was positioned in his hand, Berty said, "Catch." With a
slight movement of his hand, he tossed a flame to his friend.

Catching it on the tip of his wand, Declan held the cup over
the flame. Using his wand, he adjusted the magical flame so that it
looked as though he was heating a cup over a long, tapered can-
dle. The wafting steam carried a spicy ginger to Berty's nose.

Retracting the flame into his wand, Declan handed the cup to
Teresa. "Swirl it around as you drink," he instructed. "It should
help."

Teresa sipped as they continued on Ojore's chosen path.
When they stopped for the heat of the day to pass, she slept near
her husband.

The last drops of water in his canteen rolled across Berty's
tongue. Holding the soft leather pouch in his hands, he thought
about filling it with water. After his third attempt, the canteen
stayed a raisin instead of swelling into a juicy grape. "Why can I
make fire, but not water?" he asked.

"Different processes," said Silvia. "Magic is transforming

what is already there."

Berty did not understand why he could not transform hydrogen and oxygen to make water.

"But doesn't the sky make water when it rains?" Sean asked.

"No," said Jon with his eyes closed. "Berty, you can't make water because there's not enough water vapor. It's too hot."

He stared at his brother who leaned against a rock with his eyes closed and glasses folded in his lap. "What do you know of magic, little brother?"

Grinning, Jon answered, "Not magic. Science." His one eye took a quick peek at Berty. "I know what you're thinking. To do so would take a large explosion. Hydrogen and oxygen aren't exactly flame retardant."

On a molecular level, magic and science were probably indistinguishable. Magic was the manipulation of energy—it could not be created or destroyed. It just changed shape. Berty chuckled. "You know, Dad took magic's voltage reading."

Jon opened his eyes. He laughed a little. "Hope's known all along, hasn't she?"

Berty nodded.

"We dismissed it as childhood fantasy," Jon said. He brushed Teresa's dark hair off her face as she slept. "We're a long way from home. My wife isn't well. I have more aches and pains than I knew I had muscles. I haven't seen my daughter in ages. And for some reason, although this should defy all logic, it doesn't. My brother throws fire with his bare hand and I accept it as if it's normal. Perhaps I'll wake up soon and be back in my bed." Resting his head against the rock, he closed his eyes.

Berty did not know how to tell his brother that he, too, was a descendent of one of the Seven High Sages. And that was why magic made sense to him. He hoped that once they reached the Empire Tree everything would fall into place.

334

Nighttime settled by the time they made camp near a small spring. Drinking to their hearts' content, they made antelope stew out of what little dry pieces were left to help with hydration. Declan brewed ginger tea and liquid aspirin from willow bark next to the fire. He portioned some to Teresa and Jon, respectfully.

Swallowing the last bit, Jon grimaced. "They make pills, you know," he mentioned.

"I've been dreaming of a nice, hot bath with Epson salts," said Teresa.

Jon caressed his wife's hand. "Soon." He looked at Berty as if to ask, how soon will soon be. Berty could only shrug his shoulders.

During the dark morning, they filled their canteens. The morning dose of ginger tea helped stave off Teresa's nausea. They waded through the tall grass until a gunshot echoed through the never-ending, clear blue sky. Akia stood poised with a shotgun nestled in her shoulder.

After a frozen moment, she disappeared into the grasses. She emerged, followed by a leopard. "She was stalking us," she said. "Me, actually." Her tough exterior cracked slightly. "It spoke to me."

"She will come, bearing a staff of fire, with a leopard by her side," recited Ojore. "The Outlander."

"What is that?" she asked.

"Warrior of warriors," Ojore answered.

The leopard stopped at Akia's side, nuzzling its head in her hand. Reluctantly, she petted the cat's large head. "She said she's been waiting for me," Akia said. "How do I know this?"

"Because," Ojore explained, "while all of us who live in the Outlands are Outlanders, you are *the* Outlander. You are destined for greatness, Akia, if you so choose. My father will explain more when we get to my village."

"Does this mean we are no longer sisters?" a young voice asked.

Turning, Akia answered, "We will always be sisters, Kafi, because we share this experience." She gave Kafi a hug. "We are bound by something bigger than ourselves. We are meant to protect each other no matter what." Taking the young girl's hand, they walked with the group as the leopard trotted by Akia's side.

Stopping for the heat the day, Edwin asked Ojore, "How far to your village?"

"Unfortunately, longer than usual," he answered. "We must travel from water source to water source. I am sure you miss your wife, Lieutenant. But it is the only way if we are to survive the heat."

"I never thought I'd miss the Land of Sages," Sean muttered.

They took to napping in the heat of the day like Spaniards taking siestas. Eating was relegated to the evening when it was cool enough to make a fire. The leopard prowled in the long, beige grass, finding food where they thought was none.

Ojore brought them to a puddle of a watering hole. Through the muddy water protruded two smooth rounded snouts. Little ears flapped, splashing the dirty water.

"Hippos?" said Teresa.

"Very observant," Ojore answered. "Come, we cannot take any water from here."

As they wandered away from the mud puddle, one of the young girls screamed, "Rabia!"

The teenage girl descended into the dried banks of the watering hole. Akia ran through the group. Ojore stopped her from entering the watering hole.

Calmly, he walked towards Rabia. "Rabia," he said, "where

336

are you going?"

Tear trails glistened against her dark skin. "Let me go," she cried.

"If you wish to kill yourself, I will not stop you," he told her.

"No. *They* will do it for me," Rabia said.

"There are more honorable ways."

She slowed. "I do not deserve honor. I only ask for God's forgiveness—to cleanse me." Her body shook as sadness overtook her. Straightening, her feet continued towards the circling beasts.

"Your god will forgive you, Rabia, but there is a better way to be cleansed," Ojore called out to her.

Stopping, she turned to face the hunter.

"It is on the way to my village," he said softly. "Come, Rabia."

She obeyed. When she reached him, she took his hand and allowed him to guide her out of the watering hole.

Keeping a close eye on Rabia, Ojore led them to the next water source.

As they sat around the nightly fire, Silvia gave Berty a worried look. "I don't think we will make it in time," she said. "The Hallows are fast approaching."

Berty looked at Jon and Teresa. It would take them two weeks on foot to the Empire Tree from Ojore's village. He had no idea how much longer they would be in the Outlands' wilderness. Taking his Watcher's Locket, he wrote to Delyth. "Prepare for us not to return until after the Hallows."

His brother stroked Teresa's torn sleeve. Her head rested on Jon's shoulder. Berty knew they desperately wanted to go back to their life. Sitting there, watching the fire, they probably yearned for modernity. How was he going to tell them that they would never see their old life again? He wished that being with Hope would be all that mattered to them.

Closing his eyes, Berty saw Hope sitting at the table across from Matt and Julie. Empty plates still sat in front of them.

"Julie, if you married my Uncle Matt, then you become my Aunt Julie. Right?" Hope pondered.

"Okay," said Julie.

"So, if I call you Aunt Julie and Obie calls you Aunt Julie, will that mean that Obie and I would be related?"

Julie laughed. "Of course not."

Matt stared at the tablecloth. His fingers followed the stitches as if he were not paying attention.

Breathing a sigh relief, Hope asked, "Will you guys get married?"

Blushing, Julie laughed.

"Do you have any homework to finish?" Matt asked Hope.

Feeling a vibration, Berty opened his eyes. "Your father stabilized the Scepter," Delyth wrote in the locket. "According to the Watchers' Guild Master, the magic no longer is erratic, but it is not as strong as it once was. Your parents said that they have some decisions to make. I will keep you informed."

He looked up from the locket to see Silvia staring at him. Her eyes told him, *tell your brother.* He pulled Jon and Teresa aside. Quietly, he told them everything.

Chapter Twenty-five
No More Secrets

Teresa stared at her dirt coated sneakers. "What about Hope's future?" she finally asked. Looking at Berty, she continued, "Jon and I can start again anywhere. A little cottage would be fine. But, what kind of life can Hope make for herself here? She's not going to be just an archer."

While telling them everything, Berty did not disclose one tiny detail. "Hope has a special gift," he said. "I can't tell you more. Not until we're in a more secure location."

"Berty, we are in the middle of nowhere," Teresa exasperated.

"When it comes to Whispers, you can't be too careful."

"Whispers?" Teresa asked.

"They ride on the wind in-between the trees," said Jon. He sat up straighter in surprise. Through his rectangular spectacles, his brown eyes bored into his brother's. "Where did that come from?"

"Our DNA. Happens to me all the time," Berty answered.

Jon opened his mouth, then closed it.

"What about my parents and brother? Do I not get to say good-bye?" Teresa asked in a small voice.

"This was not what I planned on happening," admitted Berty. "Matt's been to the Empire Tree. You can write a note on the locket and Delyth will give him the message."

Slowly, Teresa nodded.

"You are the only one who was going to stay here when the portals closed," Jon observed.

"I've made a life here," said Berty. He glanced at Silvia. "A new chapter."

Jon's eyes found Silvia. "Yes, you have."

Berty slept better after telling Jon and Teresa almost everything. After throwing his pack onto his back, a delicate hand slid into his. He squeezed Silvia's hand, pulling her close.

Their eyes met in the semi-darkness. Stealing a kiss, he whispered, "Thank you." His lips grazed her ear. "Love you."

Her hands squeezed his. "Me, too," she said with a smile.

Their hands slipped apart. Walking together, they followed Ojore.

The grasses yielded to red mud flats. The wind hinted of sulfur. Steam rose from jeweled pools.

"Rabia, you wished to cleanse yourself," said Ojore. "Choose a basin. Dip yourself in fully. Emerge anew."

Holding her mouth, Teresa ran to be upwind of the steaming sulfur.

Rabia chose emerald colored water. Carefully, she took off her shoes. As she began to undress, Berty turned his head. Declan struck Sean on the arm to get him to turn around.

Berty heard a gentle splash. Water lapped against calcified rock. He noticed Jon rush to Teresa's side. Bent over, her body convulsed.

"Is there anything I can do?" Jon asked quietly.

If Teresa answered, Berty did not know. He saw Jon rub her back, then handed her his canteen. The smell made his sister-in-law sick.

Rabia passed with her dripping head held high. The leopard

led them to shade for waiting out the heat of the day.

Berty began to lose count of the days. Each day was the same—walk, sleep, eat. The heat became more tolerable or the days finally started to cool.

A large, bone structure poked through the tall beige grasses. He thought his eyes deceived him until he heard Ojore say, "Home at last."

Ojore blew a greeting on a horn. Another horn responded. Approaching the bone wall, a gate lifted. Villagers stared as the large party entered.

In the long, central, wall-less great hall, the Chief walked towards them with open arms. "We are honored by your return, my Lord," he said. Noticing the leopard, he stopped.

"Father," said Ojore, "refugees from the other side."

The Chief nodded. "The Spirit has awakened. Kivuli walked again. Tonight, we feast."

They were shown to their hammocked quarters. The former prisoners were taken to see the Shaman.

Berty lay in hammock while he watched the village pass. Jon strolled back from seeing the Shaman. Sitting in hammock across from his brother, he said, "Strangest doctor visit ever. Teresa is with him now." Jon adjusted his glasses. "Wherever Teresa is, is home," he continued. "I know you understand that. Everything else is out of my control. And I'm okay with that. Let the fates lie where they may."

"Who are you and what have you done with Jon?" Berty said, sitting up. The brothers laughed.

A young boy cautiously approached. "Excuse me, my Lord. The Shaman would like to see you both."

Berty and Jon rushed to the Shaman's hut. Inside, they found Teresa sitting on a table. "Is something wrong?" Jon asked.

With her one hand gently rubbing her abdomen, Teresa's free

341

hand grabbed her husband's. "Jon, I'm pregnant."

"What? How? Are you?" stammered Jon.

"The mother and child are fine," the Shaman answered. He smiled at Jon. "Do not worry. She has informed me about all the miscarriages."

"Miscarriages?" Berty said.

"Yes," admitted Teresa. "We didn't tell anyone. There were a few before Hope and lots after. Our parents only know about a couple of them. I was told that I could never have any more children. Technically, I shouldn't have been able to have had Hope."

Berty did not know what to say. He felt as though he was intruding on something more personal to which he should not have been privy.

"The reason I have called you here, my Lord," said the Shaman, "is because you must be aware of Teresa's limitations. You are family, after all. I am brewing medicine to take with you. I believe this baby to also be magical."

"Also?" asked Jon.

"I have met your daughter," the Shaman answered.

"Hope's been here?" Jon asked.

Berty said nothing.

"When you return to the Empire Tree," said the Shaman, "the search must begin for a good midwife. Your Astrologer will be able to find one once the signs emerge."

Berty found it hard not to look at the bone through the Shaman's nose. Glancing at Jon and Teresa, he nodded.

Smiling, Teresa said, "Promise not to tell until after the first trimester."

"I have to tell Estelle, but I will swear her to secrecy as well," he said.

Jon and Teresa giggled. As they kissed, Berty exited the hut.

Declan sat up as Berty found the hammock on which he was sitting. "The Shaman confirmed her pregnancy," Declan said quietly.

Looking at him, Berty neither confirmed nor denied Declan's words. His pocket vibrated, saving him from answering. He opened the locket to read Delyth's message.

"George and Kate have decided to stay on this side of the portal. Matt will run Chase Technologies and live in Jon and Teresa's house. Julie will stay on the other side of the portal, living in your house. Matt would like to ask Declan for his sister's hand. He will also ask Obie's permission. Be safe. See you soon."

He looked at Declan. His hand passed the open locket to his friend.

After reading it, Declan asked, "May I reply? All I want to know is if Julie loves him."

Berty nodded. "Tell them where we are."

Declan handed back the locket when he had finished his reply.

The feast began at sundown. Food spread out before them on grass mats. Laughter finally found them. They were safe—for the time being.

After dinner, they danced. They danced to celebrate Kivuli. They danced to celebrate the return of the Staff of Lightning. They danced to celebrate the fall of the Nyoka. They welcomed the girls into the tribe with dance.

Teresa retired early. The flames rocked with the hypnotic drumming. Through a drink induced haze, Berty watched the fire grow higher. The flames formed the figure of a woman. Her fiery eyes stared at Berty. Parting flame lips said, "Listen to the trees. They cry. Watcher can all see. The pry. Only you can free. Her tie." The fire erupted in a burst of yellowish orange.

She was gone.

Berty awoke with a fiery image lingering in his mind. Getting ready to leave the village, he pushed it to the side. After replenishing their provisions, Silvia handed Jon and Teresa gray bundles. "Let me know if you need help with the fastener," she said.

"What is it?" Jon asked.

"A cloak for each of you," she answered.

"But it's so warm," said Teresa.

"Not where we're going," Silvia continued. "The chilly autumn winds have begun to spill over the mountains." She glanced at Berty. "It's almost Halloween." Gravity filled her voice.

Ready for the trek home, they thanked the Chief for his hospitality.

"Emperor, you and your party are always welcome here," said the Chief. "My son has experienced much and he will be a better chief for it."

"The Empire Tree will always be open to the Ghost Tribe," Berty announced. He shook Ojore's hand. "It was a pleasure having you with us, Ojore. Hope to see you again someday."

Ojore smiled wide. "My Lord, it was an honor." Turning to Declan, he placed a sharp bone tool in his hand. "For young Oberon."

Declan gave him a deep nod.

Wind blew their cloaks away from their bodies as they crossed the grasslands. The setting sun illuminated the mountain path they climbed. Finding a campsite, they started a fire. After scouting, Edwin sat around the fire, rubbing his shoulder.

"Do you need something for your shoulder?" Declan asked.

"It's just the cold night air," said Edwin. "The Shaman told me that only the Witch of Rowan can cure it completely. Something about her relationship with the trees is good for Elves."

344

"She's not a full Witch yet," said Declan.

"I know." The Elf stared into the flames. "Might be a long winter."

"Speaking of," said Jon. "What was that in the fire last night?"

Berty stared at his brother while others denied seeing anything in the fire. Shifting his gaze to Declan, he asked, "Is there anything around?"

Declan's eyes searched the area thoroughly. "No."

"What did you see?" Berty asked Jon.

"A fire woman," Jon answered.

"Did she say anything?"

"It sounded like a garbled mess," said Jon.

The image appeared to both of them, but only Berty understood her. Catching the glittering red of his pinky ring in the dancing fire, Berty knew why. "We both saw the Pixie Priestess appear in the fire because we're brothers," he explained. "However, I heard her words." He repeated her song.

"Why riddles?" complained Sean. "Might as well be utter nonsense."

Silvia's teeth tugged on her lip. "Not nonsense" she said. "Hope, Declan, and the third will be revealed in time."

"What does Hope have to do with anything?" Teresa asked.

Smiling slightly, Silvia said, "She'll have to show you herself." Silvia and Teresa stared at each other until Silvia said, "It's nothing with which we need to concern ourselves now."

Teresa looked as though she wanted to say more, but did not. She wrapped her cloak more tightly around her body.

The morning trudge up the mountain kept them warm. Reaching the summit, rolling oranges, yellows and reds greeted them.

"How beautiful," Teresa remarked.

"Do we chance the valley?" Berty asked.

"If things go our way, we might be able to reach the Empire Tree before the Hallows end," said Sean.

Berty's head snapped in Sean's direction. He was surprised Sean said something sensible. "Then do we all agree to cross through the valley?" he asked.

Both Edwin and Declan said, "Yes." When Silvia agreed, Berty removed his sheathed sword. He handed it to Jon.

Jon stared at the sword snug in its scabbard. "What are you doing?"

"In case you need it."

"But... What about you?" Jon protested.

Flashing a fireball in his palm, Berty said, "I'll be fine."

With Berty's guidance, Jon attached the sword to his pants. "You know that I don't know how to use this," Jon said as he tucked the sword behind his cloak.

"You'll figure it out if need be," said Berty. Leaning towards Jon, he whispered, "Hold the pointy end out." Giving his brother a wry smile, he led them down the path.

"We should have Fairy Dust with us," Declan mentioned.

"I still have some," said Berty.

"And someone who can use it."

"Not going to help us now," said Edwin.

"Fairy Dust is useless against some of the creatures that were imprisoned here," said Silvia. "Hopefully, they haven't been released."

"Released? How?" asked Jon.

"Magic," Silvia answered.

"What I don't understand," said Declan, "is why they were not released when Eirawen was draining magic from the world."

"Because the Scepter was stronger than Eirawen," Silvia said.

Declan's eyes followed invisible movement through the trees.

"Whisper," he said. They continued down the mountain in silence.

When they reached the valley floor, Edwin unsheathed his sword and readied his shield. Lifting his shielded arm, he blocked an arrow.

Declan responded with two arrows. His eyes flashed wider. "Necromancer," he muttered.

"Impossible," said Silvia.

"No one else can reanimate the dead," said Declan. "Sean, let loose lightning. We are essentially useless against them."

Sean held his staff high. Lighting shook corpses blocking their path.

"We need to find another way across the river," said Berty.

They ran off the path into the woods. "There must be some way to defeat them," said Jon, trying to catch his breath.

"Kill the Necromancer," answered Declan. "If we can find him."

Berty shot Dragonfire to help them gain space between them and the corpses.

As if lying in wait, the hairy creatures that they encountered on their last venture sprang from behind the trees. They changed direction.

Taking a quick glance around, Berty said, "We're being forced deeper into God Mountain."

"Why?" Jon asked.

"I don't want to find out," Berty answered. "Run for the clearing."

Emerging from the woods, Berty stopped running. "Stay near me," he instructed. Palms out, he raised both arms over his head. A circle of Dragonfire erupted around them. The flames roared higher than their heads.

"Great. Now, we're trapped," whined Sean.

"I wonder," said Declan. He shot an arrow through the fire. The tip caught the fire before it reached its target. The creature fell to the ground aflame. He quickly released more arrows.

Berty looked up at the blue sky. "Tong," he called, "as your Match, I am calling for your assistance. I release you and only you from the bonds of the Dragonlands. Help us." Throwing a fireball into the sky, it burst like a firework.

"The clans will not be happy with you," warned Silvia.

"And if we don't return to the Empire Tree, the Empire will be lost to us," said Berty.

"I fear that, too," Silvia said.

Fire shot from an invisible source above them. The black long Dragon materialized, breathing fire in a wider circle. Tong landed on top of the ring of fire Berty made. His steps extinguished the flames. Berty heard gasps from Jon and Teresa.

"Climb on," said Tong. "Hurry. I saw something marching this way."

They scrambled to get on the Dragon's back. As soon as Tong ascended, Berty felt weightless. Seeing nothing but gray, he knew the Dragon had dematerialized.

When Tong reformed underneath Berty, he saw a painter's palette of oranges and yellows. The trees masked black stone fortifications.

Tong landed in front of a large, black, stone gate. "I promised the Prince that I would bring you here if we crossed paths, my Lord," said Tong. "I will bring you to the Sages' Grove as well."

"Thank you for coming to our aid, Tong," said Berty as he slid off the Dragon's black back.

"I am in your debt for releasing me," said Tong. "Thank you for trusting me."

The stone gate slid open. "What was marching towards us?" Berty asked Tong.

"I do not know its name," Tong answered. "All I know is that it had to be secured before the clans would agree to come to the Dragonlands."

Berty caught Silvia closing her eyes and shaking her head.

Fairies led them under the stone arch. "What?" Berty asked Silvia quietly.

"Later," she whispered.

A busy, rustic settlement of Fairies greeted them in the center of the ancient, black stone ruins.

"My Lord, welcome to Giriewald," said Telor. He ushered them inside the stone buildings. "These old ruins have become our sanctuary," he explained. "Displaced Fairies find themselves here on a regular basis."

"How do you know they are loyal?" asked Declan.

"You truly have Fairyland's best interests at heart, Declan," said Telor. "Father was right in granting your Dukeship." He brought them to a large room with small windows. "They must be loyal to me to be able to find these ruins. That is something the ancient Fairies understood well."

When they reached a large, round table, an older Fairy stood. Berty recognized the Fairy without his armor. A cane rested against the edge of the table.

"Gwron was injured in the escape from Fairyland," Telor said.

"Please, don't stand on our account, Colonel," Berty told him.

"Thank you, my Lord," said Gwron. "Your Grace," he nodded to Declan. "Lieutenant," he said to Edwin.

"Join us, please," said Telor.

Taking seats around the table, Jon and Teresa stayed silent. Berty said, "Telor, we can't stay long. We must return to the Empire Tree before the Hallows end."

With a nod, Telor stated, "I'll make this quick. I need Delyth to know that old magic is on our side. She will understand. Declan, is it possible you can help Gwron? You were able to help my father."

"In the end, it wasn't me who cured that poison," Declan said. "But I'll do what I can." He helped the Fairy out of the room.

Telor's green eyes glowed in the limited sunlight. "We weren't ready for them," Telor admitted. "They will reach the walls of the Sages' Grove. We would like to help in the fight against them. Unfortunately, we are not much of a force."

"You have Fairy Dust and the knowledge of the ancient Fairies," said Berty. "That is your greatest weapon."

When the shock wore off of Telor's face, he smiled. "Of course. You must use old magic against old magic."

Declan and Gwron re-entered the room. Telor watched them both hopefully. "The Colonel's injuries are magical," said Declan. "As a Watcher, I can see the magic in his system, but not being a Wizard, I cannot help him."

"Thank you, Declan, for trying," said Telor.

"There is one who may be able to help," Declan mentioned. "You have time, Gwron. Seek the Shaman of the Ghost Tribe in the Outlands. He is a Wizard."

"My Prince needs me here," said Gwron.

"And he will need you on the battlefield when we reclaim Fairyland," Declan said.

Smiling, Telor turned to his Colonel. "Take this chance and go. I will give you ample payment for this Wizard."

"Your Highness," Gwron protested.

"Don't make me order you as your Prince, Gwron," Telor said.

"All I need is time to prepare for the journey," Gwron conceded.

Telor turned his attention to Berty. "Let my parents know that we are okay. Fairydom is still strong."

Berty gave the Fairy an assuring nod. Telor had become the ruler Elrick and Lida had wanted him to be. Extracting his locket, he messaged Delyth. "On our way. Call for Goscislaw."

"Thank you for coming," Telor said. "Let me show you out."

The Fairy showed them to the stone gate. "Our Dragon friends have been good to us," said Telor. "I don't know what we would have done without them."

"Thank your sister when you see her," said Berty. "Good luck here, Telor. We will try to communicate when we can. I do not want to compromise your position."

Telor finally looked at the others. "Safe journey." His hand touched the stone to lower the gate.

Tong waited for them outside the ruins. "We need to return to the Empire Tree as quickly as possible," Berty told the Dragon.

"I look forward to seeing this tree with my own eyes," Tong replied. "Get on."

Looking at the large creature before him, Jon sighed.

"Hope thinks Tong is just the coolest," Berty said.

"When we promised Hope an adventure with her uncle, this is not exactly what I had in mind," said Teresa. She gave Berty a smile. Tugging on Jon's hand, Teresa said, "She's waiting for us. I want to tell her about Lily." Her hand touched her stomach.

"After your mom," said Jon. "Perfect." He followed his wife.

Silvia smiled at Berty as she climbed onto the Dragon's back. After everyone was seated, Berty said, "Take us home, Tong."

The Dragon pushed off the ground. In a matter of seconds, they were suspended in gray free fall.

A cool, autumn evening materialized around them. Berty saw

the lights of the Sages' Grove while Tong encircled the Empire Tree.

Descending, Berty heard shouting. "Dragon!"

"Hold your fire!" Alvar's voice carried in the cool air. "I know that Dragon. Open the gates!"

Chapter Twenty-six
A New Chapter

Tong landed in the void between the forest and the treed wall. Before sliding off the Dragon's back, Berty tossed spheres of light over their heads.

"Whoa," he heard his brother say.

Alvar and Delyth stood at the opened gates, greeting them with lanterns.

"Thank you, Tong," said Berty.

"Thank you, my Lord," said Tong. His boxy head lifted to see the top of the Empire Tree. Smiling, he said, "I will be seeing you, Sorcerer." His dark body leapt into the sky.

"Come," Berty said to Jon and Teresa. He ushered them inside the walls.

Jon's head spun to see everything. Teresa, too, looked around, then asked, "Where's my daughter?"

Inside the tree, Berty allowed Teresa and Jon to climb the steps before him.

"Mommy! Daddy!" he heard Hope cry.

Emerging from the staircase, he saw Jon and Teresa clutching to Hope. His mother cried. Lark embraced Edwin. Lida wiped her cheek. His eyes found Silvia.

He did not have to say a word. The descendants of the Seven High Sages climbed the stairs to the Scepter Room.

Berty stepped over the twisted copper cable lying across the floor. Darkness still held the Scepter.

"Do you think these crystals still hold the incantation?" Alfred asked, touching his colorless crystal.

"There's only one way to find out," said Silvia. "Hold on to your columns."

The seven of them stumbled around the dark room. Somehow, Berty found his column. He wrapped his left arm around the carved wood.

"Is everyone in place?" Silvia asked.

"Yes," they murmured.

"Let's send the crystal our magic," Silvia said.

Berty concentrated his magic onto the crystal. The dark room strobed with different colored lights. When magic pulsed from the Scepter, they paused.

Dim light returned to the crystal sconces on the round walls. A small point of light glowed in the depths of the large, colorless crystal in the center of the room.

"We need that incantation," growled Goscislaw.

Copper wiring drew Berty's eyes. His father had constructed a seven pronged circular copper housing to stabilize the Scepter's magic. "I'll be back," he said.

"Dad," Berty called as he ran down the steps. He saw everyone lingering in the Reception Room. "Dad, can you quickly remove the copper wiring?"

"I'll need some help," George said. "Hope, Obie, go collect my tools. We are going to have to throw it down the tree."

"I can fly it down," Delyth offered.

George nodded. "Colvin, take who you need outside. Delyth will meet you," he said. Obie and Hope returned, carrying his bag between them. "Kate and Declan, can you hold flashlights for Jon and me?"

Berty led them up the steps. George placed his bag on the landing. "Some light, but not enough," said George. He handed flashlights to his wife and Declan. In Jon's hands, he placed gloves and snips. "You work on one side and I'll work on the other."

After stepping into the Scepter Room, Jon froze. Shaking his head, he hurried after his father. Berty watched his father and brother snip copper.

George wadded the snipped copper enclosure. He glanced at Delyth waiting near the door. "Jon, give Delyth your gloves," he said. Obeying, he handed them to the Fairy.

Delyth pushed her small hands into the man-sized, thick, leather gloves. "These are much too big," she said.

"You must wear them," said George. "They're insulated. They will protect you from getting shocked or from the wire conducting your magic."

Nodding, she made sure the gloves were on her hands. The Fairy took the wad from George. He made sure the wire did not touch her as she walked to the bridge. She opened her wings, then dove off the side.

Jon gasped.

"She's on the ground," said George, leaning over the railing. "Declan, I need your eyes. Can you grab my bag, Jon?" He placed his hand on Berty's shoulder. "Do what you need to do, son."

Kate smiled at Berty before following the three men down the stairs. When he returned to the room, he took his place amongst the Sages.

Berty closed his eyes. His back rested against a column. His feet could feel the wooden floor through the soles of his boots. Symbols—some he recognized, some he did not—covered every inch of wood in the Scepter Room. He opened his mouth. As if he were one chair of a symphony, he said, "*Safna váratfarð. Slá fróðleikeld. Fylla hringríki. Øruglaun innan sjádraug. Fest al-mennvéurr. Sjau vitha varðveita inmenband."*

A whitish, electrically charged glow filled the room. The power converged onto the crystal. Like a vacuum, the Scepter absorbed everything.

The top crystal cluster shot a white beam into the ceiling. The beam bored through the core of the tree. When it reached the stargazing platform, the beam spread into a dome that reached the treed wall. The magic traveled through the wall into the ground. Cutting through the dirt, it reached the tree's taproot. Magic geysered through the center of the Empire Tree until it hit the bottom of the Scepter, coming full circle.

When Berty opened his eyes, the six of them still stood next to the columns. In the center of the room, the Scepter's crystal shone white.

"Is it fixed?" Lida asked.

"I believe so," said Alfred.

Looking around the room, he noticed that the colors returned to the crystals around their necks. Yellow, orange, green, brown, blue, red, and instead of gray, Sean's was a silvery purple.

"Your debt to the tree has been filled, Seanlaoch," said Berty. "You're free to go wherever you'd like."

Sean touched his crystal. "I'll collect my things." With a glance towards the Scepter, he left.

"Declan needs to survey," Berty told the others. With Silvia by his side, he led them down to the Reception Room.

Entering from a bridge, Declan approached the Sages. "I've watched thoroughly," he said. "The magic is stronger than ever and the tear has been repaired."

"Did anything get trapped inside?" Berty asked.

"Nothing. We can now speak freely," Declan answered. "However, the copper that was used has retained some magic.

356

Colvin has the Dwarves digging it out as we speak."

"If it has the magic of the Scepter in it, then it will need to be hidden," said Goscislaw. "Somewhere none of us knows."

"We need the Goblins," Silvia said.

"I will send Darnell a message," said Alfred.

Berty caught Sean entering through a far door. He dressed for a long journey. When he saw Berty, he walked over to him. Words seemed to have been stuck in Sean's throat.

"Why not stay the night and leave in the morning?" Berty asked.

"There should be a connection every time I touch the staff," Sean answered, "but, save for a few moments in the Scepter Room, there is not. I need to travel to where I should have found the staff. Then, I'm going to go home to see my family."

"You have enough provisions?"

Sean half smiled. "I do. Thank you."

"Good luck and safe travels," Berty said.

Sean gave Berty a proper bow, then descended below the floor.

"Uncle Berty," said Hope as she tugged on his cloak, "does this mean the portals won't close?"

Finding Teresa sitting with his mother, he smiled. "The portals will stay open with the restrictions, of course. Bring your mother and father," he told his niece. "Declan, I need you to check the house's magic. And you may want to see your sister."

"Can I come, too, my Lord?" Obie asked.

With a smile, he answered, "Yes." Taking Silvia's arm, he said, "We will be back soon. Let me know when Darnell gets here."

Hope practically dragged her parents up the stairs and across the bridge to her chambers. Freesia stood when they all entered.

"You must be Freesia," Jon said.

"Yes, sir," the Fairy answered.

"It is nice to finally meet you," Teresa said with a smile.

"We will return shortly," Berty told Freesia.

"I will be here."

They climbed the steps. He looked at Declan, who nodded. "Obie, see if you can cross by yourself," Berty suggested.

Obie stood in front of the tapestry. Taking a step, he disappeared. Declan quickly followed. "We will need to speak with Hatcher," Silvia said.

Holding onto her parents' hands, Hope pulled them through the portal. Berty and Silvia stepped into the paneled hallway.

"Julie?" called Declan.

Berty allowed Declan and Obie down the steps before them.

"Declan?" said Julie's voice. She stood in the foyer, holding a bowl of orange wrapped candies. "Declan! Does this mean?"

"All fixed," Declan said. He and Obie ran down the remaining steps.

"Julie? Is everything okay?" Lillian walked into the foyer as Julie hugged her brother. She looked at who was coming down the stairwell. "Robert! Matt! Get out here!" She started crying. "Our little girl is home, Robert."

The men ran into the hall as Teresa hurried down the stairs. Jon quietly followed.

From his mid-staircase perch, Berty watched the hugging and crying. Silvia took his hand.

The doorbell rang. "My first trick-or-treater!" Julie said excitedly.

"A what?" Declan asked.

Julie opened the door. A group of costumed kids said, "Trick-or-treat!" Laughing, she gave each kid a candy. When she closed the door, she explained Halloween to her brother and nephew.

"Only time of year when strangers can ring the doorbell," said Silvia.

"You both have to try this," Julie said. She tore open an orange candy wrapper. "It's called a peanut butter cup." She gave them each a half.

Taking a bite, Declan made a strange face. Berty laughed. When the doorbell rang again, Hope looked longingly at the children.

"Do you want to go trick-or-treating?" Teresa asked her daughter.

Hope nodded. "But, I don't have a costume," she said.

"If you raise your hood, you can go as Little Red Riding Hood," Teresa suggested.

Hope shrugged.

Silvia stepped into the crowded foyer. "Think clearly about what you want to be," she said.

"Okay," Hope said. She closed her eyes for a moment. "Got it!"

"Hold that image in your mind," Silvia instructed. She touched the top of Hope's head with her palm. Hope's clothes transformed.

Looking at her reflection in the glass doors, Hope squealed, "I'm a Fairy! I even have wings!"

"The magic will wear off when you step back inside this house," Silvia said.

"Thank you," Hope said. She squeezed Silvia. "Can Obie have a costume, too?"

"If he wants one," Silvia said. "Obie?"

He nodded eagerly. When Silvia touched his head, Obie had a bow and quiver on his back. "I look like an archer," he said with a smile. "Thank you."

"Your mother and I can take you around for a little bit," Jon said.

"Don't worry about it," said Matt. "You guys rest. Julie and I will take them."

Teresa briefly touched her abdomen. "Thank you. We should also bathe before going out in public," she said.

"You two need something to carry all your candy," said Matt. "Go get some pillowcases. That's what your mom and I used to use."

Hope and Obie sprinted past Berty. When they raced back down the steps, Berty's pocket vibrated. He watched them join the hordes as he opened his locket.

After reading the message, he walked down the steps. "Declan, can you take a look around? Darnell has arrived and I want you to speak with him," he said.

When Declan left, Lillian hugged Berty. "Thank you for my daughter," she said. "Your parents told us everything."

"You're welcome," said Berty.

"Since our clothes and things are over there," said Teresa, "can we all go? Mom and Dad, too? Jon and I have so much to tell you."

"And my parents should be there, too," Jon added.

"I'll stay here and wait for them," said Silvia.

Returning, Declan said, "Everything is in order."

Berty handed Silvia the Watcher's Locket. As trick-or-treaters rang the doorbell, Berty led his family and Declan through the tapestry.

At the Roundtable Room's landing, Berty said, "Mom and Dad should be just down the steps." He and Declan entered.

Alfred and Colvin sat with the Goblin Lord at the Roundtable. Seeing Berty, they stood.

"Interesting problem, Emperor," said Darnell. "Are we sure it is Scepter magic?"

"Yes," Declan answered. "It has the same magical signature."

The Goblin's knobby fingers tapped the tabletop. "Would you like to be able to access it at some later time?"

Berty knew that it was best for no one to have access to the magic of the Scepter. However, he also knew that it could prove useful someday in the future. "Yes," he answered. "But it needs to be extremely difficult for even us to obtain."

"Very well," squeaked Darnell. "Bring it to the tunnels under the Empire Tree. The Goblins will take it from there."

Colvin left with Darnell. Turning to his two Advisors, Berty said, "This needs to stay secret. If may be best we forgot."

"We hold a lot of secrets," said Alfred. "I do not want to imagine what Leif would do with this knowledge."

"Let's let the Goblins do what they need," said Berty. "I need to speak with the Fairies."

Alfred sent Elrick, Lida and Delyth to the Roundtable.

"We saw Telor on our way back from the Outlands," Berty announced.

"How is he?" Lida implored.

"He is a great leader," Berty answered. He relayed the message that Telor wanted.

Elrick's eyes glistened. "He will be a great king. Perhaps the greatest Fairydom has ever seen. Tonight, we celebrate our strength and Fairydom's resiliency."

Lida squeezed her husband's hand.

When they entered the Reception Room, Silvia waited for him. Matt and Julie had joined the table. Hope and Obie were telling tales of their evening.

Taking Silvia's hand, he smiled. As Tenders placed food on the table, a jovial mood encircled the table. Tomorrow, he knew that living arrangements would be tackled. But, in that moment, all that mattered was that everyone was home.

About the Author

IE Castellano is an American author and poet living in the Eastern United States. Falling in love with the mechanics of the English language at an early age, she started writing poetry before venturing into fiction. With her propensity to ask, what if, she writes speculative fiction—authoring the dystopian sci-fi novel, *Tricentennial*, and the contemporary epic fantasy series, *the World In-between*.

The World In-between Series:
    Book One: The World In-between
    Book Two: Bow of the Moon

Also by IE Castellano:
    Yuletide Magic
    Tricentennial

Keep up with new book releases and other happenings on IE's blog.
    http://iecastellano.blogpost.com
    Contact IE: iecastellano@zoho.com

More by JosDCreations:
    http://josdcreations.com
    Zazzle http://www.zazzle.com/josdcreations

www.ingramcontent.com/pod-product-compliance
Lightning Source LLC
Chambersburg PA
CBHW031101030726
47496CB00002BA/323